Penguin Education

Mythology
Edited by Pierre Maranda

Penguin Modern Sociology Readings

General Editor
Tom Burns

Advisory Board
James Cornford
Erving Goffman
Alvin Gouldner
Eric Hobsbawm
Edmund Leach
David Lockwood
Gianfranco Poggi
John Torrance
Hans Peter Widmaier
Peter Worsley

Mythology

Selected Readings
Edited by Pierre Maranda

Penguin Education

Penguin Education
A Division of Penguin Books Ltd,
Harmondsworth, Middlesex, England
Penguin Books Inc, 7110 Ambassador Road,
Baltimore, Md 21207, USA
Penguin Books Australia Ltd,
Ringwood, Victoria, Australia

First published 1972
Reprinted 1973
This selection copyright © Pierre Maranda, 1972
Introduction and notes copyright © Pierre Maranda, 1972

Made and printed in Great Britain by
C. Nicholls & Company Ltd
Set in Monotype Times

Contents

Introduction

A sketch of the modern anthropological theory of myth forms the first part of this introduction. The other part consists essentially of a table summarizing the contributions grouped in the thirteen Readings that follow. Both parts make explicit the basic issues broached in this volume.

The first part comprises (1) a brief historical review; (2) a test to help the reader grasp fundamental aspects of the modern theory of myth, and (3) a glance at the codes in which our literate and technological societies couch their myths. Because of its synthetic character, the introduction should probably be read again after the book has been perused in its entirety.

What is myth?

Among those opinions which are produced by a little knowledge, to be dispelled by a little more, is the belief in an almost boundless creative power of the human imagination. . . .
     The office of our thought is to develop, to combine and to derive, rather than to create. . . .
     The treatment of similar myths from different regions, by arranging them in large compared groups, makes it possible to trace in mythology the operation of imaginative processes recurring with the evident regularity of mental law; and thus stories of which a single instance would have been a mere isolated curiosity, take their place among well-marked and consistent structures of the human mind. Evidence like this will again and again drive us to admit that even as 'truth is stranger than fiction', so myth may be more uniform than history (Tylor, 1871, pp. 273, 274, 282).

The Sherente of Central Brazil heard the story of the Original Sin. When they retell it, they modify it considerably. Among other alterations, they recast Adam and Eve as brother and sister – otherwise, the myth would be meaningless for those unclothed but sophisticated people, for how could a man and a woman be ashamed of standing naked in each other's presence?
     The Sherente reformulation exemplifies the mythic process.

Shame is a strong component[1] of their semantic system and must be a reaction to an equally strong actual situation. But the juxtaposition of a naked man and a naked woman does not constitute a strong situation in their culture. Therefore, another relation must be substituted for it. Working up from the effect – shame – to a cause that could account for it while respecting the data – a naked man juxtaposed to a naked woman – the Sherente drew an inference perfectly logical in terms of their culture, viz. Adam and Eve must be redefined as siblings. Thus, because of the incest taboo, which is a strong component of the Sherente culture, a strong situation is created whenever a risk occurs of violating the taboo. A strong reaction, shame, is then adequately motivated. Now, the alteration of the cast rests upon what Tylor called a derivation. A new relation, siblingship, is derived from the cultural system and brought to bear on the situation. This relation is deeper, semantically, than the one in the Bible, as the incest taboo is more universal than a particular form of modesty.[2]

Numerous similar cases of culture change in other areas provide the same type of evidence. In Tylor's words, and also as made clear in Lévi-Strauss's work, the life of myths consists in reorganizing traditional components in the face of new circumstances or, correlatively, in reorganizing new, imported components in the light of tradition. More generally, the mythic process is a learning device in which the unintelligible – randomness – is reduced to the intelligible – a pattern: 'Myth may be more uniform than history.'

Accordingly, the analysis of myth aims at discovering the rules governing combinations, developments and derivations, i.e. at pointing out the operations that reduce the alien to familiar structures within a given range of possible variations. It is essentially the investigation of the culture-conditioning mechanisms that mould ethnic cognitive systems.

Before proposing a more precise definition of myth, it will be useful to review briefly the emergence of its components over the

1. See p. 13 on 'strong components'.
2. Stricter considerations of this example will be found below; for additional data and interpretations, see Maranda, Dundes, Leach and Maybury-Lewis (1971).

last seventy years.[3] The first breakthrough occurred in Hubert and Mauss's monograph on sacrifice (1897–8), 'a brilliant analysis of the mechanism of sacrifice, or perhaps one should say of its logical structure, or even of its grammar' (Evans-Pritchard, 1965, p. 71); the same is true of their essay on magic (1902–3). Their approach led to the formulation of the concept of 'collective representations' which the *Année Sociologique* used and developed. Related to that fundamental work and actually inspired by it, the linguistic revolution came about. Most relevant to the present purpose is de Saussure's famous distinction between *langue* ('language') and *parole* ('speech'). In effect, as knowledge of a specific language is prerequisite to speech acts, so are specific collective representations prerequisite to language.[4]

Boas, at approximately the same time as de Saussure, stated an equivalent position which bridges the distance between collective representations and language. To him, the contrast is a matter of conscious *v.* unconscious[5] aspects of linguistic phenomena. The following passage contains germinally the substance of the contributions grouped hereafter in several Readings of this book, especially those in Part One.

To draw a parallel again between this ethnological phenomenon [modesty] and linguistic phenomena, it would seem that the common

3. Malinowski's narrow functionalist approach will be left out. The 'charter' to which he refers makes sense only with respect to cognitive and exploratory models. Frazer's contribution, despite all its shortcomings, is closer to the orientation outlined here – for a more elaborate discussion, see Maranda and Köngäs Maranda (1971).

4. The several languages in the European or other culture areas rest on partly overlapping and partly idiosyncratic collective representations. Thus, it is correct in English, but not permissible in French, to say 'the leg of the table': English does not discriminate between legs of human beings, animals and pieces of furniture whereas French calls '*jambe*' the leg of a human being and '*patte*' that of animals and of pieces of furniture. Metaphors like 'That woman is an angel', 'Time is money', are translatable and intelligible in several Indo-European languages but meaningless in many others that do not rest on the same religious and economic collective representations (see Leach, p. 46; Lévi-Strauss, 1969, pp. 341–2; Köngäs Maranda 1969, 1970, 1971).

5. Boas's definition is close to that of the French psychologist Binet, according to whom the highest mental processes are unconscious. See also Lévi-Strauss (1949, ch. 8, s. 4).

feature of both is the grouping together of a considerable number of activities under the form of a single idea, without the necessity of this idea itself entering into consciousness. The difference, again, would lie in the fact that the idea of modesty is easily isolated from other concepts, and that then secondary explanations are given of what is considered modest and what not. I believe that the unconscious formation of these categories is one of the fundamental traits of ethnic life, and that it even manifests itself in many of its more complex aspects; that many of our religious views and activities, of our ethnical concepts, and even our scientific views, which are apparently based entirely on conscious reasoning, are affected by this tendency of distinct activities to associate themselves under the influence of strong emotions. It has been recognized before that this is one of the fundamental causes of error and of the diversity of opinions (Boas, 1911, n.d., pp. 58–9; see also pp. 18–21 and 52–61).

There are indeed 'single ideas' whose semantic power is measurable in terms of the 'number of activities' which they can 'group together'. Such ideas come up in myths which map them out into cognitive and emotional charters, as it were, which vary from culture to culture. Thus, according to our own cognitive and emotional charter, according to our own collective representation of modesty, we are much more sensitive to nakedness than most peoples of the world. Our notion is more encompassing and therefore more superficial than that of, say, the Sherente (see below. pp. 11, 15). Conversely, we are proud of some 'achievements' that trigger shame reactions elsewhere, e.g. accumulation of wealth for personal use instead of for distribution or for its destruction in potlatches.

The 'unconscious formation of these (ethnic) categories' is fundamental and moulds religions, ethnical systems and even scientific thought. All of these, according to the definition to be proposed shortly are actualizations of culture-specific myths. 'Distinct activities associate themselves under the influence of strong emotions' and along the grooves of category formation staked in mythologies. 'It has been recognized before that this is one of the fundamental causes of error and of the diversity of opinions', and also one of the fundamental causes of scientific discoveries and of social consensus (cf. Kroeber, 1963). People can communicate in so far as they share common if subliminal cultural axioms and it is by virtue of such intersections or disjunctions that sects, political parties and nations are inwardly – by agreement – and outwardly – by opposition – united.

Also at approximately the same time as de Saussure and Boas, the Russian Formalist school contributed to the new approach. Propp's paper (Reading 7) offers a good summary of the theory and of the method. Further developments are found in the recent works of Meletinsky, Segal (Reading 12), and their associates (1969).

Chomsky has reactivated similar perspectives under a new terminology. He distinguishes between 'deep structures' and 'competence' on the one hand, and 'surface structures' and 'performance' on the other. His original reluctance, now at least partly overcome, to take semantics into account, keeps his model from being as powerful as those of the other scholars reviewed here.

Lévi-Strauss has been more explicit than most on the theory of myth. He formulated basic propositions as early as 1949:

the world of symbolism is infinitely varied in contents, but always limited in its laws. . . . A compilation of known myths and tales would fill an imposing number of volumes. But they can be reduced to a small number of simple types if we abstract, from among the diversity of characters, a few elementary functions (1964, pp. 203–4; cf. the quote from Tylor, p. 7 and Lévi-Strauss, 1969, pp. 341–2).

In 1956, shortly after his famous paper 'The structural study of myth',[6] he concluded an analysis:

We see, then, what a structural analysis of the myth content can achieve in itself: it furnishes rules of transformation which enable us to shift from one variant to another by means of operations similar to those of algebra (1964, p. 235).[7]

6. For an analysis and a test of his model, see Köngäs Maranda and Maranda (1971).
7. The analyst shifts from one variant to another in order to understand semantic mechanisms. The Sherente, and other peoples, do the same in order to integrate alien data into their semantic system. In the case of the myth of the Original Sin, the transformation rule used by the Sherente and recognized by the analyst is an operation of specification (increase in intension), as Adam and Eve are transformed from an unrelated couple to siblings.
The operation can be represented algebraically. Let the constant elements be N = naked, M = man, W = woman, S = shame, and let the variable relation R between M and W be r_1 = juxtaposition, r_2 = sibling-

In his continuing *Mythologiques*, Lévi-Strauss shows how elementary functions do structure vast sets of symbols (Reading 13). His transformational analysis reaches beyond linguistic processes: it tackles the operations of the invariant human mind coping with variant environments and trying to reduce them to manageable systems. Like the scientist, the mythmaker builds homomorphisms, and both make their tasks easier by always bracketing away some dimensions.[8]

Myths solve problems or declare them unsolvable as elegantly as pure mathematics, but their language is more difficult to learn. 'The kind of logic in mythical thought is as rigorous as that of modern science, and ... the difference lies, not in the quality of the intellectual process, but in the nature of the things to which it is applied' (Lévi-Strauss, 1964, p. 230).

A definition of myth will now bring this section to an end.

Definition. Myths display the structured, predominantly culture-specific, and shared, semantic systems which enable the members

ship. The general formula is $N[R(M, W)] \rightarrow S$, i.e. there is a state of naked-ness for a man and a woman standing in a relation to be specified, then shame is generated. The Christian version will be formalized as $N[r_1(M, W)] \rightarrow S$, and the Sherente version as $N[r_2(M, W)] \rightarrow S$. The shift from the Christian to the Sherente version is produced by the transformation $r_1 \Rightarrow r_2$, which is an increase in intension; correlatively, the transformation to pass from the Sherente to the Christian version is $r_2 \Rightarrow r_1$, a decrease in intension.

The analyst's and the Sherente's operations yield the same result. The former finds that $R \rightarrow S$ for $R = r_1 \vee (r_1 \wedge r_2)$, i.e. the relation generating shame is either a simple juxtaposition of a naked *man* and a naked *woman*, or the fact that the naked juxtaposed people are a *brother* and a *sister* (thus, the terms are defined by the type of relation between them). Now, the Sherente take implicitly the following steps:

(1) $R \rightarrow S$; (2) $R = r_1 \wedge r_2$; but (3) $r_1 \rightarrow S$; therefore (4) $R = r_1 \vee (r_1 \wedge r_2)$, and the Sherente now wear clothes. They have recognized that siblingship can be subtracted from their formulation and that the terms can be re-defined more broadly as *man* and *woman*; they have learned that it is not necessary that Christians of different sexes be siblings for them to be asham-ed to be naked in each other's presence. Like a great many other peoples, the Sherente have given in and adopted the ways of the technologically, if not ideologically, powerful.

For the set of transformers in folklore, see the Reading by Propp in this volume and Köngäs Maranda (1970, 1971).

8. For explications, see Maranda (1972a).

of a culture area to understand each other and to cope with the unknown. More strictly, *myths are stylistically definable discourses that express the strong components of semantic systems*.

'Discourses' refer to the articulation of narrative units into a plot (for details on units and plot models, see Meletinsky, Nekludov, Novik and Segal, 1969; Köngäs Maranda and Maranda, 1971). 'Stylistically definable' means features of formulation which are characteristic of culture areas (see references in Maranda, 1971; 1972b, and parts of Lessa's contribution, Reading 4). 'Strong components' is to be understood according to Digraph Theory, i.e. the elementary structures of myth are terms so related that they have the properties of *cycles* which are either *sources* or *sinks* (Harary, Norman and Cartwright, 1965; Maranda and Köngäs Maranda, 1970; Maranda, 1972b). Finally, 'semantic systems' add to the concept of 'collective representations' that these are structured cognitive guidelines as products of historical accretions and of mental processes.

Myths and minds

The purpose of the following test is to demonstrate Boas's fundamental point – myth as a conditioning process. Three components, which are strong ones in quite a few semantic systems, will be used. They are 'man', 'woman' and 'snake'. The test requires that the reader fill in the empty cells in Table 1 before looking at Table 2. Write in each of the four boxes what you assume the relationship would be, in a European myth, between the three components in question (for instance, if you think the snake would eat up the woman, write 'eat up' under *woman* as receiver, at the end of the first row; if you assume that there is no direct interaction, write X in the cell where the two dramatis personae intersect).

Table 1 Test

	Receiver		
Emitter	Snake	Man	Woman
Snake	X		
Man		X	
Woman			X

Now, it can be predicted (probability of over 80 per cent) that you have filled the empty cells with terms more or less synonymous with those in Table 2.

Table 2 European probabilistic model

Emitter	Receiver		
	Snake	Man	Woman
Snake	X	X	lures
Man	X	X	yields to
Woman	succumbs	lures	X

But give the same test to a Melanesian of the Eastern Solomon Islands: the matrix would be filled as follows:

Table 3 Melanesian probabilistic model

Emitter	Receiver		
	Snake	Man	Woman
Snake	X	X	mother of
Man	fears and kills	X	loves
Woman	daughter of	loves then leaves	X

Why, for a European, are European responses highly predictable and, correlatively, non-European responses difficult if not impossible to predict? 'Symbols' have different meanings in different cultures, and different relationships prevail between the same 'symbols' when we pass from one culture to another. Symbols that share the same semantic function are 'paradigmatic sets' in modern terminology; when two symbols belonging to different paradigmatic sets are connected by a relation, they form what is called a 'syntagmatic chain'. In our areas, for most people, 'snake' belongs to the paradigmatic set of 'repulsive' or 'evil' things; in many other culture areas, it belongs to the paradigmatic set of 'primeval fecundity'. 'Man' and 'woman' are cross-culturally more neutral; generally, their meaning is positional in that it is determined by their relations to other, stronger terms. The connection between 'snake' and 'woman' is a syntagmatic chain resulting from their association through a specific relation. But relations in turn are contingent upon what they connect. Of all the available relations within a semantic system, only a limited number can serve in the construction of specific chains. For example, the relation between a bear as emitter and an infant as receiver may be that of 'parent' or 'kidnapper' but hardly that of 'lover'. In our culture, the phallus–snake association suggests a relation of sexual intercourse with 'woman' as receiver, but the most common relation is that of 'deceiver'. Consequently, the association between 'snake' and 'woman', along with others that are redundant in this respect,[9] draws the latter towards the paradigmatic set 'evil' to which the former belongs by virtue of Genesis. In contrast, the Melanesian relation between the same terms is 'female parent', with snake as emitter. Consequently, 'woman' is pulled closer to the set 'fecundity' since snake is so defined semantically.

Within a semantic universe, some combinations of, i.e. relations between, elements are common, others are permissible but rare, others are poetic or archaic, and others are excluded (see note 4, above). Communication becomes increasingly difficult as one moves farther away from the semantic grooves of one's culture.[10] The interest of comparative analysis lies in the operators necessary to pass from one system to another: dimensional depth becomes measurable as well as the differential use of operators by different cultures (see Köngäs Maranda, 1969; Buchler and Selby, 1969; Maranda, 1969).

Thus, because the Sherente operator to pass from the Christian to their version of the story of the Original Sin is a restriction of extension by the addition of an attribute (siblingship), we see that our concept of shame is readily triggered by a skin-deep reaction (one step in Figure 1), whereas that of the Sherente, blood-linked, is not as easily activated (two steps in Figure 1).

9. e.g. the Pandora myth; such expressions as 'Look for the woman', 'Woman is the root of all evil', etc.
10. Riddles and poetry explore the borders of semantic systems within given languages; see Köngäs Maranda, 1971; Maranda and Köngäs Maranda, 1971.

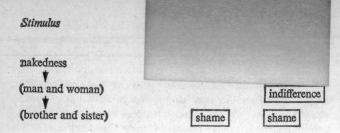

Figure 1 The Christian and Sherente Concepts of Shame

To summarize this experiment, we could say, inspired by Rousseau, that human communication is a social contract which rests on a body of subliminal laws, and that a culture's myths contain its semantic jurisprudence. Whether this can be reduced to an algebra depends on the power of the analyst. The rules are there at any rate, as evidenced by the fact that those unable or unwilling to abide and be conditioned by them are either confined into mental hospitals or marked off as foreigners.

The princess' depilatory and the hero's hair tonic

Myths, in our complex societies, are manifested in idioms different from those in which they were expressed in the past and in which they are still expressed in traditional societies. The passage from one idiom to another was effected through a recoding process that became generalized with the spread of literacy and technology.[11]

The triumph of the small but clever one over the clumsy giant may be narrated by an elder in a remote European hamlet in the form of a folktale or it can be found on television and cinema screens, not to mention comic strips. It is also repeated in wide-circulation magazines and newspapers in the North American advertisements of Volkswagen cars. Like the clever little one, like the Bible's David, the buyer of a VW has plenty of power in reserve – mental power (as he beats the system, Detroit's big vehicles).

11. 'Coding' is here to be understood in the terms of Communication Theory, slightly modified to remain congruent with the language of this introduction. A code is a set of rules of transformation to pass from one system of idioms to another one.

Then, it makes little difference, still in technological societies, that the metamorphosis of a 'beast' into a handsome male, who will conquer the glamouring princess in the Eden of ads, be the work of a tradition-consolidated magical agent or of mass-media established brands of deodorants or mouthwashes. Little does it matter, similarly, whether Cinderella becomes a mysteriously seductive woman with the help of her godmother or that of a skin-beautifying soap. Technology convinces us that it can achieve what our forefathers thought magic would do. The syntagmatic chains that moulded, and lived through, our ancestors, still perpetuate themselves among us, from the poet to the advertising agency, the cartoonist to the scriptwriter to the novelist. And our paradigmatic sets are also consistently traditional: variations in contents erode semantic grooves very little, for the functions that direct the flow of imagery are as deeply seated as our conceptual habits. Cinderella, salesgirls, devoted housewives, Jack (of the beanstalk), newspaper boys, tired executives – all feel, at the back of their minds, the nagging dream of the great adventure that culminates in long-lasting and private blissfulness.

But Melanesians find our myths boring and our advertisements tasteless. A stray issue of the *Playboy* magazine was received with shrugs in North Malaita, in the Solomon Islands. How could those girls be found attractive when the local canon of female beauty is a freshly shaven head? In those islands, the happy dream is that of a numerous progeniture so that one will be sure of a restful after-life.

Our myths are made of depilatories, royalty, pets, antiques, political ideologies, religion, hair tonics, cinemactors, scientific theories, cars, etc. – enticing avenues to the Paradise of which, ultimately we refuse to acknowledge the loss. Long ago, many strong components of our semantic systems were expressed as well as consolidated in the book of Genesis. God and the snake still thrive among us.

The contents of this book

The five Parts in which the selections are distributed as well as selection assignment to each Part will be considered arbitrary by some. Table 4 attempts to be somewhat descriptive of the contents of this volume. The table's domains and their subdivision are, inevitably, over-simplifications. The labels are crude. They purport to be only indicative and that in very general terms. They should become more meaningful, and the distortions they impose more easily discerned, if the table is examined again after the papers have been read.

Table 4 The contents of this volume

	Decade in which first published			Theoretical orientation					Fields and general topics									Analytic operations						
	1920s	1950s	1960s	Functionalist	Comparative	Cross-Cultural	Structuralist	Culture and Personality	Form and Style	Relations to Other Genres	Mythopoesis	Psycho-Socio-Linguistics	Sociology	Semantics	Philosophy	Cognition	Culture Change	Metalanguage	Transformation	Computer	Contingency	Frequency	Protocols derivable for field work	Author did field work in area
Armstrong																								
Burridge																								
Cassirer																								
Greimas																								
Guiart																								
Leach																								
Lessa																								
Lévi-Strauss																								
Lowie																								
Maranda																								
Propp																								
Roberts																								
Segal																								

The methods grouped in this book are supposed to be powerful. Each Reading is its own evidence in this respect and the readers will judge. In order to be in a position to pronounce oneself, though, one should first test the methods on other bodies of data, and preferably on data with which one is already familiar. It should be kept in mind, too, that valid as it may be for given purposes, a method does not necessarily meet the objectives of all those who try it.[12]

12. A way of assessing the scope and validity of the methods: Re-analyse the myths quoted and studied in Readings 4, 5, 7, 10, 12 and 13 with the help of the other approaches represented in this volume.

References

BUCHLER, I. R., and SELBY, H. A. (1968), 'A formal study of myth', *Monograph Series no. 1, Center for Intercultural Studies in Folklore and Oral History*, University of Texas Press.

BOAS, F. (1911), 'Introduction', 'Handbook of American Indian languages', *Bulletin 40, Part I, Bureau of American Ethnology*; published separately (n.d.), Georgetown University Press.

EVANS-PRITCHARD, E. E. (1965), *Theories of Primitive Religion*, Clarendon Press.

HARARY, F., NORMAN, R. Z., and CARTWRIGHT, D. (1965), *Structural Models: An Introduction to the Theory of Directed Graphs*, Wiley.

HUBERT, H., and MAUSS, M. (1897-8), 'Essai sur la nature et la fonction du sacrifice'. *L'Année sociologique*, vol. 2; English translation, *Sacrifice: Its Nature and Function* (1964), University of Chicago Press.

HUBERT, M., and MAUSS, M. (1902-3), 'Esquisse d'une théorie générale de la magie', *L'Année sociologique*, vol. 7; reprinted in M. Mauss (1950), *Sociologie et Anthropologie*, Presses Universitaires de France.

KÖNGÄS MARANDA, E. K. (1969), 'Structure des énigmes', *L'Homme*, vol. 9, pp. 5–48.

KÖNGÄS MARANDA, E. K. (1970), 'Perinteen transformaatiosääntöjen tutkimisesta', *Virittäjä*, pp. 277–92 (French Summary, p. 292).

KÖNGÄS MARANDA, E. K. (1971), 'Theory and practice of riddle analysis', in R. Bauman (ed.), *Toward New Perspectives in Folklore*, *J. Amer. Folklore*, vol. 84, pp. 51–61.

KÖNGÄS MARANDA, E. K., and MARANDA, P. (1971), *Structural Models in Folklore and Transformational Essays*, 2nd edn, Mouton.

KROEBER, A. L. (1963), *Configurations of Culture Growth*, University of California Press.

LÉVI-STRAUSS, C. (1949), *Les Structures étementaires de la Parenté*, P.U.F.

LÉVI-STRAUSS, C. (1964), *Structural Anthropology*, Basic Books; original French edition, *Anthropologie structurale* (1958), Plon.

LÉVI-STRAUSS, C. (1969), *The Raw and the Cooked*, Harper; original French edition, *Mythologiques I: Le cru et le cuit* (1964), Plon.

MARANDA, P. (1969), review of I. R. Buchler and H. A. Selby (1968), *Amer. Anthropol.*, vol. 71, pp. 521–3.

MARANDA, P. (1971), 'The computer and the analysis of myths', *Revue Internationale des Sciences Sociales*, UNESCO, vol. 23, pp. 244–54.

MARANDA, P. (1972a), 'Anthropological analytics: Lévi-Strauss's concept of social structure', in H. Nutini and I. R. Buchler, (eds.), *The Anthropology of C. Lévi-Strauss*, Appleton-Century-Crofts.

MARANDA, P. (1972b), 'Cendrillon et la théorie des ensembles', in *Structures et genres de la littérature ethnique*, Proceedings of the Palermo Symposium (1970), Associazone per la conservazione delle traditione popolare.

MARANDA, P., DUNDES, A., LEACH, E. R., and MAYBURY-LEWIS, D. (1971), 'An experiment: notes and queries from the desk, with a reply by the ethnographer', in P. Maranda and E. K. Köngäs Maranda (eds.), *Structural Analysis of Oral Tradition*, University of Pennsylvania Press.

MARANDA, P., and KÖNGÄS MARANDA, E. K. (1970), 'Le Crâne et l'utérus: deux théorèmes nord-malaitains', in J. Pouillon and P. Maranda (eds.), *Echange et Communications*, 2 vols., Mouton.

MARANDA, P., and KÖNGÄS MARANDA, E. K. (1971), 'Introduction', in *Structural Analysis of Oral Tradition*, University of Pennsylvania Press.

MELETINSKY, E. M., NEKLUDOV, S. J., NOVIK, S., and SEGAL, D. M. (1969), 'Problemy strukturnogo opisanija volshebnoj skazki', *Trudy po znakovym sistemam*, vol. 4, pp. 86–135. English translation in P. Maranda, ed., *Soviet Structural Folkloristics*, Mouton, in press.

TYLOR, E. B. (1871), *Primitive Culture*, Murray; Harper & Row.

Part One
Metaphor, Myth and Language

Experienced college teachers say that, in their courses, they find
Leach's paper the best introduction to the study of myth.
Quite rapidly, uninitiated students come to see the point:
myths and semantic systems have 'teeth'. Additional depth is
given to Leach's paper by Cassirer's philosophical essay and by
Lowie's empirical approach; but it is still Leach's analysis that
goes furthest in the investigation of semantic parameters.
These three Readings reveal the bearing of the metaphoric process
on mythopoesis. Cognition, as already pointed out by Aristotle,
proceeds by analogy; in the study of myth, Wundt and Frazer
with Cassirer, Jakobson and Lévi-Strauss with Leach, emphasize
the relational structure of symbols in terms of a proportion.

Part One can be reread with profit after the rest of the book
has been perused.

1 Ernst Cassirer

The Power of Metaphor

Excerpts from Ernst Cassirer, *Language and Myth*, translated by
Suzanne K. Langer, Dover Publications, 1946, pp. 83–97. First
published in German in 1923.

The foregoing considerations have shown us how mythical and
verbal thought are interwoven in every way; how the great structures of the mythic and linguistic realms, respectively, are determined and guided through long periods of their development by
the same spiritual motives. Yet one fundamental motive has so
far remained unnoticed, which not only illustrates their relationship, but offers an ultimate explanation of it. That myth and
language are subject to the same, or at least closely analogous,
laws of evolution can really be seen and understood only in so far
as we can uncover the common root from which both of them
spring. The resemblances in their results, in the forms which they
produce, point to a final community of function, of the principles
whereby they operate. In order to recognize this function and
represent it in its abstract nakedness, we have to pursue the ways
of myth and language not in their progress, but in regress – back
to the point from which those two divergent lines enamate. And
this common center really seems to be demonstrable; for, no
matter how widely the contents of myth and language may differ,
yet the same form of mental conception is operative in both. It is
the form which one may denote as *metaphorical thinking*; the
nature and meaning of metaphor is what we must start with if we
want to find, on the one hand, the unity of the verbal and the
mythical worlds and, on the other, their difference.

It has frequently been noted that the intellectual link between
language and myth is metaphor; but in the precise definition of
the process, and even in regard to the general direction it is supposed to take, theories are widely at variance. The real source of
metaphor is sought now in the construction of language, now in
mythic imagination; sometimes it is supposed to be speech, which

by its originally metaphorical nature begets myth, and is its eternal source; sometimes, on the contrary, the metaphorical character of words is regarded as a legacy which language has received from myth and holds in fee. [...]

The romantics followed the way indicated by Herder; Schelling, too, sees in language a 'faded mythology', which preserves in formal and abstract distinctions what mythology still treats as living, concrete differences (1927–8, vol. 2, p. 523). Exactly the opposite course was taken by the 'comparative mythology' that was attempted in the second half of the nineteenth century, especially by Adalbert Kuhn and Max Müller. Since this school adopted the *methodological* principle of basing mythological comparisons on linguistic comparisons, the *factual* primacy of verbal concepts over mythic ones seemed to them to be implied in their procedure. Thus mythology appeared as a result of language. The 'root metaphor' underlying all mythic formulations was regarded as an essentially verbal phenomenon, the basic character of which was to be investigated and understood. The homonymity or assonance of denotative terms was supposed to break and direct the way for mythic fantasy.

Let us consider, then, that there was, necessarily and really, a period in the history of our race when all the thoughts that went beyond the narrow horizon of our everyday life had to be expressed by means of metaphors, and that these metaphors had not yet become what they are to us, mere conventional and traditional expressions, but were felt and understood half in their original and half in their modified character. ... Whenever any word, that was at first used metaphorically, is used without a clear conception of the steps that led from its original to its metaphorical meaning, there is danger of mythology; whenever those steps are forgotten and artificial steps put in their places, we have mythology, or, if I may say so, we have diseased language, whether that language refers to religious or secular interests. ... What is commonly called mythology is but a part of a much more general phase through which all language has at one time or other to pass (Müller, 1875, pp. 372–6).

Before one can attempt any decision between these antagonistic theories, this battle for the priority of language over mythology or myth over language, the basic concept of metaphor requires scrutiny and definition. One can take it in a narrow sense, in which it comprises only the *conscious* denotation of one thought content by the name of another which resembles the former in some respect, or is somehow analogous to it. In that case, metaphor is a genuine 'translation'; the two concepts between which it obtains are fixed and independent meanings, and betwixt them, as the given *terminus a quo* and *terminus ad quem*, the conceptual process takes place, which causes the transition from one to the other, whereby one is semantically made to stand proxy for the other. Any attempt to probe the generic causes of this conceptual and nominal substitution, and to explain the extraordinarily wide and variegated use of this sort of metaphor (i.e. the conscious identification of avowedly diverse objects), especially in primitive forms of thinking and speaking, leads one back to an essential attitude of mythic thought and feeling. Heinz Werner, in his study of the origins of metaphor, has presented a very plausible argument for the supposition that this particular kind of metaphor, the circumlocution of one idea in terms of another, rests on quite definite motives arising from the magical view of the world, and more especially from certain name and word taboos. (1919, esp. ch. 3, p. 74).

But such a use of metaphor clearly presupposes that both the ideas and their verbal correlates are already given as definite quantities; only if these elements, as such, are verbally fixed and defined can they be exchanged for one another. Such transposition and substitution, which operate with a previously known vocabulary as their material, must be clearly distinguished from that genuine 'radical metaphor' which is a condition of the very formulation of mythic as well as verbal conceptions. Indeed, even the most primitive verbal utterance requires a transmutation of a certain cognitive or emotive experience into sound, i.e. into a medium that is foreign to the experience, and even quite disparate; just as the simplest mythical form can arise only by virtue of a transformation which removes a certain impression from the realm of the ordinary, the everyday and profane, and lifts it to the level of the 'holy', the sphere of mythico-religious 'significance'. This involves not merely a transference, but a real μετάβασις εἰς ἄλλο γενος; in fact, it is not only a transition to another category, but actually the creation of the category itself.

If, now, one were to ask which of these two types of metaphor begets the other – whether the metaphorical expressions in speech are produced by the mythic point of view, or whether, on the contrary, this point of view could arise and develop only on the basis of language – the foregoing considerations show that this question is really specious. For, in the first place, we are not dealing here with a temporal relation of 'before' and 'after', but with the logical relation between the forms of language and of myth, respectively; with the way the one conditions and determines the other. This determination, however, can be conceived only as reciprocal. Language and myth stand in an original and indissoluble correlation with one another, from which they both emerge but gradually as independent elements. They are two diverse shoots from the same parent stem, the same impulse of symbolic formulation, springing from the same basic mental activity, a concentration and heightening of simple sensory experience. In the vocables of speech and in primitive mythic figurations, the same inner process finds its consummation: they are both resolutions of an inner tension, the representation of subjective impulses and excitations in definite objective forms and figures. As Usener emphatically said:

It is not by any volition that the name of a thing is determined. People do not invent some arbitrary sound-complex, in order to introduce it as the sign of a certain object, as one might do with a token. The spiritual excitement caused by some object which presents itself in the outer world furnishes both the occasion and the means of its denomination. Sense impressions are what the self receives from its encounter with the not-self, and the liveliest of these naturally strive for vocal expression; they are the bases of the separate appellations which the speaking populace attempts (1896, p. 3).

Now this genesis corresponds precisely, feature for feature, with that of the 'momentary gods'. Similarly, the significance of linguistic and mythic metaphors, respectively, will reveal itself, so that the spiritual power embodied in them may be properly understood, only as we trace them back to their common origin; if one seeks this significance and power in that peculiar concentration, that 'intensification' of sense experience which underlies all linguistic as well as all mythico-religious formulations.

If we take our departure once more from the contrast which

theoretical or 'discursive' conception presents, we shall find indeed that the different *directions* which the growth of logical (discursive) and mythic-linguistic conception, respectively, have followed, may be seen just as clearly in their several *results*. The former begins with some individual, single perception, which we expand, and carry beyond its original bounds, by viewing it in more and more relationships. The intellectual process here involved is one of *synthetic supplementation*, the combination of the single instance with the totality, and its completion in the totality. But by this relationship with the whole, the separate fact does not lose its concrete identity and limitation. It fits into the sum total of phenomena, yet remains set off from them as something independent and singular. The ever-growing relationship which connects an individual perception with others does not cause it to become merged with the others. Each separate 'specimen' of a species is 'contained' in the species; the species itself is 'subsumed' under a higher genus; but this means, also, that they remain distinct, they do not coincide. This fundamental relation is most readily and clearly expressed in the scheme which logicians are wont to use for the representation of the hierarchy of concepts, the order of inclusion and subsumption obtaining among genera and species. Here the logical determinations are represented as geometric determinations; every concept has a certain 'area' that belongs to it and whereby it is distinguished from other conceptual spheres. No matter how much these areas may overlap, cover each other or interpenetrate – each one maintains its definitely bounded location in conceptual space. A concept maintains its sphere despite all its synthetic supplementation and extension; the new relations into which it may enter do not cause its boundaries to become effaced, but lead rather to their more distinct recognition.

If, now, we contrast this form of logical conception by species and genera with the primitive form of mythic and linguistic conception, we find immediately that the two represent entirely different *tendencies* of thought. Whereas in the former a concentric expansion over ever-widening spheres of perception and conception takes place, we find exactly the opposite movement of thought giving rise to mythic ideation. The mental view is not widened, but compressed; it is, so to speak, distilled into a single point. Only by this process of distillation is the particular essence found and extracted which is to bear the special accent of 'significance'. All light is concentrated in one focal point of 'meaning', while everything that lies outside these focal points of verbal or mythic conception remains practically invisible. It remains 'unremarked' because, and in so far as, it remains unsupplied with any linguistic or mythic 'market'. In the realm of discursive conception there reigns a sort of diffuse light – and the further logical analysis proceeds, the further does this even clarity and luminosity extend. But in the ideational realm of myth and language there are always, besides those locations from which the strongest light proceeds, others that appear wrapped in profoundest darkness. While certain contents of perception become verbal-mythical centers of force, centers of significance, there are others which remain, one might say, beneath the threshold of meaning. This fact, namely, that primitive mythical and linguistic concepts constitute such *punctiform* units, accounts for the fact that they do not permit of any further *quantitative* distinctions. Logical contemplation always has to be carefully directed toward the *extension* of concepts; classical syllogistic logic is ultimately nothing but a system of rules for combining, subsuming and superimposing concepts. But the conceptions embodied in language and myth must be taken not in extension, but in intension; not quantitatively, but qualitatively. Quantity is reduced to a purely casual property, a relatively immaterial and unimportant aspect. Two logical concepts, subsumed under the next-higher category, as their *genus proximum*, retain their distinctive characters despite the relationship into which they have been brought. In mythico-linguistic thought, however, exactly the opposite tendency prevails. Here we find in operation a law which might actually be called the law of the leveling and extinction of specific differences. Every part of a whole is the whole itself; every specimen is equivalent to the entire species. The part does not merely represent the whole, or the specimen its class; they are identical with the totality to which they belong; not merely as mediating aids to reflective thought, but as genuine presences which actually contain the power, significance and efficacy of the whole. Here one is reminded forcefully of the principle which might be called the basic principle of verbal as well as mythic 'metaphor' – the principle of *pars pro toto*. It is a familiar fact that all mythic thinking is governed and permeated by this principle. Whoever has brought any part of a whole into his power has thereby acquired power, in the magical sense, over the whole itself. What significance the part in question may have in the structure and coherence of the whole, what function it fulfills, is relatively unimportant – the mere fact that it is or has been a part, that it has been connected with the whole, no matter how casually, is enough to lend it the full significance and power of that greater unity. For instance, to hold magical dominion over another person's body one need only attain possession of his pared nails or cut-off hair, his spittle or his excrement; even his shadow, his reflection or his footprints serve the same purpose. The Pythagoreans still observed the injunction to smooth the bed soon after arising so that the imprint of the body, left upon the mattress, could not be used to the owner's detriment (Jamblichos, 1888, Deubner, 1922). [. . .]

In the light of this basic principle of mythic metaphor we can grasp and understand, somewhat more clearly, what is commonly called the metaphorical function of language. Even Quintilian pointed out that this function does not constitute any *part* of speech, but that it governs and characterizes all human talk; *paene quidquid loquimur figura est*. But if this is indeed the case – if metaphor, taken in this general sense, is not just a certain development of speech, but must be regarded as one of its essential conditions – then any effort to understand its function leads us back, once more, to the fundamental form of verbal *conceiving*. Such conceiving stems ultimately from that same process of concentration, the compression of given sense experiences, which originally initiates every single verbal concept. If we assume that this sort of concentration occurs by virtue of several experiences, and along several lines, so that two different perceptual complexes might yield the same sort of 'essence' as their inner significance, which *gives* them their meaning, then at this very point we should expect that first and firmest of all the connections which language can establish; for, as the nameless simply has no existence in language, but tends to be completely obscured, so whatever things bear the *same* appellation appear absolutely similar. The similarity of the aspect fixed by the word causes all other heterogeneity among the perceptions in question to become more and more obscured, and finally to vanish altogether. Here again, a part usurps the place of the whole – indeed, it becomes and is the whole. By virtue of the 'equivalence' principle, entities which appear entirely diverse in direct sense perception or from the standpoint of logical classification may be *treated* as similars in language, so that every statement made about one of them may be transferred and applied to the other. Preuss, in a characterization of magic-complex thinking, says:

If the Cora Indian classes butterflies, quite absurdly, as birds, this means that all the properties which he notes in the object are quite differently classified and related for him than they are for us from our analytical, scientific point of view (1914, p. 10).

But the apparent absurdity of this and other such classifications disappears as soon as we realize that the formation of these primary concepts was guided by language. If we suppose that the element emphasized in the name, and therefore in the verbal concept of 'bird', as an essential characteristic was the element of 'flight', then by virtue of this element and by its mediation the butterfly does belong to the class of birds. Our own languages are still constantly producing such classifications, which contradict our empirical and scientific concepts of species and genera, as for instance the denotation 'butterfly' (Dutch *botervlieg*), in some Germanic tongues called a 'butterbird'. And at the same time one can see how such lingual 'metaphors' react in their turn on mythic metaphor and prove to be an ever-fertile source for the latter. Every characteristic property which once gave a point of departure to qualifying conceptions and qualifying *appellations* may now serve to merge and identify the *objects* denoted by these names. If the visible image of lightning, as it is fixed by language, is concentrated upon the impression of 'serpentine', this causes the lightning to *become a snake*; if the sun is called 'the heavenly flier', it appears henceforth as an arrow or a bird – the sun-god of the Egyptian pantheon, for instance, who is represented with a falcon's head. For in this realm of thought there are no abstract denotations; every word is immediately transformed into a concrete mythical figure, a god or a daemon. Any sense impression, no matter how vague, if it be fixed and held in language, may thus become a starting point for the conception and denotation of a god. Among the names of the Lithuanian gods which Usener has listed, the snow-god Blizgulis, the 'Shimmerer', appears beside the god of cattle, the 'Roarer' Baubis; also in relation to these we find the god of bees, Birbullis the 'Hummer', and the god of earthquake, the 'Thresher' Drebkulys (1896, pp. 85, 114). Once a 'Roarer God' in this sense was conceived. he could not but be recognized in the most diverse guises; he was naturally and directly *heard*, in the voice of the lion as in the roaring of the storm and the thunder of the ocean. Again and again, in this respect, myth receives new life and wealth from language, as language does from myth. And this constant interaction and interpenetration attests the unity of the mental principle from which both are sprung, and of which they are simply different expressions, different manifestations and grades.

References

DEUBNER (1922), *Magie und Religion*, Freiburg.
MÜLLER, M. (1875), *Lectures on the Science of Language*, Scribner, Armstrong & Co.
JAMBLICHOS (1888), *Protreptichos*, Stuttgart.
PREUSS, K. T. (1914), *Die geistige Kultur der Naturvölker*, Leipzig.
SCHELLING, Ö. (1927–8), 'Einleitung in die Philosophie der Mythologie', *Samtliche Werke*, Munich, 6 vols.
USENER, H. (1890), *Gotternamen: Versuch einer helve von der religiosen Begriffs bildung*, Bonn.
WERNER, H. (1919), *Die Ursprünge der Metapher*, Leipzig.

2 Robert H. Lowie

Association

Excerpts from Robert H. Lowie, *Primitive Religion*, Peter Owen, 1960;
Liveright Publishing, 1952, pp. 277–82, 285–7, 305–7.

In a previous chapter I have pointed out how largely the thoughts
and the behavior of individuals are determined by factors arising
not from the inborn characteristics of the thinker or actor but
from the cultural conditions affecting all the members of his group
jointly. This principle can be amply illustrated by the associations
of ideas that appear in different societies, for though such associations have been commonly studied only from the point of
view of individual psychology it is not difficult to prove that
exclusive attention to this aspect of the phenomenon fails to
bring adequate illumination. This, indeed, is fully recognized by
Professor Höffding, the Danish psychologist, who expresses
himself as follows:

Associations of ideas may ... be so firm and constant that it is forgotten out of what elements they have arisen. Some of the greatest
mysteries in the province of psychology owe their origin to such deeply
rooted associations of ideas, the beginning and history of which have
been forgotten ... that which presents itself to us as a unity and as
necessarily coherent, may yet have arisen from the fusing of different
elements. It demands therefore a deeper and more extensive psychological analysis than the dogmatizing psychology enters into. Such an
analysis finds an especial application in the associations which have not
been formed in the actual consciousness of the individual, but are the
bequest of earlier generations (1893, p. 152).

What concerns us at present is the extent to which the association of ideas presented by a given person can be accepted as a
genuinely individual mental product or as one functionally
dependent on his social heritage. Perhaps we can most profitably
approach the question by considering Kent and Rosanoff's
studies in word association, which by many of their colleagues are

regarded as classical. After preliminary experimentation these authors hit upon a list of one hundred words and recorded the ideas associated with those of the list by a thousand normal subjects. Thus 191 individuals thought of 'table' in response to 'chair', while only a single one gave as his reaction 'office'. Treating the results secured as a standard for testing other subjects, the investigators distinguish as 'common' those reactions represented in their tables, while those not found there are called 'individual', though not necessarily abnormal (Kent and Rosanoff, 1910). To what extent is it possible to apply a similar technique to anthropological material? Scanning Kent and Rosanoff's list, we are first of all impressed with the necessity of restricting its use to persons living under similar cultural conditions. Apart from the fact that certain abstract ideas, such as 'music', might not have equivalents in other cultures, the reactions to the concept would inevitably differ in other civilizations. For instance, 'piano', 'violin', 'harmony', '*Merry Widow*' would be excluded. It might be easy to suggest plausible equivalents in the second culture, but their precise value would be highly problematical. The utility of mass investigations of this sort rests on the exposure of all individuals to a comparable educational environment. This may be illustrated from another angle. Of the American subjects studied by Kent and Rosanoff only one responded to the stimulus 'tobacco' with 'stars'; among the Crow, who identify their sacred tobacco with the stars, it is safe to assume that considerably more than one-tenth of 1 per cent would have had this reaction. Similarly, with the word 'eagle'; not a single American associated it with 'thunder' but in any Crow list the two ideas would certainly be coupled with a relatively great frequency. Probably some reactions would coincide in the two tests: there is no good reason why some Crow subjects should not offer as the second member of the pair such words as 'beak', 'clouds', 'feathers' or 'mountains'. But evidently individuality in our psychologists' sense could not be established by the Crow list for Caucasian subjects or vice versa: the coupling of 'eagle' and 'thunder' would be 'common' for a Crow, 'individual' for an American, though the investigators' wise precaution in their Appendix, that anything should be reckoned a normal response if symbolized by the eagle, must not be overlooked.

Another word of warning must be added: the psychological appraisal of a given association is impossible without a consideration of linguistic data. For example, in Kent and Rosanoff's list the 'eagle' is linked 568 times with 'bird'. This would be impossible for the Crow for the simple reason that the eagle as the bird *par excellence* is commonly designated by the same term as the whole zoological class. Again, the constellation of the Dipper is pre-eminently associated by the Crow with the number seven. Thus, the Dipper appears to Lone-tree in a vision as a man but is identified when he rises, exposing the seven stars on his queue; and so, when Lone-tree subsequently goes through a rite to aid a woman he summons six other men, 'for with them I should make seven, and there are seven stars in the Dipper'. Again, Hillside's brother sees the constellation as seven persons singing songs for him. Still another visionary infers that *four* visitants are the Dipper because they sing seven songs for him; and when he organizes a ceremony on the basis of his revelation, he assembles seven married *couples*. The last two instances are especially interesting, for they show that so long as the number seven appears in some fashion no incongruity is felt in the representation of the Dipper (Lowie, 1922, pp. 334, 391).

Now, plausible as this association may seem, there is no obvious reason for the exceptional emphasis on the numerical aspect of the constellation until we find that the Dipper in Crow is simply called 'Seven Stars', so that we are not dealing with an ordinary association of distinct ideas at all.

These examples show how important it is to take into account the linguistic data involved. This is indeed obvious when we recall that in Jung's experiments with Swiss subjects such external factors as similarity in sound (green-greed) or the conventional coupling of terms as in set phrases (assault-battery) played an important part (Jung, 1919, p. 27).

The systematic study of individual associations among illiterate peoples is hardly even in its infancy, but an unpublished series collected by Spier among the Havasupai of Arizona strongly impresses one with the psychic unity of mankind as regards the principles at work in producing responses from cue words. Thus, there is 'coordination' in uniting concepts both of which belong to the same general head, but also 'contrast', 'predication', and, as might be expected, some residual instances remain obscure. At all events, there is every reason to look for an explanation of the associations of primitive folk towards the same psychological principles operative among ourselves.

A fruitful line of research lies in the study of variants of myths and prayers. Sometimes these may be so stereotyped that for generations not the slightest alteration has been permitted. This, for example, is reported for some Hawaiian hymns, a phenomenon in harmony with Polynesian formalism. But elsewhere some latitude is allowed, and the resulting substitutions may repay study from more than one angle. We can thus examine the versions of the same myth told by two different narrators. We can also profitably examine the variations in the same individual's account at different times, for that will indicate the range of ideas evoked in one person by a fixed stimulus. At a certain stage of the Crow Tobacco ceremony a warrior is supposed to come running and to report what he has seen on a raid and on the return journey. At three different times Gray-bull dictated to me in his own language the actor's speech. There is of course far-reaching similarity, yet enough difference to prove that the form was not standardized. Thus, in all three versions the speaker stresses the abundance of the Tobacco crop and of the wild cherries, but only once uses a superlative in that connection, which accordingly is a dispensable element. In all three variants an enemy is killed, but while the narrator twice reports how he captured a gun the third account substitutes the striking of a blow: these were both conventional deeds of valor and evidently reckoned as equivalent. That is, the cue 'victorious exploit' might arouse in Gray-bull's mind either 'gun-capture' or 'blow'.

Such individual interpretations are significant even for a purely cultural inquiry because the traditional associations described by Höffding have not always been traditional, and whenever we observe a deviation from the norm we have before us a possible starting-point for a cultural innovation. Unfortunately, when a given traditional association confronts us, it is often wholly enigmatic from a psychological point of view, that is to say, no hint remains of the principle on which the underlying ideas were ever linked by any individual mind. It is easy enough to proceed from cue to reaction, but to work backwards is more difficult, just as it is harder to extract a cube root than to raise a number to the third power. Still there are degrees of obscurity, and at all events a brief discussion of some instances may illuminate the nature of the problem. [. . .]

If, say, a certain object or idea invariably appears in connection with a certain color, the color can come to acquire symbolic value and will evoke the image or concept of its regular concomitant. Sometimes an association of this character is indirect, that is, the symbol is not immediately associated with the basic emotional value but only through a series of intervening links. Thus, a species of snake among the Andamanese is an emblem of well-being not in its own right, as it were, but because it is associated with honey, which besides its intrinsic attractiveness is again associated with the season of fine weather. Similarly, the Western Dakota may represent the whirlwind by narrow upright figures that directly stand for the chrysalis of a moth from which the whirlwind is derived (Benedict, 1923, p. 79). [. . .]

Interesting as such reflections are from a psychological point of view, for our present purpose they must yield precedence to another, to wit, the religious value of the symbol. The significance of the cross in Christianity or the lotus-flower in Buddhism is too well-known to require more than a passing reference. That there are parallel instances in primitive life is clear from the example, several times quoted, of the significance attached to a feather revealed in a Crow vision. This case is a favorable one for elucidating the source of the symbol's value. It is too readily assumed that since the symbol stands for something else, its potency is derivative from that something, and the overshadowing influence exerted by an apparently secondary phenomenon remains rather enigmatic. Thus, the spontaneous emotion evoked by the flag of one's country is not easily explicable on this view, nor the Crow's appraisal of his feather as 'the greatest thing in the world'. In both cases the difficulty lies in the assumption of an inapplicable psychological attitude. Only in an intellectualistic sense does the flag or feather represent an ulterior entity of higher order; on the affective plane, either represents *nothing* apart from itself but forms an integral part of an invaluable indivisible emotional experience that immediately asserts itself with all the force of an unanalysable manifestation of the Extraordinary in the special form of the Sacred. This reaction appears clearly in a statement made by an Hidatsa woman to the effect that Indian corn and the wild geese were one and the same thing. It was not that she was of pre-logical mentality in Lévy-Bruhl's sense, that is, incapable in ordinary life of separating the idea of the plant from that of the birds, but that in the given context both were associated in the same sacred complex and stood for that complex: whether one or the other cue was used to evoke the essential emotional state, was a matter of complete indifference. [. . .]

Now it is a significant observation that the ritualistic pattern of a tribe may embrace not merely the characteristics of observances but the very purposes for which the ceremonial is performed; or, to be more precise, for which it is *avowedly* performed. Thus, the Arapaho have eight major ceremonies, each and every one of which is initiated only as the result of a pledge made to avert danger or death. In short, because of the standardization of rationalizing about ceremonial aims, ceremonial activity has become firmly linked with one particular type of explanation. The inevitable consequence will be that when any new set of comparable observances is introduced *its* rationalization will follow the path of least resistance, that is, will fall into the accustomed groove. In principle, this of course exactly parallels the etiological pattern characteristic of the region, the inclination, so often emphasized above, to derive anything and everything from a visionary experience. When my Hidatsa informants did not know of a vision-myth to account for a given ritual, they quite automatically inferred that the ceremony was not of native origin. I encountered an instructive case among the Crow. These people had within recent times adopted a Pipe ritual from the Hidatsa and had discovered that the sister tribe lacked the Crow Tobacco ceremony. These facts were introduced into the legend accounting for the separation of the two groups by the assumption that when the division occurred the founder of the Crow tribe was blessed with a revelation of the Tobacco, the founder of the Hidatsa tribe with that of the sacred Pipe. The assurance with which this rationalization was advanced is rather amusing because the Hidatsa themselves, far from claiming authorship of the Pipe ritual, say that they obtained it from the Arikara. That was a possibility the Crow rationalizer had not considered: his craving for a causal explanation for certain differences in religious behavior between two branches of a once undivided people was adequately satisfied when he had applied the approved formula.

Can we define the phenomena described above in more definitely psychological terms? Always with the understanding that an association occurring in the individual psyche does not forthwith become a cultural fact but can only be converted into one where the relations of the individual mind to its social environment are favorable, we can proceed to an analysis of the initial association. To take a concrete example, all the Arapaho military organizations performed ceremonies to ward off danger, but some of these are demonstrably of alien origin. Now what happened when one of these foreign ceremonial complexes was adopted into the Arapaho scheme? There was evidently what psychologists generally call association by similarity and contiguity: the complex was at once put into the same category as certain well-established ceremonies and whatever general features were linked with these were thus automatically joined to the newcomer. This implies a partial blindness – doubtless only in the rarest cases a *willful* blindness – as to the phenomenon assimilated. Attention is concentrated on *likeness* to familiar performances, specific differences are of course noticed but merely as constituting a pleasing variation in detail: the new ceremony is merely a novel embodiment of the current 'idea' of ceremonialism in a Platonic sense. Hence there is what Professor Woodworth has called the 'response by analogy', based on the neglect of everything in the borrowed elements that cannot be forthwith adapted to the norm.

References

BENEDICT, R. F. (1923), 'The concept of the guardian spirit in North America', *Amer. Anthropol. Memoir*, no. 29.

HÖFFDING, H. (1893), *Outlines of Psychology*, London.

JUNG, C. G. (1919), *Studies in Word Association*, Russell.

KENT, G. H., and ROSANOFF, A. G. (1910), 'A study of association in insanity', *Amer. J. Insanity*, vol. 68, nos. 1, 2.

LOWIE, R. H. (1922), *The Religion of the Crow Indians*, American Museum of Natural History.

3 Edmund Leach

Anthropological Aspects of Language: Animal Categories and Verbal Abuse

Edmund Leach, 'Anthropological aspects of language: animal categories and verbal abuse' in Eric H. Lenneberg (ed.), *New Directions in the Study of Language*, Massachusetts Institute of Technology Press, 1964, pp. 23–63.

The central theme of my essay is the classical anthropological topic of 'taboo'. This theme, in this guise, does not form part of the conventional field of discourse of experimental psychologists; yet the argument that I shall present has its psychological equivalents. When psychologists debate about the mechanism of 'forgetting' they often introduce the concept of 'interference', the idea that there is a tendency to repress concepts that have some kind of semantic overlap (Postman, 1961, pp. 152–96). The thesis which I present depends upon a converse hypothesis, namely, that we can only arrive at semantically distinct verbal concepts if we repress the boundary percepts that lie between them.

To discuss the anthropological aspects of language within the confines of space allotted to me here is like writing a history of England in thirty lines. I propose to tackle a specific theme, not a general one. For the anthropologist, language is a part of culture, not a thing in itself. Most of the anthropologist's problems are concerned with human communication. Language is one means of communication, but customary acts of behavior are also a means of communication, and the anthropologist feels that he can, and should, keep both modes of communication in view at the same time.

Language and taboo

This is a symposium about language but my theme is one of non-language. Instead of discussing things that are said and done, I want to talk about things that are not said and done. My theme is that of taboo, expression which is inhibited.

Anthropological and psychological literature alike are crammed with descriptions and learned explanations of apparently irrational prohibitions and inhibitions. Such 'taboo' may be either behavioral or linguistic, and it deserves note that the protective sanctions are very much the same in either case. If at this moment I were really anxious to get arrested by the police, I might strip naked or launch into a string of violent obscenities: either procedure would be equally effective.

Linguistic taboos and behavioral taboos are not only sanctioned in the same way, they are very much muddled up: sex behavior and sex words, for example. But this association of deed and word is not so simple as might appear. The relationship is not necessarily causal. It is not the case that certain kinds of behavior are taboo and that, therefore, the language relating to such behavior becomes taboo. Sometimes words may be taboo in themselves for linguistic (phonemic) reasons, and the causal link, if any, is then reversed; a behavioral taboo comes to reflect a prior verbal taboo. In this paper I shall only touch upon the fringe of this complex subject.

A familiar type of purely linguistic taboo is the pun. A pun occurs when we make a joke by confusing two apparently different meanings of the same phonemic pattern. The pun seems funny or shocking because it challenges a taboo which ordinarily forbids us to recognize that the sound pattern is ambiguous. In many cases such verbal taboos have social as well as linguistic aspects. In English, though not I think in American, the word *queen* has a homonym *quean*. The words are phonetically indistinguishable (kwīn). Queen is the consort of King or even a female sovereign in her own right; quean which formerly meant a prostitute now usually denotes a homosexual male. In the non-human world we have queen bees and brood queen cats, both indicating a splendid fertility, but a quean is a barren cow. Although these two words pretend to be different, indeed opposites, they really denote the same idea. A queen is a female of abnormal status in a positive virtuous sense; a quean is a person of depraved character or uncertain sex, a female of abnormal status in a negative sinful sense. Yet their common abnormality turns both into 'supernatural' beings; so also, in metaphysics, the contraries God and the Devil are both supernatural beings. In this case, then, the taboo which allows us to separate the two ambiguous concepts, so that we can talk of queens without thinking of queans, and vice versa, is simultaneously both linguistic *and* social.

We should note that the taboo operates so as to distinguish two identical phonemic patterns; it does not operate so as to suppress the pattern altogether. We are not inhibited from saying kwīn. Yet the very similar phonemic pattern produced by shifting the dental n to bilabial m and shortening the medial vowel (kwim) is one of the most unprintable obscenities in the English language. Some American informants have assured me that this word has been so thoroughly suppressed that it has not crossed the Atlantic at all, but this does not seem entirely correct as there is dictionary evidence to the contrary.[1] It is hard to talk about the unsayable but I hope I have made my initial point. Taboo is simultaneously both behavioral and linguistic, both social and psychological. As an anthropologist, I am particularly concerned with the social aspects of taboo. Analytical psychologists of various schools are particularly concerned with the individual taboos which center in the oral, anal and genital functions. Experimental psychologists may concern themselves with essentially the same kind of phenomenon when they examine the process of forgetting, or various kinds of muscular inhibition. But all these varieties of repression are so meshed into the web of language that discussion of any one of the three frames, anthropological, psychological or linguistic, must inevitably lead on to some consideration of the other two.

1. The Oxford English Dictionary says nothing of the obscenity but records *Quim* as a 'late Scottish variant' of the now wholly obsolete *Queme* = 'pleasant'. Partridge (1949) prints the word in full (whereas he balks at f*ck and c*nt). His gloss is 'the female pudend' and he gives *queme* as a variant. Funk and Wagnalls, and Webster, latest editions, both ignore the term, but Wentworth and Flexner (1961) give:
quim n. 1 = queen; 2 (taboo) = the vagina.
That this phonemic pattern is, in fact, penumbral to the more permissible *queen* is thus established.

The American dictionaries indicate that the range of meanings of *queen* (*quean*) are the same as in England, but the distinction of spelling is not firmly maintained.

Animal categories and verbal obscenities

In the rest of this paper I shall have relatively little to say about language in a direct sense, but this is because of the nature of my problem. I shall be discussing the connection between animal categories and verbal obscenities. Plainly it is much easier to talk about the animals than about the obscenities! The latter will mostly be just off stage. But the hearer (and the reader) should keep his wits about him. Just as queen is dangerously close to the unsayable, so also there are certain very familiar animals which are, as it were, only saved by a phoneme from sacrilege or worse. In seventeenth-century English witchcraft trials it was very commonly asserted that the Devil appeared in the form of a Dog – that is, God backwards. In England we still employ this same metathesis when we refer to a clergyman's collar as a 'dog collar' instead of a 'God collar'. So also it needs only a slight vowel shift in *fox* to produce the obscene *fux*. No doubt there is a sense in which such facts as these can be deemed linguistic accidents, but they are accidents which have a functional utility in the way we use our language. As I shall show presently, there are good sociological reasons why the English categories *dog* and *fox*, like the English category *queen* (*quean*), should evoke taboo associations in their phonemic vicinity.

As an anthropologist I do not profess to understand the psychological aspects of the taboo phenomenon. I do not understand what happens when a word or a phrase or a detail of behavior is subject to repression. But I can observe what happens. In particular I can observe that when verbal taboos are broken the result is a specific social phenomenon which affects both the actor and his hearers in a specific describable way. I need not elaborate. This phenomenon is what we mean by obscenity. Broadly speaking, the language of obscenity falls into three categories: dirty words – usually referring to sex and excretion; blasphemy and profanity; animal abuse – in which a human being is equated with an animal of another species.

These categories are not in practice sharply distinguished. Thus the word 'bloody', which is now a kind of all-purpose mildly obscene adjective, is felt by some to be associated with menstrual blood and is thus a 'dirty' word, but it seems to be historically derived from profanity – 'By our Lady'. On the other hand, the simple expletive 'damn!' – now presumed to be short for 'damnation!' – and thus a profanity – was formerly 'goddam' (God's animal mother) an expression combining blasphemy with animal abuse. These broad categories of obscenity seem to occur in most languages.

The dirty words present no problem. Psychologists have adequate and persuasive explanations of why the central focus or the crudest obscenity should ordinarily lie in sex and excretion. The language of profanity and blasphemy also presents no problem. Any theory about the sacredness of supernatural beings is likely to imply a concept of sacrilege which in turn explains the emotions aroused by profanity and blasphemy. But animal abuse seems much less easily accounted for. Why should expressions like 'you son of a bitch' or 'you swine' carry the connotations that they do, when 'you son of a kangaroo' or 'you polar bear' have no meaning whatever?

I write as an anthropologist, and for an anthropologist this theme of animal abuse has a very basic interest. When an animal name is used in this way as an imprecation, it indicates that the name itself is credited with potency. It clearly signifies that the animal category is in some way taboo and sacred. Thus, for an anthropologist, animal abuse is part of a wide field of study which includes animal sacrifice and totemism.

Relation of edibility and social valuation of animals

In his ethnographic studies the anthropologist observes that, in any particular cultural situation, some animals are the focus of ritual attitudes whereas others are not; moreover, the intensity of the ritual involvement of individual species varies greatly. It is never at all obvious why this should be so, but one fact that is commonly relevant and always needs to be taken into consideration is the edibility of the species in question.

One hypothesis which underlies the rest of this paper is that animal abuse is in some way linked with what Radcliffe-Brown called the ritual value of the animal category concerned. I further assume that this ritual value is linked in some as yet undetermined way with taboos and rules concerning the killing and eating of these and other animals. For the purposes of illustration, I shall confine my attention to categories of the English language. I postulate, however, that the principles which I adduce are very general, though not necessarily universal. In illustration of this, I discuss as an appendix to my main argument the application o my thesis to categories of the Kachin language spoken by certain highland groups in north-east Burma.

Taboo is not a genuine English word, but a category imported from Polynesia. Its meaning is not precisely defined in conventional English usage. Anthropologists commonly use it to refer to prohibitions which are explicit and which are supported by feelings of sin and supernatural sanction at a conscious level; incest regulations provide a typical example; the rules recorded in Leviticus xi, 4–47, which prohibited the Israelites from eating a wide variety of 'unclean beasts', are another. In this paper, however, I shall use the concept of food taboo in a more general sense, so that it covers all classes of food prohibition, explicit and implicit, conscious and unconscious.

Cultural and linguistic determination of food values

The physical environment of any human society contains a vast range of materials which are both edible and nourishing, but, in most cases, only a small part of this edible environment will actually be classified as potential food. Such classification is a matter of language and culture, not of nature. It is a classification that is of great practical importance, and it is felt to be so. *Our* classification is not only correct, it is morally right and a mark of our superiority. The fact that frogs' legs are a gourmet's delicacy in France but not food at all in England provokes the English to refer to Frenchmen as Frogs with implications of withering contempt.

As a consequence of such cultural discriminations, the edible part of the environment usually falls into three main categories:

1. Edible substances that are recognized as food and consumed as part of the normal diet.

2. Edible substances that are recognized as possible food, but that are prohibited or else allowed to be eaten only under special (ritual) conditions. These are substances which are *consciously tabooed*.

3. Edible substances that by culture and language are not recognized as food at all. These substances are *unconsciously tabooed*.

Now in the ordinary way when anthropologists discuss food taboos they are thinking only of my second category; they have in mind such examples as the Jewish prohibitions against pork, the Brahmin prohibition against beef, the Christian attitude to sacramental bread and wine. But my third category of edible substances that are not classed as food deserves equal attention. The nature of the taboo in the two cases is quite distinct. The Jewish prohibition against pork is a ritual matter and explicit. It says, in effect, 'pork is a food, but Jews must not eat it'. The Englishman's objection to eating dog is quite as strong but rests on a different premise. It depends on a categorical assumption: 'dog is not food'.

In actual fact, of course, dogs are perfectly edible, and in some parts of the world they are bred for eating. For that matter human beings are edible, though to an Englishman the very thought is disgusting. I think most Englishmen would find the idea of eating dog equally disgusting and in a similar way. I believe that this latter disgust is largely a matter of verbal categories. There are contexts in colloquial English in which man and dog may be thought of as beings of the same kind. Man and dog are 'companions'; the dog is 'the friend of man'. On the other hand man and food are antithetical categories. Man is not food, so dog cannot be food either.

Of course our linguistic categories are not always tidy and logical, but the marginal cases, which at first appear as exceptions to some general rule, are often especially interesting. For example, the French eat horse. In England, although horsemeat may be fed to dogs, it is officially classed as unfit for human consumption. Horsemeat may not be sold in the same shop that handles ordinary butchers' meat, and in London where, despite English prejudice, there are low foreigners who actually eat the stuff, they must buy it in a shop labeled *charcuterie* and not *butcher*! This I suggest is quite consistent with the very special attitude which Englishmen adopt toward both dogs and horses. Both are sacred supernatural creatures surrounded by feelings that are ambiguously those of awe and horror. This kind of attitude is comparable to a less familiar but much more improbable statutory rule which lays down that swan and sturgeon may only be eaten by members of the Royal Family, except once a year when swan may be eaten by the members of St John's College, Cambridge! As the Editor of the *New Yorker* is fond of telling us, 'There will always be an England!'

Plainly all such rules, prejudices and conventions are of social origin; yet the social taboos have their linguistic counterparts and, as I shall presently show, these accidents of etymological history fit together in a quite surprising way. Certainly in its linguistic aspects horse looks innocent enough, but so do dog and fox. However, in most English colloquial, horse is *'orse* or *'oss* and in this form it shares with its companion *ass* an uncomfortable approximation to the human posterior.[2]

The problem then is this. The English treat certain animals as taboo – sacred. This sacredness is manifested in various ways, partly behavioral, as when we are forbidden to eat flesh of the animal concerned, partly linguistic, as when a phonemic pattern penumbral to that of the animal category itself is found to be a focus of obscenity, profanity, etc. Can we get any insight into why certain creatures should be treated this way?

Taboo and the distinctiveness of namable categories

Before I proceed further, let me give you an outline of a general theory of taboo which I find particularly satisfactory in my work as an anthropologist. It is a theory which seems to me to fit in well with the psychological and linguistic facts. In the form in which I present it here, it is a 'Leach theory' but it has several obvious derivations, especially Radcliffe-Brown's discussions of ritual value, Mary Douglas's thinking on anomalous animals, and Lévi-Strauss's version of the Hegelian–Marxist dialectic in

2. English and American taboos are different. The English spell the animal *ass* and the buttocks *arse* but, according to Partridge (1949), *arse* was considered almost unprintable between 1700 and 1930 (though it appears in the OED). Webster's Third Edition spells both words as *ass*, noting that *arse* is a more polite variant of the latter word, which also has the obscene meaning, sexual intercourse. Funk and Wagnalls (1952) distinguish *ass* (animal) and *arse* (buttocks) and do not cross reference. Wentworth and Flexner (1961) give only *ass* but give three taboo meanings, the rectum, the buttocks and the vagina.

which the sacred elements of myth are shown to be factors that mediate contradictories.

I postulate that the physical and social environment of a young child is perceived as a continuum. It does not contain any intrinsically separate 'things'. The child, in due course, is taught to impose upon this environment a kind of discriminating grid which serves to distinguish the world as being composed of a large number of separate things, each labeled with a name. This world is a representation of our language categories, not vice versa. Because my mother tongue is English, it seems self evident that *bushes* and *trees* are different kinds of things. I would not think this unless I had been taught that it was the case.

Now if each individual has to learn to construct his own environment in this way, it is crucially important that the basic discriminations should be clear-cut and unambiguous. There must be absolutely no doubt about the difference between *me* and *it*, or between *we* and *they*. But how can such certainty of discrimination be achieved if our normal perception displays only a continuum? A diagram may help. Our uninhibited (untrained) perception recognizes a continuum (Figure 1).

Figure 1 The line is a schematic representation of continuity in nature. There are no gaps in the physical world

We are taught that the world consists of 'things' distinguished by names; therefore we have to train our perception to recognize a discontinuous environment (Figure 2).

Figure 2 Schematic representation of what in nature is named. Many aspects of the physical world remain unnamed in natural languages

We achieve this second kind of trained perception by means of a simultaneous use of language and taboo. Language gives us the names to distinguish the things; taboo inhibits the recognition of those parts of the continuum which separate the things (Figure 3).

The same kind of argument may also be represented by a

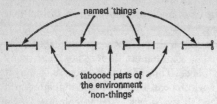

named 'things'

tabooed parts of
the environment
'non-things'

Figure 3 The relationship of tabooed objects to the world of names

simplified Venn diagram employing two circles only. Let there be a circle p representing a particular verbal category. Let this be intersected by another circle $\sim p$ representing the 'environment' of p, from which it is desired to distinguish p. If by a fiction we impose a taboo upon any consideration of the overlap area that is common to both circles, then we shall be able to persuade ourselves that p and $\sim p$ are wholly distinct, and the logic of binary discrimination will be satisfied (Figure 4).

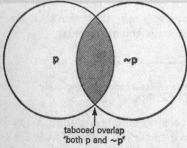

p   ~p

tabooed overlap
'both p and ~p'

Figure 4 The relationship between ambiguity and taboo

Language then does more than provide us with a classification of things; it actually molds our environment; it places each individual at the center of a social space which is ordered in a logical and reassuring way.

In this paper I shall be specially concerned with verbal category sets which discriminate areas of social space in terms of 'distance from Ego (self)'. For example, consider the three sets (a), (b), (c).

(a) Self... Sister... Cousin... Neighbor... Stranger.
(b) Self... House... Farm... Field... Far (Remote).
(c) Self... Pet... Livestock... 'Game'... Wild Animal.

For each of these three sets, the words, thus arranged, indicate categories that are progressively more remote from Self, but I believe that there is more to it than that. I hope to be able to show that, if we denote these word sets as

(a) A1 B1 C1 D1 E1
(b) A2 B2 C2 D2 E2
(c) A3 B3 C3 D3 E3

then the relational statement A1:B1:C1:D1:E1 is the same as the relational statement A2:B2:C2:D2:E2 or the relational statement A3:B3:C3:D3:E3. In other words, the way we employ the words in set (c), a set of animals, allows us to make statements about the human relationships which belong to set (a).

But I am going too fast. Let us go back to my theory of taboo. If we operate in the way I have suggested, so that we are only able to perceive the environment as composed of separate things by suppressing our recognition of the non-things which fill the interstices, then of course what is suppressed becomes especially interesting. Quite apart from the fact that all scientific inquiry is devoted to 'discovering' those parts of the environment that lie on the borders of what is 'already known', we have the phenomenon, which is variously described by anthropologists and psychologists, in which whatever is taboo is a focus not only of special interest but also of anxiety. Whatever is taboo is sacred, valuable, important, powerful, dangerous, untouchable, filthy, unmentionable.

I can illustrate my point by mentioning diametrically contrasted areas where this approach to taboo fits in well with the observable facts. First, the exudations of the human body are universally the objects of intense taboo – in particular, feces, urine, semen, menstrual blood, hair clippings, nail parings, body dirt, spittle, mother's milk.[3] This fits the theory. Such substances are ambiguous in the most fundamental way. The child's first and continuing problem is to determine the initial boundary. 'What am I, as against the world?' 'Where is the edge of me?' In this

3. An interesting and seemingly unique partial exception to this catalogue is 'tears'. Tears can acquire sacredness, in that the tears of Saints have been turned into relics and tears are proper at sacred situations, e.g. funerals but tears are not, I think, felt to be dirty or contaminating after the manner of other exudations.

fundamental sense, feces, urine, semen and so forth, are both me and not me. So strong is the resulting taboo that, even as an adult addressing an adult audience, I cannot refer to these substances by the monosyllabic words which I used as a child but must mention them only in Latin. But let us be clear, it is not simply that these substances are felt to be dirty – they are powerful; throughout the world it is precisely such substances that are the prime ingredients of magical 'medicines'.

At the opposite extreme, consider the case of the sanctity of supernatural beings. Religious belief is everywhere tied in with the discrimination between living and dead. Logically, *life* is simply the binary antithesis of *death*; the two concepts are the opposite sides of the same penny; we cannot have either without the other. But religion always tries to separate the two. To do this it creates a hypothetical 'other world' which is the antithesis of 'this world'. In this world life and death are inseparable; in the other world they are separate. This world is inhabited by imperfect mortal men; the other world is inhabited by immortal non-men (gods). The category god is thus constructed as the binary antithesis of man. But this is inconvenient. A remote god in another world may be logically sensible, but it is emotionally unsatisfying. To be useful, gods must be near at hand, so religion sets about reconstructing a continuum between this world and the other world. But note how it is done. The gap between the two logically distinct categories, this world–other world, is filled in with tabooed ambiguity. The gap is bridged by supernatural beings of a highly ambiguous kind – incarnate deities, virgin mothers, supernatural monsters which are half man–half beast. These marginal, ambiguous creatures are specifically credited with the power of mediating between gods and men. They are the object of the most intense taboos, more sacred than the gods themselves. In an objective sense, as distinct from theoretical theology, it is the Virgin Mary, human mother of God, who is the principal object of devotion in the Catholic church.

So here again it is the ambiguous categories that attract the maximum interest and the most intense feelings of taboo. The general theory is that taboo applies to categories which are anomalous with respect to clear-cut category oppositions. If A and B are two verbal categories, such that B is defined as 'what A is not' and vice versa, and there is a third category C which mediates this distinction, in that C shares attributes of both A and B, then C will be taboo.

But now let us return to a consideration of English animal categories and food taboos.

Animal and food names in English

How do we speakers of English classify animals, and how is this classification related to the matters of killing and eating and verbal abuse?

The basic discrimination seems to rest in three words:

Fish: creatures that live in water. A very elastic category, it includes even crustacea – 'shell fish'.

Birds: two-legged creatures with wings which lay eggs. (They do not necessarily fly, e.g. penguins, ostriches.)

Beasts: four-legged mammals living on land.

Consider Table 1. All creatures that are edible are fish or birds or beasts. There is a large residue of creatures, rated as either *reptiles* or *insects,* but the whole of this ambiguous residue is rated as not food. All reptiles and insects seem to be thought of as evil enemies of mankind and liable to the most ruthless extermination. Only the bee is an exception here, and significantly the bee is often credited with quite superhuman powers of intelligence and organization. The hostile taboo is applied most strongly to creatures that are most anomalous in respect of the major categories, e.g. snakes – land animals with no legs which lay eggs.

The fact that birds and beasts are warm-blooded and that they engage in sexual intercourse in a 'normal' way makes them to some extent akin to man. This is shown by the fact that the concept of *cruelty* is applicable to birds and beasts but not to fish. The slaughter of farm animals for food must be carried out by 'humane' methods;[4] in England we even have humane rat traps! But it is quite proper to kill a lobster by dropping it alive into boiling water. Where religious food taboos apply, they affect only the warm-blooded, near human, meat of birds and beasts; hence Catholics may eat fish on Fridays. In England the only common fish subject to killing and eating restrictions is the salmon.

4. The word *humane* has become distinguished from *human* only since the seventeenth century.

Table 1
English language discriminations of living creatures

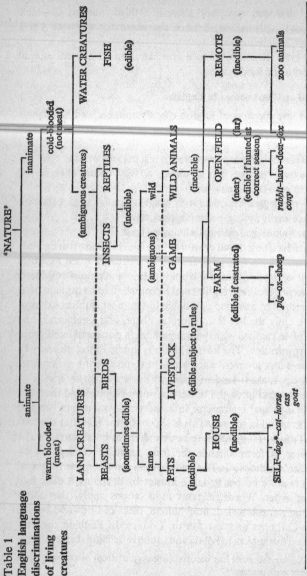

*The species *in italics* on the bottom line are those which appear to be specially loaded with taboo values, as indicated by their use in obscenity and abuse or by metaphysical association or by the intrusion of euphemism.

This is an anomalous fish in at least two respects; it is red-blooded and it is simultaneously both a sea fish and a fresh-water fish. But the mammalian *beasts* are much closer to man than the egg-laying *birds*. The Society for the Prevention of Cruelty to Animals, the Anti-Vivisection Society, Our Dumb Friends League and such organizations devote most of their attention to four-footed creatures, and as time is short I shall do the same.

Structure of food and kinship terminologies

Anthropologists have noted again and again that there is a universal tendency to make ritual and verbal associations between eating and sexual intercourse. It is thus a plausible hypothesis that the way in which animals are categorized with regard to edibility will have some correspondence to the way in which human beings are categorized with regard to sex relations.

Upon this matter the anthropologists have assembled a vast amount of comparative data. The following generalization is certainly not a universal, but it has a very wide general validity. From the point of view of any male SELF, the young women of his social world will fall into four major classes:

1. Those who are very close – 'true sisters', always a strongly incestuous category.

2. Those who are kin but not very close – 'first cousins' in English society, 'clan sisters' in many types of systems having unilineal descent and a segmentary lineage organization. As a rule, marriage with this category is either prohibited or strongly disapproved, but premarital sex relations may be tolerated or even expected.

3. Neighbors (friends) who are not kin, potential affines. This is the category from which SELF will ordinarily expect to obtain a wife. This category contains also potential enemies, friendship and enmity being alternating aspects of the same structural relationship.

4. Distant strangers – who are known to exist but with whom no social relations of any kind are possible.

Now the English put most of their animals into four very comparable categories:

1. Those who are very close – 'pets', always strongly inedible.

2. Those who are tame but not very close – 'farm animals', mostly edible but only if immature or castrated. We seldom eat a sexually intact, mature farm beast.[5]

3. Field animals, 'game' – a category toward which we alternate friendship and hostility. Game animals live under human protection but they are not tame. They are edible in sexually intact form, but are killed only at set seasons of the year in accordance with set hunting rituals.

4. Remote wild animals – not subject to human control, inedible.

Thus presented, there appears to be a set of equivalents

incest prohibition	inedible
marriage prohibition coupled with premarital sex relations	castration coupled with edibility
marriage alliance, friend–enemy ambiguity	edible in sexually intact form; alternating friendship–hostility
no sex relations with remote strangers	remote wild animals are inedible

That this correspondence between the categories of sexual accessibility and the categories of edibility is rather more than just an accident is shown by a further accident of a linguistic kind. The archaic legal expression for game was beasts of venery. The term venery had the alternative meanings, hunting and sexual indulgence.

A similar accident yields the phonemic resemblance between *venery* and *venerate* which is reminiscent of that between *quean* and *queen*. Sex and authority are both sources of taboo (respect) but in contrary senses.

A fifth major category of English animals which cuts across the others, and is significantly taboo-loaded is vermin. The dictionary definition of this word is comprehensively ambiguous:

mammals and birds injurious to game, crops, etc.; foxes, weasels, rats, mice, moles, owls, noxious insects, fleas, bugs, lice, parasitic worms, vile persons.

5. Two reasons are usually offered for castrating farm animals. The first, which is valid, is that the castrated animal is more amenable to handling. The second, which I am assured is scientifically invalid, is that a castrated animal produces more succulent meat in a shorter time.

Vermin may also be described as *pests* (i.e. plagues). Although vermin and pests are intrinsically inedible, rabbits and pigeon, which are pests when they attack crops, may also be classed as game and then become edible. The same two species also become edible when kept under restraint as farm animals. I shall have more to say about rabbits presently.

Before we go further, let me review the latest part of my argument in rather different form. The thesis is that we make binary distinctions and then mediate the distinction by creating an ambiguous (and taboo-loaded) intermediate category. Thus:

p	both p and $\sim p$	$\sim p$
man	'man-animal'	not man
(not animal)	('pets')	(animal)
TAME	GAME	WILD
(friendly)	(friendly–hostile)	(hostile)

We have already given some indication that ritual value (taboo) attaches in a marked way to the intermediate categories *pets* and *game*, and I shall have more to say about this, but we shall find that even more intense taboo attitudes are revealed when we come to consider creatures which would only fit into the interstices of the above tabulation, e.g. goats, pigs and horses which are not quite pets, rabbits which are not quite game, and foxes which are wild but treated like game in some respects (see bottom of Table 1).

In Table 2 are listed the more familiar names of the more familiar English animals. These name sets possess certain linguistic characteristics.

Nearly all the house pets, farm and field (game) animals have monosyllabic names: dog, cat, bull, cow, ox and so on, whereas among the more remote wild beasts monosyllables are rare. The vocabulary is most elaborated in the farm category and most attenuated in the inedible house-pet and wild-beast categories.

Thus farm animals have separate terms for an intact male, an intact female, a suckling, an immature female, a castrated male (e.g. bull, cow, calf, heifer, bullock, with local variants). This is not surprising in view of the technical requirements of farming, but it seems odd that the pet vocabulary should be so restricted. Thus dog has only: dog, bitch, pup, and of these bitch is largely taboo and seldom used; cat has only: cat, kitten.

If sex discrimination must be made among pets, one can say 'bitch' and 'tom cat'. This implies that a dog is otherwise presumed male and a cat female. Indeed cat and dog are paired terms, and seem to serve as a paradigm for quarreling husband and wife.

Among the field animals all males are *bucks* and all females *does*. Among the wild animals, in a small number of species we distinguish the young as *cubs*. In a smaller number we distinguish the female as a variant of the male: tiger – tigress; lion – lioness; but most are sexless. Fox is a very special case, exceptional in all respects. It is a monosyllable, the male is a *dog*, the female a *vixen*, the young a *cub*. Elephants and some other 'zoo animals' are distinguished as bulls, cows and calves, a direct borrowing from the farm-animal set.

A curious usage suggests that we are ashamed of killing any animal of substantial size. When dead, bullock becomes *beef*, pig becomes *pork*, sheep becomes *mutton*, calf becomes *veal* and deer becomes *venison*. But smaller animals stay as they are: lamb, hare and rabbit, and all birds are the same alive or dead. Goats are 'nearly pets' and correspondingly (for the English) goat meat is nearly inedible. An English housewife would be outraged if she thought that her mutton was goat!

Animal abuse and eating habits

Most of the monosyllables denoting familiar animals may be stretched to describe the qualities of human beings. Such usage is often abusive but not always so. Bitch, cat, pig, swine, ass, goat, cur (dog) are insults; but lamb, duck and cock are friendly, even affectionate. Close animals may also serve as near obscene euphemisms for unmentionable parts of the human anatomy. Thus cock = penis, pussy = female pubic hair and, in America, ass = arse.

The principle that the close, familiar animals are denoted by monosyllables is so general that the few exceptions invite special attention. The use of phonetically complex terms for 'close' animals seems always to be the result of a euphemistic replacement of a tabooed word. Thus *donkey* has replaced *ass*, and *rabbit* has replaced *coney*. This last term now survives only in the fur trade where it is pronounced to rhyme with Tony, but its

	Female	Male	Infant	Young male[a]	Young female[a]	Castrated male	Baby language	Carcass meat
Dog	Bitch		Puppy				Bow-wow	
Hound			Whelp				Doggy	
Cat		(Tom)	Kitten				Pussy	
Goat	(Nanny)	(Billy)	Kid				?	(Mutton)
Pig	Sow	Boar	Piglet	Hogget[b]	Gilt	Hog[c] Porker	Piggy	Pork, bacon, ham
Ass							Ee-yaw	
Horse[d]	Mare	Stallion	Foal	Colt	Filly	Gelding	Gee-gee	
Cow (ox)[e]	Cow (ox)[e]	Bull	Calf		Heifer	Steer Bullock	Moo-cow	Veal; beef[f]
Sheep	Ewe	Ram	Lamb	Teg			Baa-lamb	Mutton
Fowl	Hen	Cock	Chick	Cockerel	Pullet	Capon	?	Chicken
Duck	Duck	Drake	Duckling				Quack-quack	
Goose	Goose	Gander	Gosling					
Pigeon			Squab					
Rabbit	Doe	Buck					Bunny	
Hare	Doe	Buck	Leveret					
Deer	Hind	Buck Stag[g]						Venison
Swan			Cygnet					
Fox	Vixen	Dog	Cub[h]					

a Other sex distinctions:
Most birds other than duck and goose may be distinguished as cocks and hens.
The whale, walrus, elephant, moose and certain other large animals are distinguished as bulls and cows.
Lion and tiger are presumed male since they have feminine forms lioness, tigress.
The female of certain other species is marked by prefixing the pronoun 'she'; thus, she-bear.

b *Hogget*: a boar in its second year. The term may also apply to a young horse (colt) or to a young sheep (teg).

c *Hog*: may also refer to pigs in general as also *swine*.

d Note also *pony*, a small horse suitable for children.

e *Ox* (*Oxen*): properly the term for the species in general, but now archaic and where used at all refers to castrated male. The common species term is now *cow* (cows) or *cattle*. Cattle is in origin the same as capital = 'live stock'. The archaic plural of *cow* is *kine* (cf. *kin*).

f *Beef*: in singular = dead meat, but *beeves* plural refers to live animals = bullocks.

g *Hart*: an old stag with sur-royal antlers.

h *Cub* (*whelp*): includes young of many wild animals: tiger, bear, otter, etc.

etymological derivation is from Latin *cuniculus*, and the eighteenth-century rabbit was a cunny, awkwardly close to *cunt*, which only became printable in English with the licensed publication of *Lady Chatterley's Lover*. It is interesting that while the adult cunny has switched to the innocuous rabbit, baby language has retained bunny. I gather that in contemporary New York a Bunny Club has at least a superficial resemblance to a London eighteenth-century Cunny House.[6]

Some animals seem to carry an unfair load of abuse. Admittedly the pig is a general scavenger but so, by nature, is the dog and it is hardly rational that we should label the first 'filthy' while making a household pet of the second. I suspect that we feel a rather special guilt about our pigs. After all, sheep provide wool, cows provide milk, chickens provide eggs, but we rear pigs for the sole purpose of killing and eating them, and this is rather a shameful thing, a shame which quickly attaches to the pig itself. Besides which, under English rural conditions, the pig in his backyard pigsty was, until very recently, much more nearly a member of the household than any of the other edible animals. Pigs, like dogs, were fed from the leftovers of their human masters' kitchens. To kill and eat such a commensal associate is sacrilege indeed!

In striking contrast to the monosyllabic names of the close animals, we find that at the other end of the scale there is a large class of truly wild animals, most of which the ordinary individual sees only in a zoo. Such creatures are not classed as potential food at all. To distinguish these strangers as lying outside our English social system, we have given them very long semi-Latin names – elephant, hippopotamus, rhinoceros and so forth. This is not due to any scholastic perversity; these words have been a part of the vernacular for a thousand years or so.

The intermediate category of fully sexed, tame-wild, field animals which we may hunt for food, but only in accordance with set rules at special seasons of the year, is in England now

6. In general, birds fall outside the scope of this paper, but while considering the ambiguities introduced by the accidents of linguistic homonyms we may note that all edible birds are *fowl* (i.e. foul = filthy); that *pigeon* has replaced *dove*, perhaps because of the association of the latter with the Holy Ghost; and that the word *squabble* (a noisy quarrel, particularly between married couples) is derived from *squab*, a young pigeon.

much reduced in scope. It now comprises certain birds (e.g. grouse, pheasant, partridge), hares and, in some places, deer. As indicated already, rabbits and pigeons are both marginal to this category. Since all these creatures are protected for part of the year in order that they may be killed in the other, the collective name *game* is most appropriate. Social anthropologists have coined the expression *joking relationship* for a somewhat analogous state of affairs which is frequently institutionalized between affinally related groups among human beings.

Just as the obscene rabbit, which is ambiguously game or vermin, occupies an intermediate status between the farm and field categories (Table 1), the fox occupies the borderline between edible field and inedible wild animals. In England the hunting and killing of foxes is a barbarous ritual surrounded by extraordinary and fantastic taboos. The intensity of feeling aroused by these performances almost baffles the imagination. All attempts to interfere with such customs on the grounds of 'cruelty' have failed miserably. Some aspects of fox-hunting are linguistic and thus directly relevant to my theme. We find, for example, as commonly occurs in other societies in analogous contexts, that the sacredness of the situation is marked by language inversions, the use of special terms for familiar objects, and so on.

Thus foxes are hunted by packs of dogs and, at the conclusion of the ritual killing, the fox has its head and tail cut off, which are then preserved as trophies, but none of this may be said in plain language. It is the fox itself that can be spoken of as a *dog*, the dogs are described as *hounds*, the head of the fox is a *mask*, its tail a *brush*, and so on. It is considered highly improper to use any other words for these things.

Otters, stags and hares are also sometimes hunted in a comparable ritual manner, and here again the hunting dogs change their identity, becoming either hounds or beagles. All of which reinforces my original hypothesis that the category *dog*, in English, is something very special indeed.

The implication of all this is that if we arrange the familiar animals in a series according to their social distance from the human SELF (Table 1, bottom) then we can see that the occurrence of taboo (ritual value), as indicated by different types and intensities of killing and eating restrictions, verbal abuse, metaphysical associations, ritual performance, the intrusion of euphemism, etc., is not just randomly distributed. The varieties of taboo are located at intervals across the chart in such a way as to break up the continuum into sections. Taboo serves to separate the SELF from the world, and then the world itself is divided into zones of social distance corresponding here to the words farm, field and remote.

I believe that this kind of analysis is more than just an intellectual game; it can help us to understand a wide variety of our non-rational behavior. For example, anyone familiar with the literature will readily perceive that English witchcraft beliefs depended upon a confusion of precisely the categories to which I have here drawn attention. Witches were credited with a power to assume animal form and with possessing spirit familiars. The familiar might take the form of any animal but was most likely to appear as a dog, a cat or a toad. Some familiars had no counterpart in natural history; one was described as having 'paws like a bear but in bulk not fully as big as a coney'. The ambiguity of such creatures was taken as evidence of their supernatural qualities. As Hopkins, the celebrated seventeenth-century witchfinder, remarked, 'No mortal alone could have invented them.'

But my purpose has been to pose questions rather than to offer explanations. The particular diagrams which I have presented may not be the most useful ones, but at least I have established that the English language classification of familiar animals is by no means a simple matter; it is not just a list of names, but a complex pattern of identifications subtly discriminated not only in kind but in psychological tone. Our linguistic treatment of these categories reflects taboo or ritual value, but these are simply portmanteau terms which cover a complex of feeling and attitude, a sense perhaps that aggression, as manifested either in sex or in killing, is somehow a disturbance of the natural order of things, a kind of necessary impiety.

A non-European example

If this kind of analysis were applicable only to the categories of the English language it would amount to no more than a parlor game. Scientifically speaking, the analysis is interesting only in so far as it opens up the possibility that other languages analysed according to similar procedures might yield comparable patterns. A demonstration on these lines is not easy: one needs to know a language very well indeed before one can play a game of this kind. Nevertheless it is worth trying.

Kachin is a Tibeto-Burman language spoken by hill tribesmen in north-east Burma. Since it is grammatically and syntactically wholly unlike any Indo-European language it should provide a good test case. At one time I spoke the language fluently though I cannot do so now. I have a first-hand anthropological understanding of Kachin customary behaviors.

Kachin is essentially a monosyllabic language in which discrimination is achieved by varying the 'prefixes' of words rather than by tonal variation, though, as in other Tibeto-Burman languages, tones play their part. It follows that homonyms are very common in this language, and the art of punning and *double entente* is a highly developed cultural feature. A special form of lovers' poetry (*nchyun ga*) depends on this fact. A single brief example will suffice as illustration:

Jan du	gawng lawng	sharat a lo
At sunset	the clapper of the cattle bell	swings back and forth.
Mai bawt	gawng nu	sharat a lo[7]
The (buffalo's)	short tail and the base of the bell	are wagged.

Nothing could be more superficially 'innocent' than this romantic image of dusk and cattle bells. But the poem takes on a very different appearance once it is realized that *jan du* (the sun sets) also means 'the girl comes (has an orgasm)' while *mai bawt* (the short tail) is a common euphemism for the human penis. The rest of the Freudian images can easily be worked out by the reader!

On the other hand, it cannot be said that the Kachin is at all 'foulmouthed'. Precisely because of his cultivated expertness at *double entente*, he can almost always appear to be scrupulously polite. But verbal obscenities do exist, including what I have called animal abuse; the latter are mainly concentrated around the dog (*gwi*).

Kachins are a primitive people living in steep mountained forest

7. All Kachin linguistic usages cited here except the obscene connotation of *jan du* can be verified from Hanson (1906).

country. Their diet consists mainly of rice and vegetables, but they keep cattle, pigs and fowls. There are very few edible creatures which they will not eat, though they draw the line at dogs and rats and human beings. The domesticated animals are killed only in the context of a sacrificial ritual. The meat of such sacrifices is eaten by members of the attendant congregation, and sacrifices are frequent. Despite this frequency, the occasion of a sacrifice is a sacred occasion (*na*) and there is a sense in which all domestic animals are sacred.

Until very recently the Kachins had an institution of slavery. It is an indication of their attitude to animals rather than of their attitude to slaves that a slave was classed as a *yam*, a category which includes all domesticated animals. It is also relevant that the word *ni* meaning near also means tame.

The linguistic correlates of all this are not simple. In general, everything that has a place in ritual occasions falls into the wide category WU (U) meaning pollution. This has sundry subcategories:

(a) Birds.
(b) Various species of bamboo.
(c) Creatures classed as *nga*—mainly fish and cattle.
(d) Creatures classed as *wa*—mainly human beings and pigs.

Ignoring the human beings and the bamboo, this is a category of polluted foods, i.e. foods which may properly be eaten only in the context of sacrifice. It contrasts with ordinary clean food and meat (*shat*, *shan*). Other creatures such as dog (*gwi*) and rat (*yu*) may sometimes be offered in sacrifice, but these would not be eaten except as part of some special magical performance. I have arranged these and other terms (Table 3) on a scale of social distance comparable to that shown for English language categories in Table 1. The parallels are very striking. Let us consider the items in this table reading from left to right, that is to say, from very close to very far.

The closest creatures are the dog and the rat. Both are inedible and heavily loaded with taboo. To call a man a dog is an obscenity; *yu* (rat) also means witchcraft. In some contexts it may also mean affinal relative on the wife's or mother's side. For a variety of structural reasons which I have described in other

Table 3 Kachin categories of familiar animals
(for comparison with bottom three lines of Table 1)

	HOUSE (inedible)	FARM (edible if sacrificed)	FOREST (edible, no rules)	REMOTE (inedible)
	SELF-dog-rat	pig-cattle	small deer – large deer	elephant-tiger
			(near) (far)	
	gwi yu	wu	hkyi tsu shan shat	gwi raw
		wa nga		
Alternative English meanings of Kachin animal names in line above	(witch)		(feces) (ghost) (meat) (food)	(monster)

publications, a Kachin's feelings toward these *mayu ni* are ordinarily highly ambivalent. My wife's mother, a strongly incestuous category, is *ni*, which we have already seen also means very near, and tame.

The domesticated creatures that are edible if sacrificed have been considered already. These 'farm' creatures are much more closely identified with the self than the corresponding English categories. They are as human as slaves; they all live in the same house as their owners. The term *wa* (pig) also means man, father, tooth. It is veritably a part of 'me'!

In the English schema I suggested that field (game) animals have the same structural position, in terms of social distance, as the category of potential wives. In the Kachin case the category of animals comparable to English game are the forest animals hunted for meat. They live in the forest (*nam*). Now the Kachin have a prescriptive rule of marriage which requires a man to marry a girl of a certain category; this category is also *nam*. But in other respects the Kachin case is the inverse of the English situation. An Englishman has free choice in obtaining a wife, but he must go further afield than a first cousin; on the other hand he hunts his game according to precise rules. In contrast the Kachin has his category of possible wives defined in advance and, as first preference, should choose a particular first cousin (the mother's brother's daughter). But he is subject to no rules when he hunts in the forest.

The creatures of the forest which are thus obtained for meat by hunting are mainly deer of various sizes. The smaller ones are found close to the village. Like the English rabbit these are regarded as vermin as well as game, since they raid the rice fields. The larger deer are found in the deep forest. There are in all four categories of deer: *hkyi* and *tsu* are both small species living close in, *shan* and *shat* are large creatures living far out. All these words have homonym meanings: *hkyi*: feces, filth; *tsu*: a disembodied human spirit, ghost; *shan*: ordinary (clean) meat food; *shat*: ordinary (clean) food of any kind.

Thus the pattern is quite consistent. The more remote animals are the more edible, and the homonym meanings of the associated words become less taboo loaded as the social distance is increased.

However, the overall situation is not quite so simple. Monkeys of many kinds abound. They are sometimes eaten, occasionally tamed as pets, and their blood is credited with magical aphrodisiac qualities. They seem to be thought of as wild animals rather abnormally close to man, like the little deer *tsu*. A monkey is *woi*, a term which also means grandmother. The status of squirrels is very similar. The squirrel figures prominently in Kachin mythology, since it was the death of a squirrel that led man to become mortal. Squirrels are hunted and eaten, but again the attitude is ambiguous. Squirrels are *mai* (tails), but *mai* as we have already seen means a human penis.

Moreover, as remoteness is increased, we finally reach, as in English, a category of unknown and therefore inedible creatures, and the pattern is then reversed. There are two great beasts of the forest which the ordinary Kachin knows about but seldom sees. The first is the elephant, called *magwi* but also *gwi*. Since *gwi* is a dog this may seem odd, but the usage is very similar to that by which the English call the male fox a dog. The other is the tiger (*sharaw*, *raw*) which stands as the prototype for all fabulous monsters. *Numraw*, literally woman tiger, is a creature which figures prominently in Kachin mythology; she (?) has many attributes of the Sphinx in the Oedipus story, an all-devouring horror of uncertain sex, half man, half beast.[8]

This overall pattern, as displayed in Table 3, is certainly not identical to that found in English, but it is clearly very much the same kind of pattern, and the resemblances seem too close to be the product of either mere accident, as that phrase would ordinarily be understood, or the obsessional prejudices of myself as investigator. I suggest that the correspondences are at least sufficient to justify further comparative studies. On the other hand, I readily agree that it is easy to be over-persuaded by such evidence, especially when dealing with a language such as Kachin where the incidence of homonyms is very high.

In writing of English I suggested that there was a correspondence between the sequence of sex relationships: sister (incest);

8. This greatly simplifies a very complex mythological category. The *numraw* (also *maraw*) are 'luck' deities, vaguely comparable to the furies (erinyes) of Greek mythology. The *numraw* are not always female nor always of one kind. *Baren numraw* lives in the water and seems to be thought of as some kind of alligator, *wa numraw* is presumably a wild boar, and so on.

cousin (premarital relations possible, no marriage); neighbor (marriage possible); stranger (marriage impossible); and the sequence of 'edibility relationships' displayed in Table 1. How far does this apply for Kachin? How does one make the comparison? The difficulty is that Kachin has a kinship system quite different from that of English. True sisters are a strongly incestuous category, but remote classificatory clan sisters are persons with whom liaisons are possible but marriage is not. Elder sister is *na* and younger sister is *nau*. The homonyms are *na*, a sacred holiday, an occasion on which a ritual sacrifice is made; *nau*, a sacred dance occurring on *na* occasions to the accompaniment of sacrifice. This of course fits very nicely with my thesis, for Table 3 can now be translated into human as opposed to animal relationships (in Table 4) thus:

Table 4 **Kachin categories of human relationships**

	incest	no marriage, illicit relations	marriage	remote non-relative
SELF	NI	NA–NAU	NAM	RAW*
	mother-in-law	'sister'	marriageable cross-cousin	
	near (inedible)	sacred occasion (edible if sacrificed)	forest (edible)	forest fire (inedible)

*There are two relevant homonyms of *raw* = tiger. *Raw* as a verb means cease to be related; it applies in particular when two affinally related groups cease to recognize their relationship. *Raw* also means forest fire. It is thus the dangerous aspect of the forest, where *nam* is friendly.

Perhaps all this is too good to be true, but I think that it deserves further investigation.

Those who wish to take my argument seriously might well consider its relevance to Lévi-Strauss's most remarkable book *La pensée sauvage* (1962). Though fascinated by that work I have also felt that some dimension to the argument is missing. We need to consider not merely that things in the world can be classified as sacred and not sacred, but also as more sacred and less sacred. So also in social classifications it is not sufficient to have a discrimination me-it, we-they; we also need a graduated scale close–far, more like me–less like me. If this essay is found to have a permanent value it will be because it represents an expansion of Lévi-Strauss's thesis in the direction I have indicated.

References

HANSON, O. (1906), *A Dictionary of the Kachin Language*, Rangoon.

LÉVI-STRAUSS, C. (1962), *La Pensée sauvage*, Plon.

PARTRIDGE, E. (1949), *A Dictionary of Slang and Unconventional English*, 3rd edn, Routledge & Kegan Paul.

POSTMAN, L. (1961), 'The present status of interference theory', in Charles N. Cofer (ed.), *Verbal Learning and Verbal Behavior*, McGraw-Hill.

WENTWORTH, H., and FLEXNER, S. B. (1961), *Dictionary of American Slang*, Crowell.

Part Two
Myths in the Field

Here, the reader is given some field contact by proxy. Looking over the anthropologist's shoulder, one can see myths at work.

Highly qualified ethnographers analyse the data they have collected: they resort to their factual knowledge of the sociological context and to the semantic information obtained from the societies' members.

Guiart and Lessa offer striking cases of analysts working on live data. But Burridge's contribution is perhaps more cogent. There, in the dramatic complex of the Cargo Cult, traditional myths explode and charismatic men try desperately to pull together, in a new structure, the shattered parameters of their society's semantic system.

4 William A. Lessa

Discoverer-of-the-Sun:
Mythology as a Reflection of Culture

Excerpts from William A. Lessa, '*Discoverer-of-the-Sun*: Mythology
as a Reflection of Culture', *Journal of American Folklore*, Special
Issue, 1966, pp. 3–51.

*Myth does not reveal the whole of a people's culture and design for living,
though what is embedded in tradition often leads to knowledge and truth
lost to the conscious mind of a people.*

Almost anyone except the actual collector of a non-Western folktale – and sometimes even he – has experienced boredom and
frustration in trying to comprehend its content or warm up to its
style. The collector himself may develop an appreciation of the
tale only after he has studied it carefully and related it to its cultural milieu. The native listener need not be looked upon with
incredulity if he reacts with anxiety, sadness or mirth upon hearing what may seem to the uninitiated to be an insipid and confusing narrative, for the *raconteur* galvanizes his hearer's cultural
reflexes with verbal and visual stimuli well known to all from
generations of storytelling. The outsider understandably needs an
exegesis by someone in a position to analyse the tale, and it is
gratifying that at long last anthropologists have aroused themselves sufficiently to reduce some of the skepticism and disinterest
experienced by folklorists whose principal interests may lie elsewhere. It is my modest hope that my analysis of a certain body of
folktales, principally through the study of one story, will contri-
bute toward the lifting of the pall.

    Discoverer-of-the-Sun is a narrative I collected on Ulithi Atoll,
where I have pursued ethnological research on four separate
occasions beginning two years after the end of the Second World
War. It is one of forty-two tales recorded in 1960, and thus does
not belong to a previous collection of twenty-four stories gathered earlier, in 1948–9. The latter collection has already been
published (1961), but the new collection is here examined for the
first time, albeit fragmentarily and only as incidental to the

analysis of the one story under consideration. Before dealing with Ulithian oral tradition as such, and more particularly with this specific tale, it seems appropriate to look into the culture from which it emanates.

Ulithi is a seagirt land consisting of many islands arranged around a central lagoon of great expanse. The atoll is located in the Carolinian archipelago in the doldrum belt of the western Pacific, where typhoons often incubate. It lies ten degrees north of the equator. The people are Micronesians, having close affinities with the natives of such places as Yap, Truk and Ponape, as well as (to a lesser extent) Palau, the Marianas, the Marshalls and the Gilberts. They practise a simple agriculture and do much fishing. Pigs and chickens are raised to supplement the basic foods, which consist mostly of coconut and taro. The coralline nature of the soil restricts the food supply, but in addition the land surface is tiny so that the population has usually averaged only about five hundred persons, who live in small villages bordering the lagoon.

Material possessions are meager but well adapted to the environment. The people live in elongated, hexagonal-shaped huts whose interiors are divided by partitions into compartments. They make use of the true loom, with which they weave garments out of banana and hibiscus-bark fibers. Perhaps their chief pride is in their extraordinarily fast outrigger sailing canoes, in which they crisscross the lagoon for local transportation or set out for more distant islands for visits, trade and other business.

The division of labor is relatively simple, with men doing the more arduous and dangerous tasks and women for the most part working in the garden plots and the home. The specialists are all men and carry on their skills part time, particularly in canoe building, house building, navigation, divination and magic. Money is not used and goods circulate primarily through gift and ceremonial exchanges. People perform services for friends and relatives, keeping close account of their work so that they can call on their obligees when occasion demands. A good deal of labor is carried on cooperatively and communally.

The people do not live exclusively in either nuclear or extended family groups, but they have a strong sense of kinship solidarity and obligations. Marriage is monogamous, even though in theory polygyny is permissible. The prevailing rule of residence is not clear-cut but may be described as essentially patrilocal, with frequent and regular domiciliation with the wife's family for the chief purpose of working the garden plots of her group.

Matrilineal lineages constitute a strong organizing principle of social relations, entering into the ownership of land, canoes and other property, and the regulation of work, marriage and religion. A man cannot change his lineage affiliation, even though he may be adopted by someone in another lineage, a very common practise. There are some totemic macroclans which appear intrusive and have affiliations with distant places several hundreds of miles away. They do not enter seriously into the local society.

The natives are permissive in matters of sex, with premarital relations common and extramarital relations not unusual for married individuals. Divorce is simple and especially resorted to when the couple is still young and childless. Various taboos surround sex and reproduction, placing limits on the activities of new parents, specialists in magic and others. During their menstrual period women are particularly subject to proscriptions and must live apart in special huts provided for them near the shore. Abortion and infanticide are unknown; children are greatly desired, and are treated with kindness and tolerance.

Political organization has a twofold character. Internally, there is a system of district chiefs in which a so-called king is dominant. Each of the villages of the atoll has a council of male elders which decides its everyday problems and directs its communal activities. Externally, there is a highly complex linkage with Yap, which maintains a suzerainty over Ulithi, as well as over a string of other islands extending hundreds of miles to the east. Ulithi is considered to be low caste with reference to Yap, but it in turn has a superior status over the other islands of the Yapese domain.[1]

Social control is effected through the usual channels of gossip, ridicule and 'enlightened self-interest', with kinsmen playing a strong role in keeping the individual in line. Sanctions for the punishment of delicts are fairly diffuse and in any event are administered on a private basis with virtually no intervention by the king or territorial chiefs.

1. This system is explained in some detail in Lessa (1950a; 1950b).

Before the pagan religion began to crumble, it was a mixture of ancestor worship, animism and polytheism, with belief in a dualistic afterworld located in Lang, the Sky. The keeper of the lineage ancestral shrines was the closest approach to a priest that the society provided for. Other specialists in the supernatural were essentially magicians who concerned themselves with the typical anxieties of their clients, particularly illness and the hazards of wind and sea. Sorcery provided an outlet for aggression without becoming too disruptive and was especially attributed to the natives of Yap, who punished their Ulithian underlings for failure to show proper deference or to send sufficient tribute.

The first possible contacts that Ulithi had with the western world may have occurred in 1526, when Diogo da Rocha was in the vicinity, or later, in 1543, when it may have been discovered by Ruy López de Villalobos. The first undisputed visit to the atoll was made in 1712 by the Spaniard Bernardo de Egui y Zabalaga. Father Antonio Cantova set up a small Catholic mission there in 1731 but he was soon assassinated and the outside world shunned Ulithi for almost a century. After that there were occasional visits by European explorers and traders. In 1899 the Spaniards transferred the Caroline Islands to the Germans, so that from then until 1914, when the Japanese took over the German possessions in Micronesia, there was a period of moderate outside control and influence over the islands. The Japanese were interested in exploiting the atoll for copra but did little to affect the native way of life. When in 1944 the Americans took over the islands, they set in motion a process of acculturation that at first was moderately slow but has now begun to accelerate.

The culture as described above is essentially what it was just before the Second World War. The pagan religion had already been largely supplanted by Christianity. Nowadays the society is becoming particularly altered in the economic sphere, moving toward a cash economy.

After this excursion into the cultural and historical background of the atoll we may return to its folklore. This material is a conglomerate with indisputable affinities not only with the rest of Micronesia but with Polynesia, Melanesia and Malaysia as well. It shows a wide range in type and content, dealing with gods and mortals, lovers and lunatics, ogres and children, animals and fish. It does not especially serve to support magical ritual, though sometimes it indeed acts as a 'charter' for certain procedures. Occasionally it explains origins without being unduly etiological. Sometimes but not often it purports to be a chronicle of actual events outside the mythological realm. Many of the tales are lamentably truncated; others are fairly full. The people do not appear to classify the narratives. Informally they are said to deal with the *musuwe*, or times bygone. Often, specific ones are called *fiung*, a label I find difficult to define but which does not apply to purportedly historical events. Others are called *kaptal*, or story, again hard to interpret consistently.

The sixty-six tales in the complete collection were obtained from twelve informants, four of whom were women. Their ages at the time of telling ranged from twenty to seventy-two, averaging forty-seven years. Unfortunately, I did not record the native texts but took down translations with the aid of an interpreter, occasionally utilizing my own limited knowledge of the language or a direct translation by the narrator himself if he knew sufficient English. The tales were not gathered in a living context, which is not often feasible anyway, but I encouraged the narrators to deliver them as much as possible as if a native audience were listening. Most of the stories were first heard by their narrators when they were young, sometimes in early adolescence, and then again several more times, often as adults. They were learned mostly from relatives, male and female, and not only on Ulithi but on neighboring islands as well. Ulithian storytellers are monologists of a sort, much of their presentation being given in the form of a dialogue in which actors in the story are imitated by varying the voice. They do not constitute a special class, although I am willing to believe that in the past some of them may have been members of an elite group for the preservation and handing down of the more sacred of the narratives.

The narrator of *Discoverer-of-the-Sun* is Taiethau, a young man of twenty-nine who was one of my chief informants, being surpassed quantitatively only by another and much older man who had helped me in collecting both my first group of stories and my second as well. Taiethau is generally conceded to be one of the more indolent members of the community but is endowed with a flair for entertaining. He was the only Ulithian I ever encountered who had a driving desire to learn and recount as many tales as he possibly could. His manner of presentation was easily the most animated and perhaps the most skilled, and one could see that he was endowed with a vivid imagination. How much he may have superimposed his own embellishments I cannot say, although I am convinced that his materials bear the stamp of age and authenticity.

He first heard *Discoverer-of-the-Sun* when he was about thirteen years of age from an old man on Ubithi named Iungal. He heard it many times thereafter from many old men, but the parts of the narrative varied with the teller. Taiethau does not know whether his present version is as he first heard it or is a synthesis of several versions. I consider it to be as well connected and consistent as any I have heard, always remembering that in Ulithi longer tales are usually episodic in structure and therefore do not flow onward in an unbroken stream.

The text of the tale *Discoverer-of-the-Sun* that follows herewith is freely translated.

Discoverer-of-the-Sun

There were two sisters. The older sister married a man from earth. The younger sister one day went out to collect some *iuth* flowers for a head wreath, and a man from Lang came down and saw her. They agreed to get married – she said 'Yes'. So the man from Lang told her to wait for him until he should come and get her. But he used to come down and see her and she became pregnant. He went to Lang waiting until she would have a baby. When it had grown a little the man wanted to take the baby up to Lang and take its mother too, but the older sister knew this and asked the young sister if she would not leave her child with her saying she would take care of it in memory of her. So she [the younger sister] left her child and went to Lang with her husband.

The older sister had told her sister a lie. She never took care of the baby but gave it bad food and did not let the baby sleep beside her; she put the baby in her small firewood shed. The baby became thin and she always hit the child. When she took her own child for a bath in the sea, the child of the younger sister followed them to the beach. There was an orange tree near their house and the woman took a fruit from the tree and she took off the skin and gave her own child the orange and the other child the skin. After the child had eaten the orange, she took her child to the sea and gave it a bath and told her sister's child to go and

76 Myths in the Field

take a bath himself. They came back from taking a bath and the boy went to his shed and stayed there.

The next morning the woman took her child to the beach and gave it a bath, and the husband came from cutting *hachi* and saw the boy in the shed. He did not know what had been happening to the boy – that his wife was not taking care of him. He told the boy to come and drink *hachi*, and the boy came out and drank all the *hachi* in the coconut shell. After he had drunk the *hachi*, the woman and her child came from the beach and looked in the coconut shell and saw there was no *hachi* in it. She asked the boy and he said that he had drunk all the *hachi* by himself. She took a sprouting coconut and hit the boy with it in his shed, and hit him so hard he could not get up. She told the boy, 'Why did you do this? Didn't you know that your mother left you here and went to Lang and has never come back?' The boy heard for the first time that he had a real mother somewhere. When he had had trouble there he had thought that it was with his real mother.

He lay down and stayed in his house and watched the woman. When she was not looking he went out from his shed and crawled to the place where his mother used to go and collect *iuth* flowers. He came to the *iuth* tree and climbed it and went to Lang. He reached there and came to the menstrual house and walked near there, and there were lots of children playing around the house. His mother had had many children after she had gone to Lang. The women who were in the menstrual house looked at him and they said, 'Let us run away from the house, there is a *ialus* coming near us!' His hair was very long and his body was all dirty. His mother was there with a newly born child and she heard what the women said, so she came out of the house and looked for the boy. When she looked at the boy she knew that it was her own child. She ran to the boy and called him and she told the women not to run out of the house, because this was her first child. The mother of the child had married an important man from Lang. The women came and took him and gave him a bath and cut his hair and he became a handsome boy. His mother asked the boy what had happened to make him come up to Lang from earth, and he told her what had happened to him – that her sister had not taken care of him and that is why he left earth and went to Lang. She told him that it was better for him not to go back but to stay with her because her husband was his real father and he should stay with them there. They took care of him and fed him for three days.

Iolofath came the third day for recreation around the houses in the village. He happened to look in the menstrual house and saw a lot of children in and around the house, and he asked the people in the village where the children came from and who was their father and mother.

The people told Iolofath that the children belonged to that man from Lang and his wife. Iolofath went to the menstrual house to see if she would give him a child to adopt. She gave him the boy who came from earth. Iolofath asked his mother the child's name and she told him that they had no name for the boy. 'We just call him Seugau, or Baby Boy.' So Iolofath took him and called him just Seugau.

When they reached home his wife asked him where he got the boy, and Iolofath told her to be quiet and go ahead and make food for him because they were lucky to get this boy that he had adopted from somebody. She made food ready and fed some of it to the boy. When they were through eating they went to sleep.

The next morning Iolofath made *bwongbwong* over him, and when he was finished with the spell he threw him over the house. When the child fell to the other side of the house he grew bigger than he had been before. Iolofath performed the spell again and threw the boy over the house, and he got a little bigger again. He did this to him many times and he became a youth. Iolofath told him that from then on he must go and take a bath every morning in the sea. The youth did what Iolofath had told him.

After a year Iolofath told him that he should change his place for taking his bath, and to go and take a bath where he [Iolofath] used to take a bath. The boy asked him where the place was, and Iolofath told him it was at the end of the island. He told him he must also change the time for taking his bath, and that from now on he must take his bath early, before sunrise.

The lad was anxious to take the bath the next day. That night they slept and the next morning the boy got up early and was walking outside the house and saw a spirit standing outside there. His name was Limichikh [Smart, Wise or Intelligent]. He seized the boy and swallowed him, but after a few minutes he took him out of his mouth. The boy became a *limichikh*, too. The *ialus* told the boy to go ahead and do what his father had told him. All the while that the spirit was doing this and talking to the boy, Iolofath knew everything that was going on.

The boy went to the end of the island and scraped some coconut meat and rubbed himself with it for the oil. While he was doing this he looked at some sand bars and saw a spirit come from the sand bars. The spirit came to the boy and asked him who he was and why he had come here, for people were not allowed to bathe here. 'If you are a strong man you will see what I will do to you.' He took some spears made from coconut trunks – the spears are called *kei*. The boy answered, 'I am ready for a fight. If you want to fight I am ready.' The boy did not feel any fear of him. The *ialus* took a spear and threw it at the boy and hit him in the abdomen. The boy fell down dead and the spirit came and took the spear out of him and made him alive again. He told the boy that he should not come here again because he was a weak man, and only strong and able men could come here. He did this to try to make the youth angry – to feel bad. He told the boy that now he knew that the boy wanted to learn what he knew, so he gave the boy some of the spears and took some himself. He taught him how to throw spears and fight, and the boy learned very fast, because he was a *limichikh*. After practising these things he knew everything about fighting. All this happened before the sun came up. The spirit was in a hurry because he had to get back before sunrise. He asked the boy his name, and the boy told him his name was Seugau. The *ialus* laughed at him and asked him why, since he was a big man, they called him Seugau. 'You are not a baby. I will make a new name for you.' He gave him the name Thilefial, or Discoverer-of-the-Sun. He told him to remember his name and not forget it, and to tell his father. He also told him that now he was going to leave him, and that the next morning he should come to see him at the same time so they could have some fun there.

The boy went home and when he was close to his house he forgot the name the spirit had given him. He did not tell his father what had happened. Iolofath waited and waited for him to tell him, because he knew. Iolofath asked him, 'Did something happen to you when you were there?' Then he told Iolofath that he had met a spirit there and he had given him a name, but he had forgotten it. Iolofath told him that the next morning early he should go and ask the spirit what name he had given him because he knew that he would give the best of names.

The next morning the boy woke up early and went to the end of the island on the sand and started to make some coconut oil to bathe himself, and he saw the spirit coming. The spirit told the boy, 'Are you ready?' and he answered, 'Yes', and the spirit took some spears and threw them at the boy and the boy dodged them. When the *ialus* was through throwing all the spears he had not succeeded in hitting the boy. The boy said, 'All right. Are you ready? It is now my time to throw the spears back to you.' He threw the spears at the spirit but he did not strike him. When he was through, the spirit was tired from jumping around because the boy was more skillful in throwing the spears. The spirit took the spears and brought them to him, and they sat down and took a rest. The spirit asked him, 'Did you tell your father your name?' and he answered, 'I did not, because I forgot it.' The spirit said that he should go back home now and while he was going he should keep calling out his name over and over again so that he would not forget it. The spirit told him that now he was going to leave him because soon the sun would come up. He said to him, 'I am the sun. Walk back to your house and if you forget your name turn around and look at the sun.

Then you will know that your name is Thilefial, because you are the man who discovered the sun.'

The boy walked along, and whenever he forgot his name he would turn around and look at the sun and remember his name. Then he went on again, and every time he forgot his name he would turn around and remember. He reached his house and his father Iolofath was waiting for him. He shouted, 'My name is Thilefial!' His father told him that from now on he could go and take a bath any place he wanted, because the reason he had told him to go there was that he had to learn things.

One day he got up early in the morning and went to that place and took a bath there. This was just before the sun came up. He looked and saw some islands. He had a *khurukhur* stick. He took it and pointed it to the islands, and the sea became firm. He walked on it to one of the islands. There were some people on the island. He took a coconut leaf and whisked it over his hair to dry it. Some women saw him and wondered who this handsome man could be, and if one could become his wife. They went and told the people on the island that there was a handsome man on the island. The men became jealous hearing about him. The men said, 'Let us kill him.'

There was a man on the island who was the best warrior there. He was a deputy for Iolofath, and his name was Rasim. Another man, Solàl, who lived under the earth, was another deputy for Iolofath, like Rasim. Rasim and the people decided to kill the man. Rasim told the people to go ahead and kill him themselves, that he could not go with them because he was the best warrior and could not stoop to do the deed himself.

They took many spears and went to the youth. They threw them but he dodged them all, jumping farther and farther back. When the last spear came at him he was at the tip of the island, and he caught it and threw it at the men. He picked up one spear after another and kept throwing them until he came to the place where they had started. Some of the men died, and some were wounded, and the rest ran back to the village. They told the people that they could not kill him. A man with yaws all over his body was staying in the *metalefal*. He told the men they had better not try to kill him because no one could come on the island except the son of Iolofath. The men answered by telling him to be quiet, because they knew that Iolofath's wife had never been pregnant. Rasim told the men he would go with them and they would try again.

They started fighting against him and the youth did the same as before, jumping back from the spears so they would not strike him. He took the last spear, and as Rasim came in front of the men, he threw it at him. Rasim was frightened and ran away. The men went back to the village and Rasim told the men they must trick the youth to kill him.

The man who had yaws all over him told them, 'You had better stop fighting him, because we know that only the son of Iolofath can come here.'

They did not listen to the man and tried again. They fought him and he kept jumping back and back until he reached the end of the beach. While they were fighting, Rasim hid behind a coconut trunk. When the youth caught the last spear he hurled it at the men, and they ran away, some having been killed. When he got near Rasim, he did not see him, and as he walked past the tree Rasim threw a spear at his back. He fell down dead and Rasim and the men took him and buried him.

Three days after they had buried him, Iolofath, who knew what had been happening, came to the island looking for him. The old man with yaws said, 'Now we are in trouble, because if Iolofath comes what are we going to tell him?' The men were very angry at him and told him to stop saying that or else they would kill him, because they knew that Iolofath's wife had never been pregnant and they had no son. Iolofath came and sat in front of the *metalefal*. The people did not talk to him [they knew who he was]. He sat until noontime and then he talked to them. He told them, 'I have a man who came to my island before and he fought against people on my island and I tried to kill him but could not. And he ran away. I have come here to ask you if you have seen that man or not.' Rasim smiled and said, 'Do not worry, *tamol*. The man you are worrying about we have already killed.' Iolofath told the men they should show him the place where they had buried him, and they showed him the spot. He told them to dig up the man and put him in a basket, but the youth had started to rot. Iolofath took the basket and put it on a pole and put him on his back. He told the people, 'This is my son.' He took his son and went back to his island.

The men went to the *metalefal* and the old man with yaws told them, 'Now you see what I had told you – not to kill the man and you did it.' The men answered him, 'We did not know that he was the son of a chief. Iolofath is not angry with us because he knows we did not know.'

Iolofath reached home and took his son into his house and wrapped him in a mat. He told a man named Machokhochokh to go and bring back breath to his son. The man asked him where he should go and find breath. Iolofath told him to go down to Solal. Machokhochokh went down to Solal. He told him what Iolofath had told him. Solal told him, 'You have come here now but I do not have anything to give you to eat. Go and take that sprouting coconut to eat.' Machokhochokh took the coconut but did not have a husking stick, and he asked Solal what he should do with the coconut. Solal told him to go to the swordfish and use its mouth to husk the coconut. When he was through taking off the husk he asked Solal, 'What should I use to open the coconut shell?'

He told him, 'Go and break it on that turtle's back.' The man ate the coconut meat and when he was finished he asked Solal where he should go to put the shells. Solal told him to put the two pieces together and place them in an Alocasia plant, and he told him to climb a certain coconut tree and hold his breath as he climbed. The coconut tree was very high, and he told him that when he reached the top and had climbed the *ubwoth*, or growing leaves, he should look to see which way the *ubwoth* pointed and to jump in that direction. 'When you fall down to the ground, take the coconut shell and go back with it to Iolofath. The youth's breath is in the shell.' He did what he was told and climbed the tree and jumped in the direction in which the *ubwoth* pointed. When he fell and reached the bottom he took the shell and it [the breath] back to Iolofath.

As he was returning, Iolofath's son's body began gradually to be restored. He grew better and better. When he reached Iolofath's house the body was as it had been before. He was alive again. The son got up from the mat and when he looked around him he saw some maggots around him on his body, and he asked his father why he had put him in the midst of all the maggots. His father told him they had put him there because he was not a strong man and then went and told him what had happened to him on the island. His son felt bad about this and wanted to go the island sometime to fight again, but he did not tell his father how he felt.

One day early in the morning he went to the tip of the island and he took a bath there and did what he had done before – he took his stick and pointed it to the island, and the water became firm. He went to the island and took a coconut leaf and brushed his hair. The women said, 'The handsome man has come back again!' The men had a meeting and said they should kill him again. The man with yaws said, 'Why do you want to kill him? You know that Iolofath told us it was his son. Why should you want to kill him again?' The men paid no attention to him. They wanted to fight the youth. They fought and Iolofath knew that they were fighting. He turned himself into the fruit of a Barringtonia and floated on the sea to the shore of the island and watched the men and his son fighting. They could not beat him, and Rasim hid behind a coconut tree as he had done before. While he was hiding, Iolofath turned himself back into a man and stood up on the beach. He said to Rasim, 'Do not hide! Come out and fight with me! The boy is too young for you. You and I are about the same age and skill.' Rasim came out but he did not try to fight. He gave in, but Iolofath did not forgive him. Iolofath took a spear. He told Rasim that now he would throw it at him. 'Even if you run away or turn your back to me my spear will strike you in the abdomen [just below the ensiform process].

He threw the spear at that place and Rasim died. Iolofath then told his son, 'Go ahead and do what you want. If you wish to kill all the people on the island, that will be all right. Do what you want because the men on the island are of the same age and skill as you. Except for the man with yaws.'

The son went to the village and killed everyone in the village except the old man in the men's clubhouse. He went to see him and told him that from now on he was the chief of the island and that if anyone came to live there he was their chief. The youth then went back to his own island. He already knew that Iolofath had adopted him and he told him he was going to visit his real mother and father. He went to visit them and he lived there for about half a month. While he was living with them he recalled what had happened to him when he was a little boy, and he went down to earth and killed his mother's sister.

Then he returned to Iolofath and lived with him.

The content of this story is less recondite than that of most Ulithian narratives, yet for the uninitiated it poses many questions that can be answered only with a substantial amount of exposition.

I have reduced native words to a minimum in order to spare discomfort to the reader but a few of them seemed sufficiently appropriate to be retained.

The *iuth* is a shrub or small tree known to botanists as *Guettarda speciosa* and is used not only to make leis but for medicines, amulets, lumber and firewood as well. *Hachi* is palm toddy, and to 'cut *hachi*' is the native's way of saying in English that one is cutting the stalk which normally bears the inflorescence of the tree so that the sap will bleed more readily into the waiting cup tied below it. A *ialus* is any kind of a spirit, evil or benevolent, trivial or lofty, terrestrial or celestial. *Bwongbwong* is white magic, distinguished from black magic or sorcery. The *khurukhur* stick which Thilefial uses to cause the sea to become firm is literally 'orange wood', although not actually made of this substance, being made instead of any of a number of woods, such as *hangi* (*Pemphis acidula*) or *iar* (*Premna integrifolia*). Normally it is a walking staff with a slight bulge in the middle and a flare at each end. Occasionally it is used in dances. But in this story it takes on the character of a magical wand. It appears in other tales, and always has a magical meaning. It is mentioned in songs called *hachuchu*, which are sung by an audience when a medium is being possessed, it being said that the singing will not only induce a spirit to enter the medium but will keep him content during possession. A *tamol* is a chief. Literally, the word means 'my father', and is a kin term of basic importance, being applied both to one's real and classificatory fathers. A *metalefal* is a large house for men, being used for meetings, lounging, idling, and sleeping. Each village has one, and it occupies a central place in the settlement. *Ubwoth* is the whitish growing leaf of the coconut palm before it begins to unfold. It has usefulness in decorating the body as well as in imparting a certain magical potency to anything or anyone to which its leaflets are tied.

We may now deal briefly with the locale of the hero's adventures. Lang is of course the Sky or the Sky World, the abode of the celestial deities, particularly the three great ones – Ialulep, his son Lugeilang and the latter's son Iolofath. At the same time it is the home of all the dead. Those souls who come to it for admittance are interrogated, and the good are sent to that part of Lang which is reserved for them. The landscape, the mode of life and the social relations of this portion are much the same as on earth. Bad souls are condemned to either Gum Well, in which they wallow endlessly, attacked by animals, or to Garbage Pit, filled with a horrible stench. Lang has various levels, but it is never clear to Ulithians how each differs from the other, though the lower levels seem to be essentially stages that must be traversed before reaching the top. Thirteen of the stories in my Ulithian collection either wholly or partially involve Lang as a locale, although in a few of them there is no action there; instead, characters leave the Sky World and have their experiences on earth.

There is two-way traffic between Lang and earth, and the passage is traversed by both deities and mortals. The occasional mating of a god with a human is not rare; we have seen one sample of it in our story.

Cosmic pillars by means of which men ascend to or descend from the sky are found widespread in the mythology of the world, and in Ulithi there are some references to it. In *Discoverer-of-the-Sun* the young hero climbs a *iuth* tree to reach his mother in Lang. Asked to comment on the nature of an unspecified tree called Sur Lang, or Pillar of the Sky, which in another myth a hero named Haluwai climbs, an elderly informant who had not, however, narrated the myth offered the opinion that in reality the pillar is made of stone, rising upwards out of a distant place in the sea. The divergence of opinion may reflect the varying provenances of myths, for the narrator of this particular story expressed his belief that the tale came from Yap. On the other hand, in another tale from Ulithi, again of probable Yapese source, which tells how disk money came to Yap, we find that some men use a bamboo to climb to the Sky World. Perhaps the exact nature of the pillar is unimportant, and in any event the pillar itself seems of no special consequence in Carolinian mythology. If the truth be told, the hero is more apt to make his ascent on a cloud of smoke, a method especially associated with Olofat.

Who is Iolofath? Only his name and his ability to transform himself into the fruit of the Barringtonia betray him as Iolofath or Olofat, the trickster of the Caroline Islands. How changed is the wild youth of yesterday who walked alone in an unfriendly world and strove so hard to be recognized! Now he is married and staid, filled with paternal affection and responsibility.

Other Ulithian tales have chronicled his early life. In *Iolofath and Lugeilang* we learn of his birth. His father was the great celestial god, Lugeilang, who had a mortal mistress named Thilpelap. Lugeilang's wife in the sky learned of his love affair and tried to explore the matter by descending to earth, but each time she was thwarted by the magic of a dance gesture performed by Thilpelap's mother, Octopus. [. . .]

It is proper to ask if Iolofath's change of personality is not actual but merely the result of the transference of his name from one character to another. This question is proper because it is not unusual in folklore for names to be juggled about with little regard for the characters who bear them. I concede that this is a possibility.

Another possibility has already been suggested: Iolofath has merely grown older and secure. He is now accepted and need not struggle for the recognition he feels due him on account of his semidivinity.

Most likely, the answer to the difference between the one personality and the other is a combination of these two possibilities. There is enough in the literature to indicate that the new Iolofath retains most trickster traits and cleverness. At the same time, the new man conceivably could exist entirely independently of the old, to whom he owes very little in the way of personal traits. The thread of connection is there, but it is thin and weak. The transition is probably the result of an effort to retain the use and prestige of an already established mythical personage. Name dropping need not be any more alien to a primitive people than to a more sophisticated one.

There is an unmistakable resemblance between Iolofath and such other Oceanic tricksters as the Polynesian Maui, the Gilbertese Nareau and the Melanesian Qat, Ambat and Tagaro. In fact, some genetic connection is easily implied. Almost all of them are high born, experience a strange birth, manifest developmental precocity, and are parties to strong sibling rivalry. And of course all of them have universal trickster traits. The one important attribute lacking in our Ulithian hero is that he is not the originator of culture traits nor the benefactor of mankind; he is not a culture hero. Maui fished up islands, slowed the sun in its course so women had more time for their work, wrested fire from the fire god, introduced cooked food, and even tried to conquer Death. Other Oceanic tricksters too have in some way aided humanity. It is true that in some Caroline islands Iolofath succeeds in giving fire to mankind and decrees that man shall be immortal, but credit for these deeds is given in utterly inadequate fashion, as if their authenticity were not beyond debate. The strange thing is that in Micronesia the Polynesian Maui is in fact depicted by two heroes, for in addition to the tricksterism of Iolofath we have the benefactory deeds of another personage, whose name is Motikitik. Obviously, Motikitik is the same as Mauitikitiki, as he is often known as Polynesia. But Motikitik, while he fishes up an island and goes down beneath the surface of the earth, where he finds food, is a colorless conformist who knows no deceit, guile, malevolence or adulterousness. He is fairminded and sensible, and shows strong loyalty toward his dear dead mother, whom his two brothers have scorned. Even though he is confronted with the jealousy of his siblings, he cannot be aroused to retaliate. No, it is Iolofath and not Motikitik who shares Maui's colorful temperament.

Who is Discoverer-of-the-Sun's adversary, Rasim? He is a relatively obscure character whose name appears every so often in

Carolinian tales. In general he is powerful and combative, but he is not a consistent character, suggesting that the name transference associated with Iolofath may be more extreme here.

I first learned of Rasim in an Oedipal tale from Ulithi which I have called *Sikhalol and his Mother*. Rasim is a chief who discovers an abandoned baby in his fish trap and raises him as his own. He performs magic to make the boy grow rapidly. One day the lad is playing with his canoe when a woman, his mother, sees him and becomes so smitten by his comeliness that she seduces him. Her husband finally suspects that her protracted lingering at the menustrual house can only be for illicit reasons and sets out to discover who is her lover. The lad is the last one to be subjected to an identity test, consisting of the matching of fingernail scratches on the wife's face with the fingers of her lover. Rasim, who has already revealed to the boy that he has been dallying with his own mother, now prepares him in the art of self-defence. When the real father confronts the boy with the evidence of his guilt – the scratches made by his own hand – the lad resists and slays him. We do not in truth learn much about Rasim in this tale, but it is obvious that he knows something about combat.

The Rasim of *Discoverer-of-the-Sun* is less kindly than this, but even more the knowledgeable warrior. He must have had some virtues to become a deputy for Iolofath. We are not completely sure of his motivation in wishing to harm the young Thilefial. Mention is made of the men's jealousy of the youth, but what spurs Rasim to take a hand himself in the effort to murder him is the boy's skill in overcoming the men's attack, killing some and putting the others to rout. Rasim may have been additionally incensed at the audacity of a stranger in becoming Iolofath's son. It is notable that despite his own talent for fighting, Rasim finds that escape is the better part of valor. It is only when he has had a chance to recoup that he decides on the use of guile instead of a frontal assault. He kills Thilefial from behind, and then smugly assures the boy's adoptive father that he no longer has to worry about the young stranger. Later, when Thilefial comes back to life and again engages the men of the village, Rasim gets set to repeat his previous tactic, signifying a rebellion of a sort against his superior, Iolofath, who he now knows is indeed the 'father' of the youth. The demigod finds it necessary to step in and take a direct hand, throwing a well-placed spear into his body. Thus, it appears that Rasim was too stubborn to compromise with reality. It was more important for him to follow his combative instincts than to yield to his master's will.

Of course the Rasim of the patricidal tale of Sikhalol is a mortal, whereas the Rasim of our immediate story is a being in the Sky World, although the difference between these two realms, it must be conceded, is often vague. One way to explain the use of a common name for two such disparate characters is that in the course of narration a character may have his traits and millieu considerably altered. Another way is to assume that an already known name has been transferred from one character to another one.

At any rate, the Rasim of *Discoverer-of-the-Sun* is probably the same as a certain Rasim of Truk, a god who takes the form of the rainbow, a meteorological phenomenon which the people do not view sentimentally; indeed, it is especially feared by seafarers because they consider it to be a sign of death. In my collection of Ulithian tales I have an account of the killing of a woman by the rainbow (no name mentioned), and though the event occurs on earth, the rainbow is alluded to as a spirit, apparently malevolent at least toward this woman. This would seem to confirm that we are dealing with the same god. Substantiation of this assumption comes from another Ulithian tale in which Iolofath orders Rainbow, Tornado and Gale to kill a man from Yap who has played a trick on him. A further clue is provided by the traits of a god on Namoluk named Rasim, who hates women and will not permit men to have relations with them during time of war. Should a man violate this interdict, Rasim will pierce him with his spear. Men pray to him before going into battle. Surely this must be the same minor god as the aggressive warrior in *Discoverer-of-the-Sun*. On Namoluk he is even referred to, if I am correct in equating *Anu en marasi* with him, as the rainbow sent down by the highest god, Luk, to destroy an island when he is angry. This would make him a kind of deputy, as in our own Ulithian story.

Who is Solal? On Ulithi he is considered to be the god of the underworld and therefore the opposite number of Ialulep, the highest deity of the Sky World. But he seems to lack the authority of his counterpart. Indeed he is usually thought of as a benevolent sea spirit who has become the patron of fish magicians. Details concerning him are scanty, and there is little to go by in assembling a personality portrait. Solal is known throughout the west central Carolines. Generally he is said to be half fish and half human, neither male nor female, and to have created heaven and earth by rolling a grain of sand from one hand to another. He is recognized as the god of the underworld. Sometimes he is said to control the supply of fish. The literature gives few details of his personality or life history. Certainly in *Discoverer-of-the-Sun* Solal is cooperative in giving breath to Machokhochokh to take back for the resuscitation of the hero, and in addition he gives indication of being conversant with the skills of his position. [...]

The source of the magical power is not always clear and it is necessary to invoke a very broad definition of the term if one is to include the numerous instances in which supernatural power is tapped through some inner capacity rather than a ritual. Iolofath's ability to transform himself at will into a child or a bird falls into this category. So does the power that some characters have to make food or drink inexhaustible simply by willing it. Another example is that of a man who constructs a wooden bird that flies off with him inside.

The magic in *Discoverer-of-the-Sun* partakes of both the orthodox type involving ritual and the looser type involving inner capacity. When the hero is thrown over a house to make him grow, a ritual comes into play. Probably the transformation of the youth into a *limichikh* by swallowing involves contact magic, although further details would be desirable. The source of power when Thilefial firms the sea is not clear, especially since he uses a kind of a 'wand' to help him. Is the power in him, in the wand, in the gesture, or in a combination of all three? All those baths he takes are not explained, but the implication is clear that they have something to do with his conversion into a superman. I have been unable to fathom the magic behind the spear thrown at Rasim by Iolofath. It is a spear that hits the warrior in the abdomen when he is in flight, so we presume it was able to take a reverse course through the air.

Physical aggression, including battles, murders and cannibalism, constitutes a noticeable ingredient of Ulithian folklore, occurring in greater and lesser degrees of importance in almost three fourths of the tales in my collection. The nature of aggression in *Discoverer-of-the-Sun* is varied, for there is not only the blow struck against the young hero by his mother's sister wielding a coconut, but also the attack on him with spears by the *ialus* (regardless of his intent) which killed him for the time being, the attack by the jealous men prodded by Rasim, the second attack by the men, the killing of the hero by Rasim himself, the third attack on the resuscitated hero by the man, and finally the killing of everybody in the village except the old man. True, goriness and horror are not much elaborated upon but it is inescapably obvious that some concession to aggression is considered an important part of storytelling. While most of the violence is between persons, in some instances it is between a human and an animal or spirit, occurring frequently, as one might suppose, in tales involving ogres. It seems permissible for me to include also as aggression the killing of an eel by some birds because the *personae* act somewhat like humans. I have, however, not included an act of violence toward himself by a man who is so chagrined when his wife returns to her proper husband that he kills himself by striking his penis with a paddle. My criterion is that of interpersonal violence as well as group violence, including battles, which are abundant in these tales. The number of decapitations, which are usually unembellished, is small. In a few instances there is sadism, as when an ogre's intestines are pulled out of his anus by two little girls.

One might have cause to wonder if Ulithian's are themselves a violent people. The answer is not simple. Certainly today they are most gentle, and one could with justice assert either that the tales are not entirely of their own creation, or even that, original or borrowed, they are a kind of outlet for repressions. Psychologists may be able to fathom these puzzles according to their own favorite theories, but I deem it advisable that we drop the matter here.

Deception, trickery and prevarication are amply represented in Ulithian folklore, although only weakly so in *Discoverer-of-the-Sun*, as when the older sister tells the younger one that she will take care of her child, when Rasim hides behind a tree to kill the hero, and when Iolofath pretends while searching for the youth that he does not know the men have killed him.

In other Ulithian stories the deception and cunning is more obvious, being used by two brothers in a humorous tale in which they dupe their sister into becoming their sex partner by pretending that their dead parents have commanded her from the grave to submit to one of the brothers in order to save him from death as he hangs by one arm from a tree. Oceanic animal tricksters always have an abundance of guile, and here we see it applied by a ungrateful rat who has been rescued at sea by a turtle. The rat repays this act of mercy by first convincing the turtle he should allow himself to be deloused, and after he has put the turtle to sleep by this strategem he strikes him on the head with a tridacna shell and kills him. Flagrant cheating occurs in a tale in which a man removes a claim stick made with fresh coconut leaves left on a piece of land by the man who first discovered it. In its place he puts a marker made of old coconut leaves, and this convinces people that his marker is older.

Craftiness is one of Iolofath's traits as a trickster and there is no better instance of it than the ruse he employs to escape death when some men ram a post into the hole they have asked him to dig. Less distinguished heroes are also capable of cleverness. To save himself from a pursuing ogre a man uses the ruse of releasing rats to divert the ogre's attention. The same Atalanta trick is used by a girl pursued by a cannibalistic spirit. She casts behind her some head hair, pubic hair and spittle from the kindly mother of the spirit. An old standby, 'Wait till I get fat,' is used by two captive men not only to gain time but to hoodwink an ogre into giving them fat birds to eat while he is left with the lean ones.

Cunningness directed toward honest or justifiable ends is adequately represented. Thus, a girl puts coconut oil on the trunk of a banana plant to prevent an ogre from climbing up to seize her. He later catches her by imitating her younger sister's voice, and then swallows her. The younger sister then schemes to take away the fruits of his deception. She puts two barnacle shells underneath her tongue, and every time the ogre, who has been holding her captive, speaks to her she answers him word for word in echolalic fashion. Enraged, he seizes and swallows her too, but this is what she wants. Joining her sister in his stomach she gives her one of the shells and keeps the other. Together they cut through his stomach to freedom. In another tale a young hero kills nine ogres, one a day, each time putting back their severed heads and propping them up at the beach so that when their surviving brothers come up to the corpses they think they are alive and foolishly render to them the formal account required on Ulithi of men coming ashore in a canoe.

Cleverness in Ulithian folktales is manifested in a dispute over ownership of two mahogany trees. Two boys are beginning to chop them down to build a canoe when a man comes up and claims them as his own. The boys tell him that underneath each is a shell put there by their mother when she planted the trees long ago. The man is convinced of their claim when they fell the trees and the shells beneath them are revealed.

Humor is obviously an important ingredient of Ulithian folklore. Sometimes it is grim, sometimes subtle, and often blatant. It cannot always be detected in a cold text narrated without an audience of natives. The narrator who does not use his voice and body to express himself and arouse response may be incapable of imparting a sense of the comic to the interviewer. Yet even the relatively lifeless accounts appearing in writing are often patently sprinkled with the laughable, and by adding to them the fuller contexts that I was able to perceive, I feel that I have been able to extract a good deal more than appears on the surface.

In this respect *Discoverer-of-the-Sun* does not help us much, for it is almost devoid of humour. The *ialus* laughs when he learns that the hero is called Baby Boy, so perhaps this is an instance that needs to be recorded. The hero's inability to remember his new name has laughable overtones. Machokhochokh's use of a swordfish to husk a coconut is amusing. Little else is. But abundant illustrations are provided by other tales in my repertoire. However, I wish to defer consideration of them until we consider matters of folkloristic style, for I am more interested in the devices of humor than in its content. [. . .]

Any analysis of Ulithian folkloristic style must recognize that the traditional narrative is involved with a world in which a wooden bird flies carrying a man inside, a woman appears from out of the ashes of a fire, a chicken's ordure turns into yams, a taro plant becomes a girl, and a spirit sweetheart turns to bones in her lover's embrace. The fantastic and preposterous are not so predominant that they make it impossible to follow the plot or 'believe' in its contents, but they are always there and must be kept in the back of one's mind as having much to do with dominating the distinguishing traits of traditional narrative. Some of these traits will not appear foreign to western thought, yet others may seem meaningless and unreasonable.

We may make a beginning in analysis by studying the structural aspects of the stories. The lack of a native title for our tale, to which I have given the name *Discoverer-of-the-Sun* only for purposes of convenience, is characteristic of Ulithian narratives. The people themselves require no more than some catch phrase or name to enable them to identify a tale, and if more is required, then a brief introductory synopsis is offered.

Stylized introductions are characteristic of Ulithian stories. They are brief and almost compulsively insistent on opening the tale with a statement regarding the main or initial characters. The statement may be fairly minimal, but ideally it names the actors and gives their number, sex, relative age, marital state, idiosyncrasies and place of residence. Ninety per cent of the stories open in this fashion, and those that do not so begin either have a very special nature or were influenced by interview conditions. In the ensuing examples the rigidity of the opening words is sometimes diminished by the free translations I have sometimes seen fit to provide. The perspicacious reader will be able to see through this, particularly by ignoring the punctuation that for better or worse I felt called upon to furnish. He will also notice that the settings have a certain timelessness.

Discoverer-of-the-Sun is a modest illustration. 'There were two sisters,' it begins, and continues with 'The older sister married a man from earth.' Missing are the names of the sisters, which never appear even in the subsequent portion of the narrative, but we know the sex and number of the actors. Shortly after but not within the formal opening we learn of their marital condition, relative age and mortal nature. A glaring omission is the lack of mention of the place of residence or even the particular locale where the sisters reside. Names of actors in the opening statement are, however, more often supplied than omitted: 'Iongolap and Filtei were brother and sister and they were living on Yap.' 'There was a woman named Lokhsiel.' 'Haluwai and a woman lived on Yap and wanted to get married.' Once omitted, however, the name is usually never supplied in the subsequent narrative.

Two puzzling names, Iol and Iath, are recurrent in the stylized introductions. Either or both appear in the openings of ten tales, a not inconsiderable number, and mention of Iola as a half spirit is made in still another story, but not in the opening portion. In six instances, Iol and Iath are married and have children, while in a seventh they are married but childless. Once we find Iol without Iath or any other mate. Twice we find Iath married to another spouse, the name of one being Hatamaichifel and the other Hurekhrafur. The names of their offspring are never the same from one tale to the other. Nothing I have been able to do has revealed the ultimate identity of Iol and Iath and I can only conclude that they are prototypes, found also in the folklore of other Carolinians. They are fairly humble and colorless persons, and it is their children rather than they who emerge as the central personae. I have briefly toyed with the notion that Iol may be Iolofath – Ulithians usually address one another by the first syllables of their names – but this cannot be, for Iolofath is a powerful personality of semidivine origin, and however much he may seem objectionable we cannot demean him by taking away his talent for creating excitement.

Names sometimes follow a formulistic number – ten. Thus, 'Chemchem Seou [One], Chemchem Ruoa [Two], Chemchem Solu [Three] ... Chemchem Seg [Ten] were *legaselep* who ate people from island to island in the west.' Similarly, 'A woman had ten sons, called Sangaf, Rungaf, Solngaf ... and Sekh.' In another introduction we are told: 'There was a man and a woman. They were married. They had ten children – the first a girl, the next a boy, the next a girl, and so on, the last being a boy. They lived on an island that was divided into two parts ...' Here the children are not named, not even in the subsequent narration.

Locales are specified in all but nine of the tales that have formal introductions. In another nine no name is specified for the island or locale, although a feeble gesture is nevertheless made to link people with places. As one might expect, Ulithi is by far the most favored place, being designated about 40 per cent of the time, especially in the homelier and less consequential narratives. Fairly often a place outside of Ulithi but still within the Carolines is mentioned, particularly nearby Yap, where many of the folktales find their origins or counterparts. The Sky World, or Lang, is specified in only four introductions but is later designated as a scene of action in five more tales, with two additional references of weak character.

Stylized epilogues are not as consistent or clear-cut in Ulithian stories as are the introductions, but they are present. If one includes some examples that are weak, one finds that over half the tales end either by making mention of someone going to a place, or by explaining that this is the origin of such and such a practice, belief, saying, or the like. The 'place' epilogues far outnumber the etiological ones, although they sometimes occur in combination, in which event the place ending always occupies a penultimate position relative to the etiological epilogue.

All stylized epilogues are informally expressed and some may be diffuse as to place. Thus, *Discoverer-of-the-Sun* ends with 'Then he returned to Iolofath and lived with him.' Examples of other place endings both specific and vague are 'Thus, they went to the atoll to stay for good', 'He then got in his canoe and returned to Potangeras', 'He then removed her from the spirit's belly and took her home', 'They went back to Thowalu', 'The girls then emerged from the bamboo and went back to their father and mother', 'Sikhalol then took Lisor back to his village and they lived together from then on' and 'So Iol returned to his island to his family'. In an unaccustomed spirit of thoroughness one epilogue makes sure that no one is overlooked: 'The spirit returned and killed the chief and went back to the island and took the wife and husband back. The young man's helpers returned in canoes. The husband and wife and the men then stayed on Ulithi.'

Wherever etiological epilogues are found they always occupy a completely terminal position. Fifteen such clearly stated endings occur, with a few more of weak character, and in most cases they are not preceded by mention of someone going somewhere. Where the epilogues are composite (in that they combine place and explanation), no pattern of subject matter emerges. Some examples of explanatory terminations may be of interest: '... that is the beginning of why people eat fish, and that is also why the eel is mad at us and when we go out it bites us', 'That is why the people of Ulithi, when somebody is lazy, say, "You are lazy just like Furtal"', 'That is why Marespa became our *tuthup*' and 'That is why cats always try to catch rats'. In passing, it may be of interest to know that some tales contain explanatory elements mentioned only in passing and not accentuated in a terminal statement.

Ending formulas are not found in Ulithian tales. To be sure, an informant might terminate his story with 'Sasi!' meaning 'Finished!' but this seems to have been a signal to me rather than a potential audience of natives. Direct questioning on the use of the word elicited the response that it was not an integral part of the style of narration.

Emotions are expressed through action and situation rather than veralization or the *raconteur*'s commentary on the inner feelings of an actor. The narrator may substitute for this by altering his voice or moving his body, but he does not communicate emotions with words laden with affect. We learn of the deceitful and sadistic nature of Thilefial's mother's sister not through pronouncements on her personality but through the following acts: she tells her sister that she will take care of the baby in memory of her but gives him bad food, has him do his own bathing, fells him with a coconut for drinking palm toddy, and then announces that after all his real mother has gone away and left him behind. The listener can construct for himself his own image of her emotional makeup. The hero himself is not proved inwardly by the storyteller. If we know what manner of man he is – compliant, educible, trusting, perseverant, moderately enterprising, courageous without histrionics, restrained, methodical and nobly vindictive – it is because we infer this from what he does and why he does it. Only once does the narrator make a suggestion of his inner state: '[He] felt bad about this and felt he must go to the island sometime to fight again, but he did not tell his father how he felt.'

A search through all sixty-six of my stories shows that one is hard put to discover any further mention of inner feeling, and, even when it is hinted at, one cannot be entirely sure that it is not a concession to the anthropologist in an interview situation. In *The Separated Lovers* we are told more than in many other tales put together about the feelings of actors – of this or that person feeling sad, sorry, reluctant and remorseful – but all told there are only about six such references, and certainly they are minimally expressed. Ulithian folklore is steadfast in its reluctance to verbalize emotional states.

The penuriousness with which important details are conveyed is scarcely atypical of primitive folklore but it is nevertheless disconcerting for the western mind to encounter it. Take the younger sister in *Discoverer-of-the-Sun*. She goes out to collect some flowers. A man from the Sky World comes down and sees her. They agree without any ado to get married. The narrator must feel that the essence of his tale lies elsewhere and that it is needless to develop this byplay. The romantically oriented listener may be expected to fill in the details if he is so inclined. A similarly quick assent to a brusque proposal of marriage takes place in a 'swan maiden' tale I gathered on the atoll. In fact, courtships are so rarely indicated that there is nothing to conclude but that they are not appropriate material for stories; however, it should be related that they are amply described in the numerous love songs of the atoll. Perhaps there is a conventional division of expression, especially since love songs are intimate and reserved especially for segregated dancing, when they are sung to the accompaniment of erotic gyrations and thrusts. Still, it cannot be the fitness of things alone that demands brevity of detail. Who is 'that man from Lang' who fathers our young hero? We are not only never told his name but virtually nothing else about him. His wife gives up their child for adoption but nothing is said about his feelings in the matter. One must conclude that such feelings are well known to Ulithians, but they are not germane to the plot.

A stylistic trait of folktales to which Ulithi remains faithful is the dyadic nature of interpersonal activity. At any given time an actor is an interaction with only one other. Events between individuals are paired rather than participated in by three or more actors. True, more than two characters may be present but only two are in real interaction. This rule may seem to be violated occasionally but close scrutiny shows that contradictions are more apparent than real. In *Discoverer-of-the-Sun* there are approximately fifty interactions and all of them involve paired action. The first ones, covering only that portion of the story up to the acquiring of the hero's name from the spirit, are as follows: hero's mother – man from Lang; hero – hero's mother; hero's mother – hero's mother's sister; hero's mother – man from Lang; hero – hero's mother's sister; hero – husband of mother's sister; hero – hero's mother's sister; hero – hero's mother; hero – women collectively; hero – hero's mother; Iolofath – people collectively; Iolofath – hero's mother; Iolofath – Iolofath's wife; hero – Iolofath's wife; hero – Iolofath; hero – Limichekh; hero – the Sun. The remaining interactions in the tale are similarly dyadic. Sometimes more than two people are mentioned, but either they are generalized ('the men had a meeting') or one party is collective ('a man with yaws all over his body ... told the men'), or they are passive ('there were lots of children playing around the house'). There are thus no triadic conversations, making it simpler for the listener to follow the narrative, especially when it is carried on by means of direct discourse in which the narrator does not designate the participants except through change in voice.

The strain towards simplicity is further seen in the lack of embellishment for creating atmosphere or mood. The landscape is not described unless it has a bearing on the plot, as when in a ghost story a narrator, in order to signal that time is running out on a cad who fears the arrival of spirits when darkness falls, tells the listener that the sun is setting. The physiognomy of the characters is not mentioned unless it similarly affects the tale in some way, so that if an ogre is depicted as having ten heads it is only in order for him to be the tenth victim of a young giant slayer. Parsimony similarly demands that if porpoises are leaping up and down in the waters near an island they do something other than supply picturesqueness; consequently, it is not surprising to see one of them soon put to use as a 'swan maiden' who will be captured, mated with, and delivered of a daughter who becomes a totemic ancestress. Therefore when in *Discoverer-of-the-Sun* an orange tree is mentioned as growing outside the house in which the young hero is living, it is in order to provide oranges – and thus orange skins for mistreating the little boy. Child abuse is an important dynamism of the plot and is not introduced merely to provide the listener with local color. In the same story mention is made of a *iuth* tree, but only because this is the cosmic pillar by which the hero ascends to the Sky World. If the hero is described as arriving there with dirty body and long hair it is to express the neglect shown him by his mother's sister. If an old man is depicted as having yaws all over his body it is to portray him as a man despised. The lesson of all this for the scholar is that when he sees a seeming departure from penurious-ness in Ulithian tales he should be alerted from past experience to explore the discrepancy until he is satisfied that he understands its true role.

The reversal of fortune by heroes who conquer the odds and emerge triumphant constitutes an important stylistic theme in Ulithian stories. The winners are tender-aged, deformed, insane, poor, low-caste, scorned, or otherwise without apparent prospect of success. It will be recalled that the general plot of *Discoverer-of-the-Sun* is that of a maltreated boy who arrives in Lang dirty and unkempt, but succeeds in overcoming his enemies and is made chief of his island.

Out of my original collection of twenty-four tales I have ascertained that almost half have as their dominant idea the triumph of the handicapped underdog. In one of them the rejected trickster, Iolofath, finally succeeds in gaining recognition as the son of a god, although in a sequel to this there is an episode in which the seemingly unstoppable trickster is bested by his modest half-brother. In a tale of Motikitik, the youngest of three brothers is spurned by the two older ones, but when they go out fishing he is more successful than they; in fact, he even fishes up an island. A mild version of the rags-to-riches device has a low-caste man without even a canoe of his own discover an island, where he is permitted to settle with his wife and establish a colony. One of the classic stories of Melanesia, found also in Micronesia, is represented on Ulithi by a narrative in which a one-legged lad kills ten ogres, and he and his mother are made chiefs of the island by the very inhabitants who had tricked the poor woman into being left behind alone. Ogre tales are likely to give us the happy news that this or that apparently hopeless individual succeeds eventually in overcoming a monster. A madman laughed at by others succeeds by cleverness in ridding an island of an evil spirit, although all others have failed. Two small girls, whom one would suppose to be doomed, succeed through guile in killing an evil spirit who has pursued and caught up with them. Another weak version of the motif is found in a tale in which some birds succeed in tying up a dangerous eel even though the rest of the birds have warned them that their ropes were not strong enough to do so. A double reversal of fortune occurs when a poor woman and her two children, who have been scorned because of their poverty, succeed through the use of magic in gaining valuable carapaces from a distant place; but alas, a happy ending is denied when, rather than yield to the pressure of the villagers for their secret, all three jump into a blazing fire. A Ulithian version of a favorite Melanesian tale relates that the youngest of eleven daughters turns out to be an unwelcome lizard whose daughter marries a young suitor, but although the lizard pathetically hides herself from everyone except her child so that she can help the marriage, in the end she is discovered and paid honor by her son-in-law and the rest of the village.

In my new collection of tales only a little more than a fourth have the reversal of the underdog's fortune as a major theme, although six more tales have it in weak form. But there are some good examples deserving mention. In *The Very Old Wives* a handsome young man desiring a wife is assigned an old hag because all the younger women have been married off. The old woman and he become the objects of ill-concealed laughter, but he gives no sign whatsoever that he is unhappy with the arrangement. The woman works hard for him and is grieved that she has been inflicted on him, yet he treats her with utmost kindness and solicitude and even pretends to the people that he is in love with her. One day at first light she pleads with him to cut off her head, and only after her constant demands and with a heavy heart does he consent. Her skin falls off and she stands as the most beautiful woman of the island.

Three of the stories in this later collection present a happy reversal in the tide of fortune, but it does not last. One tale tells of Feces Girl, who for some unexplained reason is selected by the son of a chief to be his wife in preference to all the other girls who were beautiful, but after this initial triumph she angers a heap of excrement by failing to say good-bye to it, and in revenge the heap magically causes her to turn into feces herself. I was informed that this odoriferous tale is told for the amusement of children. In *The Magical Earth Oven* a girl who during a famine has been driven away by her parents succeeds in magically creating some cooked fish, but when the hungry villagers try to imitate her deed they end only in bringing about the death of a child, so in anger they kill the girl. Another short-lived success is related in *The Story of Lokhsiel*, wherein an ugly woman with only two hairs on her head marries the son of the chief; however, in jealousy the women of the island drown her.

A plot device almost ubiquitous throughout Oceania (except for the isolated continent of Australia) is the supernatural growth of the hero, and it is abundantly represented in Ulithi. It will be recalled that before Baby Boy became Thilefial he underwent special treatment at the hands of Iolofath to make him grow rapidly. And as we have seen, Iolofath himself had a quick growth. Additionally, in a Ulithian tale, *The Deserted Woman and her Ogre-Killing Son*, a woman hiding from some ogres delivers a boy who rapidly attains the size of an adolescent. In the Oedipal *Sikhalol and his Mother*, the hero starts life as a discarded foetus and yet grows to young manhood in a single month as the result of magic administered to him by Rasim. Another Ulithian story, *How Men were Taught Fish Magic*, relates how a woman visited by a kindly spirit gives birth to a boy who attains rapid growth and then she gives birth to a second son who grows rapidly. Finally, if one may be permitted to stretch the notion of supernatural growth to include precocious development extending beyond physical growth alone, we can include '*Palulop*' *and his Family*, for here an as yet unborn deity listens to some important conversations while he is still in his mother's womb, and later attains rapid growth.

I have made a fairly extensive study of supernatural growth, broadly defined so as to include children who talk at birth or speak from their mother's wombs, children who are already full-sized or nearly so when they emerge from the uterus, and children who become enormously strong in short order. In much of Oceania it is almost an automatic attribute of the child that he be heroic in character, be conceived in some miraculous or unusual manner, experience an exaggeratedly short or long gestation, and be delivered in a strange manner. Not all Oceanic heroes can boast of all these criteria, but for the most part the really important ones can. Olofat, Lugeilang and Ialulwe of the Carolines qualify, and so do Maui and Ru of Polynesia, Tangaro, Qat,

Sido, To Kabinana and To Korvuvu of Melanesia, and Ibonia of Madagascar. This is only a sample out of a long list. Among the unusual kinds of conception are impregnation from drinking some substance, eating an animal, making contact with an object, ingesting orally a larva or a homunculus-like, previously born creature, intercourse with an animal, and exposure of the pudenda to the wind. The term of pregnancy may be as long as ten years or as short as a single night. Micronesians, it should be noted, are more apt to favor short gestations for their heroes than long ones. Among the unusual Oceanic parturitions are delivery from a person's head, nose or elbow; delivery from a fruit, stone or flower; and delivery from a dead mother. The distant Malagasy favor a birth in which the enterprising hero cuts his way out of his mother's belly.

A distinction can be made between precocious development resulting from an innate capacity and an acquired capacity. Our hero Baby Boy, as he was known at the time, was not endowed with the capacity to grow rapidly; he was favored by white magic employed by his adoptive father, Iolofath. True, I have not been able to fathom the symbolic significance of his being tossed many times over a house, but one cannot always understand the rationale behind a magical rite unless given some clue. Baby Boy became a *limichikh* in short order when a spirit swallowed him and then after a few minutes removed him from its mouth. I suppose that Frazer has some rubric for the classification of this procedure but I fear that I do not know what it is. At any rate, it is not important that we know it. The point I wish to make is that our hero falls in the tradition of many great Oceanic figures, inasmuch as he undergoes a developmental precocity that simple mortals can never achieve. He had the uncommon good luck of being high born, then later adopted by a demigod and trained by a spirit.

The prophet without honor, as it were, is encountered not only here in *Discoverer-of-the-Sun*, where a man covered with yaws warns the people that they are threatening the son of Iolofath, but in an important myth which I have called '*Palulop*' *and his Family*. A blind stranger is at the beach making a canoe. People go up to him to ask him to forecast the weather because they are eager to embark on an important journey. They do not recognize him as the son of a certain deity, for they believe him to have been lost long ago at sea. Day after day he warns that the weather will be unfavorable. Indignant and impatient they finally decide to ignore his warning and embark anyway in their canoe, only to meet up with a fierce typhoon that destroys all of them except a young woman and a man. Just as Iolofath knew about his son's difficulties with the men who set out to kill him but did not intervene, so the father of the blind canoe builder is a great navigator god who does not reveal to the people, whom he himself has sent down to the beach to ask the man for his forecast, that he is his father. In fact the god embarks with the others, knowing they will meet disaster, and perishes with them. All he need have done was intervene with a few well-placed words.

We can speculate on the role of such ignored admonishers. They seem to constitute a literary device for heightening tension by exposing the truth to men who will not hear. The two above-mentioned gods, who have the power of near-omniscience, do not interfere because intervention would spoil the bold events in store for the listeners. We have something approximating the inexorable denouements that the Greeks loved so well.

The resuscitation of the dead is a common stylistic device in Ulithian folklore, and is so much expected that the listener knows his slain hero will be restored to life just as surely as American television viewers know the men with the white hats will triumph over those with the black. So Thilefial is in good company when Iolofath restores him after Rasim has succeeded in driving a spear into him. Iolofath himself as a youth had had the benefit of a resuscitation after he had been killed by the halfbeak whose wife he had seduced. When Iolofath's father found him buried beneath a shaking plant which had grown out of the trickster's wreath, and pulled up on the plant, young Iolofath complained that he wanted his father to stop tugging because he was sleepy.

Elsewhere the revised person in Ulithian tales shows similar reluctance about the whole thing. Thus, in a tale about an ogre who had eaten Iol's daughter, the father cuts off the head of the spirit, and after opening the ogre's belly and proceding to remove his daughter, she says, 'Do not pull me because I am sleepy.' Iol replies, 'Are you sleepy or are you lazy?' This is not the only time when such a question is asked. Thus in a tale I have luridly entitled *The Island in the Blood-Red Sea* a young hero goes through great dangers to kill numerous spirits who have cooked his father over a fire, and after he has magically restored his father to his former self the son is rewarded with the remark, 'Don't move me, because I am sleepy.' The son counters with, 'Are you sleepy or are you a lazy man? Get up and come with me.' [. . .]

Other plot devices which I shall merely mention without elaborating upon are the creation of islands from objects thrown upon the waters; the fishing up of islands by a demigod; the transformation of a man into a bird or animal; the transformation of a bird or animal into a woman; the employment of a magical object to answer for a fugitive; the inexhaustible object; the journey to the lower world; the acquiring of wisdom or knowledge through a dream.[2]

Humor is a part of Ulithian stylistic tradition in folklore, even though it may not always be apparent to a person studying it in written form. Narrators obviously know how to use the ludicrous to arouse a feeling of mirth. An example in which it is combined with another device, the unexpected transition, comes from *The Ghost of the Woman with Yaws*. In this grim story a sudden moment of relief comes when a young wife talks to her mother-in-law, who, unknown to her, has died and become an evil spirit.

As they were talking, the mother of the boy, when she knew his wife was not looking at her, lifted off her head to frighten her. Then she put it on her lap and began to delouse it. When the wife looked at her she saw she had no head and asked, 'Why did you take off your head?' She answered, 'I always do this because I am very weak and cannot do much moving.'

The old woman puts back her head but later decides to take out her eyes in order to clean them, offering as a reason that she is too weak to clean them in any other way. As they are walking along, the wife looks at the woman and notices her body is facing the village to which they are going, while her face is turned back.

The wife asked her,' What is wrong with your head?' And she answered, 'I want to be able to see you wherever you go.'

2. More plot devices are listed in Lessa (1961).

This comes as close as anything to a joke in Ulithian humor.
[...]

I have in my files a collection of 1485 responses to TAT (Thematic Apperception Test) cards prepared especially for Ulithi in conjunction with a personality study that I made some years ago (1954, pp. 243–301). The responses are spontaneous 'stories' provoked by showing Ulithians fifteen cards, fourteen of which depict native people and scenes and one of which is blank. Ninety-nine persons of both sexes and various ages, from five to over forty, were administered the tests in 1948–9, being told simply that they were to look at the cards and tell what they thought each of them portrayed in terms of the present situation, the events leading up to it, and the outcome. The TAT is a projective technique designed to stimulate the imagination and to cause each individual to react in accordance with his own personality. It of course reflects cultural conditioning as well as individual temperament. The protocols were analysed according to manifest content rather than depth psychology and were treated quantitatively. It occurs to me that some comparison of the TAT responses with the folktales would be interesting and rewarding, as long as the limitations of the comparison are kept in mind.

Needless to say, there is by no means strict comparability between each of the two bodies of narratives. For every folktale there are over twenty-two TAT responses. The tales were told by adults, mostly males, whereas the TAT responses were given by persons of all ages, almost equally distributed between males and females. The tales differ of course from the protocols in a very important respect; they are traditional in form, content and style rather than individually and spontaneously created. The TAT responses were influenced to a large extent by the directions given by the testers, who structured them in advance by telling the subjects to narrate the plot in terms of the present, past and future. Even more than that, they were influenced by the very content of the test cards, which contained figures of people, animals, landscape and so on.

We can nevertheless assume that the TAT responses were greatly influenced by cultural factors, among them being the folkloristic tradition to which the persons tested had been exposed. By ignoring the personality features of the tests, we should be able to ascertain the extent to which the artificially induced stories resemble or differ from the others. I have made an impressionistic analysis of these resemblances and differences without trying to quantify them, and I think the tentative results are worth revealing.

More or less equal portrayal of certain aspects of Ulithian life is contained in both the tales and the protocols. The importance of the family and kinsmen is clearly brought out, and so are the terms of relationship. The *metalefal* as a center of political and social activity for men is made evident. Frequent mention is made of the menstrual house and its functions, and while the exclusion of men from the area of the house is either taken for granted or implied in some way, in two instances young men go there to visit their girl friends. Filled with curiosity over this impossible situation I looked up the identity of the test subjects involved and discovered that one of them was Taiethau, the *raconteur* of *Discoverer-of-the-Sun*, whose virtuosity as a storyteller had not then been revealed, for he was only eighteen years of age when he was administered the test. The other subject was also a young man of eighteen, who had spent a little time on Guam; but I cannot say he had the potential for virtuosity in storytelling. These two atypical responses, therefore, cannot be taken seriously as relating to an actual practice of taboo violation. Brother–sister avoidance after siblings have approached maturation is strong in Ulithian society but in the tales this avoidance is occasionally disregarded, as it is once in the TAT responses, although here the situation is innocuous, with the siblings merely gathering food to take to their father. The tales and the protocols make some reference to suicide, but only occasionally, which is as it ought to be, for there has not been a suicide in Ulithi for about six decades. [. . .]

The TAT protocols contain a good deal of cultural and social content and it is important to compare them in this respect with the sixty-six stories. On the whole, the TAT protocols give a much more accurate and complete picture of Ulithian life than do the tales. They more satisfactorily depict the habitat, exploitative activities, technology and material culture. They better portray the everyday routine and the daily problems of living. They do not show social interaction in the over-simplified dyadic fashion of the tales. Their lesser stress on ingroup conflict, which is usually confined to stealing, and their failure to stress internal stratification, are more true to life than are the tales. Their portrayal of children as being treated with affection, even though occasionally chastised for the customary missteps of childhood, is much more faithful than the impression imparted by the stories of the folklore. The causes of quarreling among children and adults are truer to life. The main thing is that the tests reveal prosaic human beings rather than the artificial figures of fantasy. These are ordinary mortals who cut their fingers, burn their hands, have toothaches and sundry illnesses, cry, suffer from the cold and are blind or lame. [. . .]

Whereas the tales have a mere reference to a gun and another reference to a piece of paper with writing on it, the protocols have many indications of contact with and knowledge of the outside world beyond the native isles. [. . .]

The one great content gap in the TAT protocols is in religion and magic. There is a fleeting reference to magic, three or so references to ghosts, and a few to Christmas and going to church on Sunday. Thus, both the pagan and the Christian systems of supernaturalism are neglected, whereas in the folktales the former, at least, has of course a prominent place. When the TAT's were administered, the present resident missionary had not yet established himself on the atoll, although missionization had begun over two decades before. A current administering of the tests would undoubtedly show a stronger Christian influence.

Related in part to the omission of religion and other aspects of the supernatural from the TAT responses is the rare reference to taboo of any sort, though taboos are often mentioned and constantly observed in daily life, even with the advent of Christianization. The folktales are more useful in reflecting their importance. [. . .]

The intention of this study has been to stress that the outsider must be provided with exegetic assistance to gain as much as a minimal understanding of a tale from a culture even as simple of that of Ulithi. Most stories transferred out of their native setting and recorded on paper obviously lose much of their charm and virility when stripped, not only of their narrator's use of gesture and intonation, but, more seriously still, of their cultural meaning as well. *Discoverer-of-the-Sun*, the sample selected for analysis, is more lucid than most Ulithian tales, and yet demands as much from an audience as it gives to it. As a yarn it has elements which almost anyone can respond to with interest, but when a reader lacks adequate comprehension of the many little understandings needed to transform the skeleton of its plot into a live and vibrant story, his appreciation is greatly reduced.

In considering the extent to which culture is reflected in *Discoverer-of-the-Sun* and other Ulithian narratives, it is at once obvious that some aspects are more favored than others, many being given no attention at all. It is fortunately possible, owing to the availability of an ethnographic study of the atoll, to contrast folkloristic content with cultural reality. Whatever may be the merits of other bodies of folklore, it cannot be said that Ulithian tales are an adequate source on which to rely for a reconstruction of the native culture. They omit or slight many of the important details of ordinary life, at the same time incorporating practices that are either alien or obviously in the realm of fantasy. Nor can they be regarded, except for a few tentative accounts, as reliable records of historical events. Speaking of folktales in general, it is always puzzling to know why certain real happenings, documented by written records, fail to gain inclusion into a corpus of folklore, and it will perhaps never become clear why Ulithians fail to include in their stories historical episodes of dramatic and severe impact, such as the massacre of Father Cantova's missionary party in 1731. If major episodes disappear without leaving a trace in contemporary tales, there is even less reason to believe that the trivial ones will have been preserved, at least in recognizable form.

Part of the dilemma of both historicity and cultural reflection is indubitably linked with the problem of provenance. Many, perhaps most, Ulithian tales are from sources elsewhere in the Carolinian archipelago and beyond. Of course, diffusion characterizes folklore anywhere, yet we know that in the transference there is sufficient recasting and adjustment of the details so as to fashion the tales in the direction of local values and forms.

Another source of difficulty lies in the probability that the body of Ulithian tales which has here been considered represents only a diminished corpus of the original, either because of deterioration of the folklore tradition or failure to collect all that is actually extant. Notwithstanding this possible lack of completeness, it is likely that there is something inherent in all bodies of folktales which renders them inadequate – even though useful – as sources of cultural content. If only we could detect the principles operating to incorporate or reject cultural elements, it would be possible to make more useful assessments of any given set of tales, especially in instances where the ethnographic materials are wholly or partially deficient. A vast assault on these problems through cross-cultural analysis might shed light on the suitability or nonsuitability of cultural and historical facts for incorporation into a society's traditional narrative. Unevenness of acceptance may disclose that fundamental differences in function and values may be operative, in one setting as compared with another, although at the same time it may be demonstrated that some mechanisms of selection are universal.

More recognizable style is contained in Ulithian folktales than immediately meets the eye. Features of structure, characterization, humor and so on, become obvious only upon analysis, after which they are clearly apparent, even though not as formalized as in the tales of many other peoples. Except for certain of the myths, Ulithian narratives have the same stripped-down character as typical European tales. Simplicity is seen particularly in noncomplexity of plot, paucity of personal details, dyadic interaction between characters, placelessness of locale and timelessness of action.

A sidelight of the present study has been the comparison of responses to Thematic Apperception Tests, and while this was done without recourse to rigorous methodology, it seems to indicate many points of agreement with the tales, especially in the common emphasis on food. However, the test results are more faithful reflectors of the real life and culture of the atoll than are the tales. Comparison with the stylistic features of the TAT responses showed that certain features are common to both the test stories and the folktales, especially in the matter of concreteness, specificity and simplicity. The test responses, however, are impoverished in plot, and, without the cruelty, guile, violence and extravagances of the tales, they are fairly bland. One misses in them the marvelous and the miraculous; they do not compete at all with the folktales as story systems, largely because they fail to release themselves from the laws of nature and society. The respondents to the tests cannot, however, be blamed for this, since most of them were not narrators of tales nor even sufficiently aware of their own traditional lore to be able to project folkloristic fantasy into their responses.

References

LESSA, W. A. (1950a), 'Ulithi and the outer native World', *Amer. Anthropol.*, vol. 52, pp. 27–52.

LESSA, W. A. (1950b), 'The place of Ulithi in the Yap Empire', *Human Organization*, vol. 9, pp. 16–18.

LESSA, W. A. (1961), *Tales from Ulithi Atoll: A Comparative Study in Oceanic Folklore*, University of California Publications: Folklore Studies, vol. 13.

LESSA, W. A., and SPIEGELMAN (1954), *Ulithian Personality as seen through Ethnological Materials and Thematic Test Analysis*, University of California Publications in Culture and Society, vol. 2.

5 Jean Guiart

Multiple Levels of Meaning in M

Excerpts from Jean Guiart, 'Des multiples niveaux de signification du mythe', *Archives de Sociologie des Religions*, vol. 26, 1968, pp. 55–71. Specially translated for this volume by John Freeman.

It was through Claude Lévi-Strauss that myth first ceased to be the rehashing of classical antiquities, whether Mosaic or Christian. Objectivized, stripped down, it has become by definition neutral, finding its contingent determination in a process which refers back to the complex structures underlying each culture. [. . .] Instead of establishing that culture contains conscious memories of a great past, we are now required to decipher a message and to read between the lines, where the detailing and the style are less important than the syntax and vocabulary of the themes. The result is an admirable technique for analysing myth, which becomes again the bearer of eternal truths about mediation between life and death, the opposition of nature and culture, and so on. This undertaking to reinstate myth is almost condemned by its very perfection and success, since the reader can only be discouraged even at the idea of refining upon it. Some things are destined to remain unique.

To move beyond, or to come back to, what Lévi-Strauss brings us, we should first consider the analytical method he proposes in relation to the materials it makes use of. *The Raw and the Cooked* (1964) and *From Honey to Ashes* (1966) show how, thanks to the structuralist method and to a judicious mixture of logic and rigour, it is possible to use incongruous and often badly collected material, together with multiple versions too often summarized by ancient writers, to reconstruct whole new aspects of cultures on the run from annihilation. We can be sure the result would not have been so remarkable if Lévi-Strauss had not toiled at the same time in the highlands and in the Amazonian forest and experienced for himself the daily life of the Indians. Intuition is plainly necessary in such work, since method is not enough without an exact, personal understanding of places, things and men.

How can we expect myth to have much to say to us without such an exceptionally rigorous comparative method – now that we are no longer tied to a method based on taking account of all known data and consequently founding its generalizations on the lowest common denominator, i.e. on the least reliable documents. It is all the more remarkable, and at the same time a proof of the scientific validity of the analytical technique involved, that any commentary can so illuminate such a chaotic situation.

The structuralist's enthusiasm springs from the existence of variants of the same myth, or from recomposing incomplete myths from disparate themes and sequences; he can establish their vocabulary, and contrast the syntax and the themes. Yet should we not ask the reason why these variants exist, apart from the messages they carry? In my opinion, the answer lies in the way myths, and indeed all traditional texts, are appropriated by the group, or by the representatives of dynastic kinds of succession.

The repetitive aspect of the social coordinates of myth irritates many observers, who belittle it, failing to see that if the botanist and zoologist must localize all their samples, the ethnographer is bound to do the same, and to justify his reasons for collecting such information as well. It will not do to compile it mechanically. Often the most that ethnographers provide is the name of their informant and the place and date of the narration, without bothering to find out how the informant knew, why he decided to speak, or what determined in detail the actual form of the text collected (what was said, what was left out). The ethnographer is the prisoner of his literary or philosophical training; he is afraid to load his future reader with boring details. As a result, he unconsciously departs from the linguistic model. Though, as a structuralist, he takes pains to tabulate themes and work out systems of their logical oppositions, he may balk at relating this information – the most easily acquired since it can be worked out in the study at home – to the complex and apparently repetitive nominal system which defines the groups, individuals and places in the terrain he is concerned with.

Even if this operation ought to be seen as necessary, it is certainly not easy. These names can be assimilated to the myths, in the sense that their properties must be sought 'beyond the usual level of linguistic expression'. Each name of a man, group or place bears multiple resonances. Not one of them can be considered to be by definition 'out of context.' It has been given, taken and chosen. It is, at least partially, the symbol of a given grouping of stochastic social relations, the symbol of rights and privileges, a declaration of oppositions. It is the cipher of a mass of cultural and contingent data, varying at least slightly from one case to the next. Be it a place, an individual or a group, the bearer of a name can never be entirely assimilated to its nearest neighbour in the same category.

The whole social fabric must be memorized once it goes beyond a very humble everyday specificity. Neither a name nor a series of names are enough for this task; and so we resort to myth and other *genres* of oral literature. It must not be forgotten that the informant is partially a prisoner of his variant. Reciting a text is not an arbitrary act. It requires effort and decision. There is a wish that a certain statement should be recorded by an external witness so that the witness should at least have to take account of it. Not to please the foreigner, whatever he may believe, but because it has been noticed how such a transmission, however unusual or marginal the material may be, can secure status for the informant. The sociological definition of the informant is at least one element contained in the text received, in the same way as in the informant's own society, general consciousness of the subject determines the particular version. That is, unless the informant was going as far as his audience permitted and playing quite another game; trying to put over an invented status for himself, altering or even reversing his own, or faking a text known by hearsay and belonging in fact to others. In spite of himself, the ethnographer can become the means of compounding error or even injury, contributing to the delay or more likely the bypassing of traditional strategies. This is the danger of myths collected in confidence, if they are not checked every time against the constellation of social relations, inherited or built up, which determine the informant as well as he can freely manipulate them.

Myth, then, contains at the very least two messages: the one the structuralist deciphers, studying his text as a vehicle of the culture as a whole, and the one the narrator impresses on it, which is the summary of his social position, affirming a disappointed ambition or one on the point of success, protesting against the wrong done him. If, at least to start with, the ethnographer is generally considered an innocent, the audience is entirely capable of understanding everything the narrator implies, from the value of the smallest symbol to the information conveyed tacitly. The resulting desire not to provide food for the village gossip explains the unsatisfying look of many texts, the product of a self-censorship which must take account of multiple variables; it also explains the relatively greater richness of written texts, composed at leisure in the privacy of a dwelling. [...]

For these reasons, in an archaic society myth as much as the structure of land tenure is the fruit of a cumulative process, under the pressures of private or collective interests; consequently, it must even be said that in principle, no two versions of a myth can be the same, even if given by one individual. [...]

Gregory Bateson (1936) explained rather than described the existence of a very extensive nominal system, consisting of names memorized in pairs, belonging to each of the patrilinear groups. These are the so-called 'secret' names; the possession and revelation of them are disputed; they are stolen and pilfered; the desire to appropriate them determines marriage more than the preferential categories of kinship, and authorizes social status and land control. Acquiring series of names implies recieving at the same time territorial rights to the ground on which the purchased names depend; these rights are to sago-palm gathering areas, a form of soil exploitation that favours the plasticity of the system.

Unfortunately, Bateson has not provided us with the documentation which would have allowed us to verify and go beyond his analysis. Tables of names seemed to be unpublishable, when all that was required of him was a brilliant analysis putting him in line with the current theoretical vogue. This is all the more regrettable in that he is one of the first writers to have clearly shown the relative value of a tradition which can be manipulated or transformed at will, where the apparently most secret and sacred nominal categories are consciously used as instruments of power and prestige. [...]

Some time later, Douglas Oliver, freed from the grip of funcionalism, was the first to carry through the patient work involved in a cadastral survey of the people he was studying. He remains one of the very few to have had the courage and clear-sightedness to do this. His work (1949) remains the model of this kind, every aspect of land tenure being dissected in its localization and relative fluidity. Most ethnologists before him were repelled by the job and contented themselves with a brief glimpse, stating the accepted principles without justifying them and without distinguishing between the cultural norm and the reality. [. . .]

In my own research, I had long recognized the need for a survey of land distribution. I was afraid to broach research on this tack, however, as I knew how high passions can be raised by direct allusion to the soil, the very mention of which makes the researcher the target of all sorts of strategies. The method adopted, therefore, consisted of establishing a first frame of reference, the very one, in fact, which Gregory Bateson failed to supply, while announcing its existence; an inventory of the onomastic system and of everything concerning the status of individuals. This was the inventory of the body of social symbols. Manipulating it, more or less prudently, more or less adroitly, provides the means of influencing the modalities of land control, while claiming to be a faithful image of it. [. . .]

One thus arrives at the concept, which I believe to be scientific, that there is no other authenticity than that of the present. Setting aside the inventory, there is only what, for various reasons, is accepted; and this can be questioned even by a minority, publicly or secretly, according to how it judges its chances of success. Tradition is an unstable balancing of conservatism and ambition, at once a justification of the *status quo* or what one would like it to be, and an instrument of its overthrow, at least for those who have the intelligence or genius to use *the techniques of manipulation implied in the very utterance of tradition.* We are always among a civilization of forgers who have excellent consciences. A little lucid reflection on our own culture would lead us to the same kind of observation, even if we merely look at the teaching of history at primary-school level. There is nothing that is not perfectly normal about it. From the divine genealogies of the Roman Caesars to the manipulations, also genealogical, of the modern Mormons, the readjusting of tradition is well established in the West. [. . .]

I have already shown the importance of Douglas Oliver's discovery of the value of all the topographical information contained in myth. The so-called 'totemic' myths of the Siuai of Bougainville Island establish the migration of a symbolic animal, whose itinerary is marked out by place-names, the list of which corresponds exactly to the territorial claim made by the clan availing itself of a link with the symbol. The itineraries of ancestors, also called totemic, in the 'historical' myths of the Australian Aborigines, fulfil the same function.

It follows that myths can have a precise, objective sociological content. Whenever we are insufficiently in tune with the symbols which make up their code, we have of course no other resource than the structural method proposed by Lévi-Strauss, which shows up the profound link between the myth and the culture from which it springs. But the very informant who used or abused the myth could directly decipher at least a large part of this content; and observation of his behaviour might have borne witness to it.

At this stage it is suitable to give a specific example. I will choose the one that originally posed the problem to me; for that reason the least easy to answer, and hence a valuable example.

Rshua me Yanu

1. *Ke ho vejet anyin wa hingat adrem.*
   Story of ancestors of the past.
2. *Kehna vejeta, whân anyin ke li lap.*
   Story of the beginning of two clans.
3. *Haba lo e, me xaca thibi.*
   Two there, really only one.
4. *Walang ien li lab e, ka habe,*
   These are the names of the two clans,
5. *Rshua me Yanu.*
   Rshua and Yanu.
6. *Thu ke hnyai, ame belökâ ke somweca, öiö Yanu.*
   There is an old woman farmer, her name Yanu.
7. *Haba hna belöke, ma ku tho sa ot hni kakeihen.*
   In plantations there the grass grows on the low slopes.
8. *Me ehu ke behelök, ame iâû eu hnyi sa ot,*
   and him lizard creep him in the grass.

9. *Me sö thibut hmokunen behelök le ot; ame iâû*
   and she cut the tail of the lizard, the grass leaf, when he creep.

10. *Me hingölö thibut dren ka hnyi le ica, akû hnyi sa ot.*
    and the blood flows on the taro leaf which was growing in the grass.

11. *Me hne thithö dren hmokunen behelök, me wa he.*
    and the blood of the lizard's tail dries, and he go.

12. *Me hlâ thibut seûnö ka le mada wadra hnyi le ica.*
    and the sun comes out, and dried the blood on the taro leaf.

13. *Ke ehu ke meno ame hanyei ame gâ ka heleû an.*
    there is the bird who eats the crops, who flies, who seeks her food.

14. *Haba ien meno e me höcö. Ame han ovie, kumara, eo.*
    The name of the bird, sultan hen. Who eats banana and sweet potato.

15. *Ame heleu an meno eang, me othibut ka hnyi wadra.*
    She seeks her food, the bird, and she arrives in the blood.

16. *E laba thiju ka mokulec wadra ahup to; hela ta wakuny.*
    Her then lying the solid blood looking like an egg.

17. *Ke othibut somweca öiö Yanu, me gâh tho höcö.*
    She arrive then old woman named Yanu, the sultan hen she fly.

18. *Me wa he somweca ka wa dok a gâh hnyen höcö.*
    she come she old woman, when the sultan hen she fly away.

19. *Me othibut ka wâ, wadra ame mokulec hnyi le ica.*
    and she come then scratch the blood which lying in taro leaf.

20. *Me ka oûnyibâuâ bul, ke wa he hmetu.*
    and her observe then, and her go away to come back again.

21. *Ame ka labo helae hnyi ke bong me ke bong.*
    it is this way day after day.

22. *Ke hnyi ke bong ama ohmetu somweca.*
    Another day she comes back the old woman.

23. *Me long thithö wha tenge hnyi dog ame gâh hnyi höcö.*
    and listens then to the noise of crying in the place where fly the sultan hen.

24. *Me wahe ka elam at ametenge, me o thibut ka wanakat.*
    and seeks to find out what man cries, and arrive who child.

25. *Aghâ tho höcö, ke ahmouca but wadra me wanakat.*
    the sultan hen she flies off, she finds the blood and the child.

26. *Me hom thithö somweca ka had me gan thibut.*
   and take then (the child) the old woman who bring up to grow.
27. *Walejue matran li laba, ke ne obut walsang ang.*
   That is beginning of the two clans till now.

Wakuba Yanu[1]

This text justifies, in a thoroughly classical fashion, the simultaneous existence and the individual status of the two clans Rshua and Yanu, locally considered as *wai*, aboriginal; this is to say, they are held to represent the oldest-established groups in the region of the present village of Banut, on the south-west coast of the island of Uvea in the Loyalty Islands, as opposed to the clans recognized as originating from the nearby island of Lifu or from the mainland of New Caledonia. The myth introduces a distinction between the two clans. Yanu appears here as lasting from all eternity in the form of an old woman – though the term *somwaca* indicates respect rather than age – and as founder of the Rshuas. In ceremonial life, as if in compensation, the Yanu is considered subject to the chiefdom of Kauma, which originates from Lifu; the Rshua, on the basis of his marvellous origin, is accountable to this chief only for a *tang sahac*, a present whose amount and timing depend on the chief's good will, whereas the Yanu owes the *fat*, the offering of the first fruit of the yam harvest.

The Yanu has a magic stone which is capable of revealing to him if by any chance anyone in the chiefdom has secretly eaten fish without saving some for him; this means that his personal status with regard to the chiefdom is not without theoretical privileges. On his side, the representative of the Rshua at the court of the Kaumas is the *hingat in than*, the 'chief's ancient', that is, the advisor who is listened to and has the right to offer his opinions without being asked – but not the one who has the right to close the discussion in the chiefdom council by stating the opinion which the chief himself must conform to and which is called *obotrkong*. The Rshua also has the ownership of a magic rite which enables him to protect a field against the depredations of sultan hens; the clan's priest presides over a rite of mourning

1. French text published in Guiart (1963, p. 564). This transcription is the one accepted by local tradition.

dedicated to these birds' death, after which it is permissible to hunt them mercilessly. Let it be noted in passing that the content of the myth itself could have testified to the existence of such a control ritual. The myth is thus linked, directly or indirectly, to social privileges and particular rituals known to the speaker and his listeners.

Let us explain the value of the symbols used. The sultan hen, which lives comfortably from pilfering fruit in the fields (especially bananas), is considered to be committing a particularly odious crime; it is the more despised for the fact that its flesh, though edible, is little sought after. Its name is used, at least in the Loyalty Islands, as the symbol of the woman who habitually lends herself to illegitimate loves, or of a chief's concubine. The intervention in the story of the grass, an adventitious plant which must be torn from the hillocks so that its roots will not pierce the yam tubers, accentuates the already clear sign of the illegitimacy attached to the birth of the child found in the field by the woman Yanu – to say 'found in the path' would have been an explicit insult. The Rshua clan is thus presented in this text as a bastard line of the Yanu, and this explains the veil, as poetic as it is transparent, thrown by the myth over the original relationship of the two clans.

The intervention of an element of miracle was still needed to allow the Rshua to hold up their heads, even though nothing was said that might humiliate them since the usual images of current speech were not used, and by tacit convention everything was placed on a level which avoided the everyday. This does not in the least mean, either, that the Rshua had an illegitimate birth at the origin of their line; but that they have at least found it useful to create the image of it to justify a specific link with the Yanu. This usefulness is bound to relate to land ownership. But the information collected is not clear enough on this point. The land the Rshua hold, which is concentrated in sixty-eight neighbouring smallholdings, is more or less confused with that of the Hojodra, another *wai* clan, who support the chief Kauma's officer-of-the-mouth and treasure-keeper and owe no other dues besides occasional attendance at the rare occasions when the chief's court meets. The Yanu also lay claim to a concentrated land holding, less broken up (twenty-nine plots), which meets the

Rshua at only three points; Wejiji, Qamök and Gethop, all situated between the villages of Banut and Hulup (which is a dependency of the Kauma chiefdom). The conjunction of Rshua and Hojodra could have another meaning concerning their common origin, the link between Rshua and Yanu – since land is not transmitted by the female line – being explained by the intervention of this third group not mentioned in the myth.

On another level, the central theme of the myth is, as always, a symbolic representation of sexual union; the lizard is a phallic symbol in all Melanesia and beyond, and oral literature makes frequent mention of it; the taro leaf, said Maurice Leenhardt, is the *genetrix*. The blood of the lizard's tail falls on the female organ and coagulates into an egg. But in the act itself the lizard is not matched with another animal which could be a female symbol; the sultan hen only enters later. Similarly, the taro leaf – it is the leaf, not the plant, which is the female symbol[2] – is not correlated with the yam root, the classic masculine symbol, but with a lizard. The reason is a structural one; it was necessary to contrast an inanimate element with a moving one. By a sort of outward projection of the matrix, passing from the biological image to a symbol of behaviour, the taro leaf comes to play a mediating role between the vagabond lizard and the sultan hen of easy virtue; the cutting blade of grass provides a second mediation, by some kind of surgery provoking ejaculation on the receptacle dissociated from the body. The presence of blood, rather than sperm, keeps the operation on a symbolic level.

We have here one of the texts where the fundamental theme in the formal fabric of Oceanic myths appears most clearly, namely, coition. If the first paragraph of the myth had been cut out it would have been incomprehensible; there is nothing in it that can be cut out, and nothing that need be added for anyone who knows the symbolic language. It is one of the models of the *genre*. There is besides no need to see anything in it that is not respectable; the

2. We should have every reservation about the value of the method which contrasts the symbolisms attached to any plant in its totality. Only the root of the yam is a male symbol; the leaf of the taro plant is a female symbol but not its root. For examples of similar misinterpretations, see Barrau (1965).

old pastor Wakuba Yanu who voluntarily wrote down the vernacular text had no idea of presenting us with an item of erotic literature.

What would the structural analysis of this text have achieved, except likening it to other texts of the same kind while taking away from it its local specificity? It would have confirmed its reference to a part of the current bestiary and brought out the oppositions which summarize the argument:

male–female
lizard's tail – leaf of the taro (mediated by the grass)
lizard – sultan hen (mediated by the egg of blood)
old woman – child (mediated by the sultan hen)
flying sultan hen – coagulated blood (mediated by the old woman)

The elements of the oppositions each find themselves mediators in turn. This series of oppositions could be illuminated by parallel series, taken in particular from the love songs or the funeral songs (*wahaihai*) which I have published elsewhere (1953), or from the little erotic texts with which the old amuse themselves, commenting on the string games taught to children; this would definitely enable us to penetrate mental structures, and the conclusions would be likely to be valid for a vast area, since there is so little variability in Oceania on this level. We would not find information on the functioning of local societies; without this information we can only be in the presence of theoretical mental structures which can be reduced to the internal logic of their concatenations of symbols, and thereby demonstrate the formal perfection of structures identical to those which underlie the literary or artistic structures for which structural analysis is so well suited. Beyond the fabric torn away from the collective unconscious by scholarly means, there still remains the freedom to make use of this fabric for more conscious ends.

This text was given by the pastor Wakuba as a testimony; it was the affirmation of the social status to which he had the right, but which his position as a retired and impoverished ecclesiastic undermined. It was also a precaution against others who might have omitted to mention a link left in the dark. It was thus essentially a political act. To confide to a notebook in this way a myth so interwoven with symbols was neither a gratuitous act, nor a demonstration of confidence in the ethnographer. It was nothing other than a gesture which had become necessary.

I have published elsewhere (1963, pp. 476–7) another text which is more literary and easier to interpret; the myth of the great chief Zeula, of the Gaica district of Lifu, put to death by the *isola*, his legitimate wife, who was jealous of his dealings with two girls who had come from Uvea for a feast day by means of a subterranean passage. Here the sexual symbolism is at first applied to amorous approaches: the two girls, almost entirely naked according to custom, delouse the naked Zeula – there was no penis sheath in Lifu – whose hands do not remain idle. The intensity of the erotic atmosphere among the threesome, an intensity silently implied in the text, makes the protagonists forget the existence of the servants sent by the wife to spy on the chief. The mosquito, the last envoy, eludes the doorkeeper's vigilance, and his report provokes the fury of the wife, who is hurt that the adultery should have taken place in the hut reserved for legitimate love. She pursues the chief, finds him alone and puts him to death while the two young women are away looking for something to eat; food provided by the woman represents the normal return to 'pay for' sexual relations with the man, or vice versa.

The chief's 'deceased' state takes a while to show, or at least his desire for the two girls manages to survive the murder. We now witness the blooming of sexual symbols. The fire which the chief leaves behind him when going off fishing, with instructions not to let it go out, goes out through negligence, and the girls go to look for an ember to relight it; a light appears which draws their attention, and finally disappears and goes out in a hole. The toning down of this pious comedy played by the dead man has resulted in the substitution of the fire for his vanished virility.

The chase of the chief's girlfriends through the rocks to seize the fleeing light follows a carefully plotted itinerary of named holdings: Hmadr Point, by the sea between the point and another named place, Hmangginy, Hnathe where all three set up in the forest, then Hnapotr and Hnaöni ha thenei Canyö, all of them places in the domain claimed by the Zeula clan. This assertion of the landholding right is the reason, if not for the myth's existence, then at least for its transmission, despite the far-from-brilliant role played by this chief who was taken by surprise and killed by a jealous wife. [. . .]

Having shown that myth has a content different from that revealed by structural analysis, we can now ask a fundamental question, concerning the limitations imposed on the structural method by social facts.

Structural analysis is based on demonstrating semantic unities by means of the interplay of oppositions and permutations. Looked at in the light of its link with daily life, does myth transcend this logic? Yes and no. The nominal systems it embraces certainly constitute a body of signals which is, in a word, structured. The social relations these cover would justify structural analysis if they could be reduced to a series of binary relations. But how can we expect to do this, since the answer to most of the problems lies within the content of the relation, *a content known to everyone*? At this level, of links between the symbols, behaviour, and the physical and material factors of daily life, can we, if not prove, at least point out the possibility of unconscious structures governing the mechanisms of formal systems?

Yes, if we consider the hypostasized culture, benefiting from a thought which is mythical and an unconscious which is structural. No, if we attend only to specific named individuals, the speaker and those he speaks about, instead of to an informant considered as the representative of an anonymous collectivity which determines his every act.

Of course our living man is related to the collective heritage, and the structural method can trace the ideology of his people, both in its openly recognized and its implicit aspects, perfectly well. But myth is literature and consequently art or quasi-philosophy; all it contains, underneath the perfection or cleverness of the presentation, is a collection of grids. The superposition of these reveals in turn a certain content of local knowledge, or, described less directly, of the social structures. These must be discovered by inference because the ones given overtly in the myth may be partly artificial if not indeed fictitious. On the other hand, the land-holding structures are clearly laid out in the relations between people, groups and places.

In this last case, it is only because of our ignorance that we have to resort to our usual exercises of deduction. The story-teller's usual audience knows the meaning of each reference. He has no need to go out of his way to omit this place, or add that one; it is enough for him just to re-affirm his people's convictions at the same time as he fills out their knowledge of their rights and privileges in detail.

If, then, in the myth we only consider the translation of the landholding rights claimed, there can be no question of looking for an unconscious structure. Everything is calculated very exactly, including especially the things forgotten at the moment of telling, and the way of alluding to a claim without supporting it. The allusion is transparent to everybody, but lacks the dangerous potential of a brutal affirmation.

The researcher cannot, without abdicating his responsibilities, reject the monotonous compiling of tables of names and places; it is up to him to vivify them by calling up the multiple dialectics which in fact inhabit them. There is no discovery here of universal themes, but something equally moving, since nothing other than the material means of everyone's survival is involved.

Here is no subject for dazzling demonstration. We are only at the level of apparently repetitive facts, and we cannot escape them. Nobody, indeed, attempts to, unless it is to oppose someone else's apparent possession with his own ambitious claim, mediating the resulting contradiction by introducing a new inflection into the myth or, better still, by attempting to appropriate it; the relevant possession is the traditional text matched with its toponymic content. If circumstances and the current balance of forces allow, he will come out unharmed, though he has taken the risk, despite a general and perhaps conniving silence, of creating lasting grudges which will one day put his enterprise in danger. Or else he will find himself in the centuries-old continuity of a rivalry where abuses of power and manipulations of the myths have succeeded and opposed each other shamelessly over genera-tions. The quarrel kept up in this form is part of one's status. This is all the more true in the case of a conservative agriculture where the least nuance in the soil quality of a piece of land matters considerably because of the value attributed to the least variation in methods of cultivation (which can be due, for example, to deeper or shallower soil, or to factors assuring the land a more constant humidity).

High population density – at least in the case of peoples living from hunting or harvesting – makes the accumulated tensions more obvious and the use of myth more controlled and delicate. In an extreme situation it will be necessary to create institutions that can authenticate and regularize the land appropriations or seizures that have become necessary. When, through pressure of numbers, only effective occupation justifies the right of use, myth risks being deprived of its operational value, to the gain of juridical systems for example which censure the implications of myth while trying to preserve its supernatural sanctions. [. . .]

It might then be thought – for far be it from me to question the structures which have been shown in kinship and myth – that semantic (or social) structures are pushed back beyond immediate consciousness as soon as society can afford the luxury, or at least when it can by so doing arrive at a better economy of means. A short dictionary of kinship is generally enough to cover the needs of daily life, and the textual form of a myth, through the mnemonic quality of its melody and the entertaining quality of the narrative, can cause its content and messages to be forgotten.

Since all our essential knowledge can be easily built up from the body of myth, the question arises whether the anthropologist's deductions are not self-evident truths for the informant in front of him. This relates to my comment on the link between the inadequacy of existing materials and the need to use the structural method to raise comparative studies above the gaps in our knowledge, in order to attain a level of analysis which is more general, more objective and more coherent.

No one who devotes himself to recording a landholding system, plot by plot, can escape the consequences arising from his choice of materials and their quality. If he wishes to master individual variability, he will not rise above the awkward considerations of agriculture and soil sciences unless he puts each plot in relation to the systems of symbols used to translate and manipulate all the social appearances which we all too often take literally from the narration. The clear-sightedness of his informants, long denied to the specialist, corresponds to a necessity so peremptory, since everyone's daily bread depends on it, that the continuity between two aspects of reality cannot be broken. Everything depends on the knowledge of things, and the means of making use of it.

References

BARRAU, J. (1965), 'L'humide et le sec', *J. Polynesian Soc.*, vol. 79, no. 3, pp. 329–46.

BATESON, G. (1936), *Naven*, Stanford University Press.

GUIART, J. (1953), 'Polynesian myths and songs from Uvea (Loyalty Islands), *J. Polynesian Soc.*, vol. 62, no. 2, pp. 1–26.

GUIART, J. (1963), *Structure de la Chefferie en Mélanésie du Sud*, Institut d'Ethnologie, Paris.

LÉVI-STRAUSS, C. (1964), *Le cru et le cuit*, Plon; *The Raw and the Cooked*, Cape, 1969.

LÉVI-STRAUSS, C. (1966), *Du miel aux cendres*, Plon; *From Honey to Ashes*, Harper & Row, 1968.

OLIVER, D. (1949), 'Land tenure in north-east Sinai, Southern Bourgainville, Solomon Islands', *Paper of the Peabody Museum of American Archeology and Ethnology*, vol. 29.

6 Kenelm Burridge

Cargo

Excerpts from Kenelm Burridge, *Mambu: A Study of Melanesian Cargo Movements and their Ideological Background*, Methuen, 1960; Harper & Row, 2nd edn, 1970, pp. 250–59.

Myths in general have the attributes of objective truth largely because, perhaps, they are stories having a weight of common consent. This does not mean that storytellers cannot make their own additions to a particular myth; but it does mean that the additions they make have to obtain popular consent if they are to remain parts of the myth. Myths are stories stamped large with social approval.

Once a statement or proposition is given consent it becomes true, a part of truth, assuming an existence which is not necessarily contingent on explicit withdrawal of consent. For, having achieved objectivity or truth in a myth a statement may persist in the myth long after those who retail or who listen to the story say they discount its validity for the present. Then the statement becomes a historical truth. And, so it would seem, the longer a statement is contained in a myth as truth the longer it will persist. New truths, or rather, statements which are becoming truths, and which are expressed in the additions of individual storytellers, are extremely vulnerable to, and dependent upon, consent. But once the first tentative consent begins to harden into solid approval the lodgement becomes more and more secure, more and more independent of explicit consent or inarticulate dissent. Conversely, if at first a truth is entirely a community's babe, entirely dependent on approval, as it becomes independent of the latter so does it tend to mould the thoughts of the community in the way of its implications. [. . .]

Rather than assault the imagination too violently Tangu storytellers tend to make a deft selection of significant points. Their raw material consists of incidents which they have witnessed or heard about, which might have occurred yesterday or last month, and which have caught the public imagination; of rumours which can be embellished; of fascinating pieces of misinformation which can be decked out with tact to elicit an appreciative laugh, or score a point. And, like storytellers anywhere, Tangu resort to their dreams and daydreams for material.

As has been shown, dreams are for Tangu a repository of truths which are always relevant for the self. They spring from a total experience: from an experience of society, of other unique individuals, of the physical world, of the mystical world, of both the quick and the dead. They spring, too, from psychological experience; from an awareness of the self in relation to others, from cognizance of being, and from deep in the psyche. To cross over to Tangu and enter with them into dreamland is to venture beyond the confines of civilized man. For here are lodged those truths which white men tend to hide in asylums.

It is one thing to examine the rites in which Tangu engaged and to find in them consistency in relation to the problems that beset them; quite another to be intellectually aware of those problems and then try to work out suitable rites which will express them. Yet we do not find it strange that such ceremonies could emerge from a dream. Nor, indeed, do Tangu. On the other hand Europeans do tend to think it odd that Tangu should use their dream experiences to order everyday life. However, once having granted that dreams contain truths it is at least logical, if not always advantageous in European terms, to make use of dream experiences in other contexts of life. When a Tangu talks to his father he is undergoing a real experience. When he consults with his dead father in a dream he is undergoing a quite different kind of experience – which may or may not be as clear as either might wish – but which is certainly as real.

When A converses with his elder brother B it is a real experience which happens several times a day, every day, for many years. Then B dies. In Tangu A dreams that B comes to have a chat with him. His visits are frequent during the period immediately following his death, and then they tend to become progressively rarer until A nears the end of his span – when they tend to become more frequent again. Often enough, and certainly if A and B were close confidants in life, A and B continually meet in dream. In life not every conversation that A has with B is thought to be significant: they occur several times a day. After B's death, however, every meeting is telling. For if the dead have many of the characteristics of the living they lack one that is essential: physical life. And in virtue of what they lack the dead possess attributes which the living do not. Normally invisible, in dreams they make themselves manifest. Space does not fetter them, and time does not trip them by the heels. What the dead say has significance precisely because they are dead when they say it. And the dead, because they are dead, can oversee all, and once had physical life, cannot but have a far wider experience and knowledge of the truth however hard the living might try to harness them in convention, and however inadequate the translation of an encounter into the idiom of language.

Statements communicated through dreams are, therefore, more true than the statements of living men and women. Even trickeries and deceptions are more true. They are absolute. If, in life, B tricks A, A can reply by deceiving B. But if B is dead he can trick A to his soul's content and A cannot trick B.

Myths and dreams are interdependent in the sense, first, that much of the content of dreams tends to become articulate in myth, and myths, or parts of myths, are retold in dreams. Secondly, though myths and dreams are intimately related to truth the relationships are not of the same kind. Myths contain truths, dreams are avenues for perceiving the truths which are later embodied in myths.

A European observer might say that myths are true, or more true, because they are not simply personal views but statements of dogma acknowledged by the community as a whole. Tangu themselves say that myths are true because they are myths. It is axiomatic. If pressed, Tangu will add that myths are true because they belong to the ancestors, because they exist, and because they derive from the truths of the past which are always truths. The validity of dreams is also axiomatic. They are true because they derive from the ancestors, from the dead; because even when no ancestor appears in the dream the dream had been 'sent' anonymously – not made up by the living. Myths are social repositories of truths, and dreams are accepted as windows through which individuals may perceive the truth.

The European contribution has been to throw doubt on the

content of myths without invalidating the principles by which truth may be sought or preserved. Tangu still discover their truths through dreams, and still store their truths in myths. But in the current situation, given certain problems, and not being provided with adequate tools with which to tackle them, Tangu have had recourse to the truths in their myths. To their dismay, now that they need them, they have found there a lumber grown over with cobwebs. To be sure, some pieces still shine; but they do not suffice to explain their ever widening environment. White men have not been slow to offer them substitutes, but, with doubt in their minds, Tangu have cause to wonder which is more true, more valid, more useful. What are the criteria of truth? On the whole Tangu have been forced back into traditional hinges of choice: myths, dreams and emotional responses. Even had they preferred to take operational or organizational criteria of fitness and efficiency the administrative system deprives them of the option. Tangu are not asked, nor allowed to initiate. They must obey. They are considered not to be 'ready'.

Within the ferment of truths which might only be halftruths or nothing at all, the charismatic figure emerges as an articulate vehicle bringing order and intelligibility to a largely inchoate mass of experiences and feelings. For a period he himself becomes a veritable symbol of truth, an individual, enshrined in himself, at one with society, absorbed in the myth-dream. He can never be wholly a failure. Through him – through what he says and does – what appears to be false or useless is set aside and abandoned; and what appears to be true or useful for the future is garnered in the myth-dream and further refined. But if, for a while, the charismatic figure appears as the criterion of truth, truth itself is contained in the myth-dream. He fails as a person when the directives and principles he provides do not completely reflect and validate the myth-dream as it exists when he makes his appearance; and he succeeds in so far as he has meaning and validates a part, or parts, of the myth-dream.

The new man

Tangu gossip is like gossip anywhere else in the world. Men and women say things about other men and women; accuracy is beside the point. Rumour-mongering is different. Rumours arise out of social situations containing affective alternatives: the accuracy or truth of the matter is important because the yea or nay will affect future thought and action. Several examples have been given of the way rumours collect round the possibilities of administrative action, of the particular twists they take, and their results; and it has also been shown how ready both Tangu and Manam islanders were to put their own interpretations on the role of the writer. And the misinterpretations are important because they are affective, and because the basic questions to which the original observations try to give answers may be resolved in – What is the nature of the white man? What is the nature of man?

Tangu are interested in white men in rather the same way that certain journalists are interested in the actions of Russian political figures. There is the same hunt for significance and relevance, the same What next?, the same attempts to project possibilities. Tangu do not, cannot, take it for granted that white men are human in the same way as they are. So, within the limits of their own understanding, Tangu go to some pains to find out about white men. But, as we have seen, these same limits of understanding not only shape the questions they ask, but predicate the answers. Questions arise from the problems in Cargo, and answers spring from the assumptions in Cargo. Nevertheless, the more objective information about white men, information that is freed from conflicts of interest, is lodged where it might be expected to be found: in the myth-dream. And in the myth-dream we find the new man.

Mambu the man does not emerge as an easy character to assess. Whether or not he had courage may remain a debatable point. But he must have had a keener intelligence than most or he would not have been marked down as a possible catechist. His imagination seems to have been balanced by a nice common sense, he was perceptive, and a man without ability could not have organized a movement as he did. In the myth about him, however, Mambu becomes much more influential than he was as an historical figure. Perhaps because he meant so much more than he was. Yali was certainly a capable man, but it seems fairly clear that he owed most of his reputation to his friends and his enemies. It is surely significant that as Yali the man became more and more perplexed within himself, as he degenerated into libertinism, as he began to use power to satisfy personal desires, his social stature expanded and grew large. Real principles and interests involving relatively large numbers of people were at stake. And they met in Yali. If he was the spark, the flames that he kindled were not in his power to control.

As has been shown, both Mambu and Yali made their own particular contributions to the shape of the new man. As charismatic figures they sufficed, temporarily, to contain the new man. When their days were done what appeared to be significant to the community in their deeds, words and attributes became a part of the myth-dream. Neither Mambu nor Yali was necessarily the sort of man every one would like to be in fact. But both were certainly the kind of men almost every Kanaka would like to admire and point out as an example to others as an ideal which each one of them should, or ought to, emulate.

Irakau, whose involvement with Tangu and their affairs was minimal, was still in the ascendant in 1952 when the events narrated in the *Prologue* took place. Drawing on their experiences with Yali the mission was not wholly mistaken in thinking that Irakau's friends and followers were attempting to make him more than he was. And it would surely be asking too much of a man to expect him to resist successfully the community pressures which were pushing him into a position from whence he might exert an absolute power. In resisting the pressures to positive action, in maintaining relationships with administration and mission, Irakau was being true to the myth-dream – which is widely disseminated over the Bogia region – but not being nearly spectacular enough. He was demanding of his community the same nerve and capacity for restraint as he himself had. The youth from Pariakenam illustrates the other extreme. In himself he may have been a nonentity. But he was a lad who had a dream, who saw truth, at a crucial moment in time. In other circumstances the same dream might have been laughed at.

The charismatic figure, it would seem, the centre of a Cargo movement, may or may not have abilities of his own. But because of some qualities he may have, or because of what he is doing, or through a mere accident of time and place, he takes the centre of the stage and through the myth-dream other merits are heaped on him. He himself has something. He must have. But on the whole circumstances, the men about him, rumours, and the community which gives the rumours validity, actually create him.

Although ordinary men may see in the charismatic figure the projection of a new social ideal it is only for a brief period of time. For most of their lives they are faced by themselves as individuals. Each may feel himself to be a man, but only a few may be able to recognize him as such. And not many who feel themselves to be men can have the confidence of knowing it without the signal approbation of their friends and comrades. When Tangu are among their own kind they know they have to keep proving to themselves and to others that they are men. The methods of doing so are known and accepted, the proof of their manhood is clear.

Outside Tangu these same men are lost. The criteria of manhood are many and diffuse. A proud bearing, good in Tangu among Tangu, can be 'bigheaded' in front of a European or a Kanaka foreman. And 'bigheaded' is not only a term of opprobrium, it means no work, no cash. The instant riposte, enjoined in Tangu – and habitual in Australia itself – is punished by Europeans in New Guinea. Containing one's pride with dignity may be regarded as sulking.

What makes a man? How can others recognize a man and treat him as such when they see him?

Charismatic figures have the quality of manhood, and they derive it from the ambience of the myth-dream. Ordinary men, on the other hand, are forced to deal with the realities of day-to-day life. They have to gain self-respect – which is a product both of a critical assessment of the self by the self, and of a knowledge of standing in the community. They need a clear image of what a man should be and do.

Tangu carry the image of a manager. They are also aware of other images which tend to obscure the definite outlines of the managerial ideal. A late reveller's vision, one part of the European model has money, material goods, power over others, confidence and omnipotence: items of day-to-day experience and observation. Another part, largely the result of missionary teaching, contains the Christ-image, flat and unrounded, gentle and self-sacrificing. Yali revivified the traditional warrior, portraying the warrior of tomorrow. Irakau illustrates the shrewd entrepreneur. Where is the new man – the moral entity which can be shrewd, gentle, self-sacrificing and capable withal?

Tangu would like to be men amongst men, not merely men among Tangu. Even if in themselves they feel themselves to be men, among Europeans they cannot know that they are men. Some, it is true, may wear a policeman's uniform; and others may rejoice in the title of boss-boy or boatswain. But, for the most part, in the European environment, Tangu are labourers or domestic servants doing women's work. Europeans sport their manhood, their social worth, in fine houses, equipment and access to cargo. Like Tangu managers they have behind them a solid achievement, something to show, something which accounts for their influence and power. But in the European environment Tangu have nothing, nothing material to show they are men, nothing by which they may demonstrate that as the divine creator stands to his creation so men stand to their own material goods.

In Tangu gardens and harvests are the basis on which a man's reputation is built, and the means through which a mutual equivalence can be proved. Without cargo Tangu cannot prove an equivalence with white men. And since an assumption of moral equality is lacking there is no way of maintaining any kind of equivalence with white men. Only with the moral European do the possibilities of manhood become realizable.

Without a past and a future, it would seem, a Kanaka can hardly be secure as a man. 'I am me' does not suffice. 'I am the son of a bush-Kanaka' is no matter for pride at the present time. Inevitably, the question becomes, 'What can I be in the eyes of my fellows, my children and my ancestors?' If the past can justify the ancestors it gives the living a foothold in the present, especially in relation to Europeans. And it provides a departure for the future. European teaching, however, and experiences with Europeans, have all tended to make the ancestors seem small. They got the myths wrong; they handed on deception, not truth; their memories were bad; they sinned; they were unable to write; they invented and practised distasteful customs; they had no understanding. Through them the right to cargo was forfeit.

But apart from the ancestors there can be no past. Ancestors contain the past just as the past contains ancestors. In a Cargo movement the ancestors emerge as heroes once more. They are all right; they become respectable; they can make cargo; they have not forgotten their descendants. Even now they are sending cargo to their offspring – but white men are intercepting it, changing the labels, stealing it. . . .

If Tangu were more worthy of the ancestors, if they were in some way more men than they are, inimical and amoral white men would be thwarted. Then the cargo would come. Through Mambu the myth-dream counsels a period of waiting and learning. But who, caught in the toils of the present, may wait on the future? Tangu want to be men now, while they live, not in fifty years' time when they are dead. If they must be rehabilitated ancestors they would still like to put their children on the path towards manhood. Access to cargo has become the symbol of manhood.

Part Three
Myths in Societies

In this Part, in contrast with Part Two, the relations of myth and its sociological context are investigated at a distance. Operational tools are used, and models are drawn on or built in attempts to discover the structures of semantic systems. Propp, the pioneer of metalinguistic approaches, focuses on immediate environments as semantic determinants: urban *v.* rural, Christian *v.* pagan, etc. Maranda, with the help of the computer, abstracts a structure and passes from a version to another. Greimas tackles, after Dumézil, factors in complex societies and carries the analysis on the level of political representations.

7 Vladimir Propp

Transformations in Fairy Tales

Abridged from Vladimir Propp, 'Les Transformations des Contes
Fantastiques' in T. Todorov (ed.), *Théorie de la Littérature*,
Seuil, 1965, pp. 234–62. Specially translated for this volume by Petra
Morrison. First published in *Poltika, Vremennik Otdela Slovesnyx
Iskussto*, vol. 4, 1928, pp. 70–89.

It is a fact that the characters in fairy stories, while always remaining very different in appearance, age, sex, occupation, rank,
and other permanent and attributed characteristics, perform the
same actions in the course of the plot. It is this that determines
how the constant factors of tales relate to the variables. The
characters' actions represent the constants, while everything else
can vary. For example:

1. The king sends Ivan to find the princess. Ivan leaves.
2. The king sends Ivan to find a rare object. Ivan leaves.
3. The sister sends her brother to find a remedy. The brother
   leaves.
4. The stepmother sends her stepdaughter to find fire. The stepdaughter leaves.
5. The blacksmith sends his apprentice to find the cow. The
   apprentice leaves.

And so on. The sending on the search, and the departure, are
constants. The sender and the leaver, the motivation for the
sending, etc., are variables. Furthermore, the stages of the search,
the obstacles to it, and other features, may still essentially match
up without appearing to do so; for we can separate the characters
and their functions. Now, there are thirty-one functions or kinds
of action to be found in fairy tales. Not all tales contain every
kind of action, but the absence of some of them does not affect
the sequence of the others. Together they constitute a system or
composition, and this system has been found to be extremely
stable and widespread. The researcher can prove that different

tales, such as the Egyptian tale of the two brothers, the tale of the firebird, the tale of the Morozok,[1] the tale of the fisherman and the fish, as well as a number of myths, justify joint study. And detailed analysis confirms this assumption. The system is, however, not limited to the thirty-one types of action. A motif such as 'Baba Yaga[2] gives Ivan a horse' contains four elements, of which only one constitutes a function, while the other three are static. The total number of such elements, the constituent parts of fairy tales, is about one hundred and fifty. We can name each of these elements according to their role in the story sequence. So in the example given above, Baba Yaga is the benefactor, and the word 'gives' represents the moment of Ivan's being provided with the magic object; Ivan is the character who receives the magic object, and the horse is the magic object itself. In if this way we took the names of all the hundred-and-fifty elements of the fairy tale, and tabled them in the order which is set by the tales themselves, we could enter every fairy tale in existence on that chart: conversely, every tale that could be entered on the chart is a fairy tale, and every one that cannot belongs in another class of tale. Each rubric on the chart would isolate one constituent of the tale, and reading it vertically would reveal both the series of those forms which were basic to the fairy tale, and the series of those which had evolved from the basic ones.

It is these constituent parts which lend themselves most readily to comparison. This would correspond, in zoology, to comparing vertebrae with vertebrae, teeth with teeth, and so on. There is nevertheless a great difference between organic formations and fairy tales, which makes our task easier. While in biology, a change in one part or characteristic entails the changing of another characteristic, in the tale any part can change independently of the others. Many researchers have noticed this phenomenon, although I have yet to come across any attempt to draw all the possible conclusions, both methodological and otherwise, from it[3].

1. Character who represents the cold in popular Russian tales.
2. Supernatural female character in Russian tales.
3. cf. Panzer (1905), 'His composition is a mosaic of clearly defined pieces which produce a striking picture. These pieces are easily interchangeable and consequently simple to vary as no effort has been made to combine them in depth.' Clearly the theory of stable combinations or

Thus Krohn, while he agrees with Spiess on the mobility of constituent parts, nevertheless finds it necessary to study tales according to their general plan and not according to their constituents – he does not, however, find any weighty arguments to defend his position, one typical of the Finnish School.

We may conclude, then, that constituent parts can be studied out of the context of the story which they compose. A study of the vertical columns in our chart would reveal both the conditions and mechanisms for transformation. Thanks to the automatic way in which constituent parts link up, what is true for each individual element will remain so for the general plan.[4]

This present work is not intended to exhaust the subject. I can only outline a few main points, which will later form the base for a wider theoretical study.

Even in a short *exposé*, however, before moving on to study transformations it is necessary to establish criteria which will enable us to distinguish the basic forms from derived forms.

These criteria can be of two kinds: they can be expressed either by certain general principles or by special rules.

First of all the general principles.

In order to establish these principles we must consider the tale in relation to its context, the situation in which it was created and in which it exists. Here, everyday life and religion, in the widest sense of the word, are of the greatest importance, since the reasons for transformations are exterior to the tale and we will not be able to understand their evolution without relating the tale itself to the human context in which it exists. [. . .]

Thus the study of the basic forms leads the researcher to compare the fairy tale with religions.

On the other hand, the study of derived forms in the fairy tale is bound up with reality, for many transformations are explained by the introduction of reality into the tale. We are consequently forced to perfect our methods of studying the relationship between the tale and the contemporary way of life.

---

non-variable links is being denied here. Spiess has expressed the same idea with greater emphasis and in more detail (1917). See also Krohn (1926).

4. This important paragraph shows that Propp was aware of the paradigmatic dimension of analysis. See Lévi-Strauss (1958, ch. 11).

The fairly tale, unlike other classes of tale (anecdotes, short stories, fables, etc.), is relatively poor in elements belonging to real life: the role of reality in tale creation has often been overestimated. We cannot resolve this problem of the relationship between the tale and contemporary life unless we bear in mind the difference between artistic realism and the presence of elements taken directly from life. Researchers often make the mistake of trying to make a realistic narrative correspond to real life. [. . .]

So it is clear that the problem of the relationship between tale and reality is not at all simple. We cannot draw any conclusions with an immediate bearing on life from tales.

Yet, as we shall see later, the role of reality in tale transformations is very important. Real life cannot destroy the general structure of the tale, but it produces the material for the different substitutions which are added into the old fabric. [. . .]

By way of example I will follow up all the possible transformations of a single element, in this case Baba Yaga's cottage. From a morphological point of view, the cottage represents the dwelling of the benefactor (i.e. the character who gives the hero a magic object). We will therefore compare not only cottages but also all the kinds of dwelling which belong to the benefactor. Now, we will take the basic Russian form to be the cottage on hen's feet in the forest, which revolves. Since however one element in a tale never embodies all the possible transformations, in certain cases other examples will be used.

Reduction. Instead of the complete form, the following series of transformations can be found:

1. Cottage on hen's feet in the forest.
2. Cottage on hen's feet.
3. Cottage in the forest.
4. Cottage.
5. The forest.
6. No mention of dwelling.

Here the basic form is reduced. The hen's feet, the rotation, and then the forest are abandoned; and finally the cottage itself can disappear. Such reduction represents an incomplete basic form. It can be explained, of course, by forgetfulness, which in turn has its own, more complex, reasons. It also indicates the lack of correspondence between the tale and the kind of life lived where it is known, how little the tale actually relates to the milieu, the historical period or the narrator.

Amplification. This is the opposite phenomenon. Here the basic form is enlarged and filled out by details. This form can be considered amplified:

cottage on hen's feet, in the forest, propped up by pancakes and covered with tarts.

Most amplifications are accompanied by reductions; certain characteristics are rejected and others are added. Amplifications can be classed in groups according to their origin (as I have done below with substitutions); some come from everyday life, others represent the developing of a detail borrowed from the conventional form. In the above example, this last is the case. A study of the benefactor shows that he combines qualities of hostility and hospitality: Ivan usually has a feast at his benefactor's house. (The forms of this feast vary a lot. 'Given drink, given food', Ivan addresses the cottage in these words: 'We must come in to you for a bite to eat.' He sees the table laid in the cottage, he tastes each of the dishes, or he eats his fill; he himself bleeds the bulls or the hens in the benefactor's yard, etc.) The dwelling, then, expresses the same qualities as the benefactor. The German tale of Hansel and Gretel uses this form in a slightly different manner, to fit the childlike nature of the tale.

Deformation. At the present time deformations are found quite often, since the fairy tale is dying out. These forms, deprived of meaning, sometimes become widespread and take root. In the case of the cottage, we may consider the image of its constant rotation on its axis to be deformed. The cottage has a very particular significance in the development of the plot, for it is an outpost, and here the hero undergoes a test which will show that he is worthy of receiving the magic object. The cottage presents Ivan with a blind wall, which is why it is sometimes called a 'cottage without windows or doors'. The opening is on the other side from Ivan. We might think it is easy for him to walk round and go in by the door, but Ivan cannot do this, and in the tales he never does. Instead he says a magic formula, 'turn your back to the forest and your face to me' or 'place yourself as your mother placed you'. It generally follows that 'the cottage turned round' or rather 'returned'. The word 'returned' has been changed to 'turned', and the expression 'turns when it must' is transformed simply into 'turns' or revolves, which is meaningless, though it does have a certain charm.

Inversion. The basic form is often transformed into its opposite. For example feminine images are replaced by masculine images and vice versa. This phenomenon can also affect the cottage, so that instead of a closed-up cottage we sometimes find a cottage with its door wide open.

Intensification and weakening. These kinds of transformation only affect the characters' actions. Different actions can be performed with different intensity. Transforming the sending of the hero into his expulsion is one example of intensification. His dispatching is one of the tale's constant elements, and it comes in such a number of different forms that we can see it undergoing every stage of transformation. The dispatching may occur when some rare object is asked for; sometimes it is a commission ('do me this service'), more often it is an order accompanied by threats if it is not executed and promises if it is. Sometimes, too, it is a disguised expulsion: the wicked sister sends her brother to fetch milk from wild animals in order to be rid of him; the master sends his servant to fetch the cow which is supposedly lost in the forest; the stepmother sends her stepdaughter to fetch fire from Baga Yaga. Finally, if can be just expulsion, by itself. These are only the principal stages and each of them can have several variations and intermediary forms; these forms are particularly important for the study of tales which deal with characters who are expelled.

The basic form of the dispatching can be taken as the order accompanied by threats and promises. If the promises are omitted, this reduction can at the same time be considered as an intensification; only the dispatching and the threats are left.

The omission of the threats, however, leads to attenuation, to a weakening of the form. The ultimate weakening consists of omitting the dispatching altogether; the son leaves, asking his parents' blessing.

The six kinds of transformation which we have now examined can be interpreted as changes in the basic form. At the same level of analysis we find two other large groups of transformation; substitutions and assimilations. Both can be classed according to their origin.

Internal substitution. Continuing our study of the dwelling, we find the following forms:

1. Palace.
2. Mountain by a river of fire.

These are neither reductions nor amplifications, etc. They are not changes but substitutions, which do not come from outside; they have been drawn from the tale itself. Here we are dealing with a displacement, a transposition of the material. The princess generally lives in a palace, which is usually made of gold; and this dwelling is then attributed to the benefactor. Such displacements play a major part in tales. Each element has its own form; but this form is not always attached to the same element (for example, the princess who is the person sought after can also play the role of the helper, the benefactor). One image in the tale supplants another image. Thus Baba Yaga's daughter can take on the role of the princess, and Baba Yaga no longer lives in a cottage but in a palace, a dwelling appropriate to a princess. There is a parallel in the palaces of copper, silver and gold in other tales. The maidens who live in them are both benefactors and princesses. These palaces may sometimes arise as a triple image of the golden palace, but they can also have an independent origin, which for example has no connection whatever with the images of the golden, silver and iron ages.

In the same way the mountain by the river of fire is only the dragon's dwelling place attributed to the benefactor. These displacements, like other internal substitutions, play a very important part in the birth of transformations.

Realistic substitution. If we have these forms:

1. Inn.
2. Two-storey house.

The fabulous cottage is replaced by types of dwelling known in real life. Most of these substitutions can be explained very simply, but some of them require special ethnographic research. Realistic substitutions are particularly easy to notice and researchers usually stop there.

Confessional substitution. Contemporary religion can also substitute new forms for old. Noteworthy instances are the devil in the role of airborne carrier, the angel as provider of the magic object, the test which resembles mortification. Certain legends in fact represent tales in which all the elements have undergone such substitutions. Christianity, Islam, Buddhism, are all reflected in the tales of the peoples who profess these religions. [. . .]

There remains one further, very important, problem to clarify. If we note down all (or a large number of) the forms of one element, we will see that they cannot be reduced to a single basic form. Suppose we take Baba Yaga as the basic form of the benefactor. We can explain such forms as witch, grandmother, widow, little old lady, old man, shepherd, forest dweller, angel, devil, the three daughters, the king's daughter, etc., as substitutions and other transformations of Baba Yaga. But we also find the 'moujik as small as a fingernail with a beard a yard long'. This form of the benefactor does not come from Baba Yaga. If we were to find a similar form in religions, we could consider it a form coordinated with that of Baba Yaga; otherwise it remains a substitution of unknown origin. Each element, then, may have several basic forms, although the number of these parallel coordinated forms is usually very limited.

This study would be incomplete if I did not show a series of transformations in a denser area and provide a model for applying my remarks. Let us take these forms:

The dragon carries off the king's daughter.
The dragon tortures the king's daughter.
The dragon demands the king's daughter.

From the point of view of the tale's morphology, we are dealing with the initial hostile act. This act is usually the pivot of the story. Now, in accordance with the principles established above, we must compare not only one carrying-off with another, etc., but also the different forms of the initial hostile act, since it is a constituent part of the tale.

Prudence demands that these three forms be considered as coordinated forms; but we can nevertheless suppose that the first form is the basic one. Ancient Egypt had an image of death as the dragon carrying off the soul. This image is, however, forgotten, whereas the image of illness as the settling of a demon in the body still survives. As for the last form, the image of the dragon demanding the princess as tribute has a flavour of archaic or historical realism, particularly since it is accompanied by the appearance of an army, the siege of the town and the threat of war. (This cannot, however, be affirmed with complete certainty.) So the three forms are very ancient and each lends itself to a number of transformations.

Let us take the first one:

The dragon carries off the king's daughter.

The dragon is understood as a personification of evil. The confessional influence transforms it into a devil:

The devil carries off the king's daughter.

A similar influence changes the person who is carried off:

The devil carries off the Pope's daughter.

The dragon image is already foreign to the village and is replaced by a better-known dangerous animal (realistic substitution) which is endowed with fabulous attributes (modification):

The bear with an iron hide bears away the king's children.

The evil one is associated with Baba Yaga; since one part of the tale influences another (internal substitution), and Baba Yaga is a female creature, for this reason masculinity is attributed to the person who is carried off (inversion):

The witch carries off the old couple's son.

One of the constant forms which complicate the tale is the

introduction of the brothers, who carry off the victim. Here the initial hostile act is transferred to the hero's relatives. This is the conventional way to complicate the plot:

The brothers carry off Ivan's betrothed.

The wicked brothers are replaced by other wicked relatives, borrowed from the tale's stock of characters (internal substitution):

The king (the father-in-law) carries off Ivan's wife.

Sometimes it is the princess who plays this role, and the tale takes on more amusing forms; in this case the image of the evil one is reduced:

The princess flees from her husband's home.

In each of these cases people were carried off, but it can be divine light that is stolen (archaic substitution?):

The dragon steals the kingdom's light.

The dragon is replaced by another monstrous creature (modification); the victim is associated with imaginary royal life:

The vison-beast steals animals from the king's menagerie.

Talismans play a large part in the tale. They are often the sole means by which Ivan attains his objectives, and this explains why it is they that are so often stolen. In fact, the conventions demand this theft, so as to complicate the action around the middle of the tale. This middle event can be transferred to the beginning (internal substitution). Often it is the knave, the master, etc., who steals the talisman (realistic substitution):

The mischievous child carries off Ivan's talisman.
The master carries off the moujik's talisman.

The tale about the firebird is situated on an intermediary level, before other forms where the stolen golden apples are not talismans (cf. the youth-giving apples of life). I must add here that the theft of the talisman can complicate the action only towards the middle of the tale, when the talisman has already been located; it is possible for its theft to come near the beginning only when its possession is motivated in some way. Thus we can understand why the objects stolen at the beginning of the tale are mostly not talismans. The firebird is one of the basic forms of Ivan's bearer into the thirtieth kingdom; the golden feathers, etc., are usual attributes of fabulous animals. It moves from the middle of the tale to the beginning:

The firebird steals the king's apples.

In each of these cases, the carrying off (the theft) is retained. The disappearance of the betrothed, the daughter, the wife, etc., is attributed to a mythical being. This mythical character is, however, foreign to contemporary peasant life. So witchcraft replaces the foreign, borrowed, mythology, and the disappearance is attributed to the spells of wizards and witches. The nature of the hostile act changes, but its result remains constant, it is always a disappearance which engenders a search (substitution of superstitious belief):

The wizard carries off the king's daughter.
The maid-servant casts a spell on Ivan's betrothed and makes her run away.

Next, we notice once again the transference of the act to wicked relatives:

The sisters make the girl's fiancé run away.

Now let us move on to the transformations of our second basic form, i.e.:

The dragon tortures the king's daughter.

The transformations follow the same paths:

The devil tortures the king's daughter, etc.

Torture here takes the form of an obsession, and a vampirism, which is satisfactorily explained by the tale's ethnography. We again find another wicked creature replacing the dragon and the devil:

Baba Yaga tortures the valiant knight's mistress.

The third basic form presents threats of a forced marriage:

The dragon demands the king's daughter.

Thus a whole series of transformations is opened up:

The water sprite demands the king's son, etc.

Consistently with the tale's morphology, the same form gives a declaration of war without the demanding of the king's children (reduction). The transference of similar forms to relatives gives us:

The witch-sister tries to eat the king's son (her brother).

This last case is particularly interesting, as here the prince's sister is called 'a dragon'. Consequently it gives us a classic example of internal assimilation, and shows that we must be on our guard in studying family relationships as they emerge from fairy tales. The marriage of brother and sister, and other forms, may not in the least be survivals of an old custom, but may occur as the result of certain transformations, as is clearly shown in the case I have just cited.

References

KROHN, K. (1920), *Die folkloristische Arbeitsmethode*, Oslo.
LÉVI-STRAUSS, C. (1958), *Anthropologie Structurale, Plon*.
PANZER, F. (1905), *Märchen, Sage und Dichtung*, Munich.
SPIESS, K. (1917), *Das deutsche Volksmärchen*, Leipzig.

8 Pierre Maranda

Qualitative and Quantitative Analysis of Myths by Computer[1]

Abridged from Pierre Maranda, 'Analyse qualitative et quantitative de mythes sur ordinateurs' in B. Jaulin and J. C. Gardin (eds.), *Calcul et Formalisation dans les Sciences de l'Homme*, Centre National de la Recherche Scientifique, 1968, pp. 79–86. Specially translated for this volume by John Freeman and Pierre Maranda.

The object of this paper is to describe in broad outline a segment of the computerized analysis of myths. [. . .]

In the following pages, attention will more particularly be devoted to three points. Certain preliminary conditions for the automatic analysis of myths will first be briefly reviewed. Then, a procedure for the structural analysis of myths will be sketched. Finally, there will follow some considerations of quantitative analysis and some of its relations with qualitative analysis.

Preparation of documents

The data submitted to computer processing were a corpus of 135 Gê myths. Collected by the German anthropologist Nimuendaju and in the last decade by the anthropologists of the Harvard Central Brazil Project, these texts express the cosmology of four tribes of the Gê linguistic group, the Eastern Timbria, the Sherente, the Apinayé and the Cayapo. They all live in the Mato Grosso, in central Brazil, in a context which constitutes a sort of natural laboratory eminently favourable to comparative study (see Lévi-Strauss, 1964). Indeed, while the historical, ecological and technological parameters remain constant, one abserves sociological variations in political organization, kinship, ritual and mythology. [. . .] The work is based on English translations which of course are carefully checked.

The first stage was the preparation of the documents. It is not

1. The research work partly reported in this paper was supported by the Laboratory of Social Relations, Harvard University, Fourth Pilot Grant, and by the National Science Foundation Grant GS-178.

necessary to expand on the necessity of working with an analytic language. Natural languages – even those already trimmed by the process of oral coding and transmission – could not be submitted to operational processing without previously eliminating the ambiguities with which they are permeated.

The linguistic and logical equipment available happens to be sufficient to allow a relatively simple and economical translation of the myths from natural to analytical language. The mythic discourse is thus first of all divided up into minimal units. [...] which are elementary or analytical propositions. Their limits are marked by the plus sign (+), while the period (.) is reserved for groups formed from these indivisible units functionally articulated. In fact, it can be sufficient to use a single marker; however, a second is useful to designate the units at the 'sentence' level, that is, those which consist of elementary propositions explicitly linked by conjunctions. One can also use one or more other signs if one thinks it already possible at this stage to trace the outlines larger of divisions ('episodes', 'sections', 'mythemes', etc., see Propp 1958; Lévi-Strauss 1958, 1960).

The articulations of the mythic discourse are first normalized with the aid of a battery of unequivocal connectors defined with the help of a concordance (see below). Then a 'dictionary' – grid, data filter – is built. In the process, homographs, pronouns and other sources of ambiguities are replaced by terms unambiguous or made precise by suffixes between brackets. Finally, each term and function is assigned a numerical suffix designating its propositional role. I have elsewhere discussed in detail the procedures adopted in this matter (Maranda 1967a, 1967b; see Gundlach 1965), and I prefer to reserve the main part of my paper to considerations of a different kind.

Automatic analysis
Structural analysis

The computer processing begins once the texts have been re-written in analytical language. The programmes used are the KWIC ('Key-Words-in-Context') and the General Inquirer (Dunphy, Stone and Smith, 1965: Stone et al., 1966).[2]

2. There are now four different though partly overlapping INQUIRERS. They are, in addition to the 1964 version, the STANFORD INQUIRER (at

The structural output is obtained by a series of restrictive instructions. In effect, instead of normalizing the texts in their totality, as in the case of the complete outputs for quantitative analysis, the computer concerns itself exclusively with certain aspects in which only the principal theme of the narrative is retained.

Some preliminary remarks are necessary here to explain the procedure. The documents are normalized to the first degree by manual translation from the natural language to the analytical language. A normalization of the second degree is produced by the computer assigning each term and each function to a specific analytical category. Ninety-nine descriptors had first been established for the Gê documents (a more considerable number are now available). These analytical categories are not formed *a priori* but rest on the data themselves. The K WIC programme (Stone *et al.* 1966) used at this stage provides an alphabetical concordance where all the words from the documents are found in their context. This allows on the one hand the easy finding of ambiguities which may have escaped at the time of the first degree normalization (there are also some automatic routines which can help at this stage); on the other hand, and this is its great merit, the concordance permits the compilation of an inventory of the semantic fields in which the documents are situated. Given that all occurences of a term or function appear in it with the functions or terms with which this term or function is associated – e.g. jaguar and hunting, jaguar and verbal communication with a boy, the fear a jaguar has of a toad, jaguar and possession of fire for cooking, tapir and adultery with the village women, etc. – the concordance provides the basis for a grid to establish classes of actors and actions. The categories or classes thus obtained are formed of groups of terms and functions defined by a coefficient of association. At first nominal, that is, non-operational for the most part, these categories emerge none the less from the texts themselves and do not originate in the analyst's ingenuity. His role consists, in fact, only of choosing a name for each category, of which the definition, not at all arbitrary, is provided by an exclusive and exhaustive listing. We thus have

Stanford University), INQUIRER II (University of Washington), and INQUIRER III (Harvard University).

some fixed concepts to start off with, even if this first approximation must assuredly be completed subsequently by the operational verification of the nominal definitions, or in certain cases by its elaboration (see Maranda 1967b; see Greimas, 1971). The battery of these descriptors thus constitutes a 'dictionary' of which the rules of construction, the content and the principles governing its use are described and discussed elsewhere (Maranda 1967a, 1967b).

Already at the level of nominal definitions, certain semantic domains appear strongly differentiated, others are scarcely present, etc. KWIC reveals, for example, that to encompass the Gê data, more than three times as many sociological as cosmological descriptors are necessary (Maranda, 1967a). This is already an indication of the orientation of the Gê myths, which is confirmed by more developed analyses.

Among the ninety-nine descriptors which summarize the principal Gê semantic fields, thirty-one are exclusively 'terms' or arguments, seven are exclusively 'functions', and seven are normalized connectors. Additionally, the function is indicated by analytical dispositions at the time of first degree normalization and by numerical suffixes added to the propositional elements. Thanks to these dispositions the computer can be directed, in such a way as to produce an output containing only, for each text, the structural argument of the documents.

The first instruction in this phase indicates to the computer the path to follow in the choice of structural elements at the level of the proposition. It aims the computer exclusively at the actors, whose occurrences it counts, to determine those of which the frequency is equal to at least 20 per cent of the total number of the analytical propositions of the myth. The bearing of this operation is that only the propositions which feature these actors (in whatever position) will be taken into consideration in the next phase. The second instruction concerns the conjunctions and predicates or 'functions': all the propositions which contain the most frequently mentioned actors, and only those, are described in four columns, of which the first is devoted to the conjunctions, the second to the 'subject' actors, the third to the actions, and the fourth to the 'object' actors (see output, below). To clarify reading, repetitions are eliminated so that if, for example, A occupies the 'subject' position in three consecutive propositions, it only appears once, in the first line. Finally, the computer reacts to any change of 'subject' by printing an order number immediately before the proposition where the change occurs. In this way an automatic division of the text into clearly defined episodes is obtained.

An example will no doubt be welcome at this point. I shall take a fairly short Sherente myth and leave aside the last part of it so as not to prolong my account unduly. (This decision is also justified by the fact that the short version was collected by Nimuendaju some decades before that recounted by the Sherente to Maybury-Lewis as I shall quote it; although neglecting some aspects contained in the Nimmendaju version, the Maybury-Lewis version is more easily intelligible because less elliptic with regard to the plot). We have to do with a myth of the origin of women as told in a patrilineal society. The text comes first, followed by its structural description as the computer has established it.

After their emergence, the Sherentes were hunting when they met two women. They pursued them, and the women sought refuge at the top of a tree from which they refused to come down. Then, one of the men struck the tree, one blow, and when the man had struck the tree, one of the women transformed herself into a capivara and fell into the water emitting a feeble cry. This left only one woman left in the tree. The young men then went to the edge of the water and called to the woman: 'Woman, come down!' 'No, I will not come down!' said the woman. 'Come on, get down!' shouted the Sherente. Then the woman came down and the Sherente took her with them to their village. After nightfall, all the Sherente copulated with the woman, one after another. Finally, they killed her and cut her into pieces in order to divide her among themselves. Then each Sherente wrapped up his piece. The puma took a piece of the breast, but the sariema wrapped up his very tightly so that for this reason he now has a cross-eyed wife. Then the Sherente went hunting. Then they delegated a scout to their camp, who found the village full of women cackling among themselves (Maybury-Lewis, ethnographic notes).

The continuation of the text describes how the women prepare cakes for their husbands and give them to the scout. He rejoins the hunters who return to the village with all speed.

Here now is the computer's interpretation. The frequency analysis gives 'group of hunters' and 'woman' as principal actors.

Episodes	Conjunctions	Subject actors	Actions	Object Actors
1	time	hunters	intransitive[3] hunting	
			finding	two women
			pursuit	
2		two women	refusal	hunters
3	posteriority simultaneity	a hunter	transitive transitive	
4	(simultaneity)	a woman	metamorphosis intransitive sound inaction	
5	posteriority	hunters 'a woman	intransitive communication intransitive'	
6		a woman	communication 'refusal of the intransitive'	
7		hunters 'a woman	communication intransitive'	
8	posteriority	a woman	agreement intransitive	
10[4]	posteriority posteriority implication posteriority	hunters	transitive sexual relations transformation division transitive	a woman

3. 'Intransitive' stands for 'intransitive motion', i.e. the actor's own movements; this is in opposition with 'transitive', for 'transitive motion', i.e. the movement impelled to an object by the actor.

4. The subjects of the two propositions forming episode 9 are 'puma' and 'sariema'. Since the propositions contain neither 'hunter' nor 'wom-

Episodes	Conjunctions	Subject actors	Actions	Object Actors
11	posteriority	hunters a hunter	hunting intransitive finding	large number of women

The computer next provides a second output where only those propositions are retained which belong to the document's major semantic fields, that is, where only the most frequently appearing function descriptors are found, from the point of view of the complementarity of which the document is then examined. Thus, it can be read from this output that the action of the story is characterized by a passage, by episodes, from the *intransitive* to the *transitive* followed by a return to the *intransitive*:

intransitive — transitive — intransitive (episodes 1, 3, 4)
intransitive (episodes 5, 6, 7)
intransitive — transitive — intransitive (episodes 8, 10, 11)

where the first chain of three episodes is repeated by the last itself also of three episodes. Then, in the middle chain (*intransitive*), and only there, the *communication* function appears. The *refusal* function (episode 2) is followed by the *metamorphosis* function (episode 4) while *agreement* (episode 8) is followed by *transformation* (episode 10). Finally, the functions *intransitive*, *hunting* and *finding* (followed by *possession* in episode 12 not represented in the table) form the first and the last episode, which allows us to read the document as follows:

1. Possible addition to the group of men (episode 1).
2. Subtraction of a part of the possible addition (episodes 2–4).
3. Actual addition (episodes 5–8).
4. Division (episode 10).
5. Multiplication (episode 11).

The computer is then instructed to produce an output expressing only the propositions linked by conjunctions having to do with relations other than temporal (such as inclusion, exclusion,

an', they do not figure in this output. ('Puma' and 'sariema' both belong to the same category, 'human-animal'; on the level of the normalized text, the two propositions are thus considered as forming one episode.)

implication, causality, etc.) – here, metamorphosis is implied by division.

Finally in this phase a last output extracts from the corpus all the documents which comprise the same sequence of 'structural' descriptors, that is, grouping the myths by categories like that of the passage from the *transitive* to the *intransitive* and vice-versa, from *submission* to *dominance* and vice-versa, etc.

These very rudimentary descriptions scarcely qualify as structural. But they do provide a summary of the paths followed by the action and successive switchpoints according to which the movements of the actors are directed in a sociological and cosmological exploration. It can be seen indeed that in the myth quoted, from the first to the eleventh episode, we pass from the 'finding' of the two women to their multiplication – a kind of structure which reflects the agricultural one of cutting a tuber into pieces, planting these, and harvesting a multiplied input. This result is reached by a dialectic where a transitive operation to strike the tree (episode 3) leading to a metamophosis (of the woman into a capivara, episode 4), is followed by a dialogue, which culminates in an intransitive action on the part of the woman (she comes down the tree), sexual relations and the division of the woman – in fact, a metonymical operation. While of the two women at the beginning of the myth, only one remains after the attempt of the hunter acting in isolation and in a purely physical way, ('transitive movement', to strike the tree), the woman who remains represents all women – so we have the individual for the species – and the action is raised to the level of communication. Then, we have the part for the whole since the possession of a piece of the woman represents and in fact generates the possession of a woman. I may be reading things into the output when I see in the conjunction 'implication' followed by 'division' in episode 10, the major articulation of the metonymical structure of this Sherente myth; it remains true none the less that this summary suggests a characterization of the narrative in terms which, if they are not directly structural, hint at some interesting indications.

The version of the same myth collected by Nimuendaju (1944) begins with a description of the state of the society without women where the men practise homosexuality. One of them becomes pregnant, and, as he cannot give birth to the child he carries, dies in labour. The men go hunting, find a woman perched on the top of a tree but notice nothing of her but her reflection in the water. Frustrated in their efforts to seize the image, they finally discover its source and seize the woman. The continuation of the text is as in the Maybury-Lewis version, without the final episode of making the cakes.

A comparison of the automatic interpretations of these two versions is worth briefly examining. Only one aspect will be mentioned, as it is clear that the first episode of the Nimuendaju version is clearly different and the metonymical structure is the same in both cases. The computer invites us to contrast *communication*, present in the Maybury-Lewis version and absent in the Nimuendaju version, with *false perception/true perception*, present in the latter but not in the former. Besides, while the middle *instransitive* in the Maybury-Lewis version is accompanied by *communication*, it is replaced by *transitive* in the corresponding episode of the Nimuendaju version where the woman is seized without exchanging a word once the perception is rectified. The same metonymical structure rests, then, on two different mechanisms.

The reader will be able to scrutinize the text and the automatic interpretation at more leisure. Suffice it to have mentioned that a theme emerges expressed in such a way that it is possible to compare this summary with those of other myths. Further, by permutations or inversions of the abstract properties of the documents, theoretic variants are generated: the corpus is then searched to find whether the artificial myths can be found empirically. For example, it is instructive to reverse the sexual roles in the Sherente myth – reading 'women' for 'hunters' and 'man' for 'woman' – and to compare it with the matrilineal Bororo myth of the origin of men, in which it is the women who besiege a man perched at the top of a tree, and the *false perception/true perception* opposition is absent but *communication* is found.

Quantitative analysis

Quantitative analysis is done by means of the 'dictionary' which has already been alluded to. The results are expressed by two outputs: a *tag tally*, where each document is tabulated by descriptor according to the position of the latter in the propositional structure, and proportional graphs where each descriptor is quantified comparitively for the whole corpus. For example, it shows in what proportion *blood relations* are 'subjects' in the whole corpus, and in what proportion among the Sherente, the Apinayé, etc. (for comparative tables of this kind, where twenty categories and their distribution by tribes are contrasted, see Maranda, 1967b). No sequential order appears here. The outputs thus only indicate the size of the blocks or broad constitutive units of each document as they are measured in the *tag tally*, or comparatively for all the documents as they appear in the proportional graphs.

Although incomplete and rudimentary from the point of view of the total analysis, this quantitative information is valuable in that it measures the depth of the paradigmatic groups linked in the syntagmetic chain of the stories. If it is true that repetition emphasizes the structure (Lévi-Strauss, 1958) and assures the preservation of the information in the transmission of the message (Shannon and Weaver, 1948) the quantitative emphasis which the computer reveals at the paradigmatic level points up main themes. In a general way it can thus be said that the frequencies provide a measure of the degree of concern of myths with specific paradigmatic sets. What can also be learnt from that is that for example, when the constitutive element A appears with a very great frequency, it will be in contexts where B and C are also very frequent, and D, E, F and G generally absent.

A quantitative evaluation of the fields of concentration is thus obtained which gives a paradigmatic depth to the syntactic units indicative of the relative importance of the semantic masses which they link.

References

DUNPHY, D., STONE, P., and SMITH, M. (1965), 'The general inquirer: further developments in a computer system for content analysis of verbal data in the social sciences', *Behavioral Science*, vol. 10.

GREIMAS, J. (1971), 'The interpretation of myth: theory and practice', in P. and E. Maranda (eds.) *Structural Analysis of Oral Tradition*, University of Pennsylvania Press.

GUNDLACH, R. (1965), *Ein Dokumentationssystem zur inhaltlichen Erfassung und maschinell en Erschliessung historische Sekundarliteratur*, Munich.

LÉVI-STRAUSS, C. (1958), *Anthropologie structurale*, Plon.

LÉVI-STRAUSS, C. (1960), 'La structure et la forme', *Cahiers de l'Institut de science économique appliquée* 99 pp. 3-36.

LÉVI-STRAUSS, C. (1964), *Mythologiques I: Le cru et le cuit*, Plon.

MARANDA, P. (1967a), 'Computers in the bush: notes for the automatic analysis of Gê myths', in J. Helm, (ed.), 'Essays in the Verbal and Visual Arts' *Proceedings of the 1966 Annual Meetings of the American Ethnological Society*, *Philadelphia*, University of Washington Press.

MARANDA, P. (1967b), 'Formal analysis and intra-cultural studies', *Social Science Information*, vol. 6, pp. 7-36.

NIMUENDAJU, (1944), 'Sherente tales', *J. Amer. Folklore*, vol. 57.

PROPP, V. (1958), 'Morphology of the folktale', *Publication Ten of the Research Center in Anthropology, Folklore and Linguistics*, Indiana University Press.

SHANNON, C. E., and WEAVER, W. (1948), *The Mathematical Theory of Communication*, Illinois University Press.

STONE, P. J. *et al.* (1966), *The General Inquirer: A Computer Approach to Content Analysis*, MIT Press.

9 A. J. Greimas

Comparative Mythology

Excerpt in abridged form from A. J. Greimas, *Du Sens: Essais Sémiotiques*, Seuil, 1970, pp. 117–34. Specially translated for this volume by Anthony Hammond.[1]

Historians have been able to observe the emergence from mythology of presocratic philosophy. It is very interesting to follow the mythologist in his parallel task, to see how the interpretation of myths has given rise to a new 'ideological' language, for that, in fact, is what it is. An analysis of meaning must necessarily be framed in a new 'terminology' or metalanguage. In other words, the mythologist translates from mythological language into ideological language. The progression is self evident, a connotative semiotics, is transformed, to use Hjelmslev's terminology, into a 'denotative semiology'. It can cut both ways; thus mythological research could serve as a model for the study of super-structures and for the description of social ideologies.

Mythological significata[2] are found on various levels, and they take numerous forms. Among them, myths very naturally attract our attention. They are made of syntagmatic series or chains of related elements. These are theologemes, mythemes and other units of meaning; they are often redundant and repetitious and, beyond the narrative sequence, connected by paradigmatic links. The remarkable structural study of myth which Lévi-Strauss (1955) made some time ago, leaves no doubt on this score: the analysis of myth must not be syntagmatic only and follow the story line; it must reveal the relationships between the units of the mythical meaning, which occur throughout the

1. First appeared under the title: 'Description de la signification et la mythologie comparée', in *l'Homme*, vol. 3, 1963, pp. 51–66.

2. The narrative or fragments of narratives which mythology can use can be found, as Dumézil has pointed out so well, everywhere and at every level: in sacred texts, epic poems, manuals of rituals and ceremonials, historical works, folk legends, etc. Studies of meaning are not affected by the presentation of the signifiers.

narrative. Myth carriers are not always openly conscious of such relationships, which are limited in number in the narrative despite its semantic richness. Basic relationships can thus summarize myths in the format of a mathematical proportion. Lévi-Strauss takes as an example the myth of Oedipus which can be formulated in the following manner:

$$\frac{\text{/overestimated kinship relations/}}{\text{/underestimated kinship relations/}} \simeq \frac{\text{/autochtony of man/}}{\text{/negation of the autochtony of man}[3]\text{/}}$$

The formulation of the myth in such a way presupposes two conditions:

1. As soon as the analysis of the significance of the myth is considered to be complete, the information which the signifier contains must be reduced to a small number of units of the significatum.

2. The significance must be organized into a system of binary relations:

a) Each pair of units in the proportion should constitute an opposition, characterized by the presence or absence of a distinctive feature (or features), of the type:

A *v.* not A.

b) The two pairs should be related by a *correlation*.

The formula of the myth will therefore be, in a very simplified[4] form, the following proportion:

$$\frac{A}{\text{not } A} \simeq \frac{B}{\text{not } B}.$$

I propose to take by way of example, a certain number of mythical narratives analysed by Dumézil, in order to see if these narratives can be reduced to the single formulation suggested

3. We place between slashes /.../ any word or expression which refers to the meaning and this is done in order to make clear that these do not belong to the narrative of the myth itself but to the 'terminology' of the mythological description.

4. Since we intend to carry as far as possible the description of distinctive features, we will be content with the formulation of the myth which emerges from the analysis of Oedipus, without referring to the generalized formula which Lévi-Strauss proposes in the same study.

by Lévi-Strauss. Despite some lengthiness which resulted from the polemical nature of a part of his works and from the necessity to convince and counterargue – which is no longer the case – Dumézil's analysis is so rich and perceptive that I shall not innovate but simply offer an alternative formulation and use a terminology which is sometimes different.

I am also proposing to see if a more advanced analysis into *distinctive features* of meaningful units such as defined by Lévi-Strauss is possible (an analysis which applies most in phonology): its function in the structural description of semantic substance could eventually be generalized.

Finally we will have to deal with the difficulties involved in this binary analysis when we use it in comparative analysis.

The 'myth' of the social contract

Those who are at all familiar with Dumézil's work will know the Indian story of the accession of King Prthu, to which the mythologist has subsequently added, thanks to a gradual reconstruction, the parallel schemes of the election of Servius the censor-king and the deposition of the Irish King Bress. Although disputable for a number of reasons, to which we shall return later, this initial example has the advantage of simplicity: the identity of the units of the signifier and of the distinctive features in the Indian and the Roman stories allows us to progressively solve one by one the difficulties of comparative analysis.

Dumézil demonstrates how this story signifies metaphorically the dual contract made, at the time of his accession, between the king and his people. The story, which can be divided into two almost symmetrical parts, relates firstly the qualification of the king by the people, and goes on to relate that of the people by the king. The qualification itself can be interpreted as a reciprocity within the linguistic category of the exchange of messages. The king is qualified by praises; he distributes gifts (qualifying) in return, or vice-versa. [...]

The contract that the Indian king makes with his people can then be formulated in the following way:

$$\frac{\text{king}}{\text{people}} \simeq \frac{qgV}{gq}$$

where q=qualification, g=gifts, V=valorization or over-valorization.

The first phase of the contract not only consecrates the king, it 'envigorates' him, whereas the second phase is only a simple symbolic exchange consecrating the rights and duties of the people. We can see that what distinguishes a simple qualification (gq) from the valorizing qualification (qg) is first of all, the syntagmatic order of the symbolic exchange:

$$(q \rightarrow g) \, v. \, (g \rightarrow q);$$

and subsequently the sequence of the story relating to the Cow of Abundance (which the king recaptures after his qualification) is a redundant insistence on his new power. If we disregard this syntagmatic arrangement, the relationship between the qualification of the king and that of his people appears as a relationship between two terms, the first of which is characterized by the presence of the distinctive characteristic V, while the second is characterized by its absence. The significatum category can thus be formulated:

$$V \text{(marked)} \, v. \, \text{not } V \text{(unmarked)}.$$

The reconstruction which Dumézil makes, with the help of elements and pseudo-historical sequences relative to the life of King Servius, allows him in turn to formulate the symbolic Roman affabulation thus:

$$\frac{\text{king}}{\text{people}} \simeq \frac{gq}{qgV}.$$

This, we see, is the inverse of our summary of the Indian myth.

In Rome it is the people and not the king which is qualified by valorization: Servius, elected king due to his largesses (gq), institutes a census (q) qualifying the citizens according to their rank and wealth; this, in turn, provides an influx of taxes (g). Here the Cow of Empire corresponds to the Cow of Abundance, and the story of its acquisition and sacrifice is situated chronologically after the qualification of the people (and not of the king), confirming the king's praise of the Roman people.[5]

5. One may wonder if, in the case of historical societies, it would not be possible to date the myths very approximately, taking account not of the

The same category of valorization can be seen to establish here the relationship between the two symbolical exchanges and this constitutes a doubly sealed social contract. Such a formulation allows us to give to the comparison of the Indian and Roman stories the form of a proportion:

$$\text{India } v. \text{ Rome} \simeq \frac{V}{\text{not } V} \quad v. \quad \frac{\text{not } V}{V}.$$

We may wonder whether it sheds any new light on Dumézil's analysis according to which the qualifying praise (çams-) consecrates and valorizes the king in India, while, in Rome, through the procedure of the *census*, it consecrates and valorizes the people.

Certainly with regard to the analysis itself nothing is altered: far from being enriched, it may rather appear impoverished as a result of this reduction. The same is not true with regard to methodological precision: thanks to the use of an analytic notation, the conditions for comparison, which were perhaps no more than implicit, appear in all clarity. Far from being, as we have been taught for a long time, an inventory of resemblances and differences, comparison is above all a juxtaposition of similarities on a common basis which alone allows us to measure and compare differences. [. . .]

The myth of excess

The third example, which is rather more complex than the other two, is that of the parallelism between the Scandinavian myth of Kvasir and the episode from the Mahabharata relating the brief appearance of the Indian homologue of Kvasir, Mada.

Both appear in a situation of war. Kvasir, the Scandinavian incarnation of wisdom, is created by the gods to seal the conclusion of peace; Mada, Indian symbol of superhuman frenzy, obliges the god by his appearance to conclude the peace. Both of them, too great for peace, are subsequently destroyed, Kvasir being transformed into poetry and Mada into four human passions: drink, women, hunting, and gambling.

---

significance, whose elements are without doubt very ancient, but of their global meaning: a certain political 'ideology', for example, is compatible with certain historical contexts and not with others.

The Scandinavian myth can be formulated thus:

$$\frac{/\text{excess}/}{/\text{moderation}/} \simeq \frac{/\text{better world}/}{/\text{worse world}/}$$

The Indian mythical episode is fairly similar but inverted:

$$\frac{/\text{excess}/}{/\text{moderation}/} \simeq \frac{/\text{worse world}/}{/\text{better world}/}$$

Comparing the two versions, we notice that, as in the 'myth' of the social contract, there is an inversion of the relationship in the second part of the proportion. Given that the units of the significatum in question are the same in both cases, the inversion can be considered to be one of the modalities of the structure of myth.

Moving on now to the second stage of analysis we notice that the relationship

/excess/ *v.* /moderation/,

is in the first place to be interpreted as the relationship

/whole/*v.*/part/.

Indeed we remember that Mada, just as what remains of Kvasir, is symbolically *divided* into parts. If Mada is 'actually' divided into four parts – the passions – however, Kvasir reappears, in the form of poetry, as a proportional diminution of his original state and not as a fraction of it. We are consequently confronted by two different conceptions of the *totality*, and as such, by two different relationships between the totality and the part. To use the terminology of Brøndal, the *totality* of excess in the Scandinavian story is an *integral* (cf. *totus*). whereas the totality of excess in the Indian story is a *universal* (cf. *omnis*) The relationship of Kvasir to Poetry is of the same order as the relationship of the English definite article to the partitive article, whereas the excess of Mada represents a numerable totality which is divisible into fractions.

Before going any further we can already establish that, if the category is common to both myths, the two conceptions of excess are presented as two different expressions of the totality: an original harmonious totality has its counterpart in the conception of totality as an arithmetic sum of the constituent elements. This difference can be formulated in the following manner:

Scandinavia   India
/integral/v./positive/ $\simeq$ /universal/v./cardinal/

Other distinctive features are to be added to this fundamental opposition of the two conceptions of totality to give two diametrically opposed conceptions of excess. [. ...]

It is now the moment to return to our first example, the narrative of the conclusion of the social contract. We intentionally simplified it in the first place by taking into consideration only the Indian and Roman variants, and for the time being ignoring the Irish tales about the deposition of King Bress.

An analysis of these Irish stories, taken collectively and still following Dumézil's analysis, can now be made in two ways. The *deposition* of the king is clearly a counterpart of his *accession*, and we may wonder whether the Irish variant allows us to reconstruct the Indian or Roman schemas of the deposition, which have reached us in mutilated and incomplete forms. referring to the deposition of Prthu's and Servius's predecessors. On the other hand one may equally try to discover if the story of the Irish king's deposition would provide the schema of the king's accession in the Irish context; in other words, of the comparative series:

$$\frac{\text{Vena}}{\text{Prthu}} \simeq \frac{\text{Tarquin}}{\text{Servius}} \simeq \frac{\text{Bress}}{\text{X}}$$

possesses valid heuristic qualities.

Jakobson, one of the originators of linguistic analysis into distinctive features, distinguishes clearly between two types of dissimilarity allowing us to consider the terms of a relationship as distinctive:

a v. not a,

where a is considered as marked because it possesses a distinctive characteristic, which not a, an unmarked term, does not possess. A completely different relationship exists between:

a v. $-a$.

where $-a$ is the negation of a.

In analysing the social contract of the accession of the king, we have until now, distinguished the valorizing qualification (V) from the simple qualification (not V). The Irish variant which appears as the negation of the social contract, must differ, in the archisemic analysis which we are familiar with,

$$V v. -V$$

$$\text{not } V v. -\text{not } V$$

making possible the formation of the abolition of the social contract thus:

$$\frac{\text{people}}{\text{king}} \simeq \frac{-\text{not } V}{-V}.$$

Which simply means that the people, not having been properly qualified, the king in his turn is disqualified and loses his initial vigour.

The schematic reconstruction of the accession, in the framework of the Irish ideology, may henceforth be conceived of as a dual operation: the cancelling of the negative signs and the inverting of the relationship *people* v. *king*. Thus we can say:

$$\text{India } v. \text{ Rome } v. \text{ Ireland} \simeq \frac{V}{\text{not } V} v. \frac{\text{not } V}{V} v. \frac{V}{\text{not } V}$$

which allows us to affirm that the Irish schema of the accession is identical to that of India. [...]

A mythology, considered as a metalanguage, can only be described on the condition that we first choose *units of measurement* whose manipulation – their relation and correlation – allows us to reconstruct, gradually, larger structural wholes and finally an entire mythological system. Lévi-Strauss in the study we have already mentioned on several occasions, finds these constituent units in the signifiers which correspond to the sequences of the mythical narrative and which subsequently appear as terms in the mythical proportion:

$$\frac{A}{\text{non } A} \simeq \frac{B}{\text{non } B}$$

We have already seen that those 'large constituent units' can in turn be further analysed into *distinctive features*. If, for example, we agreed to call distinctive features *semes* (sèmes), we could call *lexemes* the terms of the mythical proportion, i.e. the groups of semes only part of which is analysed in each concrete case.

The distinctive features in turn are only of interest in so far as they exist in oppositional relationships constituted of two or more terms. Semes therefore constitute *semic categories*. *Lemexes*, are transformed into *archi-lexemes* if, instead of considering simply distinctive features, we take into account all the semic categories constituting the oppositional lexemic couples. Semes and lexemes, semic categories and archi-lexemes, these it seems, are the four principal 'units of measurement' which the mythologist and the linguist use in their analysis of content. [. . .]

Reference

LÉVI-STRAUSS, C. (1955), 'The structural study of myth', *J. Amer. Folklore*, vol. 5, no. 68.

Part Four
Myths in Cultures

In the two following readings, the data range becomes broader and the investigations more specific. Samples are dealt with and statistics resorted to. A methodological discussion by Armstrong leads to a summary of a metalinguistic analysis by Sebeok, and then to the formulation of the author's own *ad hoc* metalanguage. This is brought to bear on the comparison of data from distant areas; the validity of the findings is assessed against ethnographic information. Roberts and his associates apply the well-known cross-cultural method to games and myths in order to test their hypothesis of a corrrelation between the two folkloric *genres* and child-rearing practices. In this case, the focus is the articulation to everyday life of plot types in terms of strategies. This contribution could be seminal – a game theoretical approach to myth might mean decisive new steps in the field.

10 Robert Plant Armstrong

Content Analysis in Folkloristics

Robert Plant Armstrong, 'Content analysis in folkloristics', in I. de Sola Pool (ed.), *Trends in Content Analysis*, University of Illinois Press, 1959, pp. 151–70.

In his work the folklorist typically takes note of the presence of striking dramatic or rhetorical elements in the content of texts he examines. Upon the basis of these distinctive features, he draws at least some of his conclusions, both with respect to the text itself and to relevant cultural or biographical facts.

In the vast majority of instances, the folklorist reaches these conclusions by impressionistic procedures and by a wholistic approach to his materials. Such studies are of considerable value. Their results are often pertinent not only to literary inquiry but also to the study of human behavior in general. Yet it is unfortunate that among some folklorists such procedures constitute the ultimate research techniques. Attempts to be relatively more rigorous, more analytical, and perhaps to give quantitative expression to the results of analysis are dismissed as being 'sociological'. Such a view must be carefully re-examined.

Ruth Benedict's introduction to *Zuni Mythology* offers a case (1935, 1948) for examination. Working with raw content, she notes the presence of certain culturally archaic elements, for example the mode of entrance into a dwelling. These elements of behavior are clearly disparate with contemporary Zuni values and behavior. She calls the presence of such elements a kind of 'compensatory daydreaming'. Such findings are of undoubted significance in understanding the role of myth in Zuni culture, and multiply our insights into the Zuni culture, folkloristics and myth. Indeed, the genealogical relationship between her 'compensatory day-dreaming' and Kluckhohn's analysis of myth functioning in such a fashion as to provide adjustive and adaptive mechanisms is clear (Kluckhohn, 1942).

However, inquiry must not be arrested at this point. It is the task of other investigators, building upon Benedict's observations, to ask first whether it is possible to give additional empirical validation to her results, and further to ask if there are not other kinds of information which she failed to discern. All we are maintaining, in effect, is that while some data may be collected by such impressionistic procedures, others, equally significant, will be lost. In all probability, obvious methods most often lead to the identification of none save the most obvious features of a text.

It is therefore the purpose of this chapter to examine content analysis for the benefit of folklorists, and to draw to their attention some techniques which may facilitate the objective description and analysis of the materials with which they are concerned. It is to be hoped further that such remarks will prompt others to extend the effort, and that, in particular, students of the graphic and plastic arts, dance and music will experiment with similar procedures in order to make increasingly revealing comments on the areas of human behavior with which they are concerned.

Any behavior may be studied either as (a) *mirroring* or as (b) *constituting* a condition in an individual or a society. Such a statement as that of Benedict concerning the method of entering a house referred to above illustrates data used to mirror behavior.

Mirror statements are characteristically derived from the substance of a message. On the other hand, those materials which may be held to be constitutive of conditions within the individual or culture are most frequently derived from the structure of the message. They may also, however, stem from the substance, the difference deriving from the point of view with which the researcher approaches his materials. In mirror statements reference is made to the larger behavioral context within which the message may be conceived to be embedded, while otherwise the message itself constitutes the sole frame of reference. The categories to be used in the last section of this chapter, together with the statistical operations performed upon them, represent statements at this constitutive level.

The writings of folklorists in general, in so far as they attempt to do anything more than present new data, are largely executed on the mirror model, whether they be concerned with an individual or with his cultural milieu. It would seem, accordingly, that perhaps the greatest contribution content analysis can make to folkloristics is not merely to provide a refinement in the procedures yielding such information, although that in itself is of considerable importance, but to afford students the opportunity to improve their descriptions of the constituents of behavior. Studies designed to examine the chief characteristics of an individual or a period as seen in a body of texts represent content analysis used in such a fashion as to mirror that individual or period. On the other hand, pattern studies, showing for example that certain classes of content in a total body of texts are used with a discerned and predictable frequency, or that a given class of behavior exhibits such and such formal characteristics, examine verbal behavior constituting a characteristic of the individual or group.

There are three aspects of messages which may be examined by different kinds of content analysis. Doubtless most studies concern the *substance* of the specimens. Substance, it is apparent, is simply what is manifestly stated in the message. Indeed, content analysis is often confounded with the analysis of substance. The *form* or *structure* of the content and its *condition* are equally amenable to analysis and description, however, though the procedures required may be less apparent and, at first glance, more difficult than those for the analysis of substance. The structure of the content designates its shape, its physical array of elements, determined by means of establishing and describing the parts, however defined, together with their distributions and relationships. These two terms, elements and array, represent two different kinds of analysis, the first corresponding to a morphemic analysis of language, while the second is more nearly similar to the determination of syntax. Structure, in a sense, may be said to designate the physical dimensions of the communication. Finally, the condition of the content refers to such notions as the truth, emotional and aesthetic values of the segments of the communication.

The motif index

Any discussion of the analysis of substance of folklore material inevitably invokes initial mention of Stith Thompson's motif index. A motif is a substantive unit (e.g. 'the devil falls into the well') which appears frequently in folklore, and is found in very wide cultural distribution. The list of motifs is long. Thompson has presented and discussed them in six large volumes. Here is a system devised for the purpose of cataloging the elements of certain kinds of narrative situations, and it has accrued to itself the great respect to which its breadth of scholarship entitles it. It is, in fact, a kind of trait list, analogous in essence to the lists of cultural traits once in fashion in ethnology, and it is subject to the same criticisms of definition and analytical adequacy as the culture traits themselves. Thus, for the purposes of content analysis there are certain limitations to the motif[1] system, deriving chiefly from the fact that it is an *a priori* scheme in which each individual motif is externally derived, being whatever Professor Thompson has recognized as one. The grid is so coarse as to let certain kinds of significant data slip through unnoticed.

Over and above this, because there is no clear definition of the limits of a motif, a situation results wherein a motif may in one instance comprise a complete story, while in another it may be only a segment thereof. The motifs are not made commensurate either in terms of structural characteristics of the story (e.g. a certain unit of words or sentences) or with respect to the dramatic magnitude of the action they name. Therefore, it is apparent that the motif cannot be considered a device for successful analysis. To make some such analysis more effective, the problem is to devise a way of defining natural units of the story intermediate between the single word and the total story. Moreover, not only is the motif inadequate for the analysis of substance, but of condition as well, for since the units isolated by motif analysis may perform different dramatic functions, or none at all for that matter, they are analytically valueless.

In all fairness, it must be added that Professor Thompson does not himself present the motif index as an analytical system, but only as a classification one.

According to this plan, motifs dealing with one subject are handled together, irrespective of the literary form in which they may appear.

1. There is a question involving the 'reality' of the motif. The motif, like culture, is a construct, and does not possess any value over and above that fact. It is not a kind of Platonic entity of folklore, it is plain, but rather only an association of behavior traits arbitrarily selected.

No attempt has been made to determine the psychological basis of various motifs or their structural value in narrative art, for though such considerations have great value, they are not, I think, of much practical help toward the orderly arrangement of the stories and myths of a people (Thompson, 1932, p. 3).

Accordingly, he is in no wise responsible for the attitude, implicit in the works of some who use the index in their researches, which distorts the motif to an analytical unit.

Units based upon the substance of the text

It is apparent from the above remarks that a satisfactory analytical technique must be premised upon the establishment of relative units – ones defined in terms of the contexts within which they are found, rather than determined in accordance with the criteria of an external and arbitrarily postulated system.[2] The desirability of such a procedure seems so apparent as to recommend itself. Suffice it to say that when an elastic principle of definition is achieved, it will prove possible to isolate segments which are at all times less than the total text and are, in terms of the definition, equivalent.

Since we are in this section concerned with the substantive aspect of the text, the defining characteristics for appropriate units will be found in those modes proper to the substance, for example in nouns;[3] or in the assertion patterns of the language, as for example in some carefully established actor-action phase, or in whatever segment of an utterance flow might be said to constitute a sentence.[4] The principle may, furthermore, be found in the fictive properties or dramatic movements of the text, or, if it is non-fictive discourse, or poetry, then in features of rhetoric, prosody, sense or device peculiar to treatment of

2. See Pike (1954, pp. 8–24). The distinctions he presents between the *etic* and *emic* levels of analysis are pertinent here. Etic analysis corresponds to the noncontextual motif, while emic includes the point of view from which the critical remarks of the motif have been made. While mirror analysis may be done from either emic or etic points of departure, constitutive analysis may be cast only in terms of the emic framework.

3. See Merriam, Merriam, and Armstrong (1954). This study, which infers states in the value system of the Banyaruanda, is an example of mirror analysis.

4. Sebeok and Orzack (1953). This is an example of constitutive analysis.

substance in these types. Finally, such units may be established upon the basis of the manifestation of psychological mechanisms, upon economic, political, or religious attitudes, or indeed upon any of the range of points of curiosity which originally led the researcher to the texts. Such procedures in defining content analysis units ensure the delineation of a grid adequate to the subtlety and variety of the cases which will be encountered in the texts. In addition, they will permit generalization at either the individual or cultural level.

Among the above examples of criteria for units there is to be found a kind of natural dichotomy. There are those units whose defining points are based upon the manifest content of the text, that is to say upon what the message objectively conveys. Under this rubric would fall units defined by information actually present concerning the veritable activity of the actors in the text, or by *stated* political activity, judgements, social roles, etc. In the second place, there are units defined by interpretations of the manifest content, such as would be encountered in the search, for example, for instances of personality characteristics or cultural values and attitudes in the text.

If, for example, one were interested in analysing a body of trickster tales, he might search for (a) whether the trickster dupes, (b) whether these actions contain explicit comments on the relationship between the action and the generally approved values of the group, or (c) whether such attitudes can be inferred from the text. It is clear that in the first two cases the concern is with primary (manifest) substance, while in the third instance it is with secondary (latent) substance. It follows that a different principle of segmentation would be required in each case. In the first of the three, this principle is based solely upon the activity of the trickster, that is, its purpose is to establish units of activity and subsequently to determine whether tricking or duping is involved. In the second analysis the unit becomes simply statements concerning the ethical evaluation of the trickster's acts. In the third case, actor-action phrases might be used, or 'sentences', or, indeed, the same unit of behavior established for the first analysis. It is also possible, of course, to define a unit based upon the presumed duration of some given kind of attitude.

It is clear that in the above operations the text is differently segmented, not only with reference to the actual spans of material isolated but also with respect to the extent of the textual surface itself. In the second operation, involving the search for explicit evaluations, only portions of the surface of the text would constitute relevant units, while in the first analysis for units of action, and conceivably in the analysis for inferred substance as well, the total surface would be divided into units. But in each case, presumably, the segmentation is adequate to the analytical task which is faced, and, in these terms, one is no more exhaustive than the other.

The segmentation of the total surface of a text, however, affords a certain advantage in behavioural terms in so far as it presents the opportunity to conduct a complete inventory of units. Such an analysis might conceivably be based upon such behavioral units as those suggested above, for example tricking, or else upon some language feature, for example the actor-action phase. The search in the latter case would not be for the presence or absence of tricking merely, but rather for an indication of what, in problem-oriented terms, is the significance of each unit. This is the program which was followed in the analysis of the Suriname materials presented in the concluding section of this chapter.

The determination of unit boundaries, when more than mere presence or absence of a trait is to be noted, and particularly when the complete textual surface is under analysis, is beset with subtle difficulties. Unfortunately, little more than mention of these problems can be made here. Certainly, the problems which are raised are frequently subtle, and involve the exercise of judicious arbitrariness, which, though perhaps tolerable under the hand of a skilled analyst, raises the question of reliability. However, as Pool points out, where a trait is homogeneous in a text, analysts will find it no matter how differently they cut the pie; thus often the matter of reliability of unit definition may be de-emphasized unless there is reason to believe that there is some systematic difference between the subsentence, sentence and episode levels, or to put this into more familiar terms, a regular difference among the units or among meaningful associations of such units, such that difference rather than similarity would result, and comparability would be lost. Often it is far less important to be able to get consistency in units than it is to get the meaningful unit of interaction. The final criterion for judging the relevance of unit reliability to the particular analysis is, as Osgood pointed out, the independence of results, over several analyses by different analysts, from the units employed.

It is apparent from our consideration of the motif index that the unit of operation must be defined in such a fashion as to be subtotal, equivalent, simple and unambiguous. The necessity for *subtotal* units (i.e. units shorter than the whole text) is apparent if the unit is to be useful in analysis. As we have seen in the case of the motif, this feature may be absent. Some kind of *equivalence* is also essential, in order that the units eventually isolated may have, with respect to some constant measuring concept, equivalent properties. The basis for equivalence may reside in the fact that two units perform the same function, regardless of variability in other respects; it may be found in structural considerations, as for example if two immediate constituents are to all intents and purposes equivalent when viewed from a certain vantage point. Finally, there is a kind of substantive equivalence, which is to be found when the mere presence of a certain kind of information is of interest. In this latter case all instances of the occurrence of the notion in question may be regarded as equivalent.

The criterion of unit *simplicity* suggests that no more variables than avoidable enter into the unit. An example of the failure to maintain such a control is afforded by the motif with its 'built-in contiguities', as Sebeok has noted. It must be stressed that simplicity does not mean consisting of one part only. If one analyses for dramatic action, for example, the unit will doubtless be comprised of actor, act and a recipient toward or against whom the action is directed. Simplicity in this particular case derives from building this notion of three parts into the definition of the unit and from subsequently avoiding the establishing of any units in which more than the interaction phase indicated by such terms is included. If one is explicitly aware of the level of operation at which he is to work, and confines himself rigorously to the terms of the definition as stated, he avoids the danger of secluding information. The case is somewhat similar with the level of operation. If one has elected to examine his materials for units of action dramatically defined, he must not permit confusion to enter into the analysis by including raw activity untranslated into the language of dramatic activity as defined. The simple fact of the matter is that, obviously enough, any segment of verbal behavior is a focal point for numerous phenomena: semantic, structural, conditional, dramatic, etc. A clear definition of units and cautious procedure by the analyst will preclude or severely limit the possibility of such interlevel confusion. Either the loose definition of units or the incautious establishing of domain will lead to ambiguity of analysis and, consequently, to invalidation of the results.

One further note must be added to these remarks on the analysis of substance, and it is appropriate that it come at the end of this discussion, since it is involved sometimes with substance and sometimes with structure. Aesthetic properties, along with such questions as truth or falsity, and positive or negative evaluations, are *conditions* of the material. By aesthetic we mean simply the use of devices of substance or structure which are included solely for textural quality of the surface of the message, specifically in terms of developing effect or affect, and which perform no inviolable or inescapable feature of the text as information. While this criterion may be viewed so broadly as to prove inimical to analysis, in practice it may be limited to a consideration of such peculiarly 'literary' features as the various manifestations of metaphor (defined as the whole range of verbal strategems by which the unknown is, through the mediation of an integer somewhat more known, made familiar and interpreted into the experience of those who participate in the literary transaction), and physical principles incorporated to exploit language symmetry, or the piling of activities in the interest of cumulative dramatic import. The relevance of such aesthetic features to content analysis is that they provide another focal point from which research questions may be formulated, principles of segmentation derived, and culturally significant statements eventually made.

Structural analysis

When one is concerned less with substance than with the array of that substance, then his problem becomes one of structure. Structural analysis consists of two activities: delineating units of substance or of condition, and discerning and stating the relationships which obtain among such units.

The first activity, that is the definition and delineation of units, has already been discussed. All that was said there applies equally to the segmentation of the textural surface in structural analysis. Something more remains to be said on this point, however, which is particularly pertinent to analysis for structure. If the logic of the structure is to be seen as clearly as possible, it is necessary that the units of substance or condition be generalized in such a way that the establishing of classes will permit a kind of unity to be perceived in the relatively great variety of raw information. This principle of generalization can be drawn from many areas. Sebeok, in his study of Cheremis charms, used the linguistic notion of immediate constituents. Each charm, he finds, is composed of two constituents: those which make purely factual statements about the world, and those which express the 'motif of an extremely improbable eventuality'. An example will serve to illustrate this: '(morphemes 1–9) As the apple tree blossoms forth, just so let this wound heal! (morphemes 10–13) (All blossoms must be mentioned.) (morphemes 14–21) When water can blossom forth. only then overcome me' (Sebeok and Orzack, 1953, p. 38).[5] It is this last statement (14–21) which constitutes the 'motif of the extremely improbable eventuality'.

Sebeok first devides this charm into two statements, after the principle concerning their factuality. This yields a division of 1–13 and 14–21. When it is realized that the statement 10–13 actually means 'as the [e.g.] peach tree blossoms forth, just so let this wound heal, as the —n-tree blossoms forth', etc., the reason behind this division becomes apparent. In the second step, he notes that with reference only to 1–9 (and by extension therefore to 10–13 as well) there are two actor-action phases, 'as the apple-tree blossoms forth', a dependent clause, and 'just so let this wound heal', an independent one. He observes further that the modes of the verbs (actions) in the clauses are different in that the verb of the dependent clause is 'blossoms', whereas that of the independent clause is 'let ... heal'. It is apparent that the last of these is in the imperative. This distinction is a significant one: it distinguishes the two actor-action phases from one another and provides the principle of generalization for his data, all clauses employing the

5. Morpheme numbers refer to the morphemes as found in the original Cheremis.

verb in the indicative mode falling into one class, and those using the verb in the imperative mode into another.

Other principles of generalization may be used as well. Zellig Harris, in his system of discourse analysis, again derives his model from linguistic phenomena, and determines classes based upon positional substitutability.

If we find the sequences AM and AN in our text, we say that M is equivalent to N or that M and N occur in the identical environment A, or that M and N both appear as the environment of the identical element (or sequence of elements) A; and we write M (is equivalent to) N. Then if we find the sequence B M and C N, we say that B is (secondarily) equivalent to C, since they occur in the two environments M and N which have been found to be equivalent (1952, p. 6).

The present author, in an unpublished study of some Yoruba riddles, used the formal nature of the riddle to achieve a pair of 'immediate constituents' representing the riddle itself, which was viewed as the compounding of a metaphor, and the answer, viewed as a resolution of that metaphor. Since all riddles conform to this pattern, it was possible thus to generalize all specimens in the sample under these two constituents. Categories of substance may be used, as well, as may classes of dramatic function or objective. It is this last point which provides the basis for generalization in the sample study reported in the last section of this chapter.

Generalization requires, of course, that symbols be used to represent the classes of information, and it is this act of simple substitution which seems to have alienated many folklorists from structural studies. Little can be said here to divorce such people from such a predisposition beyond disclaiming any intention upon the part of those who resort to such devices toward obfuscation and spurious accuracy. It is – or should be – apparent that such devices are employed not for their own sake but in the interest of performing operations upon the materials which cannot otherwise be done, and of obtaining 'pictures' of the structures which cannot otherwise be obtained.

There is considerable latitude with respect to the specificity of relationships which may be expressed in structural analyses. In Harris's system of discourse analysis, these relationships are merely 'before' and 'after', and these are not given explicit statement but rather are apparent from the order of the symbols. On the other hand, Sebeok, in the same study we have already discussed, employs the logical relation of implication, $\supset$, to state the nature of the involvement between the terms of his unit. This relationship of implication derives from the occurrence, in the charms, of the 'as . . . just so' construction. 'As the apple tree blossoms forth, just so let this wound heal', therefore, is recorded as $o_1 \supset s$.

The noted relationship need not be temporal or logical. It can be based, for example, upon dramatic criteria, such as whether a succeeding unit bears toward the preceding one a relationship of forward dramatic movement, whether it arrests that movement, or whether, finally, it is involved with the dramatic point of departure. This would be an example of structure arising from a consideration of condition. At a somewhat simpler level of analysis, cultural relationships between the roles of character might be examined. In this event, the relationships might be 'approved' or 'disapproved'. It is clear, in any event, that the choice of such matters depends once again upon the orientation of the researcher. Suffice it to say that the number of alternatives is probably equal to the total number of kinds of problems which can be formulated.

When a statement, such as Sebeok's $O \supset S$, which is a generalization from his many instances of $o_n \supset s$, is obtained, it is of cultural significance, since it denotes clearly the structure of all verbal behavior involved in the invocation of charms among the Cheremis. Its value is therefore apparent, and though the behavioral area to which it applies is smaller than a similar structural statement for, let us say, social organization, it is at as high a level of both generalization and significance for the understanding of human behavior. This seems to be one of the directions in which content analysis might, in the future, be profitably extended.

Sample study

In the study which will be described below, some of the points which have been made in the foregoing discussions will be seen in operation. For this study two bodies of folk tales were used, one from the Bush Negroes of Paramaribo, Dutch Guiana, and the other from the Dakota Indians of the United States. The former selection of tales was composed of two kinds, trickster tales about

Anansi and selections from another group of Suriname tales more nearly like some of our west European fairy tales than like the trickster stories. The specimens from the Dakota Indians were all of the trickster type.

The purpose of this study was to derive information at once constitutive of culture, and still, at the same time, reflective of culture, at least to the extent that the conclusions reached would be consistent with other ethnographic findings for the two groups.

A dramatic model was used as the basis for the segmentation of the texts. The rationale behind this procedure involved the fact that in stories there is present a certain kind of phenomenon which is not found in any other kind of literary behavior. This unique feature resides in the fact that only in stories does one have 'virtual action', that is to say the presence not only of an aesthetic objective, which may be defined as whatever the storyteller may have wished to achieve, but objectives arising from the depicted actors themselves. Furthermore, it must be added that the dramatic model was greatly clarified by the writings of Burke (1941) and his analysis of dramatistic behavior.

Following his suggestions, an act was conceived of as consisting of three parts, an actor, an act and an additional actor toward or against whom the action was directed. The actor was designated with an X, the recipient with a Y, and the action itself with any one of a number of actions which are given in Table 1.

It was early apparent that in defining the unit of concern it had to be (a) subtotal and comparable, (b) concerned with internal rather than external (pragmatic) objectives, and (c) manifest rather than latent. It soon became clear that on the basis of such criteria three magnitudes of units could be discerned: *maximal*, that is to say the total text under consideration; *minimal*, which is the same as Burke's 'atoms' of action, and consists of the human body in purposeful action. But since the former proved to be too great, and preclusive of analysis, and the latter too small, since obviously many such atomic elements had been gathered together about themes of common concern, it was necessary to establish a *medial* objective. The duration of this medial objective was premised upon the criteria outlined below.

It was determined that there would be a new medial objective when:

1. There occurred an alteration in the actor-constellation of the story, either through a shift in the initiation of the activity, the agents themselves remaining constant, or through the addition or deletion of one or more characters.

2. There was a change in any one of the remaining elements, that is, agency, purpose, scene or act.

The former of these terms seems sufficiently clear; however, some clarification may be given to the latter two. A change in *scene* may be defined as adjustment in the time or the place of the activity. Ordinarily one can say that a new *act* has begun when there is an alteration in the actor constellation. There is, however, an exception to this which may be noted. This exception by definition does not constitute actual alterations of the constellation; it is found in that case where a second actor merely reacts to the move of the initiation actor. In this case, the second actor neither supplements nor resists the activity initiated with respect to him or in his presence. Typically, this situation might result in a question-and-answer exchange between two characters.

3. Finally, a new objective may be said to have been instituted when there follows a segment of dramatic behavior which is not clearly the consequent of the objective which precedes it. This does not mean, of course, that two contiguous objectives cannot have the relation of event and consequent.

Let us examine a Suriname trickster tale.

Anansi was going to bet with Cockroach to see which could climb higher. But now Cockroach was able to fly, and Anansi was able to climb well. But now, when they went to compete, Cockroach said to him said, 'Let us climb to the top of an awara tree.' Now Anansi could not fly, and so Cockroach flew up, and went to the top of the tree. He sat down.

Anansi struggled to climb, but the thorns struck him. Soon he cried out, 'Friend Cockroach, the tree has ants, I cannot climb it.' At once Cockroach cried back from the tree-top, he said, 'Well, fly up.' Anansi said, 'But I do not fly, nor did you beat me, because we did not bet about flying. We were betting about climbing.' But now Cockroach said he won, because he was the first to arrive. Then they went to call Cock to settle the dispute.

When Cock came, he saw immediately that Cockroach was his delicacy. At once he cried out, 'Ko-Ko-dia-Ko!' Then Cockroach asked Cock, he said, what was the meaning of this cry which he cried?

He (Cock) said, if he wanted to hear, then he must walk over to him on foot. So just as Cockroach came toward him, Cock ate him. That is why he eats Cockroach to this day (Herskovits and Herskovits, 1936, tale 27).

Table 1 Objectives pertaining to the distribution of reward, assistance, and punishment

$\bar{A}$	reward
A	aid, befriend, plan good
A̲	hinder, prevent, conspire, discourage
A_1	punish

Praise and condemnation

$\bar{D}^1$	flatter
$\bar{D}^2$	elevate, exult, praise, boast (reflexive)
D	approve
D_1	scold, reprimand
D_2	humiliate, defame, berate, discredit, ridicule, humble oneself (reflexive)
D_3	condemn, betray, incriminate

Objectives pertaining to resistance and attack

M^1	resist, protest
M^2	save, preserve, protect
M^3	release, free, rescue, escape (reflexive)
M	do justice, vindicate or justify oneself (reflexive)
M̲	challenge
M_1	attack
M_2	overcome, defeat, conquer, capture
M_3	kill, destroy, reduce
M_4	intimidate, accuse
M_5	accede, acquiesce, surrender

Objectives pertaining to permission and prohibition

S^1	prescribe, summon, direct
S^2	insist
S^3	beg, request
S	permit, invite
S̲	proscribe, bar, forbid

Objectives pertaining to the acquisition and use of goods and services

Gratification and deprivation

$\bar{C}$ gratify, indulge, enjoy (reflexive)

C   provide, put at ease, alleviate, comfort, please

Ç   deny, displease, withhold, disturb, discomfort, torture

Acquisition and loss of property

$\bar{O}^1$ retrieve, reclaim, collect

$\bar{O}^2$ acquire, obtain, profit, enrich

$\bar{O}^3$ bargain

O   keep, retain

$\underset{.}{O}$ lose, give

Objectives pertaining to the acquisition and dissemination of information

$\bar{R}^1$ prove, convince, verify

$\bar{R}^2$ discover, investigate (get information *from*)

$\bar{R}^3$ enlighten, inform, teach, learn (reflexive) (give information *to*)

$\bar{R}^4$ suggest

$\bar{R}^5$ remember

R   communicate

R^1 believe, agree (this is in contrast with M_5 which means the acquiescence to power)

R_1 obscure, keep in ignorance, hide, misinform, falsify

R_2 disprove

R_3 forget

R_4 doubt

Objectives pertaining to the conduct of affairs

$\bar{E}$ succeed

$\bar{E}^1$ persevere, do one's duty

E   prepare

E_1 temporize

E_2 fail

Acceptance and avoidance of obligation

$\bar{B}^1$ contract, undertake

$\bar{B}^2$ seek, encounter

B^1 acknowledge, accept

B^2 pay, repay

B_2 ignore, avoid

B_3 welch, outwit, deceive

B_4 cancel

In this story three medial units can be distinguished, and these have been indicated by setting them apart into separate physical units. The last line of the story is not characterized by any internal objective, but only a pragmatic one, a condition to be found in many moralistic and etiological tales. Nor does the introductory and orientative material (i.e. 'Anansi was going to bet with Cockroach to see which could climb higher. But now Cockroach was able to fly, and Anansi was able to climb well.') contain any internal objective. In view of this fact, such introductory and terminal remarks without any manifest dramatic objective will be included with the units which respectively follow or precede them.

The first medial unit involves the attempt of Cockroach to defeat Anansi. The objective of the second unit concerns Anansi's attempt to convince Cockroach that he has not lived up to the conditions of the wager. The dialogue in this unit may be viewed as establishing the attitudes of the contenders, and as such subordinate to the objective given. Finally, it may be said that the objective of the last unit is clearly that of Cock to capture and devour Cockroach.

After the stories were analysed and checked, the chi-square test was used to determine whether there were significant differences among the units, or significant similarities.[6] The two Suriname samples might be examined toward the end of determining whether culture patterning obtains at this level of unconscious selectivity in human behavior, and the trickster samples similarly compared in order to see what characteristics might be said to belong properly to the demands of the trickster stock of situations.

Analysis demonstrated that the two Suriname patterns were extraordinarily alike (thus defining a cultural pattern) in regard to

6. Ordinarily chi-square is used for the purposes of rejecting the hypothesis that an observed difference might be due to chance alone. We start with an expected distribution and a different observed distribution and test whether the difference would occur by chance five or more times out of 100 ($p < 0.05$). Here we are reversing the procedure. We start with distributions which are much alike thanks to cultural and literary constraints on them. But conceivably the similarities could be due to chance. We apply the chi-square test to determine the probability that the distributions would be that much alike due to chance alone. Thus, for example, if we report $p > 0.95$ it means that the chi-square is small to the point where such a similarity in distribution would happen by chance only five times or less in 100. That will be the level of significance used unless otherwise indicated.

three items: the acquisition of goods (positive O); reprimands, humiliation, defamation and ridicule (negative D); and obscuring, keeping in ignorance, misinforming, falsifying, forgetting and doubting (negative R).

In regard to gratifying, indulging, enjoying, providing, comforting and pleasing (positive C), which may be thought of as being in some sense utilitarian counterparts of acquisition of property, the two kinds of Suriname stories are, however, significantly different ($p < 0.1$). Thus, while there would appear to be a patterned, high stress placed upon the acquisition of property in all the Suriname stories, the case is different with gratification, which is unpatterned, being high in Anansi Suriname trickster stories and low in Suriname 2, those stories not involving the trickster.

In the Dakota stories, on the other hand, there is little emphasis on the acquisition of goods, and a mid-high emphasis on gratification that leads to no clearly significant differences from the Suriname stories, but to some indications of probable differences. In the comparison of Anansi trickster stories with Dakota trickster stories in regard to acquisition of property (positive O) $p > 0.2$. It is at the same level for the comparison of Suriname 2 stories and Dakota stories in regard to both gratification (positive C) and acquisition or loss of property. While it is not possible on the basis of this evidence to make any very confident inference, it may be pointed out that the general difference indicated in the stories from the two cultures corresponds roughly with the fact that the Suriname Negroes live a settled life favorable to acquisition, and with a pecuniary economy, and also have a patterned high acquisition of goods, while the Dakota Indians, semi-sedentary and without a money economy, are low and unpatterned in this respect.

Condemnation (negative D), including scolding, reprimanding, humiliating, deforming, ridiculing and incrimination, are, as noted, culturally patterned elements which appear frequently in both kinds of Suriname tales. It is interesting that this category should show up as a cultural pattern in view of the fact that the public expression of censure and ridicule, particularly by indirect allusion, has been elsewhere noted as a characteristic of these as of some West African groups (Herskovits and Herskovits, 1936, p. 23).

The common elements among the two kinds of trickster stories,

Anansi and Dakota (which may therefore be presumed to constitute a trickster pattern), pertain to prescribing, summoning, directing, insisting, begging, permitting and inviting (positive S). Such actions may constitute part of the act of tricking. Both Anansi and Ikto, the Dakota trickster, are frequently found inviting their victims to participate in the affairs which will bring about their undoing.

Oddly enough, that category where one might expect to find the greatest degree of similarity among trickster stories, namely, avoidance of obligations (B), which includes acts of avoiding, welching, outwitting and deceiving, shows only a weak and not statistically significant trend toward similarity. This reveals the somewhat different functions of the trickster stories in the two cultures. Trickster stories involve a reversal of culturally sanctioned values.

Although there is no general formulation to account for the choice of which values are to be abrogated, and it is beyond the scope of this study to attempt one here, a few observations may be made. In the Dakota stories, Ikto seems preeminently concerned with self-gratification at the expense of those who can be duped. Because of his divine nature, chances of contest are precluded. Anansi, on the other hand, while undeniably interested in satisfying his desires, seems to be more intrigued with overcoming those more powerful than he. By virtue of his very size and his humble estate he flaunts power, though cautiously, and ordinarily with marked success.

Specifically, Ikto violates incest taboos, which are of great importance among the Dakota; Anansi violates the pattern of authority, so important in the African cultures from which these people came, though this violation occurs in the world of perhaps unconscious allegory. This is not to say that there is laxity in incest regulations in these parts of Africa, or a lack of concern with authority among the Dakota. It may be pointed out, however, that the pattern of political authority among the Dakota is not so faceted and complex as it is in those West African cultures.

On the other hand, there is a certain kind of value which is not, in the large view, reversed. Duties to the gods are not jested at; no more are those to the ancestors. Furthermore, the trickster is not likely to prey upon an individual who is undeserving of such attentions. He dupes the gullible, the foolish, the avaricious. It would seem that the delineation of the character types which the trickster exploits or destroys is as important as the delineation of the trickster himself. Perhaps those who tell these stories are less interested in being like Ikto or Anansi than in avoiding being like his victims.

Finally, there are certain correspondences between the Suriname 2 and the Dakota samples, among them hindering, preventing, conspiring, discouraging and punishing (negative A); these objectives occur in both with a similar distribution, but low frequency. Almost significant ($p > 0.8$) is the similarity shown in praise and condemnation (D). There are also certain differences to be noted between these two groups of stories. Significant differences are to be found in resistance and attack (M), and the acquisition and dissemination of information (R), particularly in the positive categories of these, that is, releasing, resisting and protecting, and in proving, discovering and gaining information from another. Rewarding, aiding, befriending (positive A) and prescribing, insisting and requesting (positive S) also are probably different in pattern ($p < 0.2$).

The two similarities noted in the paragraph just above should probably not be called a pattern. A pattern is a construct to which – one hypothesizes – future samples of behavior will show some high degree of predictable conformity, and there is no reason to assume a meaningful similarity between these two samples of stories. Any two groups of trickster stories would be expected to show some conformity to the description arrived at, just as any two samples of Suriname tales from the same period would be presumed to adhere to the general description made above. With respect to each other, having neither culture nor genre in common, similarities in the Suriname 2 and Dakota results are fortuitous. A hypothesis cannot reasonably be made relating them. Given any two samples of stories from any two cultures, one would expect some similarities to emerge from their comparison. For patterned predictable similarities, any two bodies of data must have either common cultural or generic bases.

It has been the purpose of this chapter to acquaint folklorists with a rationale in terms of which they might adapt the procedures of content analysis to their own studies. A perusal of the other essays included in this present collection suggest further procedures and tools to be modified to the needs of the reader's own research program. The comments on Cloze Procedure, touched upon in Chapter 2, may be briefly noted, since the Cloze notion appears to be a particularly fertile one, not only for the folklorist concerned with verbal materials but for those interested in music, dance and the graphic and plastic arts as well. The usefulness of this procedure in cross-cultural definition of units, for example, is readily apparent.

References

BENEDICT, R. (1935), *Zuni Mythology*.

BENEDICT, R. (1948), *Patterns of Culture*.

BURKE, K. (1941), *The Philosophy of Literary Form: Studies in Symbolic Action*.

HARRIS, Z. (1952), 'Discourse analysis', *Language*, vol. 28, pp. 1–30.

HERSKOVITS, M. J., and HERSKOVITS, F. S. (1936), *Suriname Folklore*.

KLUCKHOHN, C. (1942), 'Myths and rituals: a general theory', *Harvard Theological Rev.*, vol. 35, pp. 44–78.

MERRIAM, A. P., MERRIAM, B. W., and ARMSTRONG, R. P. (1954), 'Banyaruanda proverbs', *J. Amer. Folklore*, vol. 67, no. 265, pp. 267–84.

PIKE, K. L. (1954), *Language in Relation to a Unified Theory of the Structure of Human Behavior*, pt 1, Summer Institute of Linguistics, California.

SEBEOK, T. A., and ORZACK, L. H. (1953), 'The structure and content of Cheremis charms', *Anthropos*, vol. 48, pp. 369–88.

THOMPSON, S. (1932), *Motif-Index of Folk Literature*, Indiana University Press.

11 John M. Roberts, Brian Sutton-Smith and Adam Kendon

Strategy in Games and Folk Tales

John M. Roberts, Brian Sutton-Smith and Adam Kendon, 'Strategy in games and folk tales', *Journal of Social Psychology*, vol. 61, 1963, pp. 185–99.

Introduction

Earlier publications have shown that the three major divisions games in culture (games of physical skill, games of strategy, ar games of chance) have specific associations with child trainii practices and other cultural variables (Roberts, Arth and Bus 1959; Roberts and Sutton-Smith, 1962). In these studies gam were viewed as expressive models and both the players' involv ment in them and the cultural support of them was explained terms of a conflict–enculturation hypothesis (Roberts and Sutto Smith, 1962). This hypothesis holds that conflicts induced l child training processes and subsequent learning lead to involv ment in games and other expressive models which in turn provi buffered learning or enculturation important both to the playe and to their societies. Since all games model competitive situ. tions it was suggested also that these three classes of gam represent different competitive or success styles (Roberts ar Sutton-Smith, 1962; Sutton-Smith and Roberts, in press). Th present study continues this general inquiry into models, but it focused on the strategic mode of competition not only as it modeled in games of strategy but also as it occurs in folk tal with strategic outcomes.

Folk tales and games are quite different media of expressio but they are similar in that they model or represent behavio occurring in other settings, both real and imaginary. As mode they belong to an extremely important cultural category whi is both ancient in human culture (models appear in the Upp Paleolithic) and universally represented (no culture lacks model

The *model array* in any one culture may include representations in such diverse forms as graphic art, sculpture, drama, literature, toys, maps, plans, folk tales, games and many more. In most, but not all societies, folk tales and games figure prominently in the model arrays and the study of these two types is a reasonable first step in the cross-cultural study of models.

All games model competitive situations, for a game can be defined as a recreational activity characterized by organized play, competition, two or more sides, criteria for determining the winner, and agreed-upon rules (Roberts, Arth and Bush, 1959). Other recreational activities not satisfying these requirements are 'amusements'. Some folk tales resemble games in that they display definite outcomes with winners and losers, but other folk tales resemble amusements in lacking such outcomes. Folk tales of the latter type are excluded from this discussion. Indeed, this inquiry is strictly limited to those games and tales which display outcomes realized through the strategic mode of competition.

It is the general hypothesis of the present study that the strategic mode in folk tales will occur in the same general cultural setting as the strategic mode in games. Before proceeding to test this hypothesis, however, it is necessary first to outline the nature of the cultural setting in which games of strategy occur. While this outline is in part a repetition of statements made earlier (Roberts, Arth and Bush, 1959), it is required by the large amount of new material now made available as a result of the adoption of the present system of game classification in the Ethnographic Atlas (Murdock, 1963).

Games of strategy

The strategic mode of competition does not occur in all games (Roberts, Arth and Bush, 1959). Strategy does not appear in any games of chance, pure physical skill, or physical skill and chance. Strategy is present as a minor mode in games of physical skill and strategy (e.g. football) and games of physical skill, strategy and chance (e.g. tipcat). Strategy, however, is the *dominant* mode of competition in games of pure strategy (e.g. chess) and strategy and chance (e.g. poker). The strategic mode of competition, then, is most clearly modeled in games of pure strategy and games of strategy and chance and it is present as a minor mode in games of physical skill and strategy and games of physical skill, strategy and chance. It will be seen that while there are analogies to these game types in folk tales, there are not exact equivalents.

Not only is the strategic mode of competition limited to a few types of games, but the ethnographic distribution of games of strategy is limited. Of 141 tribes listed without qualification in the Ethnographic Atlas (Murdock, 1963), eight were listed as having no games at all; forty-five had only games of physical skill; forty-one had games of physical skill and games of chance; three had games of strategy only; five had games of strategy and games of chance; sixteen had games of physical skill and games of strategy; and twenty-three had games of physical skill, games of chance, and games of strategy. Only 33 per cent had games where strategy was a dominant mode of competition and another 61 per cent had games of physical skill with the possibility of the presence of the minor mode of strategic competition. Since the cross-cultural data do not permit the assessment of the degree of strategic competition found in the widely distributed games of physical skill, the following discussion of the cultural environment favoring the modeling of the strategic mode of competition is based on the presence or absence of games of strategy.

An earlier study has shown that games of strategy are associated with high political integration and high social stratification: societies which are low in political integration and in social stratification are unlikely to have games of strategy (Roberts, Arth and Bush, 1959). These findings support the generalization that tribes low in social complexity lack games of strategy while tribes high in social complexity have them.

The new data presented in the Ethnographic Atlas provide further support for this generalization. Societies possessing games of strategy are characterized by a low dependence on gathering, hunting, and fishing for subsistence, a higher dependence upon animal husbandry, and a high dependence upon agriculture. Table 1 shows the association between the presence of games of strategy and the more developed types of agriculture, particularly intensive agriculture.

Table 1 Games of strategy and intensity of cultivation

| | Games of strategy | |
	Present	Absent
Absence of agriculture	2	32
Horticulture	0	14
Casual agriculture	1	6
Extensive agriculture	13	33
Intensive agriculture with irrigation	13	7
Intensive on permanent fields with avoidance of fallow	12	3

Over and above the subsistence base, it is clear that games of
strategy are associated with relatively advanced and specialized
technologies. Only three societies possessing games of strategy
lack pottery and a majority possess weaving and leather working.
The association with metal working, however, is most relevant
(see Table 2). Metal working is often regarded as an indicator of
cultural complexity. It is safe to say that every society possessing
an advanced industrial organization also possesses games of
strategy.

Further indication of the relationship between strategy and
complexity is found in the relationship between the mean size of
the local community and game types (see Table 3). Games of
strategy are associated with large local communities. Only four
of the thirty-nine strategy societies were nomadic, semi-nomadic
or semi-sedentary, the others being sedentary in settlement pattern. Twenty-one strategy societies lived in compact and relatively
permanent settlements and four in complex settlements.

Table 2 Games of strategy and metal working

| | Games of strategy | |
	Present	Absent
Metal working present	31	11
Metal working absent	1	58

John M. Roberts, Brian Sutton-Smith and Adam Kendon 197

Table 3 **Games of strategy and mean size of local community**

Mean size of local community	Games of strategy	
	Present	Absent
50 or less	1	18
50–99	1	10
100–199	7	10
200–399	5	3
400–1000	3	4
1000+	2	0
Towns up to 50,000	5	1
Towns of more than 50,000	11	0

The societies possessing games of strategy are also distinguished by having jurisdictional levels beyond the local community:

Levels beyond local community	0	1	2	3	4
Games of Strategy Absent	66	26	2	0	0
Games of Strategy Present	5	10	14	9	4

Societies possessing games of strategy had high gods. Of the thirty-six tribes only seven lacked a high god. With fifteen the high god was otiose and with four the high god was active. Finally, with ten the high god was actively supporting human morality.

A more elaborate search of the literature would no doubt reveal other relationships. Freeman and Winch (1957), for example, have arranged societies on a scale of societal complexity. With these cultures games of strategy do not tend to appear until the societies have 'crimes punished by the government'.

In sum, then, games of strategy are associated with high political integration, social stratification, animal husbandry, advanced agriculture, advanced technology (weaving, pottery, metal working and industrialization), large settlements, more jurisdictional levels beyond the local community, high gods and crimes punished by government. In associated research it is intended to scale these and other items in terms of their significance for the development of the strategic mode of competition in culture. For the present it is enough to establish the relationship between games of strategy and cultural complexity.

Another aspect of the cultural environment which favors the

modeling of the strategic mode of competition is the presence of certain characteristic types of child training. It has already been demonstrated that games of strategy are positively associated with obedience training both cross-culturally and within American culture (Sutton-Smith, Roberts and Kozelka, 1963). Games of physical skill are associated with achievement training and games of chance are linked with responsibility training, but neither type of game is correlated with obedience training, which is associated only with games of strategy.

The strategic mode of competition as modeled in games of strategy, then, is associated with societal complexity on the one hand and with obedience training on the other. The conflict–encultural hypothesis may account for these relationships. One element of this hypothesis is the view that complex societies can function only if a significant number of adults are socialized to life in a complex system. These are adults who have learned when and how to obey and to disobey and, very importantly, when and how to command and not to command. Obedience training involving both reward and punishment is part of the socialization procedures designed to produce such fully participating adults in complex societies. This necessary training produces psychological conflicts which heighten drive and curiosity in this area and these in turn are assuaged by play with model social systems, i.e. games of strategy. In addition the play with the models also teaches the player such appropriate skills as the discernment and foresight he will need if he is to function later as commander, obeyer or decision-maker.

The above data concerning the cultural setting in which games of strategy occur lead to the following specific applications of the general hypothesis presented in the introduction. Namely, *that if the strategic mode in folk tales occurs in the same general cultural setting as the strategic mode in games, it will be possible to establish relationships between strategic outcomes in tales and: (a) the presence of games of strategy in the same cultures; (b) political complexity; and (c) high obedience training.*

Method

The investigation of folk tales parallels the study of games, but it is much more exploratory and preliminary in character. It is argued, however, that this is one of the situations in which work with a small sample merits a report in the scientific literature. The tales considered here were taken from a sample of folk tales prepared by Irving Child and his associates (Child, Storn and Veroff, 1958). Twenty-seven of the societies appearing in the folk-tale sample were also societies on which game scores existed at the time of the research. For each society the sample, except in a few instances, consisted of twelve selected tales purporting to be representative of the variety of tales found in that society. Those tales which had definite outcomes were treated as if they were games or game-like phenomena.

Three judges were used. A tale was rated as having an outcome if it was an account of a contest between two or more sides. This would be the case (a) when the fortunes of the hero are followed through, either to triumph or defeat; and (b) where one individual or a group of individuals induce or restore a state of misfortune besetting a whole group. Some stories recount happenings which may, for example, purport to explain the present state of affairs, and in these cases it is often not possible to say whether it is an outcome or not. The judges were instructed to reject such doubtful tales. Still only one judge excluded a significant proportion of the tales. One judge scored 100 per cent of the tales as having outcomes, a second scored 92 per cent, and the third scored only 56 per cent. This marked difference in the number of tales scored between the third judge and the other two probably accounts in part for the somewhat unreliable results produced. Only the tales agreed upon by two judges were used for this analysis.

While the present paper is concerned solely with strategy, it was a part of a more general inquiry into all games and their analogous outcomes in tales. The other two outcomes (physical skill and chance) are, therefore, referred to here for purposes of contrast, although they are not central to this paper. It should be mentioned, however, that the findings for the physical-skill and chance outcomes were largely non-significant. Important theoretical issues were raised by this fact, but these are sufficiently complex to merit separate treatment in a later paper. The first judge used a set of definitions of the three categories, *physical skill*, *strategy* and *chance*, first with a set of tales not included in the sample and secondly with the tales in the sample. The following definitions established by the first judge were used by the two other judges:

Physical Skill: any form of motor activity which is instrumental in furthering the outcome, including killing by physical means, *being eaten* or *eating*, *running* in flight or pursuit, skill in *dancing* or *singing*, etc. Physical skill takes primary place where it is the means by which the outcome is achieved. Even when physical skill immediately precedes the outcomes, if its importance is merely incidental, it still takes a secondary or tertiary place.

Strategy can be said to occur whenever someone makes a decision to act in a certain way; whenever someone engages in devices to deceive another; whenever he evaluates a situation, weighs up one set of considerations against another; whenever he outwits an opponent as in a fight where, for example, he tries to gain advantage by an intelligent use of the physical terrain. Discount instances where the terrain rearranges itself for the convenience of the subject in question. Only instances of someone using his wits to further his ends in the real world are considered. Magical strategies are not included, but real strategies which lead the hero to a magical being or fetish are included. In terms of the analogy between games and folk tales, strategy in a folk tale has an analogy to moves in a chess game.

Chance: The actual definitions given two of the judges differed from those worked out and used by the first judge in that an attempt was made by the latter to distinguish magic from guessing, casting lots and pure chance happenings. In the present study, however, all the ratings that refer to any of the magic or chance categories used by the two judges have been taken together and they have thus become equivalent to the category employed by the first judge, who considered as chance any instance of magic, whether it was magical ritual, the gratuitous intervention of a magical or supernatural being, or the intervention of animals as people into the world of people. Also included in this category were instances of guessing, casting lots and pure chance events.

Each tale was judged in terms of the relative extent to which the three outcome categories of physical skill, strategy and chance were involved in it. A weight of three was assigned to the competitive mode which was primary, a weight of two to the secondary mode, and a weight of one to the tertiary mode. When two of the categories seemed to be equal in importance, the same weight was assigned to each. The weights for each category were added together and a score for the total sample of tales for each tribe for each judge was thus obtained. An overall score for each tribe for the three judges taken together was obtained simply by adding these totals together. The rank-order correlation coefficients for the outcome ratings for the three judges are presented in Table 4. These show that such judgements can be made with significant if modest reliability, which is probably due to the great variability in the tales themselves. Other investigators using similar methods of analysis with folk tales have encountered very similar results (McClelland and Friedman, 1952).

In addition to scoring folk tales as if they were games, it was decided to score them for the presence of themes expressive of the child-training variables used in the earlier game studies. It

Table 4 Reliability of three judges on outcome ratings

Outcome	Judges	Rho	P
Physical skill	A and B	0·64	0·01
	A and C	0·52	0·01
	B and C	0·30	0·05
Strategy	A and B	0·42	0·05
	A and C	0·56	0·01
	B and C	0·52	0·01
Chance or magic	A and B	0·68	0·01
	A and C	0·56	0·01
	B and C	0·32	0·05

was thought that such themes (which are not obvious in games) might be more explicit in tales and, if they were, would add confirmation to the present inquiry. The child-training themes studied included responsibility, obedience, achievement, nurturance and independence. These themes are described in more detail elsewhere (Baron, Barry and Child, 1952). Although two judges made a thematic classification of the tales in these terms, these judges were not found to be consistent to an acceptable degree. The authors incline to the view that this was largely due to the inadequacy of the training of one of the judges. The other judge did yield two findings of relevance to this article which because of their exploratory value are listed here: Tribes with many games of physical skill tend to have folk tales emphasizing independence ($p < 0·01$). Tribes with games of chance tend to have tales of nurturance ($p < 0·05$).

In sum: (a) tales with outcomes were selected for study; (b) these outcomes were classified as due to physical skill, strategy or chance; (c) the presence of folk tales with strategic outcomes was related to the presence of games of strategy; (d) folk tales with strategic outcomes were related to an index of political complexity; (e) folk tales with strategic outcomes were related to the child-training ratings on obedience, responsibility, nurturance, self-reliance, achievement and independence which had been used in the earlier study of games; and (f) the tales themselves were subjected to a thematic content analysis for episodes indicative of some of the same child-training themes as were scored in the Barry, Bacon and Child, child-training ratings. In this latter study (f) tales were analysed for their child-training analogues, whereas in the preceding step (e) the tale outcomes were related to separately rated child-training practices.

Results

Table 5 demonstrates that societies possessing games of strategy tend to have folk tales in which the outcome is determined or partly determined by strategy.

It is not enough, however, to establish a relationship between folk tales and games. It is necessary to show that the strategic mode in folk tales occurs in the same general cultural setting as the strategic mode in games. Table 5 shows that the strategic mode of competition tends to be modeled in the folk tales of tribes which are politically complex. The strategic mode may appear in the tales of simpler societies, but it is less likely to be prominent in the tales of such groups. Other relationships are directional. If the sample had included a larger number of truly complex societies (e.g. American), the relationship would have been stronger.

Games of strategy are associated with high obedience training in children (Roberts and Sutton-Smith, 1962). If the strategic mode modeled in folk tales is psychologically similar to the strategic mode modeled in games, the same relationship should hold. Table 6 shows that there is a relationship between strategic outcomes in tales and reward for obedience. There were also directional relationships between strategic outcomes and anxiety about 'non-performance of obedience' ($rho = 0.24$, $p < 0.05$).

Table 5 Games of strategy and strategic outcomes in folk tales

Games of strategy present	Strategy outcome score rank	Games of strategy absent	Strategy outcome score rank
Ashanti	12	Aranda	1
Mbundu	14	Crow	2
Zuni	16	Woleaians	3
Thonga	19·5	Baiga	4
Hopi	22	Pukapuka	5
Chagga	23	Nauru	7
Azande	25	Lepcha	7
Masai	27	Marquesan	7
		Muria	9
$N_1 = 8$	$R_1 = 159·5$	Chukchee	10
		Kwakuitl	12
		Koryak	12
		Mandan	15
		Kurtachi	17
		Comanche	18
		Navaho	19·5
		Ojibwa	21
		Ainu	24
		Kaska	26
		$N_2 = 19$	$R_2 = 219·5$

$U = 29·5$

$P < 0.01$ (one-tailed)

These are the same two child-training relationships previously associated with games of strategy. It is this high emphasis on *both* reward and anxiety (punishment) that forms the cross-cultural empirical basis for the theoretical stress on conflict in the present series of studies.

In the case of folk tales there is the possibility of an internal check. If the strategic mode of competition bears a relationship to obedience training, there should be an emphasis on obedience themes in the tales themselves. This relationship did appear at least directionally (see Table 7).

It should be noted that the independent relationship between cultural complexity and obedience training is either directional or

Table 6 Levels of political integration and strategic outcomes in folk tales

Political integration	Strategic outcome low (24 or less)		Strategic outcome high (25 or more)
Absent Autonomous local communities	Arapesh (16) 1	1	Kaska (40)
	Tenetahara (21)		Kurtachi (48)
	Zuni (21) Koryak (20)		Chiracahua (38)
	W. Apache (18)		Navaho (29) Hopi (27)
	Paiute (18)		Ojibwa (26)
	Pukapuka (16) Nauru (15)		
	Jicarilla (14)		
	Chukchee (14) Aranda (10)		
	Baiga (10) Chenchu (9)		
	Crow (9)		
	13	5	
Peace groups	Klamath (24)		Masai (47) Comanche (34)
	Teton Dakota (16)		
	2	1	
Dependent societies	Lepcha (17)		Ainu (44)
	1	1	
Minimal states	Marquesan (19)		Mandan (43) Arapaho (42)
	Cheyenne (12) Crow (9)		Chagga (36)
	3	3	Winnebago (31)
Little states			Azande (41) Mbundu (37)
States		0 3	Thonga (25)
			Yoruba (39) Zulu (37)
		0 3	Ashanti (36)

confirmed in this study, and has been observed also in other independent investigations. Barry, Child and Bacon state:

Pressure toward obedience and responsibility should tend to make children into the obedient and responsible adults who can best ensure the continuing welfare of a society with a high accumulation economy, whose food supply must be protected and developed gradually through the year (1959).

The same paper by Barry, Child and Bacon shows a relationship between obedience training and animal husbandry and agriculture. The greater the reliance on domestication, the higher the obedience. Obedience training also figures in a combined score which is positively associated with such variables indicative

Table 7 Strategic outcomes in tales and rewards for obedience

Tribes in order of strategy outcomes		Reward for obedience score (Girls)	(Boys)
Masai	82	12	12
Kaska	72	8	8
Azande	70	13	13
Ainu	69	14	13
Chagga	67	14	13
Hopi	56	13	13
Ojibwa	53	11	10
Thonga	51	10	10
Navaho	51	10	10
Comanche	50		5
Kurtachi	48	6	6
Zuni	47	11	9
Mandan	43		10
Mbundu	37	11	11
Ashanti	36	13	12
Kwakiutl	36	10	10
Chukchee	35	12	12
Muria	34	11	10
Marquesan	33	4	4
Lepcha	33	9	9
Nauru	33	12	12
Pukapuka	32	9	9
Woleain	28	11	9
Crow	25	10	10
Aranda	12	9	8
		$N = 23$	$N = 25$
		$rho = 0.49$	$rho = 0.41$
		$p < 0.05$	$p < 0.05$

of complexity as size of settlement, degree of political integration, and complexity of social stratification (1959).

In sum, the constellation of variables required by the conflict-enculturation hypothesis is virtually complete, though all the relationships found are not equally convincing.

The principal findings of this inquiry were: (a) the strategic mode of competition is modeled in both games and folk tales in a number of cultures; (b) where the strategic mode of competition is modeled in one medium (i.e. games) it is likely to be modeled in the other (i.e. folk tales); and (c) the strategic mode of competition as modeled in games and in folk tales is associated

Table 8 Obedience themes in folk tales and games of strategy

Games of strategy Present	Obedience theme score rank	Games of strategy absent	Obedience theme score rank
Mbundu	7·5	Ainu	2·5
Azande	12	Navaho	2·5
Chagga	17	Lapcha	2·5
Hopi	17	Kurtachi	2·5
Masai	21	Kaska	5
Thonga	21	Chukchee	7·5
Zuni	23	Woleaians	7·5
Ashanti	27	Muria	12
		Ojibwa	12
$N_1 = 8$	$R_1 = 145·5$	Pukapuka	12
		Comanche	12
		Marquesan	12
		Baiga	17
		Koryak	17
		Mandan	17
		Kwakiutl	21
		Nauru	24
		Aranda	25
		Crow	26
		$N_2 = 19$	$R_2 = 237·5$

$U = 32·5$

with both obedience training and cultural complexity. It was also noted that games of strategy were associated with obedience themes in tales and that obedience training is associated with cultural complexity.

Discussion

The constellation of relationships which are either significant or directional and which have been explored in the present paper can be described simply. Within the full scale realm of actual competition, cultural complexity and obedience training are associated. Within the model realm, games of strategy and strategy in tales are associated and games of strategy are also associated with obedience themes in tales. Between the model realm and the full-scale realm, games of strategy and strategy in tales are associated with cultural complexity and obedience training. In sum these relationships constitute a consistent and meaningful configuration in terms of the conflict–enculturation hypothesis.

It has been argued that obedience training is necessary if adults are to function in a complex social system. This training produces conflict, which leads to heightened curiosity and drive, which in turn favor involvement in strategic models. Involvement in the models, in turn, assuages the conflict-induced drive and provides supplementary training which further enables game participants to meet the demands of a complex social system.

It is difficult to say much about the enculturation side of the hypothesis until more is learned about the psychology of strategic competence in individuals. While there is little direct research on the development of strategic abilities in children, some evidence suggests that such abilities appear relatively late. Although children play games of strategy such as checkers and tic-tac-toe in a routine fashion in early childhood, ongoing research suggests that they do not show the ability to execute deceptive strategies until about the age of ten or eleven years or later. Piaget has contended that children achieve the theoretical capacity that strategic thinking implies at these ages and that children demonstrate this ability in the way they recodify their own games systematically and variously in pursuit of more exciting play (1948). Perhaps it can be said that individuals must reach certain advanced levels of social and intellectual maturation before they can appreciate the strategic mode in models.

It is probable, too, that cultures must reach an advanced level of organization before strategy in models becomes salient. If historical depth can be inferred from cross-cultural distributions and associations, then games of strategy are most likely a relatively late invention appearing no earlier than Steward's period, 'Formative era of basic technologies and folk culture', or Coon's Level III, and no later than Steward's 'Era of regional development and florescence' (1955) or Coon's Level IV (1948, pp. 611–14). The specific association between games of strategy and the presence of metal working is informative. This is not to say that there is a direct relationship in a causal sense, but rather that a culture which has metal working is almost certain to be sufficiently complex to warrant a game of strategy. The highest development of games of strategy appears at much later periods. Folk tales, however, are less specialized and the strategic elements in them may have appeared at an earlier cultural period. Tales may have had their strategic elements derived from the expression of the minor mode of strategic competition, as in games of physical skill and strategy which are linked with achievement rather than with the major mode – the games of strategy – obedience training – cultural-complexity association. Well-developed tales of strategy with clear outcomes are probably no earlier in appearance than games of strategy.

These various speculations are based on the underlying assumption that child-training practices themselves and their associated models are cultural adaptations and inventions with their own culture histories. If we can conclude with a final speculation, the probable order of the appearance of the cultural inventories of child-training procedures and models is as follows: (a) nurturance and self reliance with no games; (b) independence, responsibility and achievement with games of physical skill and games of chance; and (c) obedience with games of strategy. The full culture history of models such as games and their associated conflicts, however, must be studied much more systematically than it has been to this time if the above order is to be regarded as being anything more than speculative. Perhaps the time will come when types of tales can be arranged in analogous fashion.

Finally, it would appear that the strategic mode of competition is modeled more sharply in games than in tales and that, in general, game associations are stronger than tale associations. The relative weakness of these associations in tales may be a result of work with a limited sample, unsatisfactory content analysis, and poorly translated tales, but it must be noted that tales, unlike games, are not confined to the modeling of competition and that in general they constitute a more flexible medium than games. In an earlier article, games were labeled *behavioral models* and tales were called *vicarious models* (Roberts and Sutton-Smith, 1962). In this frame of reference, tales appear to be more general and less specialized, while games of strategy appear to model the strategic mode of competition in particularly powerful and direct ways. Thus, the strategic mode is not modeled with equal strength in games and tales; games are the favored medium. The present discovery of linkages between both tales and games, and other cultural variables, however, is a first step in the more general study of the nature of model involvement in human culture.

Summary

Earlier cross-cultural work with games of strategy has demonstrated linkages with obedience traning and cultural complexity. These linkages were supported by further cross-cultural analysis in the present investigation. In addition, it was hypothesized that folk tales with strategic outcomes would be found in the same cultural setting as games of strategy. This hypothesis was confirmed. The results were explained in terms of a conflict–enculturation hypothesis, which seeks to locate the origins of model involvement in psychological conflicts induced by child training, but explains the culturally adaptive value of these models (in this case games and tales), in terms of the learning which arises out of this same model involvement.

References

BACON, M., BARRY, H., III, and CHILD, I. L. (1952), 'Raters' instructions for analysis of socialization practices with respect to dependence and independence', mimeographed paper, Yale University.

BARRY, H., CHILD, I. L., and BACON, M. K. (1959), 'Relations of child training to subsistence economy', *Amer. Anthropologist*, vol. 61, pp. 51–63.

CHILD, I. L., STORN, T., and VEROFF, J. (1958), 'Achievement themes in folk tales related to socialization practice', in J. W. Atkinson (ed.), *Motives in Fantasy, Action and Society*, Van Nostrand.

COON, C. S. (1948), *A Reader in General Anthropology*, Rinehart and Winston.

FREEMAN, L. C., and WINCH, R. F. (1957), 'Societal complexity: an emprical test of a typology of societies', *Amer. J. Sociol.*, vol. 62, pp. 461–6.

MCCLELLAND, D. C., and FRIEDMAN, G. A. (1952), 'A cross-cultural study of the relationship between child-training practices and achievement motivations appearing in folk tales', in Swanson, Newcomb and Hartley (eds.), *Readings in Social Psychology*, Holt, Rinehart and Winston.

MURDOCK, G. P. (1962; 1963), 'Ethnographic atlas', *Ethnology*,
vol. 1, pp. 113–34, 265–86, 387–403, 533–45; vol. 2, pp. 109–33.

PIAGET, J. (1948), *The Moral Judgement of the Child*, Free Press.

ROBERTS, J. M., ARTH, M. J., and BUSH, R. R. (1959), 'Games in
culture', *Amer. Anthropol.*, vol. 61, pp. 597–605.

ROBERTS, J. M., and SUTTON-SMITH, B. (1962), 'Child training and
game involvement', *Ethnology*, vol. 1, pp. 166–85.

STEWARD, J. H. (1955), *Theory of Culture Change*, University of
Illinois Press.

SUTTON-SMITH, B., and ROBERTS, J. M. (in press), 'Rubrics of
competitive behavior', *J. Genet. Psychol.*

SUTTON-SMITH, B., ROBERTS, J. M., and KOZELKA, R. M. (1963),
'Game involvement in adults', *J. Soc. Psychol.*, vol. 60, pp. 15–30.

Part Five
The Semantics of Myth

The two most important recent contributions to scientific
folkloristics are those of Lévi-Strauss and of the Russian School.
After Propp, Meletinsky, Segal, and others in the U S S R are
developing original research whose objective is related to that of
Lévi-Strauss. Like him, the Soviets try to decipher codes and to
discover the basic, deep structure of myths. To some extent,
this ties up with Part One, especially with Leach's paper: the
structure of relations between terms is where meaning dwells.
But myth is not only a static proportion. It is the expression of
the dynamic disequilibrium without which a semantic domain
would cease to be productive. It is the expression of the
dynamic disequilibrium which is the (acknowledged)
powerlessness to build adequate homomorphisms between
incompatible and hence disturbing facts. It is the expression of
the reluctant acknowledgement that the event is mightier than
the structure. But myth is also and more than anything else the
hallucinogenic chant in which mankind harmonizes the vagaries
of history – the chant hummed for generations in the minds of
men and humming itself in the human mind (that innate dream
to reduce continuous randomness to a final pattern) as hinted
by Plato and Jung or, better, as amplified by Chomsky and
Lévi-Strauss.

12 Dmitry M. Segal

The Connection between the Semantics and the Formal Structure of a Text

Dmitry M. Segal, 'Il Nesso tra la Semantica e la Struttura Formale del Testo' in R. Faccani and E. Eco (eds.), *I Sistemi di Segni e lo Strutturalismo Sovietico*, Milano: Bombiani, 1969, pp. 333–64. Specially translated for this volume by Robert J. Vitello. The Russian original appeared under the title, 'O svjazi semantiki teksta s ego formal'noj strukture', in *Poetika II*, Varsovie, 1966, pp. 15–44.

The subject of this inquiry is three variants of the same mythological tale published some years ago by the French Canadian ethnographer Barbeau (1961).[1] All three myths were recorded in the Canadian North-West on the Pacific coast near the Canada–Alaska border. Myths α and β were collected by Benyon in 1952 and 1954 at Metlakatla and at Hartley Bay, while myth γ was transcribed 'recently' (according to Barbeau) also by Benyon at Port Simpson. The areas are all near each other and constitute the habitat of the Tsimshian Indian tribe to whom, according to Barbeau, these myths belong. The text of myths α and β contain a direct indication that they belong to the same Tsimshian Indians, those of the gitzarhlaehl.

All three narratives can be related to a theme which is widespread among the Indians of North America, that of 'Cinderella' or the 'outcast hero' (*unpromising hero*, L., according to Thompson's classification of folklore motifs) (1955–8) They are further classified in a particular group on the basis that they all contain an aetiological motif of the supporting of the earth. This motif occurs in them as follows: the earth is balanced on a pole by an athlete. It is to be noted that according to Thompson, in North America this myth is found only among the Tlingit Indians (who are the Tsimshians' nearest neighbours to the north; it seems reasonable therefore to suppose that some geographical inter-

1. This is the book which contains the myths of 'The strong man who holds up the earth' (here referred to as myth α) and 'Amaelk, the strong man who holds up the earth' (here referred to as myth β), see Barbeau (1953). This collection contains the myth here referred to as myth γ, which has the same title as myth α.

penetration has taken place). Outside North America this myth only occurs in Finno-Ugric folklore.

Thus the three variants form an isolated group and we can therefore examine them separately, without being accused of arbitrarily extrapolating them from the body of myths which contain the motif of the 'outcast hero'.

I wish to point out, incidentally, that notwithstanding the undoubtable usefulness of a comprehensive interpretation and general inquiry into the structure of a thick cluster of myths, it is still profitable to try to subdivide such clusters into more homogeneous groups on the basis of theme and plot. An inquiry of the first kind, which shall be dealt with in due course, is contained in Randall's essay 'The Cinderella theme in North-west coast folklore' (1949). Among inquiries of the second kind we recall the work of Spenser (1957), in which he gives a detailed analysis of ritual myths among the Navajo Indians containing the theme of the 'outcast hero', which he examines in relation to a reconstruction of the Navajo value system. Naturally, the number of such examples can be increased, but these two are important because they deal most directly with the 'outcast hero' theme. It is true that Spenser's work examines the mythology of the Navajo tribes, which are geographically and culturally very far removed from the Canadian north-west. I know no works which analyse specifically the myths with this theme among the Tsimshian, Tlingit or Haida. On the other hand, a superficial examination of the summaries of 'Cinderella' myths to be found in Randall's essay show how the most diverse myths fit into this group. Some describe the way in which the outcast hero brings his tribe a ritual or rituals (often connected to a totem). Others are presented as myths of an aetiological type (explaining the origin of the rainbow). Finally, there is a fairly large group of so-called 'narrations' which are always connected with a particular tribe or clan, and, unlike other myths, take place in historical, rather than mythological, time.

All these myths are unified by the appearance in them of an outcast hero and naturally, in the interpreting of them, this must always be borne in mind. However it is clear that the meaning of each text, as it is re-established in the course of interpretation, will be different according to whether, for instance, the text contains the description of the hero's journey in search of a ritual or tells the story of successes and failures in hunting.

The aim of our inquiry is to demonstrate that the common theme of the 'outcast hero' changes, and that the significance of the text changes in relation to its structure.

We will try to indicate the relationship between the formal thematic-narrative structure of a myth and its interpretation (semanticizing it, i.e. correlating elements of the myth's structure with certain extra-mythic elements). I must quickly qualify this statement; in the formal analysis of a myth we start with the fact that its content can be understood, and that we will be able to identify the segments of the plot which are endowed with the same meaning. In the course of such an interpretation, such identifications emerge clearly. In order to simplify and abbreviate the transcription of the plot, I have adopted letter-symbols for the predicates (the narrative statements to which a set value is attributed). Each predicate is presented in symbolic form without specifying the specific referents for each symbol, since there are few actors in the myths we will be considering, and the functions are distributed in the same way in each.

The theme of the 'outcast hero' in the folklore of the Indians of north-west Canada can be represented by the following thematic-narrative scheme [*sjužetno-tematičeskaja schema*]. (It has been compiled by this author on the basis of the interpretation proposed by Randall).

A C D E Ā Č

In this statement:

A is the symbol for the predicate, 'the hero is in a state of repudiation' (in a condition of rejection). Note that in Randall's essay this predicate takes the following concrete forms: poverty (Kāhā'sî, the hero in the Tlingit myth 'Kāhā'sî 'The Strong Man' (Swanton, 1909), is poor): orphanhood (an orphan is the hero of the myth among the Bella Coola Indians (Boas, 1898)): impurity (Kāhā'sî again. This, incidentally, escaped Randall's notice. Note that incontinence (enuresis) is not merely a negative quality, but a specific hint at another possible interpretation): physical defects (ugliness, sickliness, etc.): unrequited love: the fact that the hero is younger than his brothers: vices (extravagance, passion for gambling, etc.).

C is the symbol for the predicate, 'the social group to which the hero belongs rejects him'. Properly speaking, this predicate relates to A. From the point of view of the plot we could afford to ignore it, since it connects directly with A: A →C. But for reasons of convenience in the interpreting, of which more later, we need to have C.

D is the symbol for the predicate, 'the hero acts to overcome the state of rejection'.

E is the symbol for the predicate, 'the hero receives assistance from magical powers'.

Ā is the negation of A. That is, the removal of the state of rejection (followed by the receiving of riches, victory over an adversary in battle or a contest, marriage with the beloved, liberation from ugliness, initiation into the secrets of a ritual, or participation in the magical powers of the totem).

C̄ is the negation of C. That is, the capturing of the respect of the social group, usually crowned by elevation to the position of leader or by the recognition of the hero's powers as a shaman.

This scheme A C D E Ā C̄ is interpreted by many authors as being a representation, in symbolic form, of the way the Indians view the position of a young member of the tribe in the collective social life. Randall in particular perceives in the role of C̄ an element which demonstrates that the primitive conflict of the hero's rejection has a purely social character, and that all the different kinds of As are merely tribal variants. The presence of C̄ proves that the hero deserves to get rid of A, so that the conflict ends and the hero rejoins his social group.

In the light of this interpretation the narrative scheme A C D E Ā C̄ constitutes an invariant which remains constant despite thematic changes (the filth in one myth and the poverty in another are variants of the same predicate), or changes in significance of the myth. The logic of the relation between the plot segments is here tied to a different, extra-textual logic, the logic of the social development of the personality in the tribal group.

Randall, very correctly, establishes the correspondence between the story of the outcast hero's final triumph, and the real circumstances of the social life of Indian tribes on the Canadian Pacific coast. Especially convincing in her work is the contrasting of the European story of Cinderella and the Indian myths of the outcast hero; the scholar finds one such contrast in the more dynamic, personal quality of the conflict and its resolution in the Indian myths, as compared with the European tales. Randall points out that in the European variants the hero is not reunited with his group at the end of the story, but abandons it (note the marriage of Cinderella to the prince in the Grimm brothers' tale).

From much of the aforegoing, we can see how in Randall's interpretation the concepts of 'rejection' and 'reintegration' have an essential role.

One thus understands how the predicates C and $\bar{C}$ play a fundamental role in a schematic and abstract transcription of the plot as $A\,D\,\bar{A}$ (which does not affect the personalized and dynamic character of the semantic opposition).

It seems advisable at this point to stress how important it is, in principle, to correlate the narrative scheme with the sequence of extra-textual relationships which emerge from analysis of the myth. Since in Randall's essay this correlation is imperfectly carried out, she is unable to explain certain peculiarities in the meaning of a number of myths. Only nodal 'moments' of the plot are interpreted, and that in their most general schematic form. Instead, let us consider Vladimir Propp's studies (1958; 1945); these contrast the entire narrative scheme in all its details with rituals of initiation in primitive society, and the most minute details of the plot are understood in terms of initiation. Propp seems to have succeeded in discovering the mechanism of the tale's construction precisely because he perceived the impersonal meaning of the initiation ritual behind the mechanism. Furthermore, once in possession of the structural scheme of the story, he was able to correlate the elements of the tale with those of the ritual with great accuracy.

There is a substantial difference between Propp's interpretation and that of Randall, because the first is historic and the second synchronic.

To correlate the narrative scheme of a Russian magical tale

with a rite of initiation, a reconstruction is required. On the other hand, interpreting the myths of the Canadian north-west coast in terms of the social adaptation of the members of the collectivity does not require a reconstruction since the facts of Tsimshian social life and that of the neighbouring tribes can be obtained directly, by working in the field (Swanton, 1905). Nevertheless, both these interpretations refer back, in principle, to the same phenomenon: to the facts of the social organization of primitive tribes, to the great importance of the collectivity in primitive social organization, to the enormous significance of the transition from the state of exclusion from the collectivity which goes with being young (synonymous with rejection), and to the entry into the collectivity. This transition can be proved to be the result of a particular initiation ritual even though it is possible that such a ritual no longer exists (as in primitive societies which are already in contact with civilized peoples) and that the need for entry into the collectivity is now seen in pragmatic, not ritual, terms.

Summarizing the basic elements of Randall's proposed interpretation, we recall that in her opinion, all the Indian myths about the 'outcast hero' are characterized by open conflict between the hero and his group, which ends largely through the hero's open, energetic and successful efforts, which win him the assistance of spirits, liberation from his defects, and reintegration into the community.

The three texts I have chosen to examine were published after Randall's essay appeared. Even a brief reading of them shows that the interpretation A C D E Ā Č proposed by Randall is probably too general, and that certain elements which are important for Randall (the opposition of C and Č) are presented differently in these texts. I summarize the plot briefly, to enable the reader to make up his own mind.

The hero (who is the youngest son or the youngest nephew of a head of the tribe) does not take part in the training which is obligatory for all adolescents and stays all day long in the ashes near the fire. He is apathetic, sleeps, and in addition his bed is always soaked. His brothers go through the training and continually mock him. The hero, however, trains at night, so that nobody knows. He returns home at dawn and when normal life in the village resumes, is found sleeping in the ashes by his relatives. One night in the woods he meets a supernatural being (*narhnorh*), from whom he receives aid. Despite uninterrupted mockery, the hero finishes first in the hunt, in a competition with other tribes, and in a struggle with natural elements (ferocious beasts, trees, mountains). All these victories do not change his character. He continues to be apathetic and to look filthy. His acquaintances, who immediately after each victory begin to respect him, return to mocking him. One day a boat approaches the ocean shore and the people in it carry the hero away with them. They are supernatural beings who take the hero to the depths of the earth where he will replace his grandfather to support the whole world on a pole.

I have conducted an analysis of the plot of the three myths and in the course of it have identified the different sections of the text. For this identification, I have used the following symbols.

A The meaning of this predicate has already been indicated. The essential components of A in these texts are: the hero's filth (incontinence and sleeping in the ashes by the fire), apathy and sleepiness, his apparent lack of reaction to surrounding events, his apparent reluctance to train. His condition of youngest brother, stipulated in all three variants, is ascribed to him automatically and does not, it seems to me, have an essential role in the development of the plot or, hence, of the interpretation.

$\tilde{A}$	Modification of A. Here in the sense of the hero's active reaction to events.
$\bar{A}$	Complete negation of all the components of A.
C	The same meaning as indicated earlier.
$\bar{C}$	Negation of C. Here in the sense of a good disposition toward the hero during the period of his rejection.
$\tilde{C}$	Modification of C. Here in the sense of a modification of the tribe's attitude towards the hero as a result of his successes. (Analogous to $\tilde{C}$ as given earlier.)
C^*	$\tilde{C}$ on the part of members of other tribes.
$C<E>$	C in that the hero shows himself to be a supernatural being.
B	Explicit training of the hero's brothers.
$\bar{B})$	Victorious test of strength during the brothers' training.
B)	Unsuccessful test of strength (by the brothers).

D	Secret training of the hero.
D)	Victorious test of strength during the hero's secret training.
Ď)	Hero's unsuccessful test of strength.
Dp	Hero's secret training in the past.
E	Attainment of magical help by the hero.
$\overrightarrow{E}$	Arrival of supernatural beings.
$\overleftarrow{E}$	~~Departure of supernatural beings.~~
F	Manifestation of the wish to act on the part of the hero: defiance.
F)	Satisfaction of the other members of the tribe with the hero's desire to act.
H	Refusal to act positively on the part of the members of the hero's tribe.
G	Failure of the actions of the members of the hero's tribe.
Ğ	Success of the actions of the members of the hero's tribe.
I	Success of the hero.
|d|	Concurrence of an action with an earthquake.
X	Explanation of how the earth is held up on a pole by a hero.
M	Moral.
N	Indication of the tribe to which the myth belongs.

These are the symbols which are found in all three variants. Some of them figure in all of the three texts, others in only one. The interpretation of some (Č and Ā in particular) differs from the interpretation given them in the earlier general schematic analysis of myths concerning the outcast hero, since there the most general scheme was selected; here the analysis is more detailed. Each symbol in this transcription represents a sentence in the English text of the myths. For this reason it was necessary to broaden the inventory of symbols and to introduce diacritical marks. We need to be able to distinguish between a constantly favourable attitude toward the hero (that is, the vigorous negation of C) and the modification of attitude towards the hero (Č) without placing too much emphasis on the positive nature of the modifications; the same applies to the negation of A and to its modification. It was also necessary to adopt a separate symbol for the concurrent event |d| (the earthquake) and to introduce a

Table 1 Symbolic transcription of the three variants of the myth

Myth β			Myth α			Myth γ			
N									
A B C		①	B		①	A	D		①
A	D		B			A C			
AB) C			A C			A			
A	D		A	C D					
A	C		B̄) D̄) E				F		②
	C̄		A C			C	F)		
	C		AB			A C	F) G		
A	D E		A				Y G H		
	D						F		
B) C			C*	Ḡ	③	Ā̄ C	F		
	C̄		C.				F)	I	
B	D E		C*	G		A			
	D)			G					
A	C			G			H	③
B			C C	F		C*			
		F	②	Ā̄ C		AC C	F		
	C̄C̄		C	F)		Ā C	F		
	F) G			F)		C			
	G		C*				G H I	
	F		C̄C̄C̄	f		ĀC̄			
	C̄C̄ F) I		A A C*			AC̄<E>			
A			Ā̄A C						
	I		A A C	B		C*	G H	④
	I		A A C̄			AC D	I	
	I		A A	I		Ā̄			
						AC E		
B		③	C*	I	④	C*	G	
A A C				I		A	H	
A	D B			I		A	G|d|	
	C̄C̄		C*	I		DpE		
B			C*	H		A	G|d|H	
A	D G		A	I|d|		AC E	H	
	C* F F			I		AC̄<F>	I	
	C F F								
A	C̄C̄ C* F I				X ⑤		Ē̄ B	⑤
	C̄C̄C̄ F F		A	Ē̄ E		A	B	X
	C̄C̄C̄ I		A A Ā	C̄<E> Ē̄		C̄	E Ē̄	M
A	C* G		C̄	Ē̄		Ā̄	E	
	C̄C̄ F I			Ē̄				
				¿ X				
C* I	④		N				
C* I							
C* I							
I							
⑤	X						
A C Ē̄							
	Ē̄						
	Ē̄						
A	Ē̄						
	X						
	X	d							
	X						
	⊗						
C̄							

symbol for the motivation of $\tilde{C}$, $<E>$, to differentiate this case of $\tilde{C}$ from the others. These symbols list comprehensively the particulars of each variant and will be useful in the interpretation.

The following diagram is a symbolic transcription of the three variants. This transcription is based on the form of myth transcription proposed by Lévi-Strauss (1955). Equivalent predicates are transcribed underneath each other. In this way we are able to set down the paradigmatic and syntagmatic structures of the myth simultaneously. The symbolic notation runs from left to right as in any text.

From this table it is clear that the plots of the three variants consist of differently ordered repetitions of the basic predicates. We start with the hypothesis that two mechanisms are involved in the structure of the plot; one is a random mechanism while the other is not. Let me try to clarify this idea. The horizontal lines of the table separate sections of the myth from each other. In myth α and β there are four such sections while in myth γ there are five. The similar narrative sections share the same number as follows:

1. Introduction. Description of the preparation of the hero's brothers and of his secret training.
2. The hunt.
3. Contest with other tribes.
4. Struggle with nature.
5. Conclusion.

It seems to me that the absence of the description of the hunt in myth β, and the absence of predicate B in myth γ, are random or accidental happenings. On the other hand, the sequence of the sections of the plot is not random. It is conditioned by specific traits in the meaning of the myth which we shall discuss later.

We now analyse the structural details of each section of myths α, β and γ.

Section 1 Introduction

The most fully developed narrative scheme is offered by myth α:

Table 2 Syntagmatic structure of the introduction of myth α

```
A           B   C           (A) D
A           B)  C           (A) D
A     C         C       C    A
                                 D   E   D
B           C           Č    B
                                 D   E   D)
         A   C   B
```

The parentheses round A designate its optional character.
A B C D is a fairly complete scheme, since it contains the fundamental predicates of the opposition.

The sequence of predicates A B C (A) D is repeated twice from the beginning. Here the fundamental conflict, the basic semantic opposition, is most fully defined: this is the opposition between A D and C B, which from one perspective is the indifference and constant apathy of the hero contrasted with his secret preparation for the hunt, and from another point of view is the active disapproval of the hero's actions on the part of the members of his tribe set against the active preparation for the hunt.

The same clash is underlined by the contrasting of A with C Č C in A C Č C A. The negative reaction of the hero's surroundings is emphasized by the appearance of Č, the youngest uncle's positive attitude to the hero. As for the hero, there is no evidence that he reacts either to the negative attitude (disapproval) or to the positive attitude (approval) in his encounters. The motif D E D is repeated twice. The second time D occurs with D), the successful outcome of the hero's training with the test of strength.

B C Č B can be interpreted as a variant of the motif A C Č (C) A in which the inactivity of the hero is replaced by the activity of his brothers. The first section of myth α ends with a *sui generis* 'coda', A C B, which repeats the fundamental opposition in this part of the myth A D – C B.

The symbolic structure of this section of myth α can therefore be defined as a double repetition of the motifs A B C D, A C Č A and D E D with a 'coda' A C B. On the paradigmatic level the second repetition can be disregarded. In this case the scheme of the section can be written thus:

A	B	C	D	
A		CČ		
A			D	E
			D	'coda'

The series A is contrasted with the series C Č and the series B with D E D.

Examining the content of the predicates in this first fragment, the predicate A emerges as follows. The hero sleeps in the ashes, never takes a purifying bath, lies in something similar to filth, and never pays attention to anyone. The link between the hero and the ashes of the fire, the fact that his bed is always soiled, his apathy and his apparent refusal to purify himself by washing, seem to me to be essential. Predicates C and Č are interesting in that they are complementary, not only from the point of view of attitude to the hero, but also in their content. C in [A B C (A) D]₁ is the mockery of the hero which is expressed in the words, 'We wouldn't ask him for food unless we were starving.' Č in A C Č C A represents the following statement made by the hero's youngest uncle: 'Stop your mockery. The time for my nephew to show his strength has not yet come. When it is necessary, he will show what he can do.' We have here two contrasted statements. The opposition of B and D E D, particularly if we take into account the repetition of D E D, underlines the important role of E.

We will now embark on correlating the instances of A, B, C, D, and E which are obvious as well as those which are not so obvious.

In A the hero's apathy, his indifference (which has already been stressed), the mockery, his relation to the ashes in the fire hole, are clearly set out. Among not so clear-cut meanings are the hero's association with filth (it is emphatically stressed that his filth and that of his bed are an illusion), and his refusal of the cleansing and of the training (which are implied in D). C and B are made particularly explicit. E could be held to be only implied, or secret, since the hero encounters his magic advantage at night in the woods; D is a characteristic which is equally implicit. In

this way A combines both overt and implied 'moments' while C
and B are clearly contrasted with D and E.

We now analyse the structure of the Introduction to myth β.

Table 3 **Syntagmatic structure of the introduction of myth β**

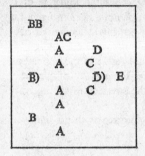

With regard to the different structure of the same section of
myth α, we note that myth β does not repeat the same motifs so
precisely in its structure. In myth β the motif B̄) D̄) E, around
which the plot coalesces, can be taken as central. In this section
of this myth the magic help is recorded only once. Unlike myth
α, where E comes after D, E follows D̄) here. Thus the 'moment'
at which the magical aid unexpectedly occurs is accentuated in
myth β as it is in α but it is almost the result of the hero's own
effort. From his strength and from D alone, the hero cannot
obtain success and so E is introduced from necessity. His
success, marked by the presence of E, is not isolated, but is
related in this part of myth β to the content of A. And here we
perceive a tendency to justify A. A is described as the hero's
failure to react to his surroundings (much as in myth α), a relation
with the fire ('he slept alongside the fire', again as in myth α),
an implied refusal of training, and the aforementioned relationship with filth ('his bed was always soaked and people thought
he wetted himself in his sleep'; earlier, 'after the secret training
he returned home; water dripped from his body because of his
bath and he went to bed just as he was'; and also, 'he returned
to his bed all wet, water dripping from his body'). Now clearly
it is only in myth α that the filth was actually in evidence. In myth
β, on the contrary, the motif of the hero's filth is inverted; that

which seemed to be filthy was in fact clean. Here the filth, whether physical or ritual, is ambivalent. Thus, myth β differs from myth α in stressing on the one hand the ambivalence of A (or rather of a part of A, since the other part of A – the hero's lack of reaction and relationship with the ashes – is presented explicitly, in real terms), and on the other the injustice of C (which is connected to A). In myth α C is not autonomous but is in conflict with C̄: in myth β C does not involve a similar conflict. Furthermore, in this myth the emotional content of the conflict between A D and C B does not reside in the opposition between the passivity of the hero and the activity of the other members of his tribe, but rather in the stressing of the injustice of C.

The narrative scheme of the Introduction to myth γ is simply:

A   D
A C
A

First, we note that the complex of predicates here is defective; there is no B. The absence of B destroys the opposition which was fundamental in myth α and which was present in myth β; the opposition of passivity and activity between the hero and his brothers. The idea of the injustice of C, however, does appear here. It can be seen especially in the content of A.

Like myths α and β, myth γ includes the association of the hero with the ashes of the fire, and the implied refusal of training. The interpretation of the motif of the hero's filth is different, however, from myth α where it is implied and myth β where it is ambivalent; in myth γ the filth is manifest and real ('he wetted himself where he slept'). The motif of the apathy indicated by his failure to react is likewise different. Here it is only implied ('he pretended not to hear anything'; earlier, 'he rose from his bed and asked almost with indifference . . .'; and again, 'the young man seemed to sleep, and at first sight nothing interested him').

The composition of A and the interrelation of the various parts of A in so far as they are explicit–implicit in the three myths, can be represented in the following table, where ambivalence is indicated by a zero, explicitness by a plus, and implicitness by a minus sign.

Table 4

A	The hero's filth	Indifference, apathy	Refusal of training	Relation with ashes of the fire
Myth α	—	+	—	+
Myth β	0	+	—	+
Myth γ	+	+	—	+

Section 2 The hunt

Now let us examine the next section. It occurs only in myths α and γ. First, the structure in myth α. The Table should be read, as before, from left to right.

Table 5 **Syntagmatic structure of section 2 of myth α**

```
            F   C   C̄   F)
      GG    F   C̄        F)
      I         C
  A   III
```

We should note the secondary role of predicate A in this section. A appears only in the 'coda' and merely as an observation on the hero's unchanging nature. The basic contrasts in this plan are the opposition G – I (the repetitions of I in the 'coda' are particularly characteristic), and the emphasis on the superiority of the hero's power to that of the other members of the tribe. We also see the reappearance of the opposition C – C̄, previously noted in the Introduction, as well as that of the contrasting negative and positive prophecies. In the last I, the positive prophecy is confirmed. The other basic oppposition is between F and F), and C C̄. This could be considered to be a modification of the opposition A C C̄ A which occurred in the Introduction. Where in A C C̄ A the passivity of the hero and the activity of his brothers were contrasted, the passivity of the hero is here set against the active attitude of other members of the tribe. Now, given the relative absence of A, we move on to look at the hero's actions and the functional, impersonal role they play in affirming his identity. It is interesting, in this context, to find C̄ appearing after I.

The second section of myth γ follows this sequence:

Table 6 Syntagmatic structure of section 2 of myth γ

```
                    F   C   F)
   A                    C   F)
         GG   H    F    C
   Ā                F       F)
         I
   A
```

In myth γ we find the oppositions A Ā – C, G – I, H – F F), and C – F F). The opposition C – A Ā, absent in myth α, is particularly interesting. Here the personal, but not functional, activity of the hero (anger, violent reaction to his surroundings) is opposed to the negative inactivity around him ('nobody paid him any attention').

The active personality of the hero, which is not in evidence underneath his superficial apathy, is made perfectly clear here. The oppositions H – F F) and C – F F) also illuminate the functional aspect of the hero's activity. However, in contrast to myth α, very little attention is paid to the purpose of the activity, as can be seen from the modest role of I. The most important factor in this section of myth γ is not the success of the activity, but the self-affirmation which is indicated by the triple interaction of F F). In this sense, the second sections of myths α and γ turn out to be complementary.

Section 3 The contest

The third section of the plot, the contest, occurs in all three myths.

The third section of the first myth duplicates the sequence of motifs found in the Introduction, though naturally in a reduced form. However, both the fundamental oppositions A D – C B and A – C Č – A are represented. The scheme of this section is as follows:

```
B      A      C
       A                    D        E
              C    Č
B      A                    D
```

Here the introduction appears to be free of the repetitions of internal motifs which are so consistently found in Sections 1 and 2. However, the narrative scheme of the contest shows again the repetitious tendency so typical of myth.

Table 7 Syntagmatic structure of section 3 of myth α

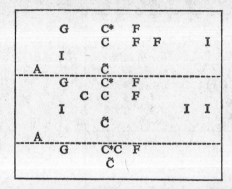

The second part of this scheme repeats the structure of the first part with scarcely any modification. Really, the structure of this section duplicates, perhaps more precisely, the same semantic oppositions already found in myth α; from one point of view, the opposition between the hero's passive personality and his functional actions, from another, that between his active personality and the functionally passive personality of the rest of the hero's tribe. The functional activity is seen in the repetition of F and by the three repetitions of I (after each part). The hero's activity in myth α has positive results, regularly and inevitably, without any striving towards self-affirmation on his part. The tribe's specific attitude is indicated by C̃, which inevitably appears at the end of all the subsections of Section 3.

We note that C̃ does not at all prevent the reappearance of C in the following part of this section. This fact in particular is one which is not dealt with in Randall's essay. She considered it a part of the overall structure, a 'layer' of the myth, and did not subject it to separate interpretation. It would seem, however, that such a component substantially changes the nature of the relation C – C̃ (or C̃). We will discuss this later in detail.

Dmitry M. Segal 231

The structure of the longer Section 3 of myth β, which contains the story of the contest in which the hero participates, is characterized by frequent repetition of pairs of predicates and of single predicates, but not of whole segments of the plot.

Table 8 **Syntagmatic structure of section 3 of myth β**

		C*				Ḡ		
	C	C*				G G G		
		C	F					
		C						(I)
Ā			F	F)				
	C*	C					I	
		Č						
A								
		C*						
A								
Ā					E			
		C						
		C						(II)
A		C*					I	
A		Č						

Remember that in Section 1 of this myth there is the predicate Ď). In each of the three myths this is the unique instance in which the hero's activity does not result in success. The analysis of the relevant section demonstrates that this is not a random phenomenon. In the first myth we have so far noted the opposition between the passive personality and functional activity of the hero, and between the active and passive personalities of the members of his tribe: meanwhile, in the third myth γ we have singled out the opposition between the passive and functional personality of the tribe and the active and functional activity of the hero: in myth β, however, the basic conflict is in the emphasis on the difficulty of achieving success. It is not the other members of the tribe who constitute the principal opposing force, but the enterprise itself.

This conflict is clearly expressed in the structure of Section 3 of myth β. The first and second parts of this section are built around the idea of growing difficulty. In fact, we note a Ḡ at the beginning and a string of three Gs following. In myth α the hero's victory occurred easily and inevitably; in myth β, in the second part of this section, magical aid is necessary in order for the hero to triumph (see the Introduction). In the second part G is missing. This indicates that no one except the hero accepts the challenge of the members of the foreign tribe, since the challenge is so arduous.

Ā serves to establish the difficulty of the task. The content of Ā here is different from the content of Ā in myth γ. In both myths, Ā represents the negation of the hero's passivity, his apathy and his lack of response. However, in myth γ Ā is the positive negation of such qualities as anger, scorn and violent activity, while in myth β Ā is the negation of a different group of qualities; desperation, weeping, sorrow. In both cases Ā leads by definition to F) and I. However, in the second part of Section 3 of myth β Ā → E. This underlines once again the difficulty of the victory and the important role of the supernatural forces.

In myth β as in myth α, each plot is regularly concluded by Č, while C appears in the segment that follows:

Table 9 Syntagmatic structure of section 3 of myth γ

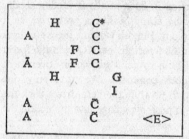

In myth γ, in contrast to the other two, this section contains only one I and consequently, the repetitions (FC) which are contained in it constitute, so to speak, microrepetitions of a particular kind. At the same time, the section is not set up in its ensemble on a cyclical principle, but, like the second section of the same myth, on a principle of expansion. The fundamental opposition is the one in section 2, the active and functional personality of the hero set against the passive and functional personality of his surroundings. The emphasis on the tribe's passivity is reinforced in the relation F – H. The active personality of the hero is expressed in the opposition C – A Ā.

As in the other sections, I → $\tilde{C}$; here however the implication is divided up into I → $\tilde{C}$ and I → $\tilde{C}$ <E>.

Section 4 The struggle with nature

The penultimate part of the plot – the hero's struggle with nature – is presented differently in each of the three myths.

We begin with an analysis of the most frequently repeated variations contained in myths α and β. They are as follows:

Table 10 **Structure of section 4 of myths α and β**

Myth α		Myth β				
	I					
C*	I		C*	I	I	I
C*	I		C*	I		
C*	I		C*	H	I	|d| I
	I		A			

The structure of this section in both myths is fundamentally the same. The story is related abruptly, like a postscript, as it were, to the hero's main exploits. In both variants there are three basic challenges; that from the ferocious beasts, from the forest and from the mountains. The hero gains his victory over them instantly, without superfluous comment. We note only one interesting exception; in myth β, while the hero drives back the mountains which threaten to push his village into the ocean, the whole earth reverberates.

The structure of this section is very different in myth γ. There the section which narrates the hero's struggle with the forest and the mountains (the challenge from the ferocious beasts is missing) occupies the most space.

The section is composed of two unequal parts. In the first we find the opposition C – A Ā. Properly speaking, this first part contains no repetitions, being on the whole constructed according

Table 11 Structure of section 4 of myth γ

Ā	A	A	C	Dp	D	E	I	G	H
			C*					G	H
	A		C	Dp			I		
Ā		A	C			E			
			C*					G	
A									H
A								G|đ|	
					D	E			
A								G|đ|	H
A			C						H
						E			
							I		
A			C <Ẽ>						

to our second principle of expansion. The appearance of E at the end of this part is interesting. It anticipates, so to speak, the basic conflict in the second part, which can be represented by the following combination:

A D E $\longleftrightarrow$ I
C H G |d|$\longleftrightarrow$Č

We do not find Ā here any more. The hero's implied, apparent indifference is contrasted to H, the tribe's desperation over its inability to accept the challenge of the natural elements. This apparent incapacity is heightened by repetitions. It is stressed not only because it is inherent in the character of the other members of the hero's tribe (see H in the third section), but also because the task seems insurmountable. G, the attack on the mountains, is accompanied by earthquakes, |d|. The tribe seems doomed to ruin. The hero has to face the most terrible ordeal. And at this point the character of E changes. Supernatural aid does not come to the hero spontaneously; he prays to the *gagaru*, his magical helper, to give him the power of his grandfather to control the mountains and demonstrate his strength to the tribe. The hero pushes back the mountains only when endowed with the magic power. On the surface, the situation recalls the motifs of the three sections of myth β, but its meaning is actually different. It is not weakness or desperation (or some other personal emotion) which compels the hero to ask help, but his awareness of the uniqueness of the situation and of its absolute importance.

The conclusion of this section reveals the final modification of the tribe's attitude toward the hero. There was already a $\check{C}$ at the end of Section 3. But here the modified attitude to the hero is decisive. 'All were persuaded that he was more powerful than any shaman and that his power had supernatural origins.'

Section 5 Conclusion

The conclusion of the three variants has a different structure than the other sections. It contains neither the 'hero-tribe' opposition nor the 'failure of the tribe-success of the hero' opposition. The narrative plan of the finale is not organic to the story of the 'outcast hero'. In myths α and β the motif of the strong man who balances the earth on a pole actually appears at the beginning of the Conclusion, even before $\vec{E}$ which in fact constitutes the beginning of the motif.

In myth α the main part of the conclusion is focused on the explanation of the hero's exploit. This information is given by a supernatural messenger who has come to look for the hero. The hero's grandfather, whose place the hero must take, tells what fate awaits the hero. And finally, the same myth contains a detailed account of the exploit which is also an explanation of all the hero's past behaviour. This explanation, which has no counterpart in myths β and γ, is very important for an interpretation of the myth.

In myths β and γ the relation $\bar{A} - \check{C}$ occurs. That is, when the magical boat comes to take the hero away, he loses all his connotations as an 'outcast' and the tribe recognizes once and for all his great magic powers. This relation recalls analogous motifs of other Indians myths about the 'outcast hero'. However, the conclusions of those myths are quite different.

The hero does not remain within the social milieu of his tribe. His new social condition – that of being the most powerful man in the whole world – does not have a place within the confines of the tribe. We should, then, note that in myth α we do not find the final motif $\check{C}$. The tribe therefore does not ever discover the hero's true nature. Here is how the narrator summarizes and explains the hero's behaviour.

236 The Semantics of Myth

It is necessary to point out that the youth was from the beginning under the influence of the old man (the grandfather who supported the earth). The old man caused him to be always happy with his company and not to want the companionship of others. Thus, the young man was to get used to the solitude which accompanied his new obligations. He avoided friends and never showed any desire to approach a woman. Though women often tried to gain his favour, he avoided them. Therefore he was fully satisfied when he assumed his new duties.

Here we find an explanation completely based on the hero's behaviour. The tribe did not have anything to do with the hero's future duties. Essentially, the hero does not depend in any way on the tribe, being from the beginning under magical protection. Because of this, $\bar{C}$ is not essential in the structure of this section.

We shall now examine the differences between myth β and myth γ. Whereas in myth α we have continually singled out the passive personality of the hero, in myths β and γ the hero has given proof of individualistic activity. In these myths, therefore, the $\bar{A} - \bar{C}$ relation appears. Finally, myth γ goes even further in this direction. As will be remembered, the individualistic activity of the hero in myth γ was marked by an aggressive, self-affirming character. The natural result of this is the appearance of M, the moral: 'Do not mock those whom you do not understand. You have mocked me. Do not do it again in future.'

In this manner the structure of the Conclusion is dependent on the completion of the structure of the earlier sections of the myth. We can therefore summarize the fundamental particulars of the three myths, as they have emerged from the plot analysis.

From this comparison it is possible to see that in the three variants the hero is placed in various semantic relations with the same surroundings. This is shown both in the content of the predicates which describe the action in the myths, and in the construction of the plot.

Above all, it becomes obvious that Randall's interpretation incompletely describes the semantic relations of myths α, β and γ.

In the first place, she sets out the character of the 'outcast hero' differently. She writes that

The Indian's emotions are given tangible expression, and they are always either shame, sorrow, sulkiness, or a desire for suicide after ridicule. . . . There is rarely any intermediate form of emotion attributed

Table 12 Basic Semantic Oppositions of Myths α, β and γ

	Myth α	Myth β	Myth γ
Functional activity of the hero	The hero triumphs easily and inevitably throughout the myth. His power does not depend on the tribe. The main thing in the hero's actions is his aims.	The hero has to strive to triumph, because of the difficulty of the task. The hero's power manifests itself only towards the end of the myth. Success is just as important as prestige.	The hero triumphs easily, but only after having overcome the tribe's great opposition. The hero's power is continually questioned by the tribe. Prestige is the main aim of his activity.
Functional activity of the tribe	Failure in all activities. The hero saves the tribe from famine, dishonour and ruin.	Some success. Initially, the hero's brothers triumph in contests. Later the hero saves the tribe from dishonour, famine and ruin.	The tribe is not able to accept the challenge. The difficulty of the contest frightens the hero's tribe. The tribe appropriates for itself the fruits of the hero's activity.
Personality of the hero	Apathy, solitude, indifference, sleepiness.	The hero is drowsy and apathetic, but still active during his failure; he despairs and weeps.	The hero shows apparent indifference and apathy. He is often angry and aggressive. After his victory he is contented.
Personality of the tribe	The tribe's antipathy to the hero is contrasted with his youngest uncle's sympathy. The tribe's attitude is actively hostile.	The hero is continually mocked by his successful brothers. No one shows sympathy for him.	The whole tribe scorns the hero and they obstruct his activities.

	Myth α	Myth β	Myth γ
Role of the supernatural forces	In the course of the myth the hero receives help in training. It is he who conquers but he is constantly under supernatural protection.	The determining agent in every difficult moment. The hero could not win without the help of the supernatural powers.	Not essential for the whole myth, as the hero achieves his victory by himself. But decisive for the repulsion of the natural elements.
Filth	Apparent; the hero seems to urinate on himself.	Ambivalent; the wet bed denotes the hero's filth. Lichens seem to be growing on the hero's face.	Real; the hero is filthy and wets himself in his sleep.
Attitude to training	The hero does not take part in the communal training. Trains secretly.	Does not take part in the communal training. Trains secretly.	Does not take part in the communal training. Trains secretly.
Relation with the ashes of the fire	Sleeps by the fire.	Sleeps by the fire.	Sleeps by the fire.
Modification of the tribe's attitude to the hero	Each of the hero's successes is accompanied by a modification of the tribe's attitude. Each time, however, their attitude returns to hostility. C̄ does not recur at the end of the myth.	Each of the hero's successes is accompanied by a modification of the tribe's attitude. Each time, however, their attitude returns to hostility. C̄ recurs at the end of the myth.	Each of the hero's successes is accompanied by a modification of the tribe's attitude. Each time, however, their attitude returns to hostility. C̄ recurs at the end of the myth.

either to the main protagonist or to the other mythological characters. Moreover there is rarely a myth in which the protagonists evince no emotion (Randall, 1949, p. 254).

All this is only partly true. In fact the hero continually excites the banter and scorn of the tribe and yet in each of the three myths the hero's apparent or real apathy, his indifference and general absence of emotion are stressed. Ā (Ã) and C̄ (C̃), as we have repeatedly emhasized, have a totally different character in Randall's interpretation and in the semantic characterization given here of the three myths.

In Randall, Ā signifies the 'attainment of riches', 'liberation from ugliness', 'marriage with a woman with whom it was formerly impossible to marry'. In our myths the accent is not placed on these aspects of Ā. The hero's rejection, shown in the tribe's antipathy toward him, does not disappear after the hero's victory; and neither do the apathy or the filth (whether apparent or real). The hero is not transfigured. In this sense, myths α, β and γ contradict the entire interpretation given by Randall as follows:

Cinderella is as good when she is the beautiful bride as she is when she is the poor servant, and the 'dumb' son is not necessarily any 'brighter' when he becomes king. . . . But the north-west coast 'dirty boy' trains to cure his scabby skin, and then is rewarded as chief; or the deserted, lazy boy industriously hunts and feeds his grandmother and wife. Then the villagers recognize his achievements and award him a position of leadership (Randall, 1949, p. 254).

Though the hero of our myths trains himself, it is not with the aim of being freed from his state of rejection. He does not become in some sense better, more acceptable to the tribe. Only myth γ contains the contrast between his personal activity of self-affirmation and the tribe's antipathy. This is the only myth which fits partially into Randall's scheme, and then only in so far as the constant redefining of the hero's actions is concerned. According to Randall, the basic aim, conscious and explicit, of the protagonist's behaviour in all of the myths she analysed is to gain prestige. I do not see this goal as fundamental to our myths and moreover, it is completely absent in myth α. I must stress that C̄ appears early in the course of the story. In myths α and β it comes after the first I and in myth γ after the second I. According to Randall's scheme, at this point the story should end. The repeating cycles A C I Č could be considered as more or less typical mythic repetitions (see Lévi-Strauss, 1955, for discussion of the role of repetitions in narrative motifs in myth, especially his emphasis on and detailing of the paradigmatic structure of myth). The absence of the motifs of the return, reintegration and final triumph of the hero within the tribe (all of which are typical in myths of the 'outcast hero') leads me to think that the repetition of A C I Č does have a significance in the development of the plot. In all our three myths, C is not the only motif which indicates the resolution of a mythological conflict (the opposition between the hero's rejection and the tribe's negative attitude to him, on the one hand, and between the termination of the rejection and the hero's triumph, on the other). The motif X appears alongside Č in these myths and this is fundamental in the narrative chain, both from the point of view of the hero's behaviour (myth α) and from the point of view of the modification of the tribe's negative attitude toward the hero (myth γ, in which X→Č). Consequently the role of Ā as it figures in Randall's scheme (liberation of the hero from the state of rejection) is reinforced not by I, which can be followed by Cs (impossible in Randall's scheme), but by X. Is the placing of X in the plot fortuitous? As we have seen, Č in this scheme is fortuitous. It can appear after any I, as in the second and third sections of myths α and β; can appear in opposition to a single I, as in myth γ, but cannot appear after I in the fourth section of myths α and β. In any case, Č does not appear only once in the Conclusion, as Randall maintains, but turns up many times. X, on the other hand, is rare. It appears solely in the fifth section and its repetitions do not have the same significance as those of Č. In the fifth section, X, referring to the hero, does not come until after Ē and their repetitions cannot follow each other. In this way we see that the position of X in the scheme is not random. It can be properly placed only at the end of the tale, and thus fulfils the function of a concluding formula which explains and resolves the central conflict.

Such a role of X cannot be justified in terms of Randall's proposed interpretation. Rather, the role of X can be explained by advancing the hypothesis that the hero has a double character.

In fact, as we have seen, an explanation in terms of the rejection–reintegration dichotomy does not fully explain particular details of these myths. Is it feasible to propose a different, though related, interpretation of the link between these three myths and the initiation ceremony? At first sight it would seem natural to pose this problem. In all three myths one of the hero's characteristics is his refusal to train with his brothers. This training has the clear appearance of an initiation rite. In the myths this training, which comprises a bath, ritual and physical purification and physical abstinence, has the purpose of preparing the participant for the sea-lion hunt or for competition with other tribes. According to various researchers (Garfield, 1951; Leechman, 1956), this same preparation was obligatory for adolescents during the period of sexual maturation. Only through a rigid course of training, which consisted of a daily bath, particularly in winter, flogging with a special whip made from a larch or cedar switch, purification by means of a purgative and fasting, could the adolescent become ritually and physically clean enough to receive help from his spiritual guardian. The idea of cleanliness or purity plays a predominant part in any magic act. One must be clean not only to receive supernatural protection, but also to perform any important action.

In this way initiation (or an analogous ritual) is clearly and most directly discernable in our myths. However, this relation is too direct, the interpretation being based on the simple indication of it. In stories of the Cinderella variety or in Russian stories about magic, a reconstruction of the rite of initiation is necessary in order to establish the link between the story plot and the rite. Because the reconstructed rite is external to the myth, the link consequently acquires an effective semantic value, since it is a relation between the symbol and an object situated in another system. In our case, however, the indication of a similar relation is not meaningful since the myths themselves are the account of the initiation. Consequently, we must look elsewhere for the significance of these myths; in the hero's attitude towards the initiation and in the confrontation between his attitude and the ethical values of the tribe as a whole. This will then indicate the duality of the hero's character and the duality of the plot.

The structure of the plot can be presented in the following way.

The hero is filthy (impure) but scorns purification, which earns him the rejection of the group. He suffers from this, begins to train secretly, eventually triumphs and gains the respect of the tribe. This is the way the narrative scheme of a number of myths cited by Randall works (Myths 1b, 1e, 3a, 3e of the section, 'The Filthy Boy'). Within such a scheme the rejection can be considered a just punishment for refusing to be purified, and the secret purification, a consequence of the rejection. In spite of taking place in secret, the purification retains all its beneficent value, and the hero triumphs.

In the myths which we have examined it is certainly possible to extract a similar meaning. In fact, the hero's disdaining of the training is only apparent. An overt refusal of the purification rite is never found. Such a refusal would contradict too many of the tribe's values; and yet there must be conflict and here it is presented from two points of view, that of the tribe and the 'true' one. From the point of view of the tribe, the hero is dirty (impure), but from the point of view of the objective observer, he is clean (pure). This kind of ambivalence appears explicitly in myth α in the motif of the hero's filthy bed. In myth β it is given an explanation; the hero must shrink from everyone since he is predestined to carry out another task, the balancing of the earth.

For the rest, in the secret nature of the hero's training we find a correspondence with aspects of Tsimshian magical activities. We must not forget that the hero's secret training is necessarily accompanied by his encounter with a supernatural being and by subsequent aid from the latter. According to the Tsimshian value system, this is why the hero's secret training is successful, since it has resulted in aid from supernatural forces. In addition, Garfield writes that among the Tsimshian the individual, solitary quest for magic force, especially in the forest where the adolescent is not disturbed or seen by anyone, is very common. The indispensable condition for receiving personal magic force is solitude, which can be true solitude or the state of sleep or trance; that is, any interval of time when the soul has no contact with other members of the tribe. It is also essential that anyone accustomed to receiving magical help should not speak about it to anyone.

The secret nature of the hero's training is, therefore, fully in the spirit of the Tsimshian value system. The double character of the hero's training, however, also contains other traits. In myths α, β and γ there is no indication that the hero begins to train secretly because of the scorn shown him by the tribe. The secretive attitude is an organic trait, inseparable from the hero, and not the result of his conscious recognition of the necessity of being purified.

Consequently, the secret nature (and success) of the hero's purification must be situated in a varied series of semantic relationships. In particular, it must be located in the reference in myth α to the fact that it was necessary for the hero to be isolated from the tribe since he was awaiting another mission. Myth α also supplies the explanation of this requirement; the hero must be alone because otherwise he might get bored supporting the earth without any company. There is another curious element in this explanation; the hero must abstain from the company of women, in particular, as well as of the rest of the tribe. This motif recalls a peculiarity of ritual purification among the Tsimshian, sexual abstinence. Therefore, in the final analysis the hero's solitude can be interpreted as ritual purification related to other initiation rites.

I have already established the duality of the plot. On the one hand, it explicitly contains the pragmatic motif of the necessity of purification for a member of the Tsimshian tribe; this motif is supported by the indication that the hero triumphs as a result of his secret purification and of his subsequently gained magic force. On the other hand, the actual plot (secret training – hunt – contest – struggle with natural elements – conclusion) represents a second initiation rite, one to which the hero is subject not as a member of the tribe but as a supernatural being. The plot of the myths is therefore related semantically to an initiation rite though not to the one with which it is directly concerned. This interpretation of the plot which I propose is supported by the introduction of X, that is, by the demonstration of the hero's success in accomplishing the tasks which follow his preliminary initiation. Furthermore, in myths β and γ there is the motif $\bar{C}<E>$, the conscious realization by members of the tribe that the hero is a supernatural being.

If we accept that the plot is concerned with the initiation rite of a supernatural being, then the identical order in which the sections of the three myths are arranged becomes understandable. In effect, this initiation proceeds according to growing difficulty

It begins with the tribal initiations, which constitute the first and easiest, though nevertheless absolutely necessary, stage. Then comes the hunt, that is, the providing of the tribe with all that is necessary for life. Then comes contest (or a war, as indicated in Boas's résumé of the same Tsimshian myth, cited by Randall) in order to defend and safeguard the tribe's prestige. (It is interesting to note that the episode where the tribe's prestige is defended occurs in all three variants, while the provision of necessities for the tribe occurs as a narrative section only in myth β.) And finally, the struggle with the natural elements, the ferocious beasts, the forest and the mountains. This last undertaking entails in myth γ a special magic force and represents the apogee of the hero's achievements.

The plot order cannot be altered since to pass through any one stage it is first necessary to pass through the one which precedes it. Apparently the episodes can all be dropped except one, which can be any one of the five; but their order must remain the same, because it reflects the sequence of the difficulties which are overcome, and the order in which all reality is conquered.

The double nature of the hero also explains the repetition of Č, in the course of the plot. Č has to be repeated since the triumph of the hero as a member of the tribe demands the modification of the tribe's attitude towards him, though the definitive Č cannot, naturally, appear until the hero has passed through all the stages of the initiation which is imposed on him as a supernatural being. On the other hand, for the hero as supernatural being, Č has minimal importance. It is here that he differs from other 'outcast heroes'.

Let us note that the apathetic and impure hero, who lies in the ashes and reveals himself powerful, can be found in other mythologies. I borrow some examples from Meletinski's work on the origin of heroic poetry (1955). According to Bogaraz, the 'strongest' among the Čukči are the shamans, who are marked by magical physical abnormalities (scabs, warts, effeminacy) (Meletinski, 1955, p. 79). In the Čukči legends exceptional physical strength acquired during the course of systematic training replaces, in the hero, the 'tests' imposed on shamans. Vytryva's prolonged repose, in which he is oblivious to everything, hides not relations with spirits, as in the legends of shamans, but a secret training, an acquiring of power (p. 91).

Among the Narty, Batradz

is sometimes given the traits of a 'sedentary', who gradually builds up his power, and he then takes on the appearance of the 'unpromising' democratic hero of fables. He is filthy, grovelling in ashes and dung. He is a good-for-nothing (p. 200).

In Jakuta epic poetry, the hero's prodigious origin is sometimes marked by his temporary ugliness (p. 324).

In our myths the hero is repeatedly associated with the ashes of the fire. Let us look at the variants of these myths cited by Boas (1902, p. 112). Generally, neither the initiation ritual, nor the struggle with the natural elements, nor the contest are referred to in them and moreover, the supporting of the earth on a pole, as the life purpose of the hero, is not mentioned at all. The internal content of the variants is summarized by Boas in the statement, 'a man attains supernatural strength by sleeping at the edge of a smoke-hole'. The myth is entitled Amàlá (cf. Amaelk in Barbeau, the name of the hero of myth β), a word which is translated as *smoke-hole*.

In fact, if presented in such an abbreviated form, the myth contains only the above-mentioned motif.

We know that among the Tsimshian, Haida and Tlingit Indians, ideas of magic power were connected with fire and ashes. Barbeau quotes as an example a Haida myth in which magical power is attained as a result of leaping into the fire (1953, p. 305). The rite of initiation among the Tsimshian called for an ordeal by fire, during which the adolescents had to stand very near the flames. The Tlingit burnt their slaves and scattered their ashes on the totem poles of their new homes; they believed that these ashes protected the home from malevolent forces (Leechman, 1956, p. 305).

It is interesting to note that among the Indians of the Canadian Pacific coast it is particularly the Tsimshian, Tlingit and Haida who cremated their dead, and the Tlingit also preserved the ashes in special caskets. The mourning ceremony required the relatives of the dead to smear their faces with ashes from the funeral pyre (p. 322).

It is consequently clear that there was full awareness of the ritual and magical role of fire and ashes in the mythological and social value system of north-west Canadian Indians, particularly among the Tsimshian.

Thompson, in his index of mythological plots, cites many examples of ashes developing a positive magic power (magic ashes render invisible D 1361.44, protect D 1380.8, cure D 1500.46, resuscitate E 42, E 66.1, E 132, and so on). There are also cases in which the ashes possess a negative force or are the result of a negative force (one instance is money being changed to ashes). This ambivalent role of ashes in mythology is explained, in my opinion, by its double nature. From one point of view the ashes are a result of the fire (cf. purificatory, magical nature of fire in D 1733.1, D 1797, etc., in Thompson's index). From another, it is filth, and thus by definition ambivalent. For being undesirable and negative, filth often possesses magic power. This agrees perfectly with Lévi-Strauss's observations on the magical role of garbage and ashes (1955). I wish only to refer to the point at which Lévi-Strauss speaks of the role played by ashes in mediating between the fire and the roof (in Indian mythology in particular).

The hero's sleeping outdoors instead of in the house is repeatedly stressed in myths α, β and γ and in Boas's summaries (see this beginning of a myth in Boas; 'There was a man who never slept in his house. He always lay by the smoke-hole'). The ashes' role in mediating between the fire and filth therefore seems clear.

Our Tsimshian myths also contain an indication of a link between the hero and his own waste (urine). We showed earlier that this relation could be explicit (myth γ) or implicit (myth α). It is none the less characteristic of all three myths that from the point of view of the tribe the hero is associated with his own excreta. The magical role of waste, especially of urine, is stressed both overtly and implicitly in many mythologies (cf. Thompson; bringing back to life through the medium of urine in E 29.6, magical role of excrement and urine in D 1002 and D 1002.1). On the other hand, what could be called the chthonic nature of filth is also interesting. In many primitive mythologies and especially in the mythology of North American Indians, the earth is created from the body of the creator or from his excretions (urine, faeces, sweat, dirt from his fingernails), or from mud and dust (Dundes, 1962).

It seems to me that the hero also has a chthonic nature because the whole earth trembles during his encounter with the mountains, and it also trembles when the mountains advance on the hero's village (myth γ) and when the old man, the hero's grandfather or uncle, changes position. The hero cannot be separated from the earth or from his post (myths β and γ); he also sleeps on the earth. He shows, therefore, clear signs of a relation with the earth, and his relation with his own filth (urine, ashes wetted with his urine) reinforces his chthonic nature. Indeed, his chthonic characteristics, which can be reconstructed from comparison with the heroes of other myths, explain why he was chosen to support the earth and why he had to undergo a second initiation.

In this way, at the base of all three variants, we find a combination of two types of mythological story; that of the 'outcast hero', typical of North American Indian mythology, and that of the initiation of supernatural beings with chthonic traits. Naturally, such an arrangement is quite conventional, though in fact the two themes are inseparable, particularly since the hero remains the same. The three variants stress the two aspects of the plot differently. The more chthonic hero is probably the one in myth α. This would account for the appearance of X, which is intended to clear up the puzzles of the hero's behaviour. The account given of the hero, however, is sufficiently esoteric for there to be no clear indications in the myth of his chthonic qualities. On the other hand, myths β and γ (especially myth γ) develop the theme of the 'outcast hero' far more coherently, and consequently need to give explicit indications of the relation between the hero and the earth ($|d|$) in order to change the normal course of the plot of the 'outcast hero'.

References

Barbeau, M. (1961), *Tsimshian Texts*, Department of Northern Affairs and National Resources.

BARBEAU, M. (1953), *Haida Myths Illustrated in Argillite Carvings*, National Museum of Canada.

BOAS, F. (1898), *The Mythology of the Bella Coola Indians*, American Museum of Natural History.

BOAS, F. (1902), *Tsimshian Texts*, Washington Government Printing Office.

DUNDES, A. (1962), 'Earth diver: creation of the mythopoeic male', *Amer. Anthropol.*, vol. 64, pp. 1032–51.

GARFIELD, V. E. (1951), *The Tsimshian: Their Arts and Music*, Augustine.

LEECHMAN, D. (1956), *The Native Tribes of Canada*, Gage.

LÉVI-STRAUSS, C. (1955), 'The structural study of myth', in Thomas A. Seboek (ed.), *Myth: A Symposium*, Indiana University Press.

MELETINSKIJ, E. M. (1963), 'Proischozdenie geroiceskogo esposa', *Rannie formy i archaiceskie pamjatniki*, Moscow.

PROPP, V. (1928), *Morfologija skazki*, Leningrad; *Morphology of the Folk Tale*, American Folklore Society, 1968.

PROPP, V. (1945), *Istorideskie Korni, Roliebnoj*, Leningrad.

RANDALL, B. U. (1949), 'The Cinderella theme in North-West Indian folklore', in M. W. Smith (ed.), *Indians of the Urban North-West*, Columbia University Press.

SPENSER, K. (1957), *Mythology and Values*, American Folklore Society.

SWANTON, J. R. (1909), *Thigit Myths and Texts*, Washington Government Printing Offices.

THOMPSON, S. (1955–8), *Motif-Index of Folk Literature*, Indiana University Press.

Table of symbols for Reading 13

$\triangle$	man
$\bigcirc$	woman

$\triangle = \bigcirc$ marriage (disjunction of marriage: $\neq$)

$\begin{matrix} \triangle \\ \triangle \end{matrix}$ $\begin{matrix} \bigcirc \\ \bigcirc \end{matrix}$ father and son, mother and daughter, etc.

$\longrightarrow$ is transformed into

$\left\{ \begin{matrix} : \\ :: \end{matrix} \right.$ is to ...
as ...

$/$ contrast

$\left\{ \begin{matrix} \equiv \\ \not\equiv \end{matrix} \right.$ congruence, homology, correspondence
noncongruence, nonhomology, noncorrespondence

$\left\{ \begin{matrix} = \\ \neq \end{matrix} \right.$ identity
difference

$\approx$ isomorphism

f function

$x^{(-1)}$ inverted x

$+, -$ these signs are used with various connotations depending on the context: plus, minus; presence, absence; first or second term of a pair of opposites

13 Claude Lévi-Strauss

The Raw and the Cooked

Excerpts from Claude Lévi-Strauss, *The Raw and the Cooked*, translated by John and Doreen Weightman, Jonathan Cape, 1969; Harper & Row, 1969, pp. 35–73 and 136–95.[1]

Bororo song
The bird-nester's aria

The following is one of many myths told by the Bororo Indians of central Brazil, whose territory used to extend from the upper reaches of the Paraguay River to beyond the valley of the Araguaya:

M_1 *(key myth). Bororo: o xibae e iari. 'The macaws and their nest'*

In olden times the women used to go into the forest to gather the palms used in the making of *ba*. These were penis sheaths which were presented to adolescents at their initiation ceremony. One youth secretly followed his mother, caught her unawares, and raped her.

When the woman returned from the forest, her husband noticed feathers caught in her bark-cloth belt, which were similar to those worn by youths as an adornment. Suspecting that something untoward had occurred, he decreed that a dance should take place in order to find out which youth was wearing a similar adornment. But to his amazement he discovered that his son was the only one. The man ordered another dance, with the same result.

Convinced now of his misfortune and anxious to avenge himself, he

1. The following abridged version of the first two hundred pages of the first volume of *Mythologiques* will hopefully serve as a guide to Lévi-Strauss's analytic operations. The aim is to bring out the essential steps of the author's procedure by reducing contentual aspects to a minimum. Lévi-Strauss's structural approach leads him to map out the transformations through which transformers make possible the passage from a myth concerned, among other things, with wind and rain, to a group of variants dealing with the origin of fire (see, in the excerpt, especially the three last paragraphs of '2nd Movement: Ge', the five paragraphs before M_{120}, and the last section, Part Four). The master lines of the approach were already defined in chapters 11 and 12 of *Structural Anthropology*, originally written, respectively, in 1955 and 1956 [Ed.].

sent his son to the 'nest' of souls, with instructions to bring back the great dance rattle (*bapo*), which he coveted. The young man consulted his grandmother who revealed to him the mortal danger that such an undertaking involved; she advised him to obtain the help of the hummingbird.

When the hero, accompanied by the hummingbird, reached the aquatic region of souls, he waited on the shore, while the hummingbird deftly stole the rattle by cutting the short cord from which it was hanging. The instrument fell into the water, making a loud noise – *jo*. Alerted by this noise, the souls fired arrows from their bows. But the hummingbird flew so fast that he reached the shore safe and sound with the stolen rattle.

The father than ordered his son to fetch the small rattle belonging to the souls; and the same episode was repeated, with the same details, only this time the helpful animal was the quick flying juriti (*Leptoptila* species, a kind of dove). During a third expedition, the young man stole some buttore; these are jingling bells made from the hoofs of the caititu (*Dicotyles torquatus*, a type of wild pig), which are strung on a piece of rope and worn as anklets. He was helped by the large grasshopper (*Acridium cristatum*, Albisetti and Vertvelli, 1962, vol. 1 p. 780), which flew more slowly than the birds so that the arrows pierced it several times but did not kill it.

Furious at the foiling of his plans, the father invited his son to come with him to capture the macaws, which were nesting in the face of a cliff. The grandmother did not know how to ward off this fresh danger, but gave her grandson a magic wand to which he could cling if he happened to fall.

The two men arrived at the foot of the rock; the father erected a long pole and ordered his son to climb it. The latter had hardly reached the nests when the father knocked the pole down; the boy only just had time to thrust the wand into a crevice. He remained suspended in the void, crying for help, while the father went off.

Our hero noticed a creeper within reach of his hand; he grasped hold of it and with difficulty dragged himself to the top of the rock. After a rest he set out to look for food, made a bow and arrows out of branches, and hunted the lizards which abounded on the plateau. He killed a lot of them and hooked the surplus ones to his belt and to the strips of cotton wound round his legs and ankles. But the dead lizards went bad and gave off such a vile smell that the hero fainted. The vultures (*Cathartes urubu, Coragyps atratus foetens*) fell upon him, devoured first of all the lizards, and then attacked the body of the unfortunate youth, beginning with his buttocks. Pain restored him to consciousness, and the hero drove off his attackers which, however, had completely gnawed away his hindquarters. Having eaten their fill, the birds were prepared to save his life; taking hold of his belt and the strips of cotton round his arms and legs with their beaks, they lifted him into the air and deposited him gently at the foot of the mountain.

The hero regained consciousness 'as if he were awakening from a dream'. He was hungry and ate wild fruits but noticed that since he had no rectum, he was unable to retain the food, which passed through his body without even being digested. The youth was at first non-plussed and then remembered a tale told him by his grandmother, in which the hero solved the same problem by molding for himself an artificial behind out of dough made from pounded tubers.

After making his body whole again by this means and eating his fill, he returned to his village, only to find that it had been abandoned. He wandered around for a long time looking for his family. One day he spotted foot and stick marks, which he recognized as being those of his grandmother. He followed the tracks but, being anxious not to reveal his presence, he took on the appearance of a lizard, whose antics fascinated the old woman and her other grandson, the hero's younger brother. Finally, after a long interval, he decided to reveal himself to them. (In order to re-establish contact with his grandmother, the hero went through a series of transformations, turning himself into four birds and a butterfly, all unidentified; Colbacchini, 1925, pp. 235–6).

On that particular night there was a violent wind accompanied by a thunder storm which put out all the fires in the village except the grandmother's. Next morning everybody came and asked her for hot embers, in particular the second wife of the father who had tried to kill his son. She recognized her stepson, who was supposed to be dead, and ran to warn her husband. As if there were nothing wrong, the latter picked up his ceremonial rattle and welcomed his son with the songs of greeting for returned travelers.

However, the hero was full of thoughts of revenge. One day while he was walking in the forest with his little brother, he broke off a branch of the api tree, which was shaped like a deer's antler. The child, acting on his elder brother's instructions, then managed to make the father promise to order a collective hunt; in the guise of a mea, a small rodent, he secretly kept watch to discover where their father was lying in wait for the game. The hero then donned the false antlers, changed into a deer, and rushed at his father with such ferocity that he impaled him on the horns. Without stopping, he galloped toward a lake, into which he dropped his victim, who was immediately devoured by the Buiogoe spirits who are carnivorous fish. All that remained after the gruesome feast were the bare bones which lay on the bottom of the lake, and the lungs which floated on the surface in the form of aquatic plants, whose leaves, it is said, resemble lungs.

When he returned to the village, the hero took his revenge on his father's wives (one of whom was his own mother).

This myth provides the theme of a song, called *xobogeu*, belonging to the Paiwe clan of which the hero was a member (Colbacchini and Albisetti, 1942, pp. 224–9, 343–7).

An older version ends as follows. The hero declared: 'I no longer want to live with the Orarimugu who have ill-treated me, and in order to have my revenge on them and my father, I shall send them wind, cold and rain.' Then he took his grandmother into a beautiful and distant land, and returned to punish the Indians as he said he would (Colbacchini, 1925, p. 236). [...]

Ge variations (six arias followed by a recitative)

The story of the bird-nester, which forms the central part of the key myth, occurs in an initial position in the case of the Ge, in the myth about the origin of fire, which is found in all the central and eastern Ge tribes that have been studied up to the present.

I shall begin with the versions peculiar to the northern group, the Kayapo, who may be the Kaiamodogue previously mentioned (p. 60 n. 11; cf. Colbacchini, 1925, p. 125, n. 2), although the tendency nowadays is to identify the latter with the Shavante (Albisetti and Vertvelli, 1962, vol. 1, p. 702).

First variation

M₇. Kayapo-Gorotire. 'The Origin of Fire.'

Noticing that a pair of macaws had built their nest on top of a steep rock, an Indian took his young brother-in-law, Botoque, with him to help him to capture the nestlings. He made Botoque climb up an improvised ladder; but when the boy got up to the nest, he said that he could find only two eggs. (It is not clear whether he was lying or telling the truth.) His brother-in-law insisted that he should take them; but as the eggs fell down, they changed into stones which hurt the older man's hand. This made him furious, with the result that he dismantled the ladder and went away, not realizing that the birds were enchanted (*oaianga*) (?).

Botoque remained caught on top of the rock for several days. He grew thin: hunger and thirst obliged him to eat his own excrement. Eventually he noticed a spotted jaguar carrying a bow and arrow and all kinds of game. He would have liked to call out to it for help, but fear kept him silent.

The jaguar saw the hero's shadow on the ground and, after trying in vain to catch it, looked up, asked what had happened, repaired the ladder, and invited Botoque to come down. The latter was afraid and hesitated a long time; in the end he made up his mind, and the jaguar, in friendly fashion, suggested that if he would sit astride its back, it would take him to its home to have a meal of grilled meat. But the young man did not understand the meaning of the word 'grilled' because in those days, the Indians were unacquainted with fire and ate their meat raw.

At the jaguar's home the hero saw a big jatoba trunk burning; beside it was a pile of stones such as the Indians now use to build their earth ovens (*ki*). He ate his first meal of cooked meat.

But the jaguar's wife, who was an Indian, disliked the young man and referred to him as *me-on-kra-tum* 'foreign, or abandoned, son'; in spite of this, the jaguar, being childless, decided to adopt him.

Each day the jaguar went off to hunt, leaving the adopted son with the wife whose aversion for him steadily increased; she gave him only old wizened pieces of meat to eat, and leaves. When the boy complained, she scratched his face, and the poor child had to take refuge in the forest.

The jaguar scolded the wife, but in vain. One day it gave Botoque a brand new bow and some arrows, taught him how to use them, and advised him to use them against the woman, should the need arise. Botoque killed her by shooting an arrow into her breast. He fled in terror, taking with him the weapons and a piece of grilled meat.

He reached his village in the middle of the night, groped his way to his mother's bed, and had some difficulty in making his identity known (because he was thought to be dead); he told his tale and shared the meat. The Indians decided to get possession of the fire.

When they arrived at the jaguar's home, there was no one there; and since the wife was dead, the game caught the day before had not been cooked. The Indians roasted it and took away the fire. For the very first time it was possible to have light in the village at night, to eat cooked meat, and to warm oneself at a hearth.

But the jaguar, incensed by the ingratitude of its adopted son, who had stolen 'fire and the secret of the bow and arrow', was to remain full of hatred for all living creatures, especially human beings. Now only the reflection of fire could be seen in its eyes. It used its fangs for hunting and ate its meat raw, having solemnly renounced grilled meat (Banner, 1957, pp. 42–4).

Second variation

M₈. Kayapo-Kubenkranken. 'The origin of fire'

Formerly, men did not know how to make fire. When they killed game, they cut the flesh into thin strips, which they laid out on stones to dry in the sun. They also ate rotten wood.

One day a man noticed two macaws coming out of a hole in a cliff. To get at their nest, he made his young brother-in-law (his wife's brother) climb a tree trunk in which he had cut foot holds. But there were nothing but round stones in the nest. An argument ensued, degenerating into a quarrel, which ended as in the previous version. In this case, however, it seems that the lad, annoyed by his brother-in-law's taunts, threw the stones deliberately and wounded him.

In response to his wife's anxious inquiries, the man said the boy must have got lost, and to allay suspicion, he pretended to go and look for him. Meanwhile, suffering extreme hunger and thirst, the hero was reduced to eating his excrement and drinking his urine. He was nothing but skin and bone when a jaguar came along carrying a caititu pig on his shoulders; the animal noticed the boy's shadow and tried to catch it. On each occasion the hero moved back and the shadow disappeared. 'The jaguar looked all round, then covering its mouth, looked up and saw the lad on the rock.' They entered into conversation.

Explanations and discussions took place as in the preceding version. The hero was too frightened to sit directly on the jaguar but agreed to bestride the caititu, which the latter was carrying on his back. They reached the jaguar's home, where his wife was busy spinning. She reproached her husband, saying 'you have brought home another's son'. Unperturbed, the jaguar announced that he was going to adopt the boy as his companion, and intended to feed him and fatten him up.

But the jaguar's wife refused to give the lad any tapir meat and allowed him only venison and threatened to scratch him at the slightest opportunity. Acting on the jaguar's advice, the boy killed the woman with the bow and arrow given him by his protector.

He went off with the jaguar's belongings: the spun cotton, the meat and the burning ash. When he reached his village, he made himself known first to his sister, then to his mother.

He was summoned to the *ngobe* 'men's house', where he related his adventures. The Indians decided to change themselves into animals to take possession of the fire: the tapir would carry the trunk, the yao bird would put out the burning ash that might be dropped on the way, while the deer would take charge of the meat, and the peccary of the spun cotton. The expedition was a success, and the men shared the fire between them (Métraux, 1960, pp. 8–10).

Third variation

M₉. *Apinaye.* '*The origin of fire*'

A man found a macaw's nest with two young birds in a high and vertical cliff. He took his little brother-in-law along, chopped down a tree, leaned it against the wall of rock, and bade the boy climb. The boy went up, but the parent birds rushed at him with fierce screams; so he got frightened. Then the man got angry, knocked the tree aside and left.

The boy, unable to descend, remained sitting by the nest for five days. He nearly died of thirst and hunger. He was completely covered by the droppings of the macaws and swallows that flew above him. Then a jaguar came past, saw the boy's shadow, and tried in vain to catch it. Then the boy spat down, and now the jaguar raised his head and saw him. They entered into conversation. The jaguar demanded to have the two young macaws, which the hero flung down to him one after the other, and which he immediately devoured. Then the jaguar brought up the tree and asked the boy to step down, promising him that he would not eat him, and that he would give him water to quench his thirst. Somewhat hesitantly, the hero complied. The jaguar took him on his back and carried him to a creek. The boy drank his fill and fell asleep. At last the jaguar pinched his arm and awakened him. He washed the dirt off him and said that, having no children, he would take him home as his son.

In the jaguar's home a huge jatoba trunk was lying on the floor and burning at one end. In those days the Indians were unacquainted with fire and ate only flesh dried in the sun. 'What is smoking there?' asked the boy. 'That is fire,' answered the jaguar. 'You will find out at night when it warms you.' Then he gave the roast meat to the boy, who ate till he fell asleep. At midnight he woke up, ate again and then again fell asleep.

Before daybreak the jaguar went hunting. The boy climbed a tree to await his return. But toward noon he got hungry, returned to the jaguar's house, and begged his wife for food. 'What!' she shouted, baring her teeth. 'Look here!' The hero cried out from fear and ran to meet the jaguar and told him of the occurrence. The jaguar scolded his wife, who excused herself, saying that she was merely jesting. But the same scene occurred again the next day.

Following the advice of the jaguar (who had made him a bow and arrow and told him to shoot at a termite's nest), the boy killed the aggressive wife. His adopted father said, 'That does not matter', gave him a lot of roast meat, and explained to him how to return to his village by following along the creek. But he was to be on guard: if a rock or the aroeira tree called him, he should answer; but was to keep still if he heard 'the gentle call of a rotten tree'.

Claude Lévi-Strauss 257

The hero moved along the brook, replied to the first two calls and, forgetting the jaguar's warnings, to the third as well. That is why men are short-lived: if the boy had answered only the first two, they would enjoy as long life as the rock and the aroeira tree.

After a while the boy again heard a call and replied to it. It was Magalon kamduré, an ogre, who tried unsuccessfully to pass himself off as the hero's father by means of various disguises (long hair, ear ornaments). When the hero finally discovered the ogre's identity, the latter wrestled with him until he was quite worn out, whereupon he put the boy in his big carrying basket.

On his way home the ogre stopped to hunt coatis. Speaking from inside the basket, the hero called to him to make a trail through the woods first, so he could carry the load better. While the ogre was doing this, the hero escaped, after weighting the basket with a heavy stone.

When the ogre reached home, he promised his children a choice morsel, even better than the coatis. But all he found in the bottom of the basket was a stone.

Meanwhile the boy had found his way back to his village, where he related his adventures. All the Indians set off to look for the fire. Various animals offered their help: the jaó was to extinguish the fallen embers; the jacu was spurned, but the tapir was considered strong enough to carry the tree. The jaguar gave them the fire. 'I have adopted your son', he said to the boy's father (Nimuendaju, 1939, pp. 154-8).

Another version (M$_{9a}$) differs in several respects from this one. The two men are a father-in-law and his son-in-law. The jaguar's wife, who is an expert spinner (cf. M$_8$), welcomes the boy first of all; and when she starts to threaten him, he kills her on his own initiative. His action is disapproved of by the jaguar, who does not believe in his wife's wickedness. The three calls that are then mentioned in the story are uttered, the first by the jaguar himself who from afar guides the hero back to his village; the others by stone and rotten wood; but we are not told how the hero reacts to the last two calls. When the Indians arrive in search of the fire, the jaguar is even more friendly than in the previous version, since it is he who engages the services of the helpful animals. He objects to the caititus and the queixadas but agrees that the tapirs should transport the log, while the birds pick up the fallen embers (Oliveira, 1930, pp. 75-80).

As can be seen, the version above maintains the bond of affinity and age difference between the two men; and these, as will subsequently appear, are the invariant features of the set.

But at first glance we have here such an unexpected inversion of the functions of the 'wife-giver' and the 'taker' that we are tempted to suppose that there must be some linguistic error. As a matter of fact, the narrative was given directly in Portuguese by an Apinaye Indian who, together with three companions, had come to Belem to see the authorities. In every case where it is possible to make a comparison with texts that Nimuendaju collected in the field about the same time, it is noticeable that the versions by the Belem Apinaye, although more long-winded, contain less information (cf. p. 174). It is significant, however, that the jaguar's wife appears less hostile in M_{9a} than in all the other versions, and that the jaguar is even more friendly than in M_9, where he was already extremely friendly: although he does not believe his wife to be guilty, he bears the hero no grudge for having killed her; he shows great eagerness to give the Indians fire and organizes its transport himself.

Once this has been noted, the anomaly pointed out in the preceding paragraph becomes clearer. Among the Apinaye, as among other matrilineal and matrilocal communities, the wife's father is not, properly speaking, a 'giver'. This role falls rather to the young girl's brothers, who furthermore do not so much 'give' their sister to her future husband as 'take' the latter and compel him to accept, simultaneously, marriage and matrilocal residence (Nimuendaju, 1939, p. 80). In these conditions the father-in-law–son-in-law relation in M_{9a} appears less like an inverted form of affinity than as a distended form, since it occurs, as it were, at two removes. This aspect of the situation clearly emerges from a comparison between M_{9a} and the key myth, in which the matrilineal line of descent and matrilocal residence are also relevant factors:

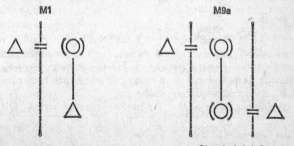

M1   M9a

In M_{9a} we have, therefore, a variant in which all family relations, as well as the corresponding moral attitudes, are equally relaxed. In all respects this version is probably the weakest known to us.

Fourth variation

M_{10}. *Eastern Timbria. 'The origin of fire'*

Formerly men were unacquainted with fire and dried their meat by laying it out in the sun on a flat stone, so that it was not completely raw.

In those days a man once took his young brother-in-law on an expedition to rob macaws' nests in a cleft of a vertical cliff. But the fledglings made such an outcry that the boy did not dare take hold of them. The man grew angry, knocked down the ladder, and went off. The hero remained sitting by the nest, suffering from thirst, his head covered with birds' droppings, 'so that maggots grew there; and the young birds soon lost all fear of him'.

What follows is identical with the Apinaye version. It is explained, however, that the jaguar's wife was *pregnant* and could not bear the slightest noise she therefore flew into a rage whenever the hero made a noise as he chewed the grilled meat his adopted father had given him. But try as he might, he could not eat silently, since the meat was too crisp. With the weapons given him by the jaguar, he wounded the wife in the paw and fled. The wife, hampered by her pregnancy, was unable to follow him.

The hero recounted his adventure to his father, who summoned all his companions. They placed runners at intervals all the way to the jaguar's house and organized a relay system: the burning log was passed from hand to hand and finally reached the village. The jaguar's wife begged them in vain to leave her a burning ember; the toad spat on all those that remained, and put them out (Nimuendaju, 1946a, p. 243).

Fifth variation

M_{11}. *Eastern Timbira (Kraho group). 'The origin of fire'*

The two civilizing heroes, Pud and Pudlere, formerly lived with men and put fire at their disposal. But when the heroes went away, they took the fire with them, and men were reduced to eating their meat raw, sun-dried, and accompanied by *pau puba*.

It was during this period that the brothers-in-law undertook their expedition. The younger of the two men was abandoned on the cliff face, where he wept among the angry birds: 'After two days the birds became used to him. The macaw deposited its droppings on his head, which swarmed with vermin. He was hungry.'

The end is similar to the other versions. The jaguar's wife was pregnant and liked to frighten the boy by threatening to eat him. The jaguar showed the boy the secret of the bow and arrows; and, following his advice, the boy wounded the wife in the paw and ran away. The Indians, after being informed of what had happened, organized a system of runners to get possession of the fire. 'But for the jaguar, they would still be eating their meat raw' (Schultz, 1950, pp. 72–4).

In a different context, a Kraho myth, which deals with a visit by a human hero to the jaguar's home, contains the following remark which forms a direct link between the fire theme and the pregnancy theme: 'The jaguar's wife was very pregnant [sic] and on the point of giving birth. Everything was ready for the confinement, and in particular a good fire was burning, because the jaguar is master of fire' (Pompeu Sobrinho, 1935, p. 196).

Sixth variation

M_{12}. *Sherente.* '*The origin of fire*'

One day a man went into the woods with his little brother-in-law in order to take young macaws out of a nest in the hollow of a tree. The man made his brother-in-law climb a pole; but when he got up there, the young man declared that there were only eggs there. When the man said he knew there were young in the nest, the hero took a white stone in his mouth and threw it down. The stone turned into an egg that was smashed against the ground. The man was angry, pulled away the ladder, and went home, leaving the hero in the tree where he was forced to remain for five days.

Then a jaguar passed by and asked what he was doing up there, made him first throw down the two young macaws (which were in fact in the nest), told him to jump after them, and, growling, caught the boy between his front paws. Then the boy was very much afraid, but nothing happened to him.

The jaguar carried the hero on his shoulders until they came to a creek. Although the boy was suffering greatly from thirst, he was not allowed to drink, because, as the jaguar explained, the water belonged to the camon vulture (*urubu*). The same thing happened at the second creek, because the water there belonged to 'the little birds'. Finally, at the third creek, the hero drank so much as to drain the whole creek, in spite of the entreaties of the alligator,[2] the owner of the creek.

The hero was given a chilly welcome by the jaguar's wife, who reproached her husband for having brought back 'a lean and ugly boy'. She called the boy to delouse her, but when she had him between her paws, she frightened him with her growls. He complained to the jaguar, who made him a bow and arrows and ornaments, gave him two basketfuls of roast meat, and helped him back to his village, after advising him to aim for the wife's carotid, should she try to pursue him. Everything happened as had been foreseen, and the wife was killed.

Shortly afterward the young man heard people coming. It was his two brothers, to whom he revealed his identity, and who ran home to tell their mother. 'You lie,' said their mother. 'He's been dead long since.' But the boy concealed himself again. He came out of hiding on the occasion of the Aikman funeral festival.

Everybody was amazed when they saw the roast meat he had brought back. 'Why, how is it roasted?' 'In the sunshine,' the boy kept repeating, although he finally revealed the truth to his uncle.

An expedition was organized to capture fire from the jaguar. The mutum and the water fowl, both good runners, seized the trunk, but the jacu, following them, picked up the scattered embers (Nimuendaju, 1944, pp. 181–2). [...]

Second movement: Bororo

Let us now return to the myths assembled in Part One. What has the key myth (M_1) in common with the Ge set about the origin of fire (M_7–M_{12})? At first sight, only the episode of the bird-nester. Otherwise, the Bororo myth begins with the story of incest which does not occur explicitly in the Ge myths. The latter are constructed around the visit to the jaguar, who is master of fire; and this visit is taken as explaining the origin of the practice of cooking food; there is nothing comparable in the Bororo myth. Hasty analysis would lead one to suppose that the bird-nester episode had been borrowed either by the Bororo or the Ge and introduced by either group into an entirely different context from the original one. If so, the myths are made up of odds and ends.

2. TRANSLATORS' NOTE: In the myths 'alligator' is the term commonly used as an equivalent for the Portuguese *jacaré*. The animal referred to is a cayman (*Caiman niger*), except perhaps along the northern and northeastern coasts where crocodiles proper exist. To avoid confusion, the usual tradition of using the word 'alligator' has been followed throughout the text wherever Lévi-Strauss has *crocodile*.

I propose to establish, on the contrary, that in all these instances we are dealing with the same myth, and that the apparent divergences between the versions are to be treated as the result of transformations occurring within a set.

In the first place, all versions (Bororo: M_1; and Ge: M_7–M_{12}) refer to the use of a bow and arrows made out of branches. Some imply that this explains the origin of hunting weapons which, like fire, were unknown to men, and the secret of which was also in the jaguar's possession. The Bororo myth does not contain the jaguar episode, but the lost and famished hero at the top of the cliff face makes a bow and arrows with the material to hand; and this creation or re-creation of hunting weapons is a theme common to the whole series of myths under consideration. It will be noted, moreover, that the invention of the bow and arrows in the jaguar's absence (he is absent from the myth) is perfectly congruous with the invention of fire by the monkey in the (momentary) absence of the jaguar in M_{55}; whereas, according to the Ge myths, the hero receives the bow and arrows directly from the jaguar (instead of inventing them), and the fire is already kindled.

We now come to the most serious disparity. All the Ge myths (M_7–M_{12}) are patently myths about the origin of fire, a theme that seems to be completely absent from the Bororo myth. But is this certain?

The authors of *Os Bororos orientais* make an important comment on this myth, in two different places. According to them, it deals with 'the origin of wind and rain' (Colbacchini and Albisetti, 1942, pp. 221, 343), and they go into such geological questions as erosion by rain, laterization of soil, and the formation of steep rock faces with potholes at their base, through the dripping of water. During the rainy season these potholes, which are normally full of earth, fill up with water and look like receptacles. This remark, which has no reference to any incident in the myth (although it occurs as a preliminary statement), is particularly significant if, by any chance, it comes direct from the informant, as is often the case in the work in question. The Ge myths, which I am trying to link with the key myth, refer expressly to the origin of cooking.

But the Bororo myth refers to only one storm and nothing in

the text indicates that it was the first. It will be remembered that the hero returns to his village, and that a violent storm occurs during his first night there and puts out all the fires except one. However, the conclusion of the first published version of M₁ plainly suggested its etiological character (see p. 254) and although the sentence has disappeared from the second version, the commentary confirms that the natives interpret the myth in this way. It follows that the Bororo myth, too, is about origins: the origin not of fire but of rain and wind which (as the text clearly states) are the opposite of fire, since they put it out. They are, as it were, 'anti-fire'.

The analysis can be carried further. Since the storm has put out all the fires in the village, apart from the one in the hut where the hero has taken refuge, the latter finds himself temporarily in the position of the jaguar: he is master of fire, and all the inhabitants of the village must apply to him to obtain firebrands with which to rekindle the lost fire. In this sense the Bororo myth also relates to the origin of fire, but by a procedure of omission. The difference between it and the Ge myths therefore lies in the weaker treatment of the common theme. The occurrence is situated within the known history of village life, instead of in mythical times to mark the introduction of the arts of civilization. In the first case the fire is lost by a limited community which had previously been in possession of it; in the second it is bestowed on humanity as a whole, after being totally unknown. However, the Kraho version (M₁₁) provides an intermediary formula, since in it mankind (as a whole) is deprived of fire by the culture heroes, who carry it away with them.

The preceding demonstration would be still further strengthened if it were possible to interpret the name of the hero in the key myth, Geriguiguiatugo, as a compound of *gerigigi* 'firewood' and *atugo* 'jaguar'. This would give 'the firewood jaguar', with whom we are acquainted as a Ge hero, and who is obviously absent from the Bororo myths, but whose existence would be indicated by the etymology of the name attributed to a character who, as we have seen, performs his precise function. However, it would be dangerous to pursue this idea, since the available transcriptions are doubtful from the phonological point of view. On the other hand, the accuracy of the etymology put forward by

Colbacchini and Albisetti will be confirmed below, without its being necessary for us to exclude *a priori* the possibility that the same name may admit of several interpretations.

Be that as it may, we do not need any further proof in order to accept the fact that the Bororo myth belongs to the same set as the Ge myths and constitutes a transformation of the same themes. The transformation appears in the following points: (1) a weakening of the polar opposites, in regard to the origin of fire; (2) an inversion of the explicit etiological content, which in this instance is the origin of wind and rain: anti-fire; (3) the mutation of the hero who occupies the position attributed to the jaguar in the Ge myths: master of fire; (4) a correlative inversion of the relations of kinship: the Ge jaguar is the (adopted) father of the hero, whereas the Bororo hero, who is congruous with the jaguar, is a (real) son of a human father; (5) a mutation of family attitudes (equivalent to an inversion): in the Bororo myth the mother is 'close' (incestuous), the father 'remote' (murderous); in the Ge versions, on the contrary, it is the adopted father who is 'close': he protects the child *like* a mother – he carries it, cleans it, satisfies its thirst, feeds it – and *against* the mother – whom he encourages his son to wound or kill –whereas the adopted mother is 'remote', since her intentions are murderous.

Lastly, the Bororo hero is not a jaguar (although he discreetly performs the jaguar's function), but we are told that, to kill his father, he turns himself into a deer. The problems raised by the semantic position of the Cervidae in South American mythology will be discussed elsewhere; here I shall restrict myself to formulating the rule that allows us to transform this episode into a corresponding episode of the Ge set. The latter presents us with a real jaguar, who does not kill his 'false' (adopted) son, although such an act would have been in keeping both with the nature of the jaguar (a flesh-eater) and with that of the hero (who is in the position of the jaguar's prey). The Bororo myth reverses the situation: a false deer (the hero in disguise) kills his real father, although this act is contrary to the nature of the deer (a herbivorous animal) and to that of the victim (a hunter stalking his prey). It will be remembered that the killing takes place during a hunt directed by the father.

Several North and South American myths present the jaguar

and the deer as a linked and contrasting couple. To mention for the moment only tales that are comparatively close to the Bororo, it is significant that the Cayua of the southern part of the Mato Grosso, whose linguistic connections are doubtful, consider the jaguar and the deer as the first masters of fire (M_{62}: Schaden, 1947, pp. 107–23). In this case the two species are associated (but in very early times), whereas they are contrasted in a Mundurucu myth (M_{37}). And, according to Tucuna myths (M_{63}), which have equivalents in North America (among the Menomini, for instance), deer were once man-eating jaguars; or heroes, having been changed into deer, became capable of playing the part of either the victim or the killer (Nimuendaju, 1952, pp. 120, 127, 133).

Third movement: Tupi

There are further reasons for supposing that the Bororo myth relates to the origin of fire, in spite of its extreme discretion on this point. Certain details, which must be attentively examined, seem to be echoes of other myths relative to the origin of fire which, at first sight, offer no resemblance to those of the Ge group and in fact come from another linguistic family, the Guarani group.

According to the Apapocuva (M_{64}), who lived in the extreme south of the Mato Grosso in the middle of the nineteenth century:

The civilizing hero, Nianderyquey, one day pretended to die, so realistically that his body began to decay. The urubus, who were the masters of fire at the time, gathered around the corpse and lit a fire in order to cook it. No sooner had they put the body among the hot ash than Nianderyquey began to move, put the birds to flight, took possession of the fire, and gave it to men (Nimuendaju, 1914, p. 326 ff.; Schaden, 1955, pp. 221–2).

The Paraguayan version of the same myth is richer in detail:

M65. Mbya. 'The origin of fire'

After the first earth had been destroyed by a flood, which had been sent as a punishment for an incestuous union, the gods created another and placed on it their son, Nianderu Pa-pa Miri. He created new men and set about obtaining fire for them; at the time it was in the sole possession of vulture-sorcerers.

Nianderu explained to his son, the toad, that he would simulate death, and that the toad must seize the burning embers as soon as Nianderu, having recovered consciousness, scattered them.

The sorcerers approached the corpse, which they found suitably plump. Pretending that they wished to revive it, they lit a fire. The hero moved about and shammed death alternately, until the sorcerers had brought together enough embers; the hero and his son then took possession of the latter and put them inside the two pieces of wood that would henceforth be used by men to produce fire by a process of rotation. As a punishment for their attempted cannibalism, the sorcerers were doomed to remain carrion-eating vultures 'with no respect for the big thing' (the corpse) and never to achieve the perfect life (Cadogan, 1959, pp. 57–66).

Although the old authors do not mention this myth as existing among the Tupinamba, it occurs among several tribes who speak the Tupi language or are known to have come under Tupi influence. Several versions of it are found in the Amazonian basin, among the Tembe, the Tenetehara, the Tapirape and the Shipaya. Others occur in the Gran Chaco and in north-eastern Bolivia, among the Choroti, the Tapiete, the Ashluslay and the Guarayu. It also exists among the Botocudo (Nimendaja, 1946b, pp. 111–12) and among immediate neighbours of the Bororo, the Bacairi and the Tereno. From Guiana right up to the northern areas of North America, it occurs frequently, but in a modified form; the fire-stealing theme is missing and is replaced by the capture of a daughter of the vultures, by a hero who outwits them by taking on the appearance of a piece of carrion (cf., for instance, Simpson, 1944, pp. 268–9, and Koch-Grünberg's general discussion, 1916, p. 278 ff.). Here, for example, are three Tupi versions of the myth about the origin of fire:

M₆₆. Tembe. 'The origin of fire'

In the old days the king vulture was the master of fire, and men had to dry their meat in the sun. One day they decided to get possession of fire. They killed a tapir; and when the body was full of worms, the king vulture and his relatives came down from the sky. They took off their feather tunics and appeared in human form. After lighting a big fire, they wrapped the worms in leaves and put them to roast (cf. M_{105}). The men had gone into hiding not far from the dead body, and after a first unsuccessful attempt, they managed to obtain possession of fire (Nimuendaju, 1915, p. 289).

M_{67}. Shipaya. 'The origin of fire'

To get fire from the bird of prey who was master of it, the demiurge Kumaphari pretended to die and to decay. The urubus devoured his body, but the eagle had put the fire in a safe place. The demiurge then pretended to die in the form of a roebuck, but the bird was not taken in. Finally Kumaphari took the form of two shrubs in which the eagle decided to put his fire. The demiurge got possession of it, and the eagle agreed to teach him the art of producing fire by friction (Nimuendaju, 1919–20; 1921–2, p. 1015).

$M_{.68}$ Guarayu. 'The origin of fire'

A man who did not possess fire bathed in putrid water, then lay down on the ground as if he were dead. The black vultures, the masters of fire, settled on him in order to cook and eat him, but the man got up suddenly and scattered the embers. His ally, the toad, who was waiting for the opportunity, swallowed some. He was caught by the birds and forced to cough it up again. The man and the toad then repeated their attempt, and this time they were successful. Since then men have had fire (Nordenskiöld, 1922, p. 155).

The Bororo myth does not explicitly mention the origin of fire, but one might say that *it knows* so well that this is its real subject (prefacing it, moreover, with a flood, as in the Guarani myth) that it almost literally reconstitutes the episode of the hero who is changed into carrion (in this case he is dressed as carrion, being covered with putrefied lizards) and arouses the greedy appetites of the urubus.

We can confirm the link by pointing out that one detail of the Bororo myth is incomprehensible until it is interpreted as a transformation of a corresponding detail in the Guarani myth. How are we to explain the fact that in the key myth the urubus, instead of completely devouring their victim, interrupt their feast to save him? In the Guarani myth, as we know, the vultures claim to be healers, who cook their victim while pretending to revive him, and do not succeed in eating him. The sequence is simply reversed in the Bororo myth, in which the vultures consume (part of) their victim – raw – and afterward behave like genuine healers (life-savers).

It is a well-known fact that the Bororo way of thinking was greatly influenced by Tupi mythology. In both groups the same myth – the one about the jaguar's human wife, who is the mother of the two civilizing heroes – occupies an essential position. And the modern Bororo versions (Colbacchini, 1919, pp. 114–21! 1925, pp. 179–85; pp. 190–96) remain astonishingly close to the one that Thevet recorded as existing among the Tupinamba in the sixteenth century (M_{96}; Métraux, 1928, p. 235 ff.).

But how must we interpret those peculiar features that distinguish the key myth from the myths about the origin of fire, with which we have compared it? They may be a result of the historical and geographical position of the Bororo, who – being caught, as it were between Guarani and Ge groups – have borrowed from both and fused certain themes, thus reducing or even destroying their etiological significance.

The hypothesis is plausible enough, but inadequate. It does not explain why each mythology, or each separate set of myths, should form a coherent system, as my discussion of the question has shown to be the case. The problem must therefore also be studied from the formal point of view, and we must ask whether both the Ge and the Tupi sets of myths are not part of some larger set, within which they exist as different subordinate subsets.

It is immediately obvious that these subsets have some features in common. To begin with, they attribute the origin of fire to an animal, who gave it to man or from whom man stole it: in one instance it is a vulture; in the other, a jaguar. Secondly, each species is defined in terms of the food it eats: the jaguar is a beast of prey who feeds on raw meat; the vulture is a carrion-eater, who consumes rotten meat. And yet all the myths take into account the element of decay. The Ge set does so very faintly and almost allusively, in the episode about the hero covered with feces and vermin. The Bororo set, which we studied first, is rather more explicit (M_1: the hero dressed in carrion; M_2: the hero defiled by the droppings of his son who has been changed into a bird; M_5: the hero 'putrefied' by his grandmother breaking wind; M_6: the heroine exudes illnesses as if they were an intestinal evacuation). And, as we have just seen, the Tupi-Guarani set is quite clear on this point.

It is thus confirmed that the Ge myths about the origin of fire, like the Tupi-Guarani on the same theme, function in terms of a double contrast: on the one hand, between what is raw and what is cooked, and on the other, between the fresh and the decayed.

The raw–cooked axis is characteristic of culture; the fresh–decayed one of nature, since cooking brings about the cultural transformation of the raw, just as putrefaction is its natural transformation.

In the total system thus restored, the Tupi-Guarani myths illustrate a more radical procedure than the Ge myths: according to the Tupi-Guarani way of thinking, the significant contrast is between cooking (the secret of which was in the possession of the vultures) and putrefaction (which is a characteristic of their present diet); whereas, in the Ge myths the significant contrast is between the cooking of foodstuffs and eating them raw (the jaguar's present procedure).

The Bororo myth may therefore express a refusal, or an inability, to choose between the two formulas; and the refusal or the inability needs to be explained. The theme of decay is more strongly emphasized among the Bororo than among the Ge, while that of the carnivorous beast of prey is almost entirely absent. On the other hand, the Bororo myth sees things from the point of view of victorious man – that is, from the point of view of culture (the hero of M_1 invents the bow and arrow, just as the monkey in M_{55} – who is a counterpart of man – invents fire, which is unknown to the jaguar). The Ge and the Tupi-Guarani myths (which are closer in this respect) are more concerned with the despoiling of animals, which is an aspect of nature. But the dividing line between nature and culture is different, according to whether we are considering the Ge or the Tupi myths: in the former it separates the cooked from the raw; in the latter it separates the raw from the rotten. For the Ge, then, the raw + rotten relation is a natural category, whereas for the Tupi the raw + cooked relation is a cultural category.

Fugue of the five senses

Because of its incomplete and provisional nature, the synthesis that emerged tentatively from Part Two is not absolutely convincing, since it fails to deal with important sections of the key myth, and the fact has not been established that these elements also occur in the Ge set. The method I am following is legitimate only if it is exhaustive: if we allowed ourselves to treat apparent divergencies among myths, which are at the same time described as belonging to one and the same set, as the outcome either of logical transformations or historical accidents, the door would be thrown wide open to arbitrary interpretations: for it is always possible to choose the most convenient interpretation and to press logic into service whenever history proves elusive, or to fall back on the latter should the former be deficient. Structural analysis would, as a result, rest entirely on a series of begged questions, and would lose its only justification, which lies in the unique and most economical coding system to which it can reduce messages of a most disheartening complexity, and which previously appeared to defeat all attempts to decipher them. Either structural analysis succeeds in exhausting all the concrete modalities of its subject, or we lose the right to apply it to any one of the modalities.

If we take the text literally, the episode of the expedition to the kingdom of the souls, by which a wronged father hopes to ensure his son's death, occurs only in the Bororo myth. This seems all the more evident in that the episode is a direct consequence of the hero's incestuous behaviour, which is also absent from the Ge myths.

Let us look at the episode more closely. The hero is sent into the aquatic world of the souls on a precise mission. He is to steal three objects in the following order: the great rattle, the small rattle and the string of little bells. Three objects, that is, capable of producing a noise, and this explains – the text is absolutely explicit on this point – why the father chose them: he hopes that his son will be unable to gain possession of the three objects without moving them and thus raising the alarm among the souls, who will punish him for his temerity. Once this point has been made clear, certain connections with the Ge myths come to light.

But before venturing on an explanation, I must stress that the Ge myths undoubtedly constitute a set. We already know this to be the case, through the simple fact that the different versions with which we are acquainted, although not all equally elaborate or detailed, are identical in their main outlines. Moreover, the communities in which these myths originated are not all really separate entities, and none is completely distinct: the Kraho and the Canella are two subgroups of the eastern Timbira, who belong to a much broader community, of which the Apinaye – and the

Kayapo, too, no doubt – are the western representatives; the separation must have taken place only a few centuries ago at most, as is testified by the legends commemorating it. The separation between the Kubenkranken and the Gorotire is even more recent, since it took place as recently as 1936.[3]

Methodologically speaking, we are in the opposite situation to the one I described a little while ago. When one adopts a structural approach, one has no right to resort to historico-cultural hypotheses whenever principles already enunciated run into difficulties of application. Historico-cultural arguments are in the circumstances no more than conjectures, improvised to meet the needs of the moment. On the other hand, it is certainly our right, even our duty, to take into careful consideration conclusions that ethnographers have arrived at by means of linguistic and historical research, and that they themselves hold to be sound and well founded.

If the present Ge tribes spring from a common historical origin, those of their myths that show resemblances do not merely constitute a set from a logical point of view; empirically they also form a family. It is therefore permissible to use the most detailed versions to testify for the others, provided the poorer versions are distinguished from the former only by what they omit. If the two versions contain different treatments of the same episode, it becomes necessary, within the limits of the subset, to appeal again to the concept of transformation.

After stating these methodological rules, I can now turn to an aspect illustrated by at least two versions (M_9, M_{10}), out of the six summarized, of the Ge myth explaining the origin of fire. Like the Bororo myth, although by means of a different story, the Apinaye and Timbira myths state a problem relating to noise.

This is very clear in the Timbira myth (M_{10}). After being rescued by the jaguar, the hero, like his counterpart in the Bororo myth, finds himself in mortal danger if he ventures to make a noise: by dropping the noisy instruments (Bororo), and by noisily masticating the grilled meat and thus annoying his protector's pregnant wife (Timbira). The problem – we might almost say the ordeal – with which both heroes are faced consists in not making a noise.

3. For the history of the eastern and western Ge, cf. Nimuendaju (1946a) and Dreyfus (1963), ch. 1.

Let us now move on to the Apinaye myth (M_9), from which this theme is apparently absent. It is, however, replaced by a different theme which is not found elsewhere: the origin of man's loss of immortality. Forgetful of the jaguar's advice, the hero replies to more calls than he should; in other words, he allows himself to be affected by noise. He had permission to reply to the echoing calls uttered by the rock and the hardwood; and had he been satisfied to reply only to these, men would have lived as long as those mineral and vegetable entities: but since he also replies 'to the gentle call of a rotten tree', the duration of human life is henceforth curtailed.

The three myths (M_1, M_9, M_{10}) – Bororo, Apinaye and Timbira – can therefore, in this connection, be seen to have a common denominator, which is: a cautious attitude toward noise, because the penalty is death. In M_1 and M_{10} the hero must not *provoke others by making a noise*, otherwise *he will die*; in M_9 he must not *let himself be provoked by all the noises he hears*, because, according to the acoustic threshold at which he reacts, men – that is, *others – will die more, or less, rapidly*.

In M_1 and M_{10} the hero is *the subjective producer of noise;* he makes a *little noise* but *not a lot*. In M_9 he is *the objective receiver of noise* and can hear *a lot of noise, not a little*. May we not suppose that, in these three cases, the nature of life on earth, which is – by its limited duration – a kind of mediatization of the contrast between existence and non-existence, is being thought of as a function of man's inability to define himself, unambiguously, in relation to silence and noise?

The Apinaye version is the only one to formulate this metaphysical proposition explicitly – an unusual feature which is accompanied by another, for the Apinaye myth is also the only one in which the episode of the ogre occurs. The two peculiarities are linked, as a preliminary demonstration will show. [. . .]

The Apinaye myth (M_9) is therefore not making an arbitrary use of 'the call of a rotten tree' in order to effect the transition from the obtaining of fire for cooking to the meeting with a cannibalistic ogre. I have already shown that there is an intrinsic link between the theme of man's loss of immortality and the obtaining of fire for cooking purposes. And it is now clear that, for natives who practise the 'slash and burn' technique, even vegetarian cooking cannot be dissociated from a kind of 'cannibalism', which is also vegetarian. Man's mortality manifests itself in two ways: either through a natural death – old age or disease – as is the case with trees when they 'die' and become firewood; or by a violent death at the hands of an enemy, who may be a cannibal – therefore an ogre – and who is always a cannibal, at least in a metaphorical sense, even in the guise of the tree feller attacking the living tree. It is therefore logical that in the Apinaye myth the episode of the meeting with the ogre (who is a 'shadow' or a 'ghost') should follow immediately on the episode of the call of rotten wood (which is also a ghost). In this way death is introduced in both its aspects.

Nevertheless, the Apinaye myth poses a problem that we have not yet solved. What meaning can be attributed to the strange conception of a call coming from a vegetable or mineral entity that has no power of articulate expression?

The myth lists three calls to which the hero must reply or keep still. In order of diminishing loudness, these are the calls of the rock, the hardwood aroeira tree, and the rotten tree. We have some information about the symbolic value of rotten wood in Ge mythology; it is a vegetable antifood,[4] the only food eaten by men before the introduction of agricultural techniques. Several Ge myths, to which I shall return later, attribute the obtaining of cultivated plants by man to a star-woman who came down to the earth to marry a mortal. Formerly men used to eat their meat accompanied by rotten wood instead of vegetables (Apinaye: Nimuendaju, 1939, p. 165; Timbira: Nimuendaju, 1946a, p. 245; Kraho: Schultz, 1950, p. 75; Kayapo: Banner, 1957, p. 40, Métraux, 1960, pp. 17–18). It can be concluded from this that, in the nature versus culture context, rotten wood represents the reverse of cultivated plants.

Now the episode of the ogre shows how the hero tricked his

4. The same idea also occurs in North America, especially in the north-west area, where the story of the 'ogress with the basket' is found in numerous versions, the details of which are remarkably similar to the Ge version. No doubt many American myths are widely diffused throughout the two parts of the continent. However, so many features are common to the north-west area of North America and to central Brazil that we are inevitably faced with a historico-cultural problem; but the time has not yet come to discuss it. [See Lévi-Strauss, 1971, ed.]

abductor by leaving him a stone to eat instead of a body. Stone, or rock, appears, then, as the symmetrical opposite of human flesh. By filling in the empty space with the only culinary term still available, animal flesh, we arrive at the following table:

```
        rock              human flesh⎫ meat
wood ⎧hard wood           animal flesh⎭
     ⎩rotten wood         cultivated plants
```

What does this mean? The series of three 'calls' corresponds, in reverse order, to a division of the sources of food into three categories: agriculture, hunting and cannibalism. Furthermore, these three categories, which could be called 'gustatory', are coded in terms of a different sensory system: that of hearing. Finally, the auditory symbols used have the remarkable property of immediately suggesting two other sensory coding systems – one olfactory, the other tactile – as can be seen from the following table:

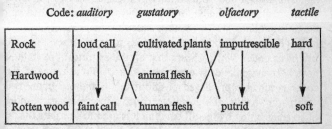

Code:	*auditory*	*gustatory*	*olfactory*	*tactile*
Rock	loud call	cultivated plants	imputrescible	hard
Hardwood		animal flesh		
Rotten wood	faint call	human flesh	putrid	soft

We can now understand the very precise meaning that must be attributed to the calls uttered by the rock and the wood: the things that emit sounds must be chosen in such a way that they also possess other sensory connotations. They are operators, which make it possible to convey the isomorphic character of all binary systems of contrasts connected with the senses, and therefore to express, as a totality, a set of equivalences connecting life and death, vegetable foods and cannibalism, putrefaction and imputrescibility, softness and hardness, silence and noise.

The point can be proved; for we know of variants of the myths already examined, belonging to the same communities or to more or less neighboring ones, from which the transformation of one sensory coding system into another can be confirmed. [. . .]

The Opossum's Cantata

Je veux peindre en mes vers des mères le modèle,
Le sarigue, animal peu connu parmi nous,
Mais dont les soins touchants et doux,
Dont la tendresse maternelle,
Seront de quelque prix pour vous.

(I wish to describe, in my verse, a model mother, the opossum, an animal little known in our country, but whose gentle, touching care and maternal affection cannot fail to appeal to the reader.)

FLORIAN, *Fables*, Book II, I.

The Opossum's solo

I hope that in the preceding section several truths have been established. First of all, when considered from the formal point of view, myths which seem very different but all deal with the origin of man's mortality transmit the same message and can only be distinguished one from another by the code they use. Second, all the codes are similar in type; they use contrasts between tangible qualities, which are thus raised to the point of having a logical existence. Third, since man possesses five senses, there are five basic codes, which shows that all the empirical possibilities have been systematically explored and used. Fourth, one of the codes occupies a privileged position; this is the one connected with eating habits, the gustatory code, whose message is more often transmitted by the others than it is used to translate theirs, since it is through myths explaining the origin of fire, and thus of cooking, that we gain access to myths about man's loss of immortality; among the Apinaye, for instance, the origin of mortality is only one episode of the myth relating to the origin of fire. We thus begin to understand the truly essential place occupied by cooking in native thought: not only does cooking mark the transition from nature to culture, but through it and by means of it, the human state can be defined with all its attributes, even those that, like mortality, might seem to be the most unquestionably natural.

However, I must not conceal the fact that, in order to obtain these results, I have to some extent glossed over two difficulties. Of all the Ge versions, only the Apinaye variant contains the episode about man's loss of immortality. I did, of course, explain at the beginning of the third section why it was legitimate, in the case of the Ge myths, to fill in the gaps in certain versions by referring to more complete versions. It is nevertheless essential to try to discover whether the other Ge groups have a different conception of the origin of man's loss of immortality, and, if so, what exactly that conception is. Furthermore, in order to ensure the reciprocal convertibility of the codes, I have put forward the equation hard wood = animal flesh, and it must be checked. Fortunately all this is feasible, since there exists a set of Ge myths in which the hardwood theme is associated with the theme of man's loss of immortality. Now although these myths – unlike M_9, on which I have chiefly based my argument – do not deal with the origin of fire, they nevertheless have an essentially culinary theme, since they deal with the origin of cultivated plants. Finally, by an unexpected twist, these myths make it possible to obtain decisive confirmation of conclusions I have already put forward. [. . .]

Concluding aria: fire and water

I have on several occasions more or less explicitly accepted the fact that in the mythological thought of South America there are two distinct kinds of water: creative water of celestial origin and destructive water of terrestrial origin. Similarly, there seem to be two kinds of fire: one celestial and destructive, the other terrestrial and creative, that is, fire for cooking purposes. We shall see presently that the situation is rather more complex than this. But first of all we must go more deeply into the significance of the basic contrast between water and fire.

For this purpose we must return to the key myth, which, as I showed (on pp. 262–70), is a myth about the origin of fire in the guise of a myth about the origin of water, and restore it to its place among the series of Ge myths dealing with the origin of fire $(M_7–M_{12})$. Although, because of their matrilineal and matrilocal social structure, the Bororo form a more complete contrast with the patrilineal and patrilocal Sherente than with any of the other Ge tribes (and perhaps precisely for this reason), an extraordinary symmetry can be observed among the myths of these two groups, the hero of which is a bird-nester (M_1 and M_{12} respectively).

In the first place, and only in the set of myths 1 to 12, the myths deal simultaneously with fire and water. The Bororo myth creates water in order to destroy fire or, more precisely, to allow the hero to become the master of fire. The Sherente myth states that, in order to become the master of fire, the hero had first of all to behave as master of water: we might say that he obliterated it by drinking it all. It will be remembered that, after being rescued by the jaguar, the hero complained of acute thirst, which he succeeded in satisfying only by drinking the stream dry, without leaving a single drop for the alligator (*Caiman niger*) who owned it. Light is thrown on this incident by a Cayua myth (M_{62}), which states emphatically that the alligator was the master of water, and that it was his task to prevent the earth from drying up: *Jacaré é capitão de agua, para não secar todo a mundo* (Schaden, 1947, p. 113).[5]

Secondly, the hero of both myths is shown as a trickster, not always at the beginning (where the contrast is chiefly between the Kayapo and Sherente versions: the eggs he throws down become stones, and the stones he throws down are changed into eggs, respectively), but at the end. The Bororo birdnester deceives his own people for a long time by disguising himself as a lizard. His Sherente counterpart also deceives his own people by claiming that the jaguar's meat was cooked simply through exposure to the sun. In both cases his distrustful attitude is unjustified.

His extreme behavior corresponds to another feature peculiar to the two myths, in which the theme is not, as in the Apinaye version, a human life whose duration is henceforth to be *measured*, but death followed by resurrection. The theme occurs twice in the Bororo myth, where the hero betrays his identity during a 'dance of the ancestors', then succeeds in returning safe and sound from his expedition to the kingdom of the souls. The Sherente myth, on the other hand, suggests that the hero remained hidden from his people for a long time because he was dead. He only reappears

5. With regard to the jaguar-alligator couple (one master of fire, the other master of water), it will be recalled that Tupinologists have compared the Tupi name for the jaguar, *jagua*, with the word *jacaré* meaning alligator, which can be split up into *iagua-ré* 'the other sort of jaguar'. I do not know what value philologists would attach to this etymology, but it is interesting to note that it was rejected as soon as it was put forward, for the sole reason that no possible equivalence could exist between the two species (Chermont de Miranda, 1944, pp. 73–4).

on the occasion of the Aikman funeral rites which were performed in honor of the illustrious dead. By stretching the sense of the texts very slightly, we might say that the timid hero procures a restricted life for men, whereas the brazen hero brings them a promise of resurrection. The contrast between prolonged life and a shortened life, on the one hand, and death and resurrection, on the other, seems isomorphic with that which can be perceived between myths that deal either separately with the origin of cooking ($\equiv$ fire) or cultivated plants ($\equiv$ water), or jointly with the origin of fire and water.

Let us begin by establishing, by means of a lemma, that the following relation is definitely present in native thought:

fire = water $(^{-1})$.

The theme of one of the most widespread South American myths, for which ample evidence is found among the Ge, is a challenge that the mythological twins, Sun and Moon, or the anteater and the jaguar, address to each other in connection with their respective diets. Depending on the versions, the diets consist, respectively, of ripe fruits and green fruits, meat (raw food) and ants (decayed food, cf. M_{89} and M_{54} by reason of the transformation opposum $\rightarrow$ ant), animal foods and vegetable foods, etc.:

(Sun: Moon, anteater: jaguar) :: (rotten: raw, ripe: green, vegetable: animal. . .).

Except for the above difference, the great anteater and the jaguar might be said to be interchangeable. Brazilian folklore has a wealth of stories that treat as equals the two most powerful animals of the *sertão*: one because of its powerful fangs, the other because of the grip of its powerful forepaws. It is said, for instance, that the jaguar never fails to overcome the anteater in the savannah, but that the opposite is true in the forest, where the anteater stands erect by supporting itself against a tree trunk with its tail and suffocates the jaguar between its front legs.

Each animal claimed that the food it ate was the 'strongest', and to settle the dispute they decided to defecate, while keeping their eyes shut, and then to compare their excrements. The anteater pretended that it had difficulty in performing, and took advantage of the respite surreptitiously to exchange its excrement for that of the jaguar. A quarrel ensued, during which the ant-eater tore out the jaguar's eyes. Or sometimes the story goes as follows:

M₁₁₉. Cauya. 'The jaguar's eyes'

The jaguar learned from the grasshopper that the toad and the rabbit had stolen its fire while it was out hunting, and that they had taken it across the river. While the jaguar was weeping at this, an anteater came along, and the jaguar suggested that they should have an excretory competition. The anteater, however, appropriated the excrement containing raw meat and made the jaguar believe that its own excretions consisted entirely of ants. In order to even things out, the jaguar invited the anteater to a juggling contest, using their eyes removed from the sockets: the anteater's eyes fell back into place, but the jaguar's remained hanging at the top of a tree, and so it became blind.

At the request of the anteater, the macuco bird made the jaguar new eyes out of water, and these allowed it to see in the dark.

Since that time the jaguar only goes out at night. Having lost fire, it eats its meat raw. It never attacks the macuco – in the Apapocuva version, the inhambu bird, also one of the Tinamidae (Schaden, 1947, pp. 110–11, 121–2).

This version is particularly instructive in that it links the rivalry between the jaguar and the anteater with the theme of the jaguar, master of fire, which I have been using as a guideline from the outset. According to Schaden's informant, the link is even stronger than at first appears, since had the jaguar retrieved the fire stolen from it by the animals, it would have used it to set fire to the earth. The fact that the jaguar lost its original eyes ('the reflection of fire could be seen in its eyes': M₇) was a final warning to humanity of this danger: henceforth even the jaguar's eyes were to be *pura agua*, only water. . . .

How then are we to interpret the connection between the excretory contest and the eye contest? I have said that, diet apart, the jaguar and the anteater are interchangeable. Now in regard to interchangeability, excretions and eyes are in direct and, one might say, anatomical opposition: excretions constitute an eminently interchangeable part of the body, since it is their function to leave the body, whereas eyes are not removable. The myth therefore assumes simultaneously that:

a) fire = water (-1),
b) jaguar = anteater (-1),
c) excretions = eyes (-1),

If excretions are interchangeable but eyes are not, it follows that an exchange of eyes (unlike an exchange of excrement) cannot involve a change of owner, since the parts of the body remain identical, but involves a change of the parts of the body, since the owner remains identical. In other words, in one instance the jaguar and the anteater exchange excretions; in the other the jaguar exchanges its own eyes with itself. It loses its fiery eyes, which were in keeping with its nature as master of fire, and having lost fire, it replaces them with eyes made of water, which is the opposite of fire.

The fact that in other versions of the same myth, the jaguar's artificial eyes were made of resin, not water, merely leads us to develop the equation.

$$:: (\ldots \text{vegetable} : \text{animal}, \text{water} : \text{fire})$$

This lemma brings us back, then, to the inversion of fire and water which seemed to characterize the contrast between the Bororo myth (M_1) and the Sherente myth (M_{12}): one destroyed fire and created water; the other destroyed water and created fire. But the water in the two myths was not of the same kind: in M_1 it was celestial, maleficent and exteriorized (tempest); in M_{12} it was terrestrial, beneficent and interiorized (drinkable). Nor was death introduced into each construct in the same way:

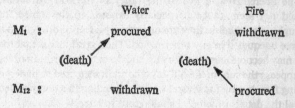

In other words, the Bororo hero's death is the *condition* of the procuring of water, and the death of the Sherente hero is the *consequence* of the procuring of fire.

I have already referred to the fact that the Bororo and the Sherente had entirely different social structures. But to account for the relation of inversion that exists between their etiological myths relating to fire and water, we must refer to other aspects of the culture of the two groups. Unlike the Ge tribes, the Bororo did not live exclusively on the plateau or in the valleys that cut across it. They were settled chiefly along the western edge, or at the foot of the plateau, in the lowlands which slope toward the southwest and eventually become submerged under the waters of one of the largest swamps in the world – the Pantanal. It follows that their mode of life has remained partly that of land dwellers, partly that of marsh dwellers. Water is an element with which they are familiar, and they believe that by chewing certain leaves they can remain under water for several hours to fish (Steinen, 1940, p. 452). This mode of life is accompanied by religious beliefs in which water plays a big part. The Bororo bury their dead twice: a brief initial burial takes place in the village plaza where for several weeks relatives water the corpse lavishly, in order to hasten the process of decomposition. When decay is sufficiently advanced, the grave is opened, and the skeleton is washed until all trace of flesh has been removed. The bones are painted red, decorated with mosaics made from feathers glued together with resin, placed in a basket, and ceremoniously dropped to the bottom of a river or lake, 'the abodes of the souls'. Water and death are therefore always connected in native thought. In order to procure the one, it is necessary to undergo the other. This is exactly what the Bororo myth about the birdnester is, in its peculiar way, trying to convey.

The Sherente, who live in the valley of the Rio Tocantins, would not seem to be particularly exposed to the danger of drought. Nevertheless they are obsessed by a fear of drought to a degree unequaled in any other region. Their great fear is that the sun may become angry and dry up and destroy the earth. In order to appease the sun, in the old days the adult men used to undergo a long fast, lasting for several weeks and ending in a complicated ritual the details of which I shall return to later.

It is enough for the time being to remember that in Sherente thought the human race lives under the threat of a universal conflagration. Corresponding to this belief in fire as the chief cause of death, there is a myth that, as we have seen, maintains that you must endure death in order to obtain fire.

It is only by taking these ecological and religious factors into account that the inversion of the Bororo and Sherente myths can be understood. The Bororo live – and, above all, think – in terms of water; for them, water connotes death, and many of their myths – which explain cultivated plants or other cultural blessings as emerging from the ashes of heroes who are dying, sometimes voluntarily, on a burning woodpile (cf. for instance, M_{20}, M_{27}; and Colbacchini and Albisetti, 1942, pp. 199, 213–14) – testify to their belief in a connection between fire and life. The opposite is true in the case of the Sherente: they think in terms of drought – that is, of negativized water. In their myths, far more emphatically than in any others, fire connotes death; and they contrast it with water, which is not lethal (in rites performed during the long fast, stale water is offered to the participants only so that they can refuse it) but life-giving. And yet all the water in the world is hardly enough to quench the thirst of a thirsty man.

In support of the contrast between fire and water, it may be noted that, in common with their Bacairi neighbors, the Bororo also possess a myth about destructive fire; but it is significant that their fire myth appears in a secondary form, as if it were the consequence of the loss of water. The danger resulting from it is easily overcome:

M_{120}. *Bororo*. '*Destructive fire*'

Formerly Sun and Moon used to live on the earth. One day when they were thirsty, they went to see the aquatic birds who kept water in huge heavy jars.

Disobeying the birds, Sun tried to lift one jar to his lips, but it slipped out of his hands and broke, and the water spilled. The birds became angry. Sun and Moon ran away, and the birds followed them to the hut where they had taken refuge.

By now Sun had become too hot. Feeling discomfort through being so near to him, the birds flapped their woven straw fans and caused such a powerful wind that Sun and Moon were carried up into the sky; where they have remained (Colbacchini and Albisetti, 1944, pp. 237–8,; Bacairi version (M_{120a}) in Steinen, 1940, pp. 482–3).

Other myths concerning Sun and Moon show them destroying fire by water: either as in M_{121} by urinating on the otters' fire (Colbacchini and Albisetti, 1944, p. 233), or as in M_{122} by pouring water on the fire made by men (p. 231). Consequently here again water is proved to have primacy over fire.[6]

It is not enough to say that for the Bororo water is the final cause of death, whereas for the Sherente fire is its efficient cause. This difference between them is accompanied by another, which can be seen in the parallel series of myths explaining the origin of cultivated plants. The Sherente completely dissociate the origin of plants from that of fire. Unlike the other Ge tribes, they include the myth about cultivated plants in the cosmogonic cycle describing the terrestrial adventures of the two culture heroes, Sun and Moon (M_{108}). Conversely, the Bororo take the origin of cultivated plants as a theme for legendary, rather than mythical, tales. They are concerned less with explaining the origin of agriculture as a civilizing art than with establishing to what extent each individual clan can legitimately claim a particular plant, or even a particular variety of a single species, as an eponym. Privileges of this kind go back to the sacrifice made by clan heroes who went voluntarily to a burning woodpile (destructive fire–cooking fire). In all respects, therefore, Bororo and Sherente mythologies relating to the transition from nature to culture occupy extreme positions, whereas the mythology of the other Ge groups is situated in the middle of the scale. Both the Bororo and the Sherente associate fire with water,

6. A whole series of Bororo myths about the origin of fire describe the latter as being extinguished by rain (M_1), spilled water (M_{122}), and urine (M_{121}). In the set explaining the origin of cultivated plants, the Sherente myth (M_{108}) describes manioc as having germinated from the drops of milk spilled by the mothers. This gives the following transformation:

(*Fire series*)   (*Plant series*)

$$[\text{urine} \to \text{fire} (-)] \longrightarrow \qquad [\text{milk} \to \text{plants} (+)]$$

It is interesting to note that a Mexican myth from the Nayarit region (M_{123}) offers a reverse transformation, which makes it possible to arrive at the first term by starting from the second: the iguana having taken the fire to the sky, the crow and the hummingbird failed to get it back. The opossum succeeded by pretending that he only wanted to warm himself at it (return to M_{56}, via the opossum → prea transformation). But he let the fire drop, and the world burst into flames. However, the Earth succeeded in putting out the fire with its milk (Preuss, 1912, vol. 1, pp. 169–81).

I have already pointed out that the Cuna of Panama, like the Bororo, change the origin of fire into the origin of water: in one instance rain puts out all fires except one (cf. M_1, M_{61}); in another urine puts out a single fire (M_{121}, M_{61}).

although they attribute opposite functions to them: water > fire–fire > water; exteriorized water–interiorized water; celestial, maleficent water–terrestrial, beneficent water; culinary fire–funerary woodpile, etc.; and the main events to which they all refer are situated now on a sociological and legendary level, now on a cosmological and mythological level. Finally, both the Bororo and the Sherente stress resurrection, not the shortening of life.

As we have seen elsewhere, the other Ge groups dissociate the origin of cooking (connected with fire) from the origin of cultivated plants (connected with water): the two themes are given parallel and independent treatment, instead of forming an asymmetrical pair within the same mythological series. Furthermore, they associate cultivated plants with decayed matter; and not with the burned, like the Bororo; or with the fresh, like the Sherente.

This pattern of relations can be illustrated by a diagram (Figure 1).

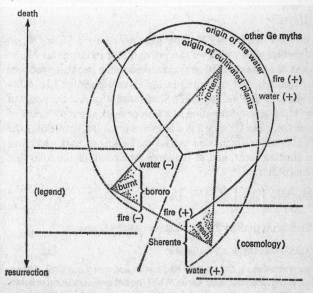

Figure 1 Interrelationship of the Bororo and Ge myths about the origin of fire or cultivated plants

Three-part inventions

I propose to give the name *armature* to a combination of properties that remain invariant in two or several myths: *code* to the pattern of functions ascribed by each myth to these properties; and *message* to the subject matter of an individual myth. Referring back now to the remarks with which I concluded Part Three, I can define the relation between the Bororo myth (M_1) and the Sherente myth (M_{12}) by stating that when we move from one to the other, the armature remains constant, the code is changed, and the message is reversed.

The results of this analysis would be definitively confirmed if it were possible to arrive at the same contrasting structure by a regressive process, which would be a kind of *a contrario* proof. The problem thus posed can be formulated as follows:

Let us suppose two myths, which we will call M_x and M_y, and which happen to be linked by a transformation relation:

$$M_x \rightarrow M_y$$
$$(f)$$

If we agree that $M_y = fM_x$, does there exist a myth $M_z = fM_y$, in connection with which we can prove that it reconstitutes M_x by means of a transformation symmetrical to the one that produced M_y from M_x, but operating in the reverse direction? In other words, after establishing that a Sherente myth about the origin of fire (M_y) is a transformation of a Bororo myth about the origin of water (M_x), can we now find a Sherente myth (M_z) explaining the origin of water which takes us back to the Bororo myth which was our starting point, and at the same time confirms the following isomorphism:

$$\begin{bmatrix} M_z \rightarrow M_x \\ (f) \end{bmatrix} \approx \begin{bmatrix} M_x \rightarrow M_y \\ (f) \end{bmatrix} ?$$

Such a myth does in fact exist among the Sherente:

M_{124}. Sherente. 'The story of Asare'

Once there was an Indian who had a wife and many sons, all of them adult except the youngest, Asare. While the father was hunting one day, the brothers sent Asare to fetch their mother and bring her to the bachelors' house, bidding her to cut their hair and decorate them. But when she entered, her own sons seized and ravished her.

Asare revealed what they had done, and the culprits were severely thrashed by their father. They took their revenge by setting fire to the hut where the couple were living. The parents changed into falcons of the kind that like to fly in the smoke, and thus escaped.

Then the sons went far away. On the way Asare suffered from thirst, and the water from tucum nuts (*Astrocaryum tucuma*) knocked down by his brothers was not enough to quench it. Then one of them began digging a well in a hollow, and so much water gushed forth that Asare, however much his brothers urged him to drink, could not exhaust it. The water spread more and more, finally forming the sea.

Then Asare recollected that an arrow he particularly prized had been left on the opposite bank. He swam across, found his arrow, and was swimming back when in the middle of the water he found an alligator (jacare), which had developed out of a swarm of lizards which Asare had killed while traveling, and which the spreading waters had carried away. Asare begged the alligator to let him sit on him, and when the latter refused, Asare called him names, making fun of his ugly nose. The alligator gave chase. Meanwhile the brothers saw the arrow drifting on the water, concluded that their youngest brother had perished, and marched on.

Asare reached land when his pursuer was already close behind. He ran into the woods where the woodpeckers were pecking the bark from the trees in order to eat the insects under it. At his request the birds covered him with strips of bark and sent the alligator off on a false scent. Once the danger was over, Asare went on his way and crossed another river where he met another alligator, with the same consequences. He escaped from it, thanks to partridges who happened to be digging out groundnuts (*Arachis hypogaea*) and who hid him under the straw. The same incidents occurred again when Asare swam across a third river, but this time he hid under the rinds of the jatoba fruits which monkeys were busy eating. One of the monkeys, from inborn talkativeness, came near divulging the secret, but another struck it on the lips, so he kept silent.

Asare finally got to his uncle, the skunk, who was not afraid at all. When the alligator came, the skunk squirted his fluid at him, and the alligator died of the stench. The skunk called the little inhambus (*Tinamus* species) to drag the corpse into the river. Asare, however, stayed with his uncle.[7]

When the sea was formed, Asare's brothers had at once tried to bathe. Even today, toward the close of the rainy season, one hears in

7. The skunk is identified in the text with *Mephitis suffocans*, '*cangamba*' (Maciel, 1923, p. 431). In reality, the South American equivalent of the North American skunk is a member of the Conepatus family.

the west the sound of their splashing in the water. Then they appear in the heavens, new and clean, as Sururu, the Seven Stars (the Pleiades) (Nimuendaju, 1944, pp. 185–6).

There is a great deal to be said about this myth. Let me begin by establishing, in accordance with my stated intention, that, with the help of a certain number of transformations affecting either content or code, it faithfully reconstitutes the Bororo myth about the bird-nester (M_1).

The initial situation is the same: a mother is raped by her son (or sons). Two differences, however, will be noted: in the Bororo myth the mother was raped in the forest where she had gone to carry out a task only performed by women. Here it is the father who is away in the forest hunting – that is, engaged on a masculine occupation – and the rape is carried out, not just somewhere in the village, but in the men's house, which women are not usually allowed to enter. Secondly, M_1 laid stress on the culprit's youth (he has not yet been initiated), whereas M_{124} describes the culprits as being initiated adolescents, obliged to reside in the men's house cf. Nimuendaju, 1942, p. 49).

A third difference follows inevitably from the two I have just noted. The Bororo father is unaware of his misfortune and makes inquiries to confirm his suspicions; once they are confirmed, he tries to kill his son. The Sherente father, on the other hand, is immediately informed of what has taken place, and it is his sons who want to kill him. The Bororo father has recourse to water in order to satisfy his passion for revenge (fire was to appear later); to satisfy their passion for revenge, the Sherente sons use fire (water appears later).

The Sherente parents escape death by changing into falcons, which are fond of kitchen fires: the Bororo son escapes death thanks to rescuers in the form of urubus, who are enemies of kitchen fires (since, according to the myth, they feed on carrion and raw flesh).

The vertical disjunction (low → high) affects both the Bororo son and the Sherente parents. On the other hand, whereas in the first case, the son is separated vertically – by air – from his parents, the Sherente hero is separated horizontally from his brothers by water.

The Bororo hero, far from the village, and after climbing to the top of a rocky cliff, suffers from hunger: also far from his village, and after covering a great distance, the Sherente hero suffers from thirst. Each one tries two remedies, which are contrasted by the two myths. In M_1 there is, in the first place, raw animal food, which decomposes because there is too much of it; then raw vegetable food, which is never adequate because the hero is unable to retain it. In M_{124} there is first a vegetable drink in short supply, then non-vegetable (chthonic) water, of which there is so much that the hero is unable to consume it all. In both cases the quantitatively insufficient remedy is vegetable and beneficent (palm-nut juice, fresh fruit) and the quantitatively sufficient (and even superabundant) remedy is non-vegetable in origin and maleficent (decomposed lizards and sea water, which both threaten to bring about the hero's death).

Both the Bororo and the Sherente myths take the form of myths explaining the origin of water; in the first case the water is rain or celestial water; in the second, it is chthonic: that is, it gushes out from the earth.

The Bororo hero has to cross water in order to bring back the ritual instruments; the Sherente hero crosses the water in order to bring back an arrow – that is, a weapon used in hunting.

On three occasions the Sherente hero meets with an alligator that has sprung from the lizards he killed before the water spread out over the earth. Lizards are also killed by the Bororo hero, in order to appease his hunger and to provide a reserve food supply. It is because this food decomposes very quickly that the vultures attack him.

If we were to keep strictly to the text of M_1, the episode would remain incomprehensible. Or, to be more accurate, the absence of any syntagmatic context would, if we were bent on finding an interpretation, lead us to comb through the whole of American mythology, which would supply us with more answers than we could cope with: for the Kubenkranken, the lizard is a precultural food (Métraux, 1960, p. 14); for the Warao, the Choco and the Cuna, a master of fire; elsewhere it is a master of sleep because it has no eyelids; and among populations as far apart as the Jicarilla Apache of North America and the Amuesha of Peru it is a symbol of incest and witchcraft. . . .

But whereas research into the etymology – one might almost

say the 'mythemology' – of the lizard would be a rash undertaking, research into its significance is not. As is indicated in no
uncertain terms by the Sherente myth, the lizard is the terrestrial
counterpart of the aquatic alligator. M_1 and M_{124} therefore shed
light on each other: one takes place on land and makes the hero a
hunter of lizards for the same reason that the other, which takes
place on water, makes the alligator a 'hunter of heroes'. The fact
that a Bororo myth and a Ge myth present this reciprocal view of
things perhaps allows us to derive confirmation for the former
from an Apinaye text:

It is said that when an Apinaye male child is born, the urubus rejoice
because there will be yet another hunter to leave them dead flesh in the
bush. But when a female child is born, the lizards rejoice, because it is
the women's duty to prepare *berubur* – that is, meals – and the fallen
scraps provide food for lacertians (Oliveira, 1930, p. 67).

If it were legitimate to extrapolate, we could say we were
dealing with a twofold contrast: one is an internal contrast, in
M_1, between lizards and urubus with the double valency:
female–male, cooked–raw;[8] the other is external, covering both
M_1 and M_{124}, and opposes the lizards and the alligator, also with
a double valency: land–water, cooked–raw.

Finally, we know that the Sherente believe the alligator to be
the master of water and the jaguar master of fire (M_{12}). It is
therefore perfectly consistent that in their myth about the origin
of terrestrial water (M_{124}) the hero should encounter an alligator,
just as in their myth about the origin of terrestrial fire (M_{12}) he
should encounter a jaguar. And since we have established that
fire = water (-1), it is equally consistent that in both myths the
respective behavior of the animal and the hero should be
inverted. The hero in M_{12} behaves courteously toward the jaguar
who offers to help him: the hero of M_{124} behaves insolently
toward the alligator who refuses to help him.

Let us pause for a moment and consider the episode of the helpful
animals, which occurs at the beginning of the Bororo myth and
at the end of the Sherente myth. In descending order of effective-

8. And perhaps vegetable/animal, too, if we follow another indication
from the same source, where lizards are grouped with grasshoppers, rats,
and rabbits as garden parasites (Oliveira, 1930, p. 65).

ness, these animals are, in the Bororo myth, the hummingbird, the pigeon and the grasshopper. Although the Sherente myth does not mention the respective abilities of the woodpeckers and the partridges, it clearly indicates that the monkeys are the least effectual, since they almost betray their protégé. We can therefore take as our starting point the following hypothetical correspondence between the two series:

Bororo		*Sherente*	
hummingbird	(1)	woodpeckers	(1)
pigeon	(2)	partridges	(2)
grasshopper	(3)	monkeys	(3)

But the correspondence seems to be reversed when we try to define the species according to the categories of high and low. In the Sherente series the monkeys eat fruit (high), the woodpeckers attack the bark of trees (medium), the partridges dig up seeds (low). If we take into account the fact that in the Bororo series the grasshopper naturally occupies a lower place than the birds, and that the respective missions assigned to the three animals consist in gaining possession of the large and small rattles (which are held in the hand, therefore more or less in the 'high' range, and unequal in size), than of the ankle bells (low), we should arrive at the following table:

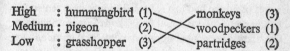

High	: hummingbird	(1)	monkeys	(3)
Medium	: pigeon	(2)	woodpeckers	(1)
Low	: grasshopper	(3)	partridges	(2)

Let us see if it is possible to overcome the difficulty. It will be remembered that the Sherente myth about the origin of fire (M_{12}) supplied a different series of three animals who played the part of masters of water. These were in the following order:

urubus	(1)
'small birds'	(2)
alligator	(3)

We do not know what these 'small birds' were, unless we suppose they were inhambus, which in the Asare myth are also described as 'small'. The inhambus (like the 'partridges' in the same myth) are gallinaceans which live on the ground, flying only occasionally and clumsily. In respect of the high and low categories, they could perhaps be placed between the urubus and the alligator. On the other hand, the ancient Tupi along the east coast used white feathers flecked with black taken from these birds to decorate their weapons when they went to war, or when they were getting ready to execute their prisoners (Abbeville, 1614, p. 237). This custom clearly corresponds to the role of 'undertakers' assigned to the small inhambus in the Asare myth (although the *inambu-tin* referred to in the old source may have belonged to a larger species).

The myths already examined refer on several occasions to gallinaceans (Tinamidae or Cracidae) and seem always (apart from M_{14}, in a passage of no great significance) to treat them as beings of little merit, if not downright sinister. The gallinaceans destroy the scattered remnants of fire, being too weak to transport it (M_8, M_9, M_{12}). The inhambu is an inferior fowl which provides a bitter soup (M_{143}) and is not accepted in exchange for the flesh of the caititu, a nobler variety of game (M_{16}): it is the sole diet of a boy who is being kept in seclusion (Murphy, 1958, p. 74; Strömer, 1932, p. 133). A certain constellation in the night sky is the mother of the Tinamidae (M_{28}); the reason the jaguar does not attack birds belonging to this family and has acquired nocturnal habits is that the Tinamidae made him eyes with water to replace the eyes of fire he had lost (M_{119}). The link between stars, night and gallinaceans can no doubt be explained by the Sherente custom. 'The hours are counted during the day by the sun and at night by the stars and by the scream of the inhambu' (Oliveira, 1913, p. 394).[9]

We possess more definite information about the semantic value of the other animals. According to the Ge myths analysed below (M_{163}), the woodpeckers are the masters of destructive fire, which means that they are both correlated with, and opposed

9. Evidence of the same belief is given by Ihering ('Inhambu' entry) in connection with *Grypturus stirgulosus*, whence its popular name '*Inhambu relogio*': the clockbird. See also Cavalcanti, 1883, pp. 159–60: the cujubim bird (one of the Cracidae) announces daybreak, but the inhambu sings at night. Finally, the mutum, which is also a member of the Cracidae family 'sings at night at such regular intervals that it can be heard every two hours ... thus for the natives it is a kind of forest clock' (Orico, 1937, p. 174).

to, monkeys which, according to a Bororo myth we have already studied (M_{55}), are masters of creative fire (fire for cooking). The dove or pigeon is a master of water, as is attested not only by the key myth but also by a Sherente myth (M_{138}), which shows a whole family escaping from the flood thanks to a pigeon's carcass (*Leptoptila rufaxilla*) which grows miraculously bigger and bigger until it becomes another Noah's ark (Nimuendaju, 1942, p. 92). In several versions of the 'opossum and his sons-in-law' (M_{97}, M_{98}), Pigeon (one of the sons-in-law) catches fish from a lake by drying it up through drinking all the water it contains (Murphy, 1958, p. 119; Wagley and Galvão, 1949, p. 152). The water the pigeon has to conquer or nullify is defined by its negative properties, like destructive fire. We can therefore establish the principle that the pigeon and the woodpecker are isomorphic, in respect of water and fire.

The Bororo myth (M_1) describes the grasshopper (*mammori: Acridium cristatum*, Albisetti and Vertvelli, 1962, vol. 1, p. 780) by its slow flight (similar to that of the partridge), which causes it to run the risk of death during its mission. In the Sherente series, it therefore corresponds on the one hand to the monkeys (one of which also almost betrays its mission), on the other to the partridges which, in the form of small inhambus come into – physical, not moral – contact with death, since they play the part of gravediggers. If we postulate that M_{124} is based essentially on the second of these homologies, only the hummingbird, about whose semantic position we have less information, remains to be explained. The Ge myths have very little to say about the hummingbird; we have to look farther afield.

In the mythology of Guiana the hummingbird is presented as being in correlation with, and opposed to, the bunia bird; together they help a man who is trapped at the top of a tree to get down, then to find his way back to his village. But whereas the bunia bird is a foul-smelling creature whose droppings are transformed into creepers (Roth, 1915, pp. 209, 371), the hummingbird emits a delightful perfume, although it is occasionally soiled by excrement (pp. 335, 371). We have therefore a twofold contrast: bad smell–pleasant smell, and defiling–defiled. On the other hand, the role usually assigned to the hummingbird in the myths of Guiana is to look for tobacco and bring it to men.

The tobacco grows on an island in the middle of a lake which the hummingbird succeeds in crossing, as in the Bororo myth; the myths make it clear that the tobacco will serve to 'call forth' spirits, provided it is used in conjunction with the ceremonial rattles (Roth, 1915, p. 336), that it is the hummingbird's task to bring back in the Bororo myth. Leaving aside for the time being the problem of tobacco, to which I shall return later (in volume 2), we should note the relation between the hummingbird and water, a point on which some light is shed by the myths of the south-eastern United States. These myths, of which we possess several versions – Natchez, Alabama, Koasati, Hitchiti, Creek and Cherokee – contrast the hummingbird and the crane as diurnal-nocturnal (in Guiana, according to a Warao myth, defiled-defiling, Roth, 1915, p. 335); on the other hand, they explain how the hummingbird staked water and fish on the result of a race, and lost: for this reason the hummingbird never drinks (Swanton, 1929, pp. 202, 273, and *passim*).

In Brazil, the Botocudo and the Caingang tell very similar stories: the hummingbird who was formerly master of all the water in the world had it taken from him by the other creatures (Nimuendaju, 1946b, 9, p. 111: Métraux, 1946, vol. 1, p. 540; Baldus, 1937, p. 60). A Kraho myth gives the hummingbird a negative relation to water, since it is the only creature capable of flying through flames (Schultz, 1950, p. 127). According to a Surura myth, it causes disjunction between fire and water by making the alligator laugh, so that it can seize fire from inside the jaws of the alligator and bring it to men (Becher, 1959, p. 105). In a Toba myth it steals fire (Métraux, 1946, pp. 107–8, 110).

If we agree, as a working hypothesis, to generalize the above convergent details, the hummingbird can be defined as a function of water but in negative terms, and it can be placed in correlation with, and in contrast to, the pigeon which was a great drinker.[10]

We arrive, then, at the following coherent system:

10. A myth belonging to the Pima of Arizona associates the humming-bird with a divinity called El Bebedor, 'The Drinker', who was responsible for the flood (Russell, 1908, p. 226, note). If the negation of water is taken to its extreme limit, the hummingbird may be confused with the wood-pecker, the master of destructive fire. This in fact occurs in a Caingang myth (M_{124a}), in which the hummingbird and the woodpecker jointly steal fire from the jaguar (Baldus, 1958, p. 122). But the remarkable thing is that in

Bororo (M₁)   *Sherente* (M₁₂₄)

(1) hummingbird (≢water)——(1) woodpecker (≡destructive fire)
(2) pigeon   (≡water)——(3) monkey (≡creative fire)
(3) grasshopper (life–death)——(2) 'partridge' (life–death)

in which we again have, on the one hand, the contrast between
water and fire and, on the other hand, the linking of one or the
other element with the transition from life to death, which struck
us as being characteristic of the way problems are posed in the
Bororo and Sherente myths respectively.

Let us now look at the matter from a different viewpoint. In
the course of their missions the animal helpers come into contact
with things: lifesaving musical instruments in the Bororo myth,
materials used as lifesaving hiding places in the Sherente myth:

Bororo (M₁)   *Sherente* (M₁₂₄)
hummingbird : large rattle   woodpeckers : bark of trees
pigeon   : small rattle   'partridges' : straw
grasshopper : little bells   monkeys   : rinds

The things in the Bororo myth are sonorous objects that 'must
not be heard'. The things in the Sherente myth no doubt prevent
the alligator from *seeing* the hero; but at the same time they have
the unusual feature of being food refuse – that is, things *that are
not to be eaten*. They are therefore antifoods forming a series
comparable, in this respect, to the series in the Apinaye myth
(M₉): rock, hardwood, and rotten wood, which are also antifoods
but, like the Bororo instruments, 'consumable' by the ear, if not
by the mouth. Through the medium, in this instance, of M₉ the
symmetry between M₁ and M₁₂₄ can be confirmed once again.

In M₁ as in M₁₂₄, a person offers assistance in addition to the
series of three animals: a human grandmother in one context, an
animal uncle (a skunk) in the other. The grandmother saves the
hero by lending him a magic wand; the uncle, by releasing his
foul-smelling fluid. I shall come back later to the parallel between
the two myths, which admits of different interpretations.

this instance it is the woodpecker who undergoes a transformation: first he
gets wet, then he becomes a master of cooking fire – not completely, however, since this fire (which becomes destructive) sets the earth alight, and
since creative fire (for cooking), is reduced to a secondary factor.

Lastly, and to complete the comparison, M_1 refers to the start of the rains – that is, to the end of the dry season; whereas the last few lines of M_{124} refer to its beginning.

The existence of a correlation between M_1 and M_{124} has thus been confirmed down to the smallest details. It has in fact been proved that if $M_y = fM_x$, there exists a myth $M_z = fM_y$ which has the same relation to M_x as M_x has to M_y.

References

ABBEVILLE, C. D' (1614), *Histoire de la mission des pères Capucins en l'isle de Maragnan et terres circonvoisines*, Paris.

BALDUS, H. (1937), *Ensaios de Etnologia Brasileira*, São Paulo.

BALDUS, H. (ed.) (1958), *Die Jaguarzwilunge. Mythen und Heilbringersgeschichten Ursprungssagen und Märchen brasilianisches Indianer*, Kassel.

BANNER, H. (1957), 'Mitos dos indios Kayapo', *Revista de Antropologia*, vol. 5, no. 1, São Paulo.

BECHER, H. (1959), 'Algumas notas sôbre a religão et a mitologia dos Surará', *Revista do Museo Panlista*, n.s., vol. 11, São Paulo.

CADOGAN, L. (1959), 'Ayvu Rapita. Textos míticos de los Mbyá-Guarani del Guaira', *Antroplogia*, no. 5, boletim no. 227, *Universidade de São Paulo*.

CAVALCANTI, A. (1883), *The Brasilian Language and its Agglutination*, Rio de Janeiro.

CHERMONT DE MIRANDA, V. DE (1944), 'Estudos sobre o Nheêngatú', *Anais da Biolioteca Nacional*, vol. 54, (1942); Rio de Janeiro.

COLBACCHINI, A. (1919), *A Tribuqdos Bororos*, Rio de Janeiro.

COLBACCHINI, A. (1925), *J Bororos Orientali 'Orarimugudoge' del Matto Grosso, Brasile* (Contributi Scientifici delle Missioni Salesiane del Venerabile Don Bosco, I) Torino.

COLBACCHINI, A., and ALBISETTI, C. (1942), *Os Bororos Orientais*, São Paulo-Rio de Janeiro.

DREYFUS, S. (1963), *Les Kayapo du Nord, Contribution à l'étude des Indiens Gé*, Paris.

KOCH-GRÜNBERG, T. (1916), *Von Roroima zum Orinoco. Zweites Band. Mythen und Legenden der Taulipang und Arekuna Indianer*, Berlin.

LÉVI-STRAUSS, C. (1971), *Mythologiques IV: L'Homme nu*, Plon.

MACIEL, M. (1923), *Elementos de Zoologia geral e descriptiva de accordo com a fauna brasileira*, Rio de Janeiro, Paris.

MÉTRAUX, A. (1928), *La Religion des Tupinamba*, Paris.

MÉTRAUX, A. (1946), 'Myths of the Toba and Pilagá Indians of the Gran Chaco', *Memoirs Amer. Folklore Soc.*, vol. 40, Philadelphia.

MÉTRAUX, A. (1946), 'The Botocudo', *Handbook of South American Indians, Bull. Bureau Amer. Ethnol.*

MÉTRAUX, A. (1960), 'Mythes et contes des Indiens Cayapo (Groupe Kuben-Kran-Kegn)', *Revista do Museo Paulista*, n.s., vol. 12, São Paulo.

MURPHY, R. F. (1958), 'Mundurucú Religion', *University of California Publications in Amer. Archaeol. and Ethnol.*, vol. 49, no. 1, Berkeley–Los Angeles.

NIMUENDAJU, C. (1914), 'Die Sagen von der Erschaffung und Vernichtung der Welt als Grundlagen der Religion der Apapocúva-Guarani', *Zeitschrift für Ethnologie*, vol. 46.

NIMUENDAJU, C. (1915), 'Sagen der Tembé-Indianer', *Zeitschrift für Ethnologie*, vol. 47.

NIMUENDAJU, C. (1919–20, 1921–2), 'Bruchstücke aus Religion und Uberlieferung der Šipaia-Indianer', *Anthropos*, vols. 14–15; 16–17.

NIMUENDAJU, C. (1939), 'The Apinayé', *Catholic University of America, Anthropological Series*, no. 8, Washington, D.C.

NIMUENDAJU, C. (1942), 'The Šerente', *Publication of the Frederick Webb Hodge Anniversary Publication Fund*, vol. 4, Los Angeles.

NIMUENDAJU, C. (1944), 'Šerenté tales', *J. Amer. Folklore*, vol. 57.

NIMUENDAJU, C. (1946a), 'The Eastern Timbira', *University of California Publications in Amer. Archaeol. and Ethnol.*, vol. 41.

NIMUENDAJU, C. (1946b), 'Social organization and beliefs of the Botocudo of Eastern Brazil', *Southwestern J. Anthropol.*, vol. 2, no. 1.

NIMUENDAJU, C. (1952), 'The Tukuna', *University of California Publications in Amer. Archaeol. and Ethnol.*, vol. 45.

NORDENSKJÖLD, E. (1922), *Indianer und Weisse in Nordostbolivien*, Stuttgart.

OLIVEIRA, C. D. DE (1930), 'Os Apinagé do Alto Tocantins', *Boletim do Museu Nacional*, vol. 6, no. 2, Rio de Janeiro.

OLIVEIRA, J. F. DE (1913), 'The Cherente of Central Brazil', *Proceedings of the 8th Congress of Americanists*.

ORICO, C. (1937), *Vocabulario de Crendices Amazonicas*, São Paulo-Rio de Janeiro.

POMPEU SOBRINHO, T. (1935), 'Lendas Mehim', *Revista do Instituto do Ceará*, vol. 49, Fortaleza.

PREUSS, K. T. (1912), *Die Nayarit-Expedition. Textaufnahmen mit Beobachtungen unter mexikanischen Indianern*, 3 vols., Leipzig.

ROTH, W. E. (1915), 'An inquiry into the animism and folklore of the Guiana Indians', *30th Annual Report Bureau Amer. Ethnol. (1908–09)*, Washington, D.C.

RUSSELL, F. (1908), 'The Pima Indians', *26th Annual Report Bureau Amer. Ethnol. (1904–05)*, Washington, D.C.

SCHADEN, E. (1947), 'Fragmentos de mitologia Kayuá', *Revista do Museu Paulista*, n.s., vol. 1, São Paulo.

SCHADEN, E. (1955), 'A Origem e a posse do fogo na mitologia Guarani', *Anais do 31 Congr. Intern. de Americanistas*, São Paulo.

SCHULTZ, H. (1950), 'Lendas dos indios Krahó', *Revista do Museo Paulista*, n.s., vol. 4, São Paulo.

SIMPSON, G. G. (1944), 'A Carib (Kamarakoto) myth from
  Venezuela', *J. Amer. Folklore*, vol. 57.
STEINEN, K. VON DEN (1940), *Entre os aborigines do Brasil central*,
  São Paulo.
STRÖMER, C. VON (1932), 'Die Sprache der Mundurukú', *Anthropos:
  Collection Internationale de Monographies Linguistiques 2*, Vienna.
SWANTON, J. R. (1929), 'Myths and tales of the Southeastern
  Indians', *Bull. Bureau Amer. Ethnol. 88*, Washington, D.C.
WAGLEY, C., and GALVÃO, E. (1949), 'The Tenetehara Indians of
  Brazil', *Columbia University Contributions to Anthropology*, no. 35,
  New York.

Further Reading

The following references aim at providing a reasonably good coverage of recent works on myth. The eighteen references prior to 1950 (against 166 later ones) are all contributions that keep their value.

Due to the rapid development of new approaches under the impact or structuralism, of a keener interest in semantics, and of innovative fieldwork methods, much will happen in the next decade. Research will continue to proliferate in the French and English speaking worlds, but it will have to take stock of important contributions by other and increasingly strong contingents. Thus, primarily in Italy, the USSR and Germany, but also in Mexico and Brazil, scholars draw the attention of their colleagues in other countries by the quality of their productions. Unfortunately, references are not given here to those works for lack of space and because neither the publications nor the languages in which they are written are commonly accessible. Let us hope that readers will soon be available where the most outstanding of those countries' numerous contributions will be presented in translations.

A. Aarne and S. Thompson, 'The types of the folktale', *Folklore Fellows Communications*, no. 184, 1961.

Karl Abraham, 'Dreams and myths: a study of folk-psychology', in Karl Abraham, *Clinical Papers and Essays on Psychoanalysis*, vol. 2, pp. 151–209, 1955.

R. D. Abrahams, 'Introductory remarks to a rhetorical theory of folk lore', *J. Amer. Folklore*, vol. 81, pp. 143–58, 1968.

H. Abrahamsson, *The Origin of Death: Studies in African Mythology*, Almquist & Wiksell, 1951.

E. Ojo Arewa and Alan Dundes, 'Proverbs and the ethnography of speaking folklore', *Amer. Anthropol.*, vol. 66, pp. 70–85, 1964.

F. C. Bartlett, 'Some experiments on the reproduction of folk-stories', *Folklore*, vol. 31, pp. 30–47, 1920.

W. R. Bascom, 'Literary style in Yoruba riddles', *J. Amer. Folklore*, vol. 62, pp. 1–16, 1949.

W. R. Bascom, 'Verbal art', *J. Amer. Folklore*, vol. 68, pp. 245–52, 1955.

W. R. Bascom, 'Four functions of folklore', *J. Amer. Folklore*, vol. 68, pp. 245–52, 1955.

W. R. Bascom, 'The forms of folklore: prose narrative', *J. Amer. Folklore*, vol. 78, pp. 3–20, 1965.

M. Beckwith, 'Polynesian story composition', *J. Polynesian Soc.*, vol. 53, pp. 177–203, 1944.

T. Beidelman, 'Further adventures of hyaena and rabbit: the folktale as a sociological model', *Africa*, vol. 33, pp. 54–69, 1963.

R. Benedict, 'A matter for the field worker in folklore', *J. Amer. Folklore*, vol. 26, no. 139, p. 104, 1923.

R. Benedict, *Zuni Mythology*, 2 vols. Columbia University Press, 1935.

R. Benedict, 'An introduction to Zuni mythology', from *Zuni Mythology*. Condensed by one-third, in M. Mead (ed.), *An Anthropologist at Work: Writings of Ruth Benedict*, Houghton Mifflin, 1959, pp. 226–45.

B. Berlin, D. E. Breedlove and P. H. Raven, 'Covert categories and folk taxonomies', *Amer. Anthropol.*, vol. 70, pp. 290–99, 1968.

J. Blacking, 'The social value of Venda riddles', *African Studies*, vol. 20, pp. 1–32, 1961.

F. Boas, 'The development of folk-tales and myths', *Scientific Monthly*, vol. 3, pp. 335–43, 1916.

F. Boas, 'Kwakiutl culture as reflected in mythology', *Memoirs of the American Folklore Society*, no. 28, 1935.

F. Boas, 'Mythology', in F. Boas (ed.), *Race, Language and Culture*, 1940, pp. 397–524.

P. Bogatyrev and R. Jakobson, 'Die Folklore als besondere Form des Schaffens', *Donum Natalicum Schrijnen*, pp. 900–913, Nijmogen-Utrecht, 1929.

L. Boyer, 'An example of legend distortion from the Apaches of the Mescalero Indian Reservation', *J. Amer. Folklore*, pp. 118–42, 1964.

C. Bremond, 'Le message narratif', *Communications*, vol. 4, pp. 4–32, 1964.

C. Bremond, 'L'analyse conceptuelle du Coran', *Communications*, vol. 7, pp. 127–38, 1966.

C. Bremond, 'La logique des possibles narratifs', *Communications*, vol. 8, pp. 60–76, 1966.

C. Bremond, 'La postérité américaine de Propp', *Communications*, vol. 11, pp. 148–64, 1968.

I. R. Buchler, 'Sémantique descriptive des catégories religieuses nuer', *L'Homme* 6, pp. 35–58, 1966.

I. R. Buchler, and H. A. Selby, *A Formal Study of Myth*, University of Texas Press, 1968.

R. Bultmann, 'The various types of traditional material', *The Study of the Synoptic Gospels*, in *Form Criticism*, trans. Frederick C. Grant, Harper & Row, 1962, pp. 36–63.

R. Bultmann, 'The laws governing popular narrative and tradition', in *Id.*, *Form Criticism*, New York, 1962, pp. 32–5.

K. Burke, *The Philosophy of Literary Form. Studies in symbolic action*, Louisiana State University Press, 1941; Vintage Books, 1957.

K. Burke, *A Grammar of Motives*, Prentice-Hall, 1945.

K. Burke, *A Rhetoric of Motives*, Prentice-Hall, 1950.

K. Burridge, *Mambu*, London, 1960; Harper & Row, 1970.

K. Burridge, *Tangu Traditions: The Mythology and Way of Life of a New Guinea People*, Clarendon, 1969.

J. Campbell, *The Masks of God; Primitive Mythology*, Viking Press, 1959.

E. Cassirer, *The Philosophy of Symbolic Forms*, vol. 2, *Mythical Thought*, Yale University Press, 1955.

A. Christensen, 'Motif et thème', *Folklore Fellows Communications*, no. 59, 1925.

S. Cohen, 'Theories of myth', *Man*, vol. 4, no. 3, pp. 337–53, 1969.

B. N. Colby, 'Cultural patterns in narratives', *Science*, vol. 151, pp. 793–8, 1965.

W. H. Davenport, 'Marshallese folklore types', *J. Amer. Folklore*, vol. 66, p. 221, 1953.

P. Delarue, *Le conte populaire français*, vol. 1, Erasme, 1957.

P. Delarue and M. Tenèze, *Le conte populaire français*, vol. 2, Maisonneuve et Larose, 1964.

A. Dundes, 'From etic to emic units in the structural study of folktales', *J. Amer. Folklore*, vol. 75, pp. 95–105, 1962.

A. Dundes, 'The morphology of North American Indian Folk tales', *Folklore Fellows Communications*, no. 19, 1964.

A. Dundes (ed.), *The Study of Folklore*, Prentice-Hall, 1965.

M. Dorson (ed.), 'Folklore research around the world', *J. Amer. Folklore*, vol. 74, 1961.

M. Douglas, *Purity and Danger*, Routledge & Kegan Paul, 1966.

M. Douglas, *Natural Symbols: Explorations in Cosmology*, Cresset Press, 1970.

G. Durant, *Les Structures Anthropologiques de l'Imaginaire*, Paris, Presses Universitaires de France, 1960.

E. Durkheim and M. Mauss, *Primitive Classification*, University of Chicago Press, 1963.

M. Eliade, *Patterns in Comparative Religion*, Sheed & Ward, 1958; Meridan Books, 1963.

V. Erlich, *Russian Formalism: History, Doctrine*, Mouton, 1955.

E. E. Evans-Pritchard, *The Zande Trickster*, Clarendon Press, 1967.

R. Finnegan, *Limba Stories and Story-Telling*, Clarendon Press, 1967.

R. Finnegan, 'Attitudes to the study of oral literature in British social anthropology', *Man* N.S. vol. 4, no. 1, pp. 59–69, 1969.

R. Firth, *History and Traditions of Tikopia*, Memoirs of the Polynesian Society of New Zealand, 1960.

R. Firth, 'The plasticity of myth', *Ethnologica* N.S. vol. 2, pp. 181–8, 1960.

J. L. Fischer, 'The sociopsychological analysis of folktales', *Current Anthropol.*, vol. 4, pp. 235–95, 1963.

J. L. Fischer, 'Folktale in the Eastern Carolines', in Andrew P. Vayda (ed.), *Peoples and Cultures of the Pacific*, pp. 380–82, Doubleday, 1968.

D. Forde (ed.), *African Worlds*, Oxford University Press, 1954.

M. Fortes and G. Dieterlen (eds.), *African Systems of Thought*, Oxford University Press, 1965.

C. O. Frake, 'A structural description of subanum "religious behavior"', in W. H. Goodenough (ed.), *Explorations in Cultural Anthropology: Essays in Honour of George Peter Murdock*, McGraw Hill, 1964, pp. 111–29.

C. O. Frake, 'The ethnographic study of cognitive systems', in T. Gladwin and W. C. Sturtevant (eds.), *Anthropology and human Behavior*, Anthropological Society of Washington, 1962, pp. 72–85.

H. Frankfort *et al.*, *Before Philosophy, The Intellectual Adventure of Ancient Man*, Penguin, 1959.

J. Frazer, *The New Golden Bough*, Anchor, 1961.

D. Freud and D. E. Oppenhein, *Dreams in Folklore*, International University Press, 1958.

J. C. Gardin, 'Procédures d'analyse sémantique dans les sciences humaines', in J. Pouillon and P. Maranda (eds.), *Echange et Communications – Exchange and Communications: Mélanges Lévi-Strauss*, 2 vols, Mouton, 1970; also in English in *Social Science Information 8*, 1969.

P. L. Garvin, *et al.*, *Predication Typing: A Pilot Study in Semantic Analysis*, Bunker Ramo Corporation, 1966; also in *Language* (special issue), 1968.

A. van Gennep, *La Formation des légendes*, Flammarion, 1910.

Genre vol. 2, no. 2, June 1969, *Symposium on Folk Genres*.

R. A. Georges (ed.), *Studies on Mythology*, Dorsey Press, 1969.

K. S. Goldstein, *A Guide for Field Workers in Folklore*, Folklore Associates, 1964.

A. J. Greimas, 'Eléments pour une théorie de l'interprétation du récit mythique', *Communications*, vol. 8, 1966, pp. 28–59.

A. J. Greimas, 'Eléments d'une grammaire narrative', *L'Homme*, vol. 9, 1969, pp. 71–92.

A. J. Greimas, *Sémantique structurale*, Seuil, 1964.

A. J. Greimas, *Du Sens*, Seuil, 1970.

M. Griaule and G. Dieterlen, *Le Renard Pâle: Tome I. Le Mythe Cosmogomique, fascicule I: la Création du Monde*, Université de Paris, Travaux et mémoires de l'Institut d'Ethnologie, vol. 72, 1965.

A. I. Hallowell, 'Myth, culture and personality', *Amer. Anthropol.* vol. 49, 1947, p. 544.

I. Hammett, 'Ambiguity, classification and change: the function of riddles', *Man* N.S. vol. 2, 1967, pp. 379–91.

J. Helm (ed.), *Essays on the Verbal and Visual Arts*, University of Washington Press, 1967.

M. J. Herskovits and F. S. Herskovits, *Suriname Folklore*, Columbia University Press, 1936.

M. J. Herskovits and F. S. Herskovits, *Dahomean Narrative*, North-western University Press, 1958.

M. J. Herskovits, 'The study of African oral art', *J. Amer. Folklore*, vol. 74, 1961, pp. 451–6.

R. Hertz, *Mélanges de sociologie religieuse et folklore*, Alcan, 1928; also in English, *Death and the Right Hand*, Free Press, 1960.

D. C. Hildum, 'Semantic analysis by computer', *Language*, vol. 39, pp. 649–54, 1963.

D. Hymes, 'Some North Pacific Coast poems: a problem in anthropological philology', *Amer. Anthropol.*, vol. 67, pp. 316–41, 1965.

V. Ivanov and V. Toporov, 'Le mythe indo-européen du dieu de l'orage poursuivant le serpent: reconstitution du schéma', in J. Pouillon and P. Maranda (eds.), *Echange et Communications – Exchange and Communications – Mélanges Lévi-Strauss*, 2 vols., Mouton, 1970.

M. Jacobs, *The Content and Style of Oral Literature: Clackamas Chinook Myths and Tales*, Viking Fund Publication in Anthropology, no. 26, 1959.

M. Jacobs, *The People are Coming Soon: Analyses of Clackamas Chinook Myths and Tales*, University of Washington Press, 1960.

M. Jacobs, (ed.), 'The anthropologist looks at myth', *J. Amer. Folklore*, vol. 79, 1966.

R. Jakobson and T. Todorov (eds.), *Théorie de la littérature: Textes des formalistes russes*, Seuil, 1965.

H. Jason, 'A multidimensional approach to oral literature', *Current Anthropol.*, vol. 10, pp. 413–25, 1969.

A. E. Jensen, *Myth and Cult among Primitive People*, University of Chicago Press, 1963.

C. G. Jung, 'The psychology of the trickster figure', in P. Radin, *The Trickster*, pp. 193–211.

C. G. Jung and K. Kerényi, *Essays on a Science of Mythology*, Bollinger, 1963.

B. F. Kirtley, *A Motif-Index of Polynesian, Melanesian, and Micronesian Narratives*, University of Michigan Press, 1955.

C. Kluckhohn, *The Scientific Study of Values*, in three lectures, University of Toronto Press, 1958.

E. K. Köngäs Maranda, 'The earth-diver (Th. A 815)', *Ethnohistory*, vol. 7, pp. 151–80, 1960.

E. K. Köngäs Maranda, 'The cattle of the forest and the harvest of water', in J. Helm (ed.), *Essays on the Verbal and Visual Arts: Proceedings of the 1966 Annual Meetings of the American Ethnological Society*, University of Washington Press, 1967, pp. 84–95.

E. K. Köngäs Maranda, 'Structure des énigmes', *L'Homme*, vol. 9, pp. 4–48, 1969.

E. K. Köngäs Maranda and P. Maranda, *Structural Models in Folklore and Transformational Essays*, 2nd edn., Mouton, 1970.

W. Labov and J. Waletzky, 'Narrative analysis: oral versions of personal experience', in J. Helm (ed.), *Essays on the Verbal and Visual Arts: Proceedings of the 1966 Annual Meeting of the American Ethnological Society*, University of Washington Press, pp. 12–44, 1967.

E. R. Leach, 'Magical hair', *J. Royal Anthropol. Institute*, vol. 87, pp. 147–64, 1957.

E. R. Leach, 'Lévi-Strauss in the Garden of Eden: an examination of some recent developments in the analysis of myth', *Transactions of the New York Academy of Sciences* Series 2, 23, pp. 386–96, 1961.

E. R. Leach, *Rethinking Anthropology*, Athlone Press, 1961.

E. R. Leach, 'Pulleyar and the Lord Buddha', *Psychoanalysis and Psychoanalytic Review*, vol. 49, 1962, pp. 80–102.

E. R. Leach, 'Telstar et les Aborigènes ou "La Pensée sauvage",' in *Annales, Economies, Sociétés, Civilisations*, vol. 6, pp. 1100–16, 1964.

E. R. Leach, 'Review of Lévi-Strauss, Mythologiques 1: le cru et le cuit', *Amer. Anthropol.*, vol. 67, pp. 772–9, 1965.

E. R. Leach (partly) 'Apologetic correction', *Amer. Anthropol.*, vol. 77, pp. 1562–3, 1965.

E. R. Leach, *Genesis as Myth and Other Essays*, Cape, 1969.

E. R. Leach, *Lévi-Strauss*, Fontana, 1970.

E. R. Leach (ed.), *The Structural Study of Myth and Totemism*, A.S.A. Monographs, no. 5, Tavistock, 1967.

M. Leach (ed.), *Standard Dictionary of Folklore, Mythology, and Legend*, Funk & Wagnall, 1949–50.

W. A. Lessa, *Tales from Ulithi Atoll: A Comparative Study in Oceanic Folklore*, University of California Press, 1961.

W. A. Lessa and E. Z. Vogt (eds.), *Reader in Comparative Religion: An Anthropological Approach*, 2nd edn, Harper & Row, 1965.

C. Lévi-Strauss, 'L'analyse structurale des mythes', in *Anthropologie Structurale*, Plon, 1958, ch. 11; original English text in T. A. Sebeok (ed.), *Myth: A Symposium* (see below); *cf.* also the English translation of *Anthropologie structurale*, *Structural Anthropology*, Basic Books, 1964; Anchor 1968.

C. Lévi-Strauss, 'Four Winnebago myths: a structural sketch', in S. Diamond (ed.), *Culture in History: Essays in honour of Paul Radin*, Columbia University Press, pp. 351–62, 1960.

C. Lévi-Strauss, 'La structure et la forme, réflexions sur un ouvrage de Vladimir Propp', *Cahiers de l'Institut de science économique appliquée,* vol. 99, pp. 3–36, 1960; also under the following title: 'L'analyse morphologique des contes populaires russes', *International J. Slavic Poetics and Linguistics,* vol. 3, pp. 122–49, 1960.

C. Lévi-Strauss, *Le Totémisme aujourd'hui,* Presses Universitaires de France, 1962; also in English, *Totemism,* Beacon Press, 1963; Penguin, 1969.

C. Lévi-Strauss, *La Pensée sauvage,* Plon, 1962; also in English, *The Savage Mind,* University of Chicago Press, 1966.

C. Lévi-Strauss, *Mythologiques I: Le cru et le cuit,* Plon, 1964; also in English, *The Raw and the Cooked,* Harper & Row, 1969.

C. Lévi-Strauss, *Mythologiques II: Du miel aux cendres,* Plon, 1966.

C. Lévi-Strauss, *Mythologiques III: L'Origine des manières de table,* Plon, 1968.

C. Lévi-Strauss, *Mythologiques IV; L'Homme nu,* Plon, 1971.

C. S. Littleton, 'The comparative Indo-European mythology of Georges Dumézil', *J. Folklore Institute,* vol. 1, pp. 147–66, 1964.

A. B. Lord, *The Singer of Tales,* Harvard University Press, 1960.

K. Luomala, 'Oceanic, American Indian and African myths of snaring the sun', *Bernice P. Bishop, Museum, Bulletin,* vol. 1, 168, 1940.

B. Malinowski, *Magic, Science and Religion,* Anchor, 1954.

P. Maranda, 'Structural models in folklore: note sur une recherche en cours', *Communications,* vol. 8, pp. 168–72, 1966.

P. Maranda, 'Computers in the bush: tools for the automatic analysis of myths', in J. Helm (ed.), 'Essays on the verbal and visual arts'; *Proceedings of the 1966 annual meetings of the American Ethnological Association,* University of Washington Press, 1967.

P. Maranda, 'Formal analysis and inter-cultural studies', *Informations sur les sciences sociales, Social Science Information,* vol. 6, 1967, pp. 7–36.

P. Maranda, 'Recherches structurales en mythologie aux Etats-Unis', and 'Lecture mécanographique des mythes', *Informations sur les Sciences sociales, Social Science Information,* vol. 6, pp. 213–22, 1967.

P. Maranda, 'Du filtre au miscroscope: Contribution méthodologique de l'informatique aux analyses de textes', Actes du Colloque *l'Informatique au Service de l'Homme,* Centre de Mathématiques appliquées, Université de Grenoble, et Centre National de la Recherche Scientifique, 1968.

P. Maranda, 'Anthropological analytics: Lévi-Strauss's concept of social structure', in H. Nutini and I. Buchler (eds.), *The Anthropology of C. Lévi-Strauss*, Appleton-Century-Crofts, 1972.

P. Maranda, 'Informatique et mythologie', *Informatique en Sciences Humaines*, Centre de Mathématiques, Logique Formelle et Informatique, Sorbonne, vol. 6, pp. 3–21, 1970.

P. Maranda, 'L'ordinateur et l'analyse des mythes'/'The computer and the analysis of myths', *Revue International des Sciences Sociales*, UNESCO, no. spécial, *L'Informatique, la documentation et les sciences sociales*, vol. 23, pp. 244–54, 1971.

P. Maranda, 'Cendrillon et la théorie des ensembles', *Proceedings of the Symposium on the Structure and Genres of Ethnic Literature*, Palermo, in press.

P. Maranda and E. K. Köngäs Maranda, 'Le crâne et l'utérus: deux théorèmes nord-malaitains', in J. Pouillon and P. Maranda (eds.), *Echange et Communications – Exchange and Communications – Mélanges Lévi-Strauss*, 2 vols., Mouton, 1970.

P. Maranda and E. K. Köngäs Maranda (eds.), *Structural Analysis of Oral Tradition*, University of Pennsylvania Press, 1971 (contributions by Lévi-Strauss, Leach, Greimas, Hymes, Dundes, da Matta, Peacock, Turner, etc.).

D. McClelland and G. A. Friedman, 'A cross-cultural study of the relationship between child-training practices and achievement motivation appearing in folktales', in G. E. Swanson, *et al.* (eds.), *Readings in Social Psychology*, Holt, Rinehart & Winston, pp., 243–9 1952.

J. Middleton (ed.), *Myth and Cosmos: Readings in Mythology and Symbolism*, American Museum of Natural History, 1967.

G. B. Milner, 'What is a proverb?' *New Society*, February 1968, pp. 199–202.

G. B. Milner, 'De l'armature des locutions proverbiales, essai de taxonomie sémantique', *L'Homme*, vol. 9, pp. 49–70. 1969.

T. Monberg, *The Religion of Bellona Island: A Study of the Place of Beliefs and Rites in the Social Life of Pre-Christian Bellona. Part One: The Concepts of Supernaturals*, National Museum of Denmark, 1966.

V. Morin, 'L'histoire drôle', *Communications*, vol. 8, pp. 102–19, 1966.

H. A. Murray (ed.), *Myth and Mythmaking*, Daedalus, vol. 88, 1959; Braziller, 1960.

S. Parker, 'Motives in Eskimo and Ojibwa mythology', *Ethnology*, vol. 1, pp. 516–23, 1962.

J. Peacock, *Rites of Modernization: Symbolic and Social Aspects of Indonesian Proletarian Drama*, University of Chicago Press, 1968.

I. de Sola Pool, *Trends in Content Analysis*, University of Illinois Press, 1959.

J. Pouillon, 'L'analyse des mythes', *L'Homme*, vol. 6, pp. 100–105, 1966.

P. S. Powlison, 'A paragraph analysis of a Yagua folktale', *International J. Amer. Linguistics*, vol. 31, pp. 109–18, 1965.

V. Propp, *Morphology of the Folktale*, University of Texas Press, 1968.

P. Radin, 'The literature of primitive peoples', *Diogenes*, Winter, pp. 1–28, 1955. Bobbs-Merrill Reprint.

P. Radin, *The Trickster: A Study in American Indian Mythology*, with commentaries by Karl Kerényi and C. G. Jung, Philosophical Library, 1956; Routledge & Kegan Paul, 1956.

O. Rank, *The Myth of the Birth of the Hero*, Vintage, 1959.

P. Richard, 'Analyse des *Mythologiques* de Claude Lévi-Strauss', *L'Homme et la Société*, July 1967, pp. 109–33; April 1969, pp. 179–91.

M. S. Robinson and L. E. Joiner, 'An experiment in the structural study of myth', in H. Nutini and I. Buchler (eds.), *The Anthropology of Claude Lévi-Strauss*, Appleton-Century-Croft, 1972.

R. Savard, 'L'Hôte maladroit, essai d'analyse d'un conte montagnais', *Interprétation* (Montreal) vol. 3, pp. 5–52, 1969.

C. T. Scott, 'Persian and Arabic Riddles: a language-centered approach to *genre* definition', *International Journal of American Linguistics*, vol. 31, pt 2, 1965.

T. A. Sebeok, 'Toward a statistical contingency method in folklore research', in W. E. Richmond (ed.), *Studies in Folklore*, Indiana University Press, pp. 130–40, 1957.

T. A. Sebeok (ed.), *Myth: A Symposium*, Indiana University Press, 1958; Midland Books 1965.

T. A. Sebeok (ed.), *Style in Language*, MIT Press, 1960.

D. C. Simmons, 'Analysis of cultural reflection in Efik folktales', *J. Amer. Folklore*, vol. 4, pp. 126–41, 1961.

E. Souriau, *Les Deux Cent Mille Situations Dramatiques*, Flammarion, 1950.

A. Stender-Petersen, 'Esquisse d'une théorie structurale de la littérature', *Travaux du Cercle Linguistique de Copenhague*, vol. 5, pp. 277–87, 1949.

P. J. Stone, D. C. Dunphy, M. S. Smith and D. M. Ogilvie, *The General Inquirer: A Computer Approach to Content Analysis*, MIT Press, 1966.

Eric Ten Raa, 'Procedure and symbolism in Sandawe riddles', *Man*, vol. 1, no. 3, pp. 391–7, 1966.

S. Thompson, *The Folktale*, Dryden Press, 1951.

S. Thompson, 'The star husband tale', *Studia Septentrionalia*, vol. 4, pp. 93–163, 1953, Oslo. Reprinted in Alan Dundes (ed.), *The Study of Folklore*, Prentice-Hall, pp. 414–74, 1965.

S. Thompson, *Motif-Index of Folk Literature*, Indiana University Press, 1955–8.

T. Todorov, 'Les catégories du récit littéraire', *Communications*, vol. 8, pp. 125–51, 1966.

T. Todorov (ed.), 'Recherches sémantiques', *Languages*, vol. 1, 1966.

V. Turner, 'Three symbols of passage in Ndembu circumcision ritual', in M. Gluckman (ed.), *Essays in the Ritual of Social Relations*, Michigan University Press, 1962.

V. Turner, 'The interpretation of symbols in Ndembu ritual', in M. Gluckman and E. Devons (eds.), *Closed Systems and Open Minds*, Oliver & Boyd, 1964.

V. Turner, 'Witchcraft and sorcery: taxonomy versus dynamics', *Africa*, vol. 34, pp. 314–24, 1964.

F. L. Utley, 'Folk literature: an operational definition', *J. Amer. Folklore*, vol. 74, pp. 193–206, 1961.

J. Vansina, *Oral Tradition: A Study in Historical Methodology*, Routledge & Kegan Paul, 1965.

J. P. Vernant, 'Ambiguité et renversement sur la structure énigmatique, d'Oedipe-Roi', in J. Pouillon and P. Maranda (eds.), *Echanges et communications/Exchange and Communications – Mélanges Lévi-Strauss*, 2 vols., Mouton, 1970.

J. B. Vickery (ed.), *Myth and Literature: Contemporary Theory and Practice*, University of Nebraska Press, 1966.

R. Wellek, 'Concepts of form and structure in twentieth-century criticism', *Neophilologus*, vol. 42, pp. 2–11, 1958.

R. G. Willis, 'The head and the loins: Lévi-Strauss and beyond', *Man*, N.S. vol. 2, pp. 519–34, 1967.

Acknowledgements

Permission to reproduce the Readings in this volume is acknowledged from the following sources:

1 Dover Publications Inc.
2 Liveright Publishing Corp. and Peter Owen Ltd
3 M I T Press
4 The American Folklore Society Inc. and Dr W. A. Lessa
5 Centre National de la Recherche Scientifique
6 Methuen & Co. Ltd
7 Editions du Seuil
8 Centre National de la Recherche Scientifique
9 Editions du Seuil
10 University of Illinois Press and Robert P. Armstrong
11 Journal Press
12 Professor Dmitry M. Segal
13 Harper & Row and Jonathan Cape

Author Index

Subject Index

Acculturation, 74
Adaptive use of myth, 124–5, 130, 134–5, 173, 220
  see also Cargo cult, Codes and recoding of myth and Tradition, manipulation of in myth
Amazonian Indians, 111
Animals, in South American mythology
  alligator, 278, 289–90
  anteater and jaguar contest, 279–81
  deer, 265–6
  'helpful animals', 290–95
  humming bird, 291, 293–5
  jaguar as master of fire, 262, 264–5, 269, 278
  lizards, 289–90
  see also Sacrifice, animal
Ancestors, 129, 134–5, 191
Andamanese, 36
Année Sociologique, 9
Apinayé, 151, 160
Arapaho, 37, 38
Arikara, 37
Association of ideas, 32, 34–5
  individual, among illiterate people, 34–5
  and religious significance, 36–8
  and study of variant myths and prayers, 35
  traditional associations and individual psychology, 35–6
  and word association, 32–4
Australia, 100, 116, 133

Bella Coola Indians, 217
Bible, the, 8, 16
Bororo Indian mythology, 159, 251

bird nester's aria and origin of fire myth, 251–3, 262–5, 266, 268–9, 270, 272–3
  and episode of helpful animals, 290–5
  and episode of visit to aquatic underworld, 271, 272–3, 282, 291
  fire and water myths of Gê and Bororo compared, 277–85
  origin of wind and rain myth, 251, 263–5
  and transformations in relation to Gê myths, 263–6, 269–70, 286–96
Brahmin food taboos, 45
Brazil, 151, 251
Buddhism, 146
Bush Negroes of Paramribo folk tales, 184–5
  see also Suriname folk tales

Caesars, 115
Canibalism, 45, 89, 91
Cantova, Father Antonio, 74
Carolinian Archipelago, 72, 74, 86, 89, 94, 101, 108
Cargo cult, 69, 131–5
  and charismatic figure, 130, 131–3
  and self-image, 133–5
Cash economies, 74, 85, 90
Catholic Church, 50, 51, 74
Cayapo, 151
Charismatic figure in myth see Cargo cult
Child rearing practices, 73, 107, 171, 194ff
  see also Games
Christianity, 12, 15–16, 36, 74, 107
  attitude to sacrament, 45